He tried reaching the Glock. Three steps. *Closer.* Reached again. Steps stopped outside his shattered window. He lay on his arm, trapped, unable to get to the weapon. He willed his labored breathing to stop. He told the rising and falling of his chest to be still. He lay quiet, listening, praying to God he could pull it off. His hand fell automatically onto his medicine bundle.

Someone shined a flashlight into Manny's car. Through his closed eyelids, Manny saw all this as if he were sitting in a theater watching some dark, foreboding movie. Light played across his lids. He wanted to open them, wanted to look at his attacker, but he didn't. The driver squatted inches from him, close enough that Manny felt warm puffs of breath on his neck through the window. He struggled to remain conscious. His cop side took over, and he listened for anything that would later identify the attacker. If he lived through this . . .

Berkley Prime Crime titles by C. M Wendelboe

DEATH ALONG THE SPIRIT ROAD

DEATH WHERE THE BAD ROCKS LIVE

DEATH ON THE GREASY GRASS

DEATH ALONG
THE SPIRIT ROAD

C. M. WENDELBOE

BERKLEY PRIME CRIME, NEW YORK

THE BERKLEY PUBLISHING GROUP
Published by the Penguin Group
Penguin Group (USA) Inc.
375 Hudson Street, New York, New York 10014, USA
Penguin Group (Canada), 90 Eglinton Avenue East, Suite 700, Toronto, Ontario M4P 2Y3, Canada
(a division of Pearson Penguin Canada Inc.)
Penguin Books Ltd., 80 Strand, London WC2R 0RL, England
Penguin Group Ireland, 25 St. Stephen's Green, Dublin 2, Ireland (a division of Penguin Books Ltd.)
Penguin Group (Australia), 250 Camberwell Road, Camberwell, Victoria 3124, Australia
(a division of Pearson Australia Group Pty. Ltd.)
Penguin Books India Pvt. Ltd., 11 Community Centre, Panchsheel Park, New Delhi—110 017, India
Penguin Group (NZ), 67 Apollo Drive, Rosedale, North Shore 0632, New Zealand
(a division of Pearson New Zealand Ltd.)
Penguin Books (South Africa) (Pty.) Ltd., 24 Sturdee Avenue, Rosebank, Johannesburg 2196,
South Africa

Penguin Books Ltd., Registered Offices: 80 Strand, London WC2R 0RL, England

This book is an original publication of The Berkley Publishing Group.

Copyright © 2011 by C. M. Wendelboe.
Cover illustration by Richard Tuschman.
Cover design by Rita Frangie.
Interior text design by Laura K. Corless.

FIRST EDITION: March 2011

Library of Congress Cataloging-in-Publication Data

Wendelboe, C. M.
    Death along the spirit road / C.M. Wendelboe. — 1st ed.
        p.   cm.
    ISBN 978-0-425-24002-1
    1. Dakota Indians—Fiction. 2. Indian reservations—South Dakota—Fiction. 3. Real estate developers—
Crimes against—Fiction. I. Title.
    PS3623.E53D43   2011
    813'.6—dc22   2010038253

PRINTED IN THE UNITED STATES OF AMERICA

10   9   8   7   6   5   4   3   2

To Milt Wendelboe,
who was a voracious reader until the day he died.

And my Lakota friends,
who kept me on my own Road.

Acknowledgments

I would like to thank my agent, Bill Contardi, and my editor, Tom Colgan, for having faith to take a chance on a rookie, and Eric Boss and Mike McGroder, for greasing the wheels and to Richard Tuschman, whose beauty with the brush portrayed so precisely the mood and theme of the novel. I thank my mentors Judy and Craig Johnson and my wife, Heather Wendelboe: Without their help, you wouldn't be reading this.

DEATH ALONG
THE SPIRIT ROAD

CHAPTER 1

Manny popped another CD into the player in the rental and fiddled with the controls. The Six Fat Dutchmen pounded out the "Tick-Tock Polka." He settled back in his seat, tapping the oomp-ba oomp-ba tuba beat on the steering wheel. How long had it been since he danced a polka? Must have been back in Germany in his army days. Oomp-ba-ba. Oomp-ba. He had tried accordion lessons back then, but he couldn't read music any better than he could drive. Oomp-ba. Oomp-ba. Tick-tock. Tick-tock. Like the song was ticking away at his life.

He bent forward to adjust the bass to accentuate the heavy tuba and caught movement in his periphery. A teen, wearing a T-shirt missing one sleeve with jeans threatening to fall down his meatless hips, stumbled between two parked cars and started across the road. The gaunt young man looked up. Eyes wide. Mouth open. Manny slammed on the brakes, and the tires of the Taurus bit into the hot asphalt. Things kicked into slow motion, like his academy instructors said happened under great stress.

The car skidded. Tires pleaded and screamed. The boy yelled, his face bombarded with loose gravel from the road. His hands hopelessly covered his face and he tried jumping out of the car's path, but he was too slow. Too drunk. The houses beside the road. Abandoned cars. Trees. All blacked out. Manny focused in front of the car, the kid walking in slow motion on instant replay.

The car rocked to a stop. The seat belt bit into Manny's shoulder and held him inches away from the steering wheel. Burnt tire smoke rose up, dark and dense. It assaulted Manny's nose with its bitter accusation, and he rubbed his eyes. The boy was gone.

Manny opened the door and stepped out as the boy rose from the pavement in front of the car. Eighteen going on forty: his face red, splintery, broken capillaries. He glared at Manny through eyes watery with wine and stinging with indignation. Hate replaced terror. He picked up his hat and slapped it against his ripped jeans. Dust fell off the cap as he jammed it on his head, and he jutted his middle finger high in the air as he scowled at Manny. With that gesture their sole conversation, the kid turned and staggered down the road.

"Screw you!" Manny said. "Watch where the hell you're going."

Manny's heart pounded as forcefully as the beat of the Six Fat Dutchmen still reverberating in the car. He took deep breaths and began to see trees and weeds at the side of the road as his vision returned to normal. He watched the kid stop beside an abandoned pickup by the Pronto Auto Parts store. He climbed in the bed and lay down to start his afternoon pass-out, the top of his ball cap visible above the tailgate.

"Damned drunk."

Manny's legs still shook as he sat back in the car. The arteries in his neck pounded oomp-ba, oomp-ba, to the beat of the polka music, and his hand trembled as reached for the player and tapped the power button. The music died, and he closed his eyes and willed his breathing to slow. "Damned fool would have deserved it," he said aloud. "Walking with his head in his ass."

Manny fingered his medicine bag, held his *wopiye* to the light. The blue and black beaded deerskin turtle had become faded and tattered around the edges from being carried so long. It was always with him. Unc said his *wopiye* had powers to help him through life, though he fought hard to believe it even as a boy. When the *yuwipi* man had given him his *inyan*, somewhere in the recesses of his Lakota soul Manny wanted to believe that this bundle with the black spirit stone would protect him. As it had now. As it had then.

"That could have been me." *If Unc hadn't taken me in when the folks died, that could have been me.*

Manny drove into Pine Ridge Village. Shanties and shacks and trailer houses, missing so many windows that they looked like schoolkids who'd been busted in the chops once too often, were spaced erratically on both sides of the road. What shingles remained to protect tattered tar-paper roofs gave the shanties the illusion of a bad haircut. No one should live in them, but people did. Just as people used the abandoned cars along the road to sleep in. Or to trade sex for booze. Or to hide bodies long dead. All these things had not changed. Manny had known this even as he accepted the assignment.

The buildings stood crumbling and bowed, like the broken spirit of the Lakota people. The reservation was one hundred years of history unmarked by progress, and things were worse than when Manny lived here. Pejuty Drug Store, where he had often bought candy as a boy, his patched dungarees full of change after finishing a chore his uncle Marion had given him, was gone. And the Wright and McGill snelling factory. It had employed more than four hundred people, but the owners found poor people overseas willing to work for even lower wages than the Indians. Now the fishhook factory stood as vacant as the stares of out-of-work Oglala.

Then he laughed. "Who the hell ever gives me a choice of assignments?" Whenever Ben Niles called Special Agent Manny Tanno to his office, it was to assign him an investigation no one else wanted. Usually on some Indian reservation no one wanted to go to. "Some choice." There was a bowling alley then, as well as a moccasin factory, and Gerber's Hotel, all boarded up now. Manny guessed that travelers were shit out of luck if they wanted a place to stay for the night.

Special Agent Manny Tanno cursed Jason Red Cloud for getting killed and dragging him back here. He cursed Ben Niles for assigning him every dispute on every Indian reservation in the country because he was the FBI token Indian-of-the-moment. And he cursed himself for accepting this assignment on Pine Ridge: He had not thought of the reservation for so long that he had become comfortable thinking it was a place where other Indians lived, not the place where he was from.

>‹›‹›‹

It was midday and the customers at Big Bat's gas station and convenience store stood three-deep at the food counter waiting to place their orders. The counter girl, wearing an ANGELICA name tag, took orders and handed them back to the cook through an open window into the kitchen. Bacon crackled on the grill, and the odor of grease and frying eggs made Manny retch. The drunk in the street was still strong in his mind, the boy's near-death lingering. He was still pissed. That kid had nearly cost Manny his career, nearly missed getting himself hit— and the news would have been reported that an FBI agent ran an Indian down on his own reservation.

"Order." Angelica grabbed a stub of pencil from behind her ear and held it poised over a paper pad. He didn't recognize her, couldn't recognize her, it had been so long since he had been home. He guessed her age at eighteen, probably just out of high school, if her parents had enough discipline to send her to school. She was rushing, though, so maybe she'd had enough gumption to graduate.

"I'll just have coffee."

She smiled at him as if he'd just placed the biggest order of the day and directed him to the coffee urns along one wall. He stood in line as a couple alternated filling their sodas and pinching one another on the butt. They eyed Manny's starched white shirt, then worked their way down to his Dockers and wing tips. One whispered to the other and they both laughed. They started for a booth when one nodded to the counter. Manny followed the nod. He turned and saw a boy, younger than the counter girl but nearly as big as Manny, elbow a woman aside. Her breakfast burrito fell to the floor.

The boy ignored her and tossed two sandwiches onto the counter. "What the hell's this slop?" He asked belligerently as Angelica backed away. "Get that cook off his ass and have him make me a new order."

"That's enough, Lenny." The cook, wiping his hands on his apron, emerged from the kitchen. "I'll make a new order."

Lenny reached across the counter and grabbed the cook's shirt. Manny set his coffee on a table and approached Lenny, who had one foot on the counter ready to climb over.

"Maybe you ought to chill out."

Lenny put his foot back onto the floor and shifted his threatening stance toward Manny. The kid's fists clenched and unclenched, and the adolescent stubble rippled on his cheeks as his jaw tightened. "Maybe I don't want to chill out."

"Let it alone, kid."

"Just who the hell are you to tell me what to do?" Lenny stepped closer, and his breath stank of cheap whiskey. "You ain't the cops."

"But I am." Manny flashed his badge and ID wallet.

"This here's an FBI agent," Lenny yelled. He staggered back, then turned and started climbing back onto the counter. "Ain't that something."

Manny grabbed him by the arm, twisted it behind him, and pushed him out the door into the heat of the parking lot. Lenny jerked his arm away and stumbled on the curb. Manny caught him before he fell.

"Leave me alone. What the hell's the FBI doing here anyhow? I thought we run you off years ago."

"There's no one to hear you out here, so you can drop the macho bullshit. I don't know what your problem is . . ."

"Course you don't. You ain't even from here."

"But you better get a handle on it. It's summer and you should be working instead of killing the day killing beer."

"I got a job."

Manny didn't want to talk to the kid any longer than he had to. He'd been assigned to Pine Ridge just for the case, and he didn't have the time to be a social worker to these people.

Lenny stumbled down the street and Manny returned to the store. His coffee had been overturned and the cup still lay in the brown puddle on the table. Someone behind him laughed. He ignored it and walked back to the coffee urn and filled a fresh cup. This time he took it and walked back to his car.

He put the coffee in the cup holder, started the car, and drove toward the justice building. He should have ordered some food, since Big Bat's was the only place in town to eat, but he had to be careful. Nearing fifty, his six-pack had become a round keg sitting on top of a tap he rarely used anymore. When he woke up one morning four months ago, he entered a quit smoking program sponsored by the FBI and forced himself to put on his Nikes and running shorts, something he'd not done for years. Running came back into his daily routine and allowed him time alone to work out problems by himself.

Manny caught the only traffic light on Pine Ridge. The light made him wait, made him watch. Four young men stuffed into a tiny Mazda coupe careened around the corner. The driver half hung out the window, yelling as the other three joined the chorus. They skidded to a stop just as a 1970s Country Squire wagon, backyard-converted into a pickup, jumped through the light. The back end was cut off above the fenders, the makeshift bed topped with channel iron. A piece of plywood, which covered the hole where the back window had been, was held into the opening by bailing wire. The converted wagon bounced through the intersection like an out-of-place lowrider from East L.A. The lot lizards sitting on car hoods on the other side of the road whooped and yelled. Out-of-work Indians with nothing else to do on a 101-degree day on what used to be called Bullshit Corner. By the looks of things, it still was.

Then the light winked. Or rather, it changed. Manny passed the girl in the homemade pickup. She lit up a bowl of what he was certain wasn't tobacco. He coughed as he tasted the oily exhaust smoke and hastily rolled up the window.

He entered the chain-link-enclosed back parking lot of the justice building and parked between an Impala with a sizeable dent in one fender and a Crown Victoria with a bloody dimple on the trunk. Little had changed here since his own days as an Oglala Sioux tribal cop. Dents were worn like badges of honor, since resistive prisoners were often educated on the trunk of a cruiser before being jailed. "Wall-to-wall counseling." Manny chuckled to himself. He stepped from the rental and stretched his back. Eighteen years had made little difference in his old stomping grounds. The lot looked as if it had been paved about the time he left for D.C. Weeds still grew through cracks in the asphalt. Most of the tribal police vehicles sported old rusted dents and scrapes bleeding through the fresh ones. One cruiser was missing a front fender. Another thrust its bent radio antenna toward the building as if it were half of some divining rod.

Two officers charged through the door. They glanced at Manny as they ran to a Dodge Durango, spinning gravel on their way to a family fight. Or an accident. Or a gun call. Manny thought of the times he had answered those calls, remembered, and thanked God the FBI employed him now rather than the Oglala Sioux Tribe.

He opened the door of the justice building, stepped inside, and let his eyes adjust from the sun that filtered through his Gargoyles. He looked past the long, narrow counter through the bullet-resistant glass. It was the American Indian Movement turmoil that had forced the tribe and Bureau of Indian Affairs to harden the building on Pine Ridge, and violence frequented the police station even now.

A girl half Manny's age rose from her desk and walked to the audio port behind the glass. Manny read her name tag: SHANNON HORN.

"Any relation to Verlyn Horn?" Manny asked as he pointed to her name tag.

"My grandfather."

"Small world." Manny read her questioning look. "I used to work for him when he was police chief."

"And you are?"

"Manny Tanno."

She sucked in a quick breath. "Grandfather always talks about you. He was always proud that you left here and made good."

"How is Chief Horn?"

"He retired years ago." She dropped her eyes. "He fell in love with White Clay."

Unc always warned Manny to avoid White Clay. "Some of your young buddies will find their way down there," he told Manny on the day he got his driver's license. "Just as their parents did and their parents before them. But don't you fall for that. Nothing good will ever come out of drinking."

White Clay sat just across the Nebraska border within walking distance of Pine Ridge Village and, since the sale of alcohol was illegal on the reservation, most Indians went there for liquor. The store owners bragged that Pine Ridge made millions for them. A recent mutual aid agreement between the tribe and Nebraska allowed Oglala Sioux Tribal Police to cross the state line, but short of making alcohol legal on the reservation, nothing would change.

Given all the years Chief Horn had worked as a lawman and seen the effects of alcohol on Lakota lives, Manny couldn't understand how the chief could succumb to the lure of the bottle.

"He went the way so many of our people do." Shannon swallowed hard, and her eyes watered. She dried them with the back of her hand. Nothing Manny said could help. It was that same desperation that had shone in the eyes of Oglala men and women when he had lived here; resignation sapped their will. He damned Ben Niles again for ordering him back here.

He changed the subject and asked for Chief Spotted Horse.

"Chief Spotted Horse had an accident. Lieutenant Looks Twice is in charge while the chief is on sick leave. He's expecting you."

"Lumpy made lieutenant?"

"Pardon?"

He shook his head.

She buzzed him through the door, and he followed her through the outer office. She glanced sideways at Manny and wrinkled her nose. Some of the younger agents said his cologne smelled like old feet. But he liked it.

Officers in black Oglala Sioux Tribal uniforms looked up from computers, but Manny was certain no one recognized him. At five-foot-eight he cast an unimposing shadow, and his paunch and thinning hair with its distinct widow's peak poking through was typical here. Only his khakis and the cuff links on his ivory shirt set him apart. Of course no one had seen him on CNN last year investigating that double homicide at Standing Rock, or on FOX when he solved that infanticide in Crow Creek. It had been so long since he had been back to Pine Ridge, even his renown didn't betray him. It was his plainness that dropped people's guard. His plainness allowed them to trust him even when they shouldn't, and people often trusted him with that small piece of information that would convict them.

He spent ten active years in Violent Crime in Chicago before Ben Niles wooed him out of the field and into an academy teaching slot. Manny was slow to admit it, but he might just enjoy being back in the field until the next academy class began. He just wished it was someplace besides Pine Ridge.

Shannon motioned to the lieutenant's office.

"Lieutenant Looks Twice must have stepped out. Can I get you a cup of coffee?"

"Thanks."

By the time she returned, Manny had settled into a large, padded velvet Elvis chair. The King, guitar in hand, hips gyrating, smiled at him from the chair's cushion. It was almost a shame to sit on him, but Manny did, and the chair swallowed him in its comfort. He smiled. This was the first time he had ever sat upon a velvet Elvis, and he tilted his head back as Shannon walked away.

He resisted the urge to prop his feet on the desktop, even though his feet couldn't be any more insulting to the desk than age had been. Lumpy had been a tribal policeman for twenty-five years, working himself up to the rank of lieutenant. His desk should have represented his accomplishments, should have projected a symbol of his success. At any other agency even a rookie would have been ashamed to have that piece of trash belittling him every day.

It was only Lumpy's desk. But Manny felt sadness for him.

A cheap-motel-room Charles Russell print hung on one wall, next to a spiderwebbed photo of a young Leon Looks Twice. He wore his finest Western duds: a shirt with pearl buttons and a Stetson placed at the obligatory rakish angle. Manny strained to recall him as a young officer. Lumpy had always taken a liking to stars of the Western screen—John Wayne, Jimmy Stewart, Ben Johnson—and had fancied himself looking like those old greats. A real Hopalong Lumpy.

On the opposite wall hung a picture of him that Manny remembered best. Lumpy stood in a sharply pressed Oglala Sioux Tribal Police uniform with arms crossed. His eyes projected the look of a bully who scratched a line in the sand and dared anyone to cross it. Those eyes seemed to follow Manny as he checked out the rest of the office.

Behind Manny, two pictures framed in gold leaf were perched on a Catholic Bible on a shelf. He got out of the chair to look at Desirée Chasing Hawk in her white lace wedding dress. Lumpy hugged her, looking too short and too fat in his tux. Manny heard they got married after he left for Quantico. Manny and Lumpy had courted Desirée all through high school. But Lumpy had always impressed girls with his flamboyant clothes and extravagant gifts, and he had wooed and won her.

In another gilded frame, Desirée straddled a bicycle. A short skirt caressed shapely legs, and a low blouse revealed what Manny never had. She smiled into the camera, and his heart raced for a moment, old feelings returning.

"That was taken the summer before Desirée left me."

Lumpy blocked the doorway. He stood with his hands on pudgy hips, black hair slicked back. "She stayed beautiful until the day she ran off with that siding salesman from Wisconsin."

"What happened?"

"She always had the roving eye. You know, it's supposed to be the man that sleeps around. She was on the make before our first anniversary. I wish to hell you'd have walked down the aisle with her instead of me."

"And some siding salesman lured her away?"

Lumpy smiled. "He owned seventeen siding companies in the West and Midwest. Worth millions. He promised her a future in acting."

"She ever act?"

"Just in his company commercials."

"Well, she must be happy with him and his millions."

Lumpy's grin faded. "It didn't last. She and her prenup moved back after a couple of years. Took back her own name just to spite me."

"Ever see her?"

The grin returned. "Once in a while."

Manny looked at Desirée with regret, turned to Lumpy, and offered his hand. Manny wasn't a tall man, but he felt six feet next to Lumpy. "Been quite a while, Lumpy."

"It's 'Lieutenant Looks Twice' now."

"I'll remember that." His little-man attitude snatched Manny back twenty-five years. He was fresh out of the army, working as a tribal cop with a roly-poly, beside-himself rookie the others called "Lumpy" for the lumps of fat sticking out from under his duty belt. Now, he looked twice as lumpy. Manny wanted to laugh out loud. Lump Lump. "So you're in charge while the chief's on sick leave."

Lumpy grinned. "Chief Spotted Horse got thrown from his spotted horse and broke his leg."

"You don't sound too broke up over it."

Lumpy shrugged. "Let's just say I'm the chief-in-training while he's out. That's why I got the call this morning that you were coming here to assume the Red Cloud investigation." Lumpy ran his hand through his thick hair. "We already began an investigation, and Pat Pourier's already processed the crime scene. Contrary to your boss's opinion, we're no rubes here. But I got ordered to remand the investigation to the FBI. I figure it would take something high-profile like Jason Red Cloud's murder to pry the legendary Special Agent Manny Tanno from his cushy academy job."

Manny wanted to tell Lumpy that he had little say in the matter. With two years until retirement, Manny couldn't refuse any request of the agent in charge. Manny had not wanted this investigation, didn't want to come back to Pine Ridge, but Ben Niles insisted.

"Besides, the press will expect Manny Tanno to investigate it. Demand it."

"I'm not going."

"Sure you are."

"Piss on you."

"I got faith in you. You've solved every homicide you've ever worked in the bureau. The media's screaming for a suspect, and you'll have this wrapped up by the time the next academy class starts two weeks from now." Niles smirked. "Besides, Jason Red Cloud's a household name."

Manny agreed, but he wouldn't admit it to Niles. The papers called Jason Red Cloud the "Donald Trump of the West," with holdings and developments from Denver to Minneapolis, Sun Valley to Salt Lake. Jason had been a hometown celebrity, an Oglala who made good, and Niles insisted this was one Pine Ridge homicide that had to be solved.

Two weeks wasn't much time to conduct an investigation on hostile ground. Lakota or no, the Oglala Sioux were distrustful of federal authorities. The government's subjugation of them went back to the repressive policies of the mid- to late-1800s, when the government's word was freely given and just as freely broken, when treaties were flamed the moment they were signed, and when the great Sioux Nation was reduced to land one-sixth the size of the agreed-upon acreage.

"Maybe I asked for this assignment because I missed you so

much, Lumpy." Lumpy's face flushed, and he balled his fist up beside his leg. "But now you say it's 'Lieutenant Looks Twice.' I'll remember that."

The years of rivalry as kids, the tension between them as tribal cops, returned in this one moment. Lumpy glared at Manny, and Manny took the bait, playing a juvenile game of stare down. Finally Lumpy blinked and bellowed to the dispatcher, "Where the hell's Willie?"

In the parking lot a car door slammed, and an officer burst through the door. He ran into the room just as Lumpy stared at Manny again, demanding a rematch. The young policeman walked directly to Manny and held out his hand.

"This is Willie With Horn."

"William," Willie corrected.

Lumpy ignored him. "Willie here's your, shall we say, liaison officer while you're here on Pine Ridge. He'll be assisting in your investigation. Feel free to use his vast expertise. His innumerable contacts." He winked at Manny. "I handpicked him myself."

Manny ignored Lumpy as he eyed the young tribal officer towering over him. Willie was uncommonly heavy in the chest and shoulders and hadn't yet developed the paunch that identified him as a Lakota. He would be right at home handling any bar fight or family dispute, but he was young. Manny had expected to work with a veteran, since Niles wanted the case wrapped up in two weeks. Manny could have asked for someone else, but William threw off good vibes, and Manny often relied on his intuition.

"Fine. Officer With Horn will do just fine."

Lumpy's smile faded. He walked around the desk, sat, and propped his feet up. His ostrich boots, so big that they hung over the desk, made him look like a caricature. He strained his short arms to reach into his top desk drawer and tossed a folder on the desktop. "Crime scene photos, Hotshot. You might take a look-see before Willie shows you to the scene."

Manny handed Willie the folder. "All the same to you, I'll wait until I view the scene. Maybe make some observations of my own. If that's OK with you."

Lumpy shrugged. "Suit yourself. Just a suggestion. And by the way, you need anything here that Willie can't get you, you come see me. With the chief laid up, I'm the go-to man around here."

"I'll remember that."

"And here." Lumpy pulled a key ring from his pocket and tossed it onto the desk. "This is for the apartment the tribe's letting you use while you're here. Willie will show you where it is in the housing."

"That's thoughtful of you."

"It's the least I can do. I picked the apartment myself." Lumpy grinned. "You might find it quite enjoyable while you're here."

Manny thanked him and turned to Willie. "I'd like to view the scene while it's still light out."

"Sure thing, Agent Tanno. Your ride or mine?"

Lumpy tilted his head back and laughed. "If you're smart, you'll do the driving. Agent Tanno here was never the best driver in the world."

He'd tell William about his accidents some other time. "Your car will do fine. And it's 'Manny.' "

Willie grinned. "Sure thing, Manny." As they walked through the front office, everyone stopped typing and watched him leave the station. Indeed, by now the masses were all aware that the "Living Legend" of Pine Ridge had come back home. At least for one last case.

CHAPTER 2

Willie started east out of Pine Ridge on Highway 18. "He doesn't like you very much."

"Lumpy?"

"Lieutenant Looks Twice."

"No, he doesn't, William."

"I'd like the lieutenant to call me by my Christian name, but he doesn't. I always thought it sounded more dignified. But you can call me 'Willie.'"

"OK then, Willie, but don't let that man back there take anything from you. And no, Lumpy doesn't like me. It goes way back."

"From when you lived here before?"

Manny nodded. "We wrestled the same weight class when we were kids." Public Pine Ridge High versus Catholic Red Cloud School was a matchup people anticipated. "Each time we met Red Cloud, I had to wrestle the only boy in my weight class:

Leon Looks Twice. I beat him on the mat every time. He's held on to that grudge all these years."

And they competed for the hottest girl on the reservation, Desirée Chasing Hawk. Manny had even gone out for cross-country his freshman year, confident that Lumpy would never be in good enough shape to be a runner and get close to Desirée. The girls' and boys' cross-country teams traveled together, something that Lumpy resented.

Manny also wanted to tell Willie how he had gone out of his way to torment Officer Looks Twice when they were both rookie cops. From the time Manny poured putrid coyote lure into the heat vents of Lumpy's squad car, to the time he sent a gay porn subscription to Lumpy at the station house, he had made Lumpy's life miserable. Even though Lumpy couldn't prove it, he'd known it was Manny, and he had never forgotten it.

Highway 18 was newly paved and smooth, the traffic nonexistent, yet Willie fidgeted in his seat. He said nothing as he was avoiding looking at Manny, wanting to say something. "You know I was assigned to help you just 'cause I'm the rookie, don't you?" he blurted out. "The same reason they give me this old beater to drive."

Manny smiled. "Don't worry. You'll do just fine."

"Jeeza. I got no experience. I've never done an investigation. The lieutenant threw you a bone with me, and a not-too-juicy bone either. I got nothing to offer you."

"You want to help me?"

"Of course I do."

"Then that's more than I had when I walked into Lumpy's office this morning. I got me a sidekick."

"Like Gabby Hayes."

"Or Hoot Gibson."

They drove past summer hay, baled and waiting pick up from

feed buyers in a five-state region. In most places of the country, the hay would have been a sign of prosperity for Indians, but here non-Indians farmed the bulk of the reservation. Indian re-organization of the last century had stripped most Lakota of land ownership. Most families' paltry section of land was di-vided and subdivided through the decades until the average In-dian on Pine Ridge owned one-one-hundredth of a section of the land his ancestors were deeded originally.

"You know, not everything you see belongs to Whites. Some belongs to Oglala. That's one of the reasons I decided to stay here."

"You ever want to leave? See what's over the next hill?"

"Once," Willie answered. "Once I wanted to be an FBI agent. So I went to college in Vermillion right out of high school. Belted out my criminal justice requirements. I even filled out a federal application. But whenever I'd come back during break, I'd al-ways hear dead elders calling me, like they wanted me to stick around. You ever get that feeling, that some lost soul was tug-ging at your arm, forcing you to return?"

"Not really," Manny lied.

"Well, I'd get those feelings, like something digging at me, something was holding me tight and wouldn't let me go."

Since crossing onto the reservation yesterday, something had tugged at Manny, too. He couldn't identify it, and the gnawing persisted.

"So now I'm enrolled at the Oglala Lakota College. Someday I'll be an investigator with the tribe."

"So you don't intend leaving the reservation like I did? Ac-cept a cushy federal position with the bureau? Maybe the Mar-shals. There's not many Indians in federal law enforcement. You could name your ticket."

Willie blushed, and Manny lightly touched his arm. "Don't feel bad, I've heard it all before. Uncle Tomahawk. Apple

Indian—Red on the outside and White on the inside. I've been called everything from a stinking bureaucrat to an out-and-out traitor to the Red race."

"I didn't mean . . ."

"Of course you didn't," Manny answered, and changed the subject. "How long have you been on the force?"

"Be a year next month." A grin lit Willie's face. Manny had Willie's enthusiasm for law enforcement—once. "With the college credits I already have, and some online work, I'll have my bachelor's within a year. Even though I'm the newbie, college will help when an investigator slot opens up."

As long as Lumpy isn't the one deciding.

There wasn't a campus on Pine Ridge back then, in Manny's college days as a tribal cop, and he had to drive to classes at Black Hills State in Spearfish twice a week. Lumpy had ridiculed him, taunted him, told him good cops didn't need college. Even though Lumpy still had no education, his intelligence, combined with his ruthlessness and ability to play reservation politics, had allowed him to float to the top. Like a turd in a toilet.

"I've been studying the old ways, too," Willie volunteered. People told Manny things, all sorts of things, most times without his asking. His balding hair and potbelly dropped people's guard and they opened up to him.

"Who are you studying with?"

"Margaret Catches."

"One of the Porcupine Catches whose dad was a holy man on the Rosebud?"

"The same. She's a true Winyan Wakan, perhaps one of the last of the sacred women here. My aunt Elizabeth studied the holy ways with Margaret. She had to give it up when her finance officer position got to be too many hours. Aunt Elizabeth is the only reason Margaret agreed to take me under her wing and teach me the old ways."

The old ways. Uncle Marion had taught Manny the old ways once, taught him the four Lakota virtues of bravery, fortitude, wisdom, and generosity, and breathed them daily. Unc believed that Lakota children chose their parents, not the other way around. Lakota call their children *inipi*, sacred, and Unc lived that as well. He'd never hit Manny, never demeaned him, never made comments that would harm him in any way. If Manny had to choose his parents, he could have done no better than his uncle Marion. Not to say that Unc's hand didn't occasionally find Manny's backside, but Unc never had a smile on his face when he did it.

Unc had been a contradiction in cultures. He had converted to Catholicism when the Jesuits determined the Lakota needed something deeper than their traditional beliefs. Unc and Manny attended every Sunday mass and every Saturday confession. He had enrolled Manny in catechism and lorded over him to ensure his lessons were to the Brothers' satisfaction. But despite all Unc's efforts, Manny had rebelled against traditional teachings. Like his brother, Reuben, who'd rebelled against authority all his life. If Reuben had been raised by a man such as Uncle Marion, perhaps he would have taken a different path. Reuben's Red Road wouldn't have landed him that long stretch in prison.

Yet, Unc's teachings remained with him always, and it was those lessons that caused him to choose this fork in his own Red Road. "There but for the grace of that loving man," he whispered to himself, "I could have gone Reuben's way and been on the opposite of the law . . ."

"I was lucky."

"I didn't catch that," Manny told Willie.

"I was lucky that Margaret knew Aunt Elizabeth so well and agreed to tutor me."

"And who is your aunt Elizabeth?"

Willie smiled. "Most people call her 'Lizzy.' "

Manny turned sideways in the seat. "Reuben's ex-wife Elizabeth?"

Willie nodded.

Manny whistled. "I didn't realize she was your aunt. How is my sister-in-law?"

"Just fine. Doing a great job as finance officer for the tribe the past eight years."

"Finance officer. Now that's impressive."

"She went to night school, and worked her tail off. She won't admit it, but she was floundering after she and Reuben got divorced. She needed something in her life, so she got her degree and began working for the tribe. When her boss died in a car wreck, Aunt Lizzy was the only one qualified for the position."

Before Manny could learn more about Elizabeth, they approached the crime scene. Willie drove toward the hill where Jason was murdered.

"Stop here for a minute." Manny left Willie in the cruiser and stepped close to the mass grave that overlooked the Wounded Knee massacre site.

Unc taught him that this site overlooking the shallow valley below was sacred, and Manny had rebelled against even that. Yet as he stood looking at the grave site, he knew it was sacred. Hairs rose on his arms, numbness weakened his legs, and his ancestors tugged at Manny's soul. Something else haunted him, taunted him. Something else he couldn't identify.

Below Cemetery Hill, a tall slender marker jutted skyward like the finger of a dying warrior proclaiming the mass grave. Manny walked up the hill to that hallowed ground. When he reached the top, he stood with his head bowed, praying to the Wakan Tanka of the Lakota, and to the Christian God of the Jesuits. He prayed for purity in doing his job and for wisdom not to violate this place where so many unarmed Lakota were slaughtered that frigid December morning in 1890.

Wakan Tanka unsimalaye. Wakan Tanka pity me. Tears distorted his visualization of the ancient crime scene, for this had been the scene of a crime. A crime that the Lakota had never resolved, a crime that Unc had never resolved.

He closed his eyes. Unarmed Sioux reached out to him for help, but there was no help as Seventh Cavalry troopers cut them down in volley after volley of gunfire. A young mother ran terrified past him as blood spurted from the infant she cradled in her arms, moments before she was shot in the back and fell to the ground.

Screaming mothers and stumbling elders sought refuge in dried creek beds, but the soldiers pursued. Faces leered with anticipation as they chased their prey and gleefully finished them off with rifle fire, then turned to look for more victims.

Wakan Tanka unsimalaye. But there was no pity for Manny, no relief as he envisioned the burial detail recovering bodies. With rude shovels, soldiers pried corpses from the frozen ground and drug them over to the edge of a single deep hole. There would be no Sending Away ceremony for these people. Manny cried.

"This was the last stand of a proud race," Unc had told him every year that they made their pilgrimage here. "The last hope of people torn from their nomadic roots, people separated from everything that nature had gifted to them." Manny had fought his feelings back then as he fought his feelings now. These dead were not like him. He was a modern man, melding what Lakota remained with what the Whites taught.

He fought the urges dragging him back to what he once was, but they jerked him back. The wind. Always the wind. It blew from everywhere. It blew from nowhere. The ghosts of long dead Lakota rode those winds, dead ancestors that kept yanking him back where Unc had always wanted him to be. Back where he resisted until his soul tore in shreds.

"You OK, Manny?"

He hadn't heard Willie come up behind him.

"You zoned out there. You all right?"

Manny faked a smile while he dabbed at the tears. "My uncle Marion brought me here once a year. Unc would pass an eagle feather through sweetgrass smoke, and ask Wakan Tanka to protect those buried at this spot. Now there's the Big Foot Memorial Ride for people to remember the massacre, but back then this is how we paid homage."

Willie nodded. "Been on that trail ride. Colder 'n a witch's tit riding two weeks from Standing Rock. But when we got here, we connected with the old ones. You feel it, too?"

"No," Manny lied again, and he turned away down the hill toward an incongruous round rock building with a concrete roof shielded from the wind. Inside the Information Center, devotees of the American Indian Movement stood eager to hand out brochures and flyers to anyone who came. The Indians who manned the center thought things would be different if the progressives were not in office; if traditionalists ruled Pine Ridge their power would return. Those people dreamed of a return to the 1970s when AIM was at its strongest. But those people were not Manny's people, and they didn't speak for the majority of the Oglala on Pine Ridge.

Manny shrugged. "Better get to looking at the crime scene while there's still light." He put his sunglasses back on to hide his red eyes and climbed in the car. Willie drove to a spot between the memorial and the village of Wounded Knee, with its dozen or so houses and trailer homes. Yellow police tape flapped loose from its stakes, waving as if to get their attention.

Willie parked just outside the tape and led Manny around the plastic perimeter. "This is where the Red Cloud Resort was gonna be built." Manny admired Jason Red Cloud's optimism at the venture, at his ability to secure such a vast amount of privately owned land. The resort was going to cover an area as big as ten football fields. By anyone's standards, and especially by reservation standards, it represented a substantial undertaking.

"How did Jason ever get the tribe and landowners together? They never agree on anything."

"You'll have to ask Aunt Lizzy about that. This is the first time this has been tried here on the rez."

They stayed just outside the yellow tape as they walked around the meadow that was to be the Red Cloud Resort. Manny nodded to metal chairs placed in a semicircle facing a lectern in the center of the field. "Expecting an audience?"

Dry Dakota dust swirled around. The gunmetal-hued grit that settled on the chairs grated on Manny's lips and he spit.

"Jason was to break ground here tomorrow. The media and dignitaries planned to be here in droves. That's another reason the lieutenant's furious about the murder. He was supposed to introduce everyone. He claimed it'd help his career, and he spent days memorizing everyone's name."

Manny remembered too well Lumpy's memory. As tribal cops, Lumpy kept everything anyone did wrong in his own special scorecard in his mind, to be dredged up at a later date when it suited him.

Manny studied the area, and fought the urge to swear at Lumpy. "Didn't he assign anyone to guard this place until I got here?"

Willie shook his head. "He said the evidence tech got all he could when he processed the scene. 'Even a Hotshot federal Apple couldn't find anything else of value here,'" he told me.

How much evidence had been destroyed since the tribal cops left? Powerless to rectify Lumpy's screwup, Manny breathed deeply to calm himself. "Where was Jason killed?"

"Over here." Willie led Manny to a shallow dip in the field where the crime scene tape was held fast by a wooden stake.

Even before they got to the spot, Manny pinched his nostrils shut. Putrid blood from corpses left rotting at a hundred crime scenes bred familiarity with that smell, and he never got used to it.

Willie started to cross the tape, but Manny stopped him. "Were you here this morning when the scene was processed?"

"Sure. Just after sunrise."

"Then show me where the evidence tech and everybody else walked in and out." *We don't need any more of the crime scene tainted.*

Willie retraced steps where other officers had entered and left the scene. Manny squatted and looked into the sun as he studied the ground. Shadows cast by the late-afternoon light provided the right contrast to reveal impressions in the dirt. He squinted: An outline made by evidence paint had been nearly blown clean. The paint depicted the faint outline where Jason had lain in death. A substantial amount of blood had soaked the dirt under Jason's head. The sun revealed distinct tire tracks.

"Is this where Jason parked his truck?"

"Yes. The lieutenant thinks he backed it in here and waited for the killer."

Manny bent low and ran his hand over the impressions. The wrecker's tire marks, where the dually had backed up to hook onto Jason's truck for the ride to the police impound, remained clear and deep. Other tracks beside the wrecker's were faint and growing fainter. "Rapidly aging," as Unc taught him. Jason's lug tires had made deep impressions. The other tire tracks beside it were narrower, lighter. "Anyone working the crime scene drive up here?" he asked.

"Jeeza! No way! My job was to make sure no one drove up here and messed things up."

"Then whose car made these tracks?"

Willie stepped closer, careful not to disturb them, and squatted beside Manny. "These are the tracks the evidence tech cast this morning. We didn't know anything about them except they weren't any of our outfits. What do you make of them?"

Manny's reputation often caught up with the real-life Senior Special Agent Tanno. He knew Willie had read his case write-ups in the *FBI Bulletin*, because he was asking about recent cases on the drive up here. Willie asked about the child abductor Manny caught at the Rosebud four years ago, and about the serial rapist and murderer at Lower Brulé two summers after that. Those cases set him apart from other investigators, and made them look at him with awe. Willie expected him to conjure up some insightful analysis, like the tracks belonged to a 1999 Chevy Lumina, and the tires are R78x14 Firestones. With one bad shock and driven by a midget transvestite missing two toes. But Manny didn't have any magic answers. "All I know is they're new mud-and-snows. And by the clarity of the impressions, they haven't been run very much."

"Jeeza. New tires. That'll narrow it down."

Manny nodded. How many times had Unc sent him out to help a friend who had blown a tire? Everyone around here rode skins on their cars, and people called them "maypops," because they may pop at any time. Manny called them "willpops," because with cords poking through the treadless rubber of the tires, flats were inevitable. Even government cars rode baldies. Only high-ranking folks with some stroke had new tires.

"You know anyone around here running new rubber?"

Willie shook his head. "The lieutenant bought a new Mustang last month, and there's a few other new cars I've seen now and again. Could be a rental. Bet your Hertz got new tires."

"Bet it does. What else did forensics find?"

"Sweetgrass," Willie answered. "I thought that was odd."

"Sweetgrass is pretty common around here."

"But not crushed up. Like someone conducted a ritual. That's what Margaret uses in her ceremonies, crushed sweetgrass."

"And nothing was said of the cut-grass?"

Willie's smile faded. "What cut-grass?"

"Here." Manny squatted and grabbed a spindly green stalk from the middle of the tire print where it had been run over and imbedded in the dirt. He touched the sharp slender leaf, and instantly blood appeared on his finger. "Now where does cut-grass grow in these parts?" he mumbled with his finger in his mouth.

Willie dropped his head. "Riverbanks. Ponds. Places that are a hell of a lot wetter than this place."

"Well, we haven't found the Holy Grail." Manny nudged Willie. "Just one more thing to keep in mind, though. Now show me precisely where Jason died."

Willie pointed to a spot three yards from where Jason had parked. The depression in the dirt was blown clear, but the large pool of blackened blood showed Jason's position where he was killed. Manny knelt and ran his hand over the dirt.

Willie knelt beside him. "Find something?"

Manny looked into the light and studied depressions around where Jason had lain. Someone had walked around the murder scene to make those prints; their flatness stood in contrast to the deep V marks made by Willie's boots. "These are shallow but they should have been obvious hours ago. Did the tech take a cast of any?"

Willie shrugged. "Not while I was watching them. What is it?"

"Shoe prints. Blowing clear pretty fast. They're older than the tech's footprints, and the soles are flat. *Hard to age*, Unc told him. *When the wind blows strong, tracks can fool you into thinking they're older than they are.* Sometimes he and Unc would close on the animals they tracked, then let the animal go its way. Other times they killed the animal for the food, but always with a deep respect for the gift of its life. It had been years since he had to study tracks such as these, but something about these footprints gnawed at him.

"It'll give you a chance to reconnect with your roots," Niles had told him when he explained Manny's temporary assignment to Pine Ridge. "Practice up on that tracking you are always so good at."

"But I got a class starting up. I've got prep work I have—"

"Reconnect like you did a couple years ago when you went to the Rosebud Reservation." Niles ignored him.

"Screw you. I got no desire to reconnect with my roots. Any more than I wanted to connect with my roots that time you sent me to Lower Brulé. Or Standing Rock. Or Crow Creek. You know Niles, if you had half a brain, your ass would be lopsided."

"Now, Manny." Niles smiled at him, and ordered another drink. "I am not going to fire you, so don't get potty-mouthed. Just take the assignment, and solve the case so you can come back here and teach."

"And wonderful Supervisory Agent Ben Niles will get the credit for solving the homicide. You might even get promoted for it."

"I might. After all, a good supervisor knows how to assign his resources."

Niles's resource would now have to take all his knowledge of Pine Ridge and more to solve this case in two weeks before the academy started.

"Here's another print," Willie announced proudly. He ran his hand over a faint depression. "And one there, going in another direction."

"You look at Jason's shoes?"

"They were hiking shoes with Vibram soles. Not smooth like these."

Manny stood and heard snap, crackle, and pop in his knees. He needed to get some road time in to work out the kinks. "Looks like the killer was worried that someone might come along and spot him. Looks like he turned all around. Watched everywhere while he waited for Jason."

"Or maybe he looked around after he killed him."

"That's another possibility." Willie's chest puffed slightly. "In any event, the killer wasn't worried about covering his tracks. These prints are so faint, the only thing I can tell about them is that they are big shoes. Maybe size ten or larger."

Willie put his foot beside the track. "At least ten."

"And Jason had Vibram-soled hikers so it wasn't his."

"I understand you knew him."

Manny hesitated. "I knew him through my brother, Reuben. I was quite a bit younger than them."

"The lieutenant said your brother and Jason were active in AIM together."

"They were." Manny had looked up to Reuben and the others in the American Indian Movement. Manny's friends constantly prodded him for stories about Reuben, stories about AIM's take-over of government offices in the name of Red rights, or stories about retribution against store owners hostile to Indians. Tales abounded of AIM Indians fighting non-AIM Indians who had sold out to the *wasicu*. People pressed him so much about his older brother's exploits that Manny was often the center of attention himself. Lumpy wasn't the only one who accused him of taking the easy way off the reservation rather than face the Lakota problem. Reuben had stayed and fought for Red rights. Too bad he chose to toe the wrong side of the line.

As a boy growing up in Reuben's shadow, Manny adored his older brother. Until Reuben was sentenced to the state penitentiary for the murder of another Indian. Suddenly, Manny was a fifteen-year-old boy without a brother to show him the way to fight for his own rights. Manny always believed Reuben was innocent, but then he was found guilty for murdering Billy Two Moons. And Manny no longer had him to look up to.

"You hungry?" Willie finally broke the silence.

"Famished. Next you'll be telling me Margaret Catches has you eating tubers or deer droppings. If that's what you had in mind . . ."

"Not hardly," Willie laughed and led Manny back to the cruiser. Willie grabbed a Budweiser cooler from the trunk and sat in the shade of the car. "Aunt Lizzy knew you wouldn't take a break, so she fixed a late lunch for us." They sat on the ground with their backs against the car and the cooler between them. Willie passed Manny a sandwich and a bottle of Hires root beer.

Before Manny unwrapped his sandwich, he grabbed his cell phone from his belt. Niles had left a message for Manny to return his call. Manny looked at the signal bars and frowned.

"They don't work so hot around the rez," Willie said. "There's not many phone towers around here because the cell company thinks us Skins use smoke signals and don't need cell service."

"I thought the Apaches used smoke signals."

"Might as well have been all the way down there for as hard as service is to get here. I can have the dispatcher place a call."

"Naw. It's just my boss reminding me about a new academy class in two weeks. He can wait. Now, let's look at those crime scene photos," Manny said between mouthfuls of turkey sandwich.

Willie reached through the car window, grabbed the manila folder, and set it on the cooler. Manny licked a bit of mayo from his finger before he opened the folder. The top photo showed the overall crime scene, including where Jason had parked his maroon Lincoln Blackwood and where Manny had spotted the tire tracks.

He placed the photo facedown and grabbed the next one. Jason's body lay on the ground in front of the truck. Manny turned the picture to the light. A war club protruded between the skull plates at the top of his head. The stone head of the club was buried so that most of it was below the skull, with the shaft resting against Jason's head. Manny knew about artifacts from a theft investigation on Standing Rock, but he was no authority on them. The single feather attached to the club's shaft fluttered, animated because the wind had been blowing strongly the moment the picture was snapped. The effect made the scene come alive.

The next photo showed Jason's head cocked toward the cameraman. The *hiakigle*, the teeth setting in death, grinned at the photographer as blood pooled beside Jason's cheek in the dirt. Manny had examined many crime scenes and photos of scenes in his years as an investigator, but even he had to put his sandwich down and look away.

"Know anything about the war club?" he asked after a long silence.

Willie finished his root beer and grabbed another from the cooler. "It's authentic. Lieutenant Looks Twice said I'm nuts. He said it was a good copy produced by some Brulé in Piedmont. I took a course in Indian artifacts last semester, and I told the lieutenant it was original, but he doesn't believe me. He's calling in some expert from the Rosebud to verify it."

"Then if it's original, it's worth a bundle."

"A big bundle," Willie agreed. "So why would anyone leave it buried in Jason's head?"

"You tell me."

Willie put down his bag of chips. "How about our man's wealthy and wanted to make a statement that money means little to him. Or maybe he didn't know it was authentic."

Manny nodded. "But why would the killer leave the club for investigators to find and process for latent prints?"

Willie paused again. "Maybe the killer figured he had no chance of being caught. Thumbing his nose at us. Taunting us to catch him."

Manny nodded approval. "Or the club's been wiped of prints. Or the killer's never been arrested, and knows the prints wouldn't be on file anywhere."

"Or wore gloves."

Manny agreed, and continued looking at the pictures. "What did your crime scene tech make of this?" Manny pointed to bruising on Jason's left cheek and nose. "It's apart from any lividity, and by the dark color it looks several days old."

Willie grabbed the photo while he reached inside his shirt pocket and grabbed a can of Copenhagen. He put a pinch under his lip and offered the can to Manny. He shook his head and instinctively reached for the pack of cigarettes no longer in his shirt pocket. "Those bruises are old. Lieutenant Looks Twice and Jason got into a fight a few days ago when Jason was making unwanted advances on Aunt Lizzy."

"Why would Lumpy jump to Elizabeth's defense?"

"She says the lieutenant's always had a thing for her."

Manny grabbed another photo of Jason lying on the ground beside his truck. "Blood splatter here." Manny pointed. Willie leaned closer. "And here. It shows Jason faced his pickup when he got clubbed. That would coincide with those faint footprints facing his truck."

Willie opened his bag of chips. "How can you tell?"

"A blood pattern shows a lot, like where someone stood or knelt at the time the weapon contacted the body." He pointed out blood on the door and seat. "He was clubbed as he faced his truck. Probably leaning in. Blood cast off here shows he was hit twice." Manny ran his finger over the arc along the outside of the pickup where blood mist had landed. "Here's where the killer cocked the club for a second blow."

"Does that help us any?"

Manny shrugged. "Jason turned to get something from inside his truck, perhaps. Maybe he was running from his attacker and started to dive in? Who knows why victims or killers do the things they do. We may never know."

Manny held the last photo to the light. A small revolver lay in the dirt several feet from Jason's hand. "Was it fired?"

"Once."

"Whose gun?"

"Jason's. The state issued him a concealed permit this spring, and the serial number matches the permit. Think he was going for it?"

Manny nodded. "Either going for it when he got into a tussle with the killer, or going for it before the fight started. He might have shot his killer before he was attacked."

"Jeeza. Like a preemptive strike?"

"Something like that. Find the slug?"

Willie shook his head. Manny made a mental note to check the Pine Ridge and Rapid City hospitals to see if anyone had been treated for a gunshot wound today. "The lieutenant figures it went somewhere into the prairie and we'll never find it."

Manny hated to admit it, but Lumpy was probably dead-on with that assessment.

By the time they finished their lunch, the sun had dropped over the hill behind them. They stood and returned to the scene a final time. They walked around it and stared into the sun to catch shadows that would reveal anything they might have missed. Manny knelt along different points of the crime scene, and looked across dusty ridges, trying to pick up signs. Satisfied nothing remained, they climbed back into Willie's patrol car and headed back to Pine Ridge Village.

"Aunt Lizzy knew Jason Red Cloud pretty well," Willie volunteered as he turned onto Highway 18. "They worked together on the resort project."

"Because Elizabeth's the finance officer?"

Willie nodded. "They worked together every day the past two

months leading up to the ground breaking. Aunt Lizzy didn't want to work with Jason's executive assistant, Clara Downing, and insisted on dealing directly with Jason."

"Jason's assistant and Elizabeth didn't get along?"

Willie shrugged. "I figure it was a woman thing."

"Woman thing?"

"Sure. You know—that thing women do to each other when they don't get along. When one wears a bigger diamond than the other. One drives a nicer car than the other. One looks a little better in short skirts than the other one does. You know—women things."

"Sure." Catfights from a dozen offices he'd worked out of came back to him. Women were far crueler than any man in an office could be. "Has anyone interviewed Clara Downing?"

Willie shook his head. "I wanted to but I was assigned the shit detail of standing guard until the tech finished. She knew Jason as well as anyone."

"Then I'll call her first thing. And where is Elizabeth living these days, so I can talk with her?"

"Batesland."

"That's a long drive into town every day."

"Twenty-six miles," Willie confirmed. "About once a week she runs it. Bikes it a couple days a week to keep in shape."

Manny could appreciate the distance. Since getting back into his running regime, the best he had been able to do was the 20K Run for the Homeless back in Langley. "Bet she still runs marathons."

"Big-time. She's taken the Black Hills Classic three years in a row."

"Still a runner." Manny laughed. "Well, she'll give me hell when she sees how I let myself go. But if we're this close to her house, let's drop by and visit."

Before Willie could turn around, the dispatcher ordered him to respond to the powwow grounds on the west end of Pine

Ridge. A drunk had staggered into the middle of the road trying to flag down passing cars.

"I'm on an investigation," Willie radioed back.

A brief lull followed before Lumpy's voice blared across the police radio. "You want to see your retirement, you'll do your follow-up another time. Take that drunk call."

Willie apologized to Manny.

"No need. Let's just say it's your lieutenant's way of keeping his fingers in the investigation." Lumpy would love to see the Living Legend fail. Niles's Living Legend. At least that's how Ben thought he always convinced Manny to take these cases. *Flatter the Indian, and he'll do anything*, he wanted to tell Willie.

They drove past Big Bat's to the Y intersection. A man teetered in the middle of the road by the powwow grounds, and the headlights lit him up. "Henry Lone Wolf," Manny breathed. For those who never remembered a face, Henry's would be the exception. His bulbous nose was red and swollen, with deep scarring that looked like someone had used it for a bulletin board. His nose was perched between two close-set eyes, on cheeks that had more lines and spiderwebs than a Rand McNally. He glared at the police car.

"I'd thought he'd be dead by now."

"He is," Willie answered, and stopped within a cruiser-length of Henry. "He's just so well pickled he doesn't know it yet." Henry danced in the middle of the road as he yelled obscenities at the police car. "I figure ol' 'Lone Wolf McQuade' will outlive us all."

As Willie walked toward him, Henry assumed his best fighting stance, balled fists held high in front of him, and flicked out slow, labored jabs at invisible opponents. He spied Willie and threw a limp right cross, and nearly lost his balance. Willie dodged Henry's fist and spun him around and had him cuffed before Manny got out of the car.

Willie eased him into the backseat behind the cage. "About Lone Wolf McQuade back there," Willie explained. "Someone started teasing Henry that he was like that Chuck Norris character, the way he always fought us, and was always belligerent when we arrested him. Now every time we haul him in, Henry feels obligated to fight because of his nickname."

"And don't you forget it, Officer With Horn," Henry yelled from the back. He banged on the Plexiglas divider with his head. "That you Officer Tanno?"

"It's me, Henry. Long time."

"Too long. Heard you came back here to clean up that Red Cloud mess these local yokels can't handle."

Manny listened to Henry vent. No use arguing with a drunk. Willie parked at the jail and opened the door for Henry.

"Just wait a minute." Henry jerked his arm from Willie's grasp and turned to Manny.

"What is it, Henry?"

"These guys didn't ask me, but I got information about that Red Cloud killing."

Manny waited for Henry to continue. "A week ago I was having a right good sleep in back of the tribal building. That girl of your sister-in-law . . . What's her name?"

"Erica," Willie volunteered, then looked sideways at Manny.

"Yeah. Erica. She and Jason had a terrible argument. Bad enough to wake me up. Nice night. The windows was open. It was like I was right there with them in that room they was so loud."

"Go on," Manny said.

"Well, Erica yelled that she was going to tell her husband everything. That things had gone far enough."

"Then what?"

"That's it. They moved off into another part of the building and I didn't hear the rest."

"What does this have to do with Jason's murder?"

Henry shrugged. "It was just suspicious. You know I'm good for it. I gave you good information once before, 'member? 'Member when I told you that your brother, Reuben, was at Lizzy's apartment the night Billy Two Moons was murdered? 'Member?"

Manny " 'membered." He had arrested Henry on a public intox charge as he lay passed out across the border from White Clay. Reuben had pleaded guilty to the Two Moons murder eight years before, and Manny desperately wanted some piece of information, some new bit of evidence to hold high and tell everyone his brother didn't kill Two Moons. Manny believed then that Henry lied to reduce his jail time, just as he was doing now.

"And what do you want for this pearl of information?"

Henry smiled. "Just to be released by Thursday. That's payday here, you know."

The ruse hadn't worked when Manny was a tribal officer, and it didn't work against Willie now. He steered Henry down the long corridor to the booking counter, while Manny walked to Lumpy's office and plopped down in his velvet Elvis, relaxing his eyes until Willie came back from booking Henry. When they got outside, Willie asked about Henry.

"You think there's anything to your brother and Aunt Lizzy being together the night Two Moons was killed?"

"Tell me, did you believe Henry when he told us about Jason and Erica arguing? Could he even remember anything as drunk as he is now?"

Willie shook his head. "I see your point."

"Henry always maintained he saw Reuben with Elizabeth that night. When he told me that, he was in the same shape he's in now. A man who hates authority like Reuben would never have confessed unless he did it."

Willie dropped Manny off at his rental and he followed Willie to the housing. He was beside his door before Manny could turn off the polka music.

"Second door on the right."

Manny dipped into his pocket for the keys. "We'll meet up tomorrow after I visit your aunt."

Willie drove away and Manny fumbled with the key.

"Manny." A soft voice stopped him.

Desirée Chasing Hawk sashayed out of the apartment next to the one Lumpy arranged for Manny. Her sheer teddy stopped just above her knees, enough to give Manny a look at the finest pair of legs he had seen since high school.

"Manny. You going to just stand there? After twenty years, I'd have thought you'd be glad to see me. You're still as hot as you were in high school."

Manny sucked in a quick breath as her perfume, applied so that just a hint of it reached him, reminding him of what gifts she might offer a man.

"I must not have been as hot as Lumpy."

"Water under the bridge."

"You live here?"

She laughed. "Yep. In the apartment next to the tribe's. When Leon told me you would be staying next to me, I thought I'd orgasm. Come in and we'll uncork a bottle of wine. Catch up on each other."

Manny wanted to accept her offer. Wanted to go inside. Wanted to catch up on her. But Desirée always had her own agenda, and the last thing he needed now was for Desirée to distract him. Even if she was a sexy distraction. "Take a rain check?" Manny dropped the keys. Fumbled for the lock. Dropped them again. "Another night. I got to get up early."

She stepped toward him just as he found the lock. "Tomorrow night," she called after him as he slammed the door behind him. He stood with his back against the door, panting faster than a lizard on a hot rock.

"You asshole, Lumpy. You could have given me any other apartment."

Tomorrow he'd have words with him. Right after he talked with Clara Downing and Elizabeth about Jason Red Cloud. And even though he discounted Henry's tale of the argument Tuesday night, he would ask Elizabeth about Erica's fight with Jason as well.

CHAPTER 3

Manny squinted the entire twenty-six miles to Batesland. When he started for Elizabeth's this morning, he had clutched the sunglass case. Now the glasses were missing in action, and his temples throbbed from the morning headache.

Willie said this had been a dry year, but some crops had thrived. Off to the left, cornfields stood higher than his car. To the right, green alfalfa fields flourished in the heat.

The smoothness of the road eased his headache. He marveled at the highway, one of the few newer blacktopped roads on Pine Ridge. As a tribal policeman he'd driven this same road faster than he had a right to. Most reservation roads back then were little more than dirt paths or two-tracks, and he'd dreaded going to emergency calls. He was constantly afraid the cruiser would drop into a rut or pothole and come apart at the high speeds. And he often lost his sunglasses in the commotion of fighting to maintain control. The memories made him squint all the more, and he held his hand above his eyes.

He turned at the Batesland Store and drove past the Wapamni Bed and Breakfast. Just as he passed the thick shelter belt of elm and cottonwood, a single house rose from the trees. He felt like some ancient conquistador first spying the Mayan pyramids jutting up from the rain forest. He didn't expect to see such a house out here. The mahogany-stained sundeck spanned the entire west side. In the center of the deck, matching lawn chairs held a meeting around a table directly under a giant yellow umbrella, inviting guests to sit and stay.

Willie said that on the side opposite the driveway flower boxes would be cupping each windowsill to catch the rising sun. Lizzy had bought the house as a fixer-upper, and did all the work herself. He bragged about her prowess with a hammer and saw. Every piece of window trim was mitered, the siding matching up perfectly with the flashing.

For a moment, Manny would have traded his suburban colonial and all the hoopla of D.C. for her secluded home. He would have traded the smog and hubbub of Arlington for the serenity and quiet of this summer day. He would drink the morning air without having to spit out the grit of pollution.

But now Washington defined Manny Tanno the FBI agent as Pine Ridge had defined Manny Tanno the Lakota. He had tried walking the Red Road here at Pine Ridge. Tried and failed. Now he was just homesick to return to Virginia.

Elizabeth bent over a laundry basket under a clothesline. She wiped the line with her daisy-printed apron and reached into a canvas bag that hung on the line. She fished out some clothespins and hung a wet top. The stiff breeze lifted her midback black hair, and the sun reflected reddish highlights, a product of her Scottish father and Brulé mother from Crow Creek. Salt-and-pepper flecks around her temples only added to her beauty.

She bent over to grab another top from the basket and spotted him. She smiled and waved, a smile that made him feel as giddy as he'd felt the first time he saw her with Reuben, a smile that could have lured any man into her arms if she wanted. Manny blushed like a schoolboy caught peeking into the girls' locker room. She waved him on and ran to his car. He climbed out and she wrapped her arms around him and hugged.

"Look at you." He held Elizabeth at arm's length. It had been years since he had last seen her, but her figure and her complexion had remained youthful. Matte mauve lipstick showed off her not-too-pouty lips, and smudged eggplant eyeliner accentuated her almond-shaped hazel eyes. She never had needed much makeup, and she remained the poster child of beauty and health. He swayed as he caught scent: subtle, inviting, distinctive. Sweet lilac perhaps. Maybe some prairie berry that had brushed against her on one of her runs. He was a teen when she and Reuben married. She was Manny's first crush, until Desirée Chasing Hawk pushed that crush aside. His face flushed at the memories.

She stepped back and looked at him. "And what's your secret?"

"Secret?"

"You haven't aged one whit. Not one. Why hasn't some lucky lady scooped you up by now?"

Manny laughed. "Reality's the only obstacle to happiness. I'd get too close to someone, and remind myself that familiarity breeds children. I don't cotton to kids much. But what about you? Why didn't you remarry?"

"I'm married to the tribe."

"Willie said you'd got your degree after Reuben was sent up."

She nodded. "I had to do something after we were divorced. People got so used to Reuben and me being joined at the hip. It didn't look right for me to mooch off the tribe. So I made up my mind to do something about it."

"Well, good for you. Bet it keeps you hopping."

"All I have time for is work and work out. But how do you keep looking so young?"

Manny laughed. *You really wouldn't think I looked young if I took off my hat.* "Hitting the road for some daily pavement pounding. And getting a hug now and again from some foxy lady, keeping foxy by running, I see." He exaggerated his gaze as he looked from her face to her toes to her face.

"Most days. Willie said you'd be driving out this way. Got coffee on."

Before Manny could answer, she wrapped her arm in his and led him up the steps across the deck to the back door. "Excuse the door," Elizabeth said. "With the land falling away like it was, I couldn't make that east door the main entrance."

"Don't apologize." Tradition dictated that the sacred entry into a Lakota home was to be on the east side, and she was genuinely sorry for not having her front door facing that direction. Elizabeth had kept up with the old ways, something Manny had not done as a city Sioux.

Her skill with home improvement became apparent when he stepped into her kitchen. Marbled floor tiles blended with an arched doorway opening to the rest of house. Copper pots hung from a small ladder suspended over a butcher-block island counter. Light glistened off the pans and they banged together in time with the breeze from the nearby window. He challenged himself to find one thing that was out of place, one thing that was askew in her kitchen, but he couldn't.

A calico cat with a stub tail sunned itself on the counter. When Manny reached to stroke it the cat hissed louder than the coffeepot perking. It bared its fangs and arched its back to spring. Manny backed away. *So much for an Oglala warrior having a special way with animals.*

"I'm sorry. Mabel never acts like that."

"I guess I have that effect on women. Even feline women."

Mabel ran from the room, and Manny waited for Elizabeth to pour coffee. Across one countertop Elizabeth had arranged the coffeepot and blender and four-slice toaster. The other counter remained bare for food preparation. He sat in one of the heavy-backed captain's chairs situated around the oval oak table.

Simmering orange, maybe tangerine, potpourri enhanced the aroma of fresh brewed coffee greeting him. Elizabeth grabbed mugs hanging from a wooden cup tree on the counter. "Erica said you hadn't changed."

"Well, she sure has." Erica and her new husband Jon met Manny last summer when they attended an Indian sovereignty conference in D.C. "She's grown. I see why she did so well in those beauty pageants as a kid. How is she?"

"Just great," Elizabeth answered, and placed a large coffee mug and a plate of oatmeal cookies in front of him. "She and Jon are getting along well, both involved in their own businesses in Rapid City."

Manny wanted to ask more about Erica. But first he had to know what Elizabeth knew. "Tell me about Jason?"

"Jason?"

"I understand you two worked together on the resort project."

Elizabeth smoothed her dress and sat across from Manny. She stirred a teaspoon of sugar into her coffee and waited until it dissolved before she answered. When she did, she spoke slowly, deliberately.

"Jason was never one of us. He was a rich kid. He was like the hangers-around-the-fort Indians in the old days." Manny nodded. He sipped his coffee and waited for her to continue. She lifted her spoon from her cup and watched coffee drip down, creating tiny swirls in the liquid.

"He liked to be near the action, but not part of it. He quit the movement after a few years to attend college."

"But you quit AIM to go to college, too." Manny wished he

could drag his question back, but he couldn't. *A closed mouth gathers no feet*, as Unc said. Elizabeth's lip quivered, and he knew he'd entered touchy territory.

"I quit AIM and everything else connected with Reuben when we split. Right before he murdered Billy Two Moons. I needed more than a clerk's check from the tribe, so I got my degree. Not an expensive Ivy League education like Erica. I couldn't afford that, but I did all right for myself."

"You must have impressed the tribal council. Finance officer is a prestigious position."

Elizabeth laughed. "LaVonne Drapeaux was finance officer back then, and I was her assistant. Everyone thought LaVonne would be there until she died. And she was—she died in that car wreck just outside Manderson. I got the job by default, so I guess you could say my degree paid off."

Manny had read about LaVonne's accident in the *Indian Country Today* eleven years ago. She had been driving her new Mercury on good roads, and when she came to the same hill where Jason's parents wrecked and died, her car veered off the road and plunged into a thirty-foot gully.

"I got the job despite my ex-husband."

Manny looked away.

"I didn't mean—"

"Don't worry. I still don't talk to Reuben. I'll have to see him during this trip, because he knew Jason back in the day, but I feel the same about him as you do."

"Maybe not quite the same." Manny read not a smile or a hint that she missed Reuben and their days as a couple, or that said she hated Reuben for what he had done to their future. For all Manny's skills as an interviewer, he could interpret nothing in her expression. She had been asked about her relationship with Reuben after the Two Moons murder, and she'd rehearsed her answer so many times it was rote, devoid of any emotion.

She took a slow sip of her coffee. When she continued, her voice wavered.

"As much pain as Reuben caused me, I still miss him now and again. I was a giddy eighteen-year-old when we first met. He was a star with AIM and I cherished being with him. I loved people looking at me like I was somebody."

Manny shrugged. "Most teen girls are pretty impressionable. I remember Reuben sometimes brought you over to Unc's for supper. I can still hear the kids grilling me about Reuben's new squeeze."

Elizabeth smiled. "We were in the movement together. Indian rights and all that. Going places for the cause. Making it hard for society to take advantage of us Skins. And in between the protests and the letter writing and the newspaper interviews, we partied. And grew to love one another. I knew—just knew— we'd always be a couple. I just knew Reuben and I would cross onto the Spirit Road together. Even after he killed Two Moons, I knew Reuben was no good for me. But it didn't matter. I'd have still been with him if he hadn't been convicted. That sound bad?"

"Not at all. People always called Reuben charismatic, like he could charm a used-car salesman out of his commission. He was a lot like Jason in that way. He used you."

Elizabeth turned her head, and tears formed at the corners of her eyes. He wanted to ease her pain, convince her that she still meant something to him despite her breakup with Reuben, but Manny couldn't find the words. He had shifted from the loving ex-brother-in-law to the investigator who needed answers, and he felt as much like a rat as Billy Two Moons had been. "You were telling me more about Jason."

"Of course." She dabbed at the corners of her eyes with a napkin and began to nibble on a cookie. "The three of us were inseparable when we were in AIM, doing all sorts of nasty things in the name of Indian rights. Bad things. Jason used to come around when he knew Reuben was gone, but he knew Reuben would kill him if he ever found out he came around and flirted like he did. That's when I started disliking him as much as Reuben did."

"But I thought they were buds?"

"They were. Until Jason got the ultimatum from his folks: go to college or forget about taking over the family business. That always grated on Reuben. He became angry when he thought of Jason selling out his traditional values for the quick Red Cloud buck, and Reuben never forgave him."

Manny chanced another cookie. Oatmeal cookies were made with oatmeal, and oatmeal was healthy. "When was the last time you saw Jason?"

"A week ago, last Thursday night in the finance office."

"Night? Like after-hours?" Henry Lone Wolf told him about Erica and Jason arguing, but not about Elizabeth and Jason meeting there.

Elizabeth laughed. "Not what you're thinking. Jason often came around when he thought everyone else had left. The office the tribe let him use was next to mine. He had a snoot full that night like he usually did, but he left before he got too frisky."

Manny recalled Jason's bruised cheek and nose in the crime scene photos. "Did Lumpy Looks Twice help him leave?"

Elizabeth sipped her coffee. She toyed with her spoon as if reading the ripples again. "Jason came into my office drunk. He put his arm around me, and I tried to push him away, but he weighed twice as much as me. When I smelled his sickening sweet whiskey breath I managed to push him off. He lost it. Jerked file drawers open, tossed folders all over the floor. Mean things. Then Lumpy came in and tossed him out. For once Jason was drunker than Lumpy. They fought, though it wasn't much of a fight."

"Did Jason often come on to you when he drank?

"When he drank?" Elizabeth laughed. "Jason came on to me whenever he had a free moment."

"Then why didn't you deal with his assistant, this Clara Downing, if he was so obnoxious?"

"Clara? Never. I wanted the resort to succeed. She'd only muck things up."

"She must have something on the ball to have become Jason's executive assistant."

Elizabeth's lip quivered. Her eyes narrowed as she fixed them on Manny. "She's got no formal education. None. Jason hired her right out of high school. She rose to the top of one of the most esteemed development firms in the West with not even one semester of college."

Manny recognized Elizabeth's resentment and quickly changed the tone. "When did you start dealing directly with Jason?"

"He started coming here two months ago, when he first started his project."

"That when he started to get frisky?"

Elizabeth nodded. "He put on a lot of weight since his AIM days, but he still dressed to the nines. He figured most women would fall for his money and his charm."

"But not you?"

"Never."

"Who else did he see when he came here?"

Elizabeth paused. Her eyes darted upward as she dug into her own memory. "Jason met with many people when he came here on day trips. He held meetings with different contractors, and talked with different factions living around Wounded Knee where he wanted to build the resort. He brought everyone together and convinced them how the tribe could benefit. His charm eventually won out, and he got the land deal for the resort.

"When he needed to be here full-time, the tribe let him stay in a house they own in Pine Ridge so he didn't have to travel from Rapid City. I had the displeasure of seeing him every day, and he thought I'd pulled strings so we could be together. That was the kind of ego he had."

Manny understood egos. Some agents needed to be the center of attention, needed people to think they shone as brightly as the spotlight they craved. He read that same ego in Lumpy since he'd returned here. By what Elizabeth just described about Jason, he and Lumpy and many agents Manny knew could be brothers. "Tell me something about the resort plans."

Elizabeth refilled their cups and restocked the plate of cookies that Manny ate. "I can't do the resort justice," she said over her shoulder. She dumped the grounds down the garbage disposal and started another pot of coffee. "You'll have to come to the finance building and look at the mock-up in Jason's office. It was ambitious for us Oglalas, we who never agree on anything. But that was Jason's persistence and skill as a negotiator. He could tell you to go to hell and you'd look forward to the trip. He might have been a jerk, but he charmed the pants right off most people."

Manny asked for an overview. Elizabeth sat in the chair and broke off another piece of her cookie. "It would have been a true five-star RV resort, with two hundred hookups located on Porcupine Butte."

"That would have overlooked Wounded Knee cemetery."

Elizabeth nodded. "Jason said just being close to the memorial alone would add to the tourist draw. To hell with what the memorial means, he just wanted to work every angle."

"And what do you think?"

She shrugged. "The resort would have been a huge draw. A fence would enclose a yard for every RV site, with shower and toilets for every two spaces. The land would be maintained like a golf course. People wouldn't expect that here on Pine Ridge."

"How did he arrange for the land?" For years, tribal members wanted a Wounded Knee Massacre shrine there, but the shrine never materialized. Too many factions and self-interests involved, and private-property owners wanted triple their land value to sell. And the tribe wanted to hold on to their portions because of spiritual reasons.

"No one could figure out how to get everyone together. Enter Jason 'P.T. Barnum' Red Cloud and his troupe of high-priced corporate lawyers. The greatest show on Earth. On the rez anyway. A little song and dance here. Some razzmatazz there. And presto, he charmed Ellie White Mouse out of that land she owned adjacent to Oglala Lake, where the tribe's been drooling to build a marina for so many years. Then presto, Jason traded that property for land the tribe owned around Wounded Knee."

"But what about the private owners? Even Red Cloud Development couldn't afford land prices there."

She held in a deep breath then let out a loud sigh. "Jason got up on his soapbox in Billy Mills Hall and preached about the profits the resort would pour out upon his people, and they believed him. They wanted to believe him. He was everyone's long-lost best friend. He was the rainmaker come to town in the midst of a drought. He was no less than the savior of all their lost souls. I guess even he started believing his pitch, because he wanted to believe in prosperity, too." She pushed her cookie away. "Or at least get his business out of debt."

"Would that RV stuff have drawn enough tourists to make the resort profitable?"

"Not if that were all." She pulled her long hair behind her ears. Beaded earrings on gold wires dangled from her earlobes and twirled as she spoke. "Jason planned to run horseback rentals with Lakota guides taking riders on day trips, and a shuttle would ferry tourists to the Prairie Wind Casino for some day gambling. He'd even planned to charter buses to Rapid City for what he referred to as a 'shopping safari.' He planned an arcade for the kids and an outdoor theater. He planned so thoroughly that everyone knew it would make the tribe wealthy."

"If he hadn't been killed perhaps the tribe would have been able to get on its feet."

Elizabeth shrugged. "Jason was way over his head."

"How so?"

"The Red Cloud Development Corporation was about to file Chapter 11." Elizabeth put another heaping plate of cookies on the table. Manny didn't want to be impolite and grabbed another.

"But Red Cloud Development thrived under him. That'd be like Bill Gates filing Chapter 11."

Elizabeth looked first at her coffee cup, then at her apron, which she twisted in her hand. When she answered Manny, tears clouded her eyes. "Jason hired Erica to help with the resort. He said she was a bright kid, that she would bring a lot to the project. I thought he hired her because of her Harvard degree, but he hired her because she's an Oglala. He used Erica to help sell the idea to the tribe. She's a good kid. You know that."

He wanted to comfort Lizzy, wrap his arms around her, tell her Erica would be all right. But that was one thing the bureau never taught its agents: how to shed a tear with a victim.

Elizabeth slumped in her seat, her energy drained, their conversation ended.

"How can I get hold of Erica?"

"You don't believe me about Jason?" she snapped, then held up her hand. "That didn't come out right. I'm sorry. I know you have to talk with her about his finances."

Manny nodded. "And there's another thing." He told her what Henry Lone Wolf said about the argument he overheard between Erica and Jason days before his murder.

"But that sounds like they were having an affair." Elizabeth stood and met his gaze. "He was twice her age. And she's happily married. Not only does she love Jon, it wouldn't look right, would it? She wouldn't risk that."

"I figured it was Henry's bottle talking again. But I had to ask."

"Of course." She smoothed her apron, her composure reclaimed. She jotted Erica's phone number on a napkin and handed it to him as she walked with him to the deck. She stood watching him from the screen door as he got into his rental, then she walked over and stood beside his door.

"One last thing. You'll hear about it sooner or later, so it might as well be from me. Last Monday, I took my lunch break at Big Bat's with one of the girls from the office. Reuben was there with a couple of his Heritage Kids when Jason came in and started toward our table. Reuben stepped in front of him, and they had words. Reuben was angry enough to kill him, people will say, but I think I know Reuben enough to say he wouldn't."

"What did they argue about?"

Elizabeth shrugged. "Reuben never got over me—never got over the divorce. I know he figured Jason and I had something going and became jealous over seeing us together, but he wouldn't have hurt Jason. Not really."

Whenever he could talk himself into seeing Reuben, Manny would ask him about it.

He started out of Elizabeth's driveway and stopped to check the bars on his cell phone. He punched in the number for the Red Cloud Development Corporation and waited until a woman answered. Clara Downing wasn't in, and the operator wasn't sure when she would be. Manny hung up, more determined than ever that Clara Downing held answers to many of the questions he had.

CHAPTER 4

"Hoka hey." Willie handed Manny a large foam cup through the open passenger-side window.

"Hoka hey." The steaming liquid instantly clouded Manny's sunglasses. He shook them in the air. That was the problem with cheap sunglasses. He missed his Gargoyles, wherever they might be. If he could kick himself in the ass for losing them he would. But it was so normal to misplace them, Manny thought he should buy them by the gross. It was hell to get old.

When the fog evaporated from his shades, he climbed in Willie's cruiser. KILI out of Porcupine blared powwow music, its hard, steady drumbeat pounding in Manny's head: like polka music, only harsher. He looked sideways at Willie, then at the radio. Willie turned the music down and cleared his throat.

"Got something to say?"

"You sure you want to do this today?" Willie asked at last.

"I got to talk with Reuben sometime. Better sooner and get it over with. Let's drop by the justice building and check for those fingerprint results first."

Manny sipped his coffee and his glasses fogged again. As they pulled into the parking lot, Manny took them off to air them out and he saw that the parking lot was full. *Lakota Country Times* logo on the side of one car. *Rapid City Journal* on another. *Indian Country Today* on yet another. A KELO news van was set up in front of the building, its T-whip antenna on top assuring some reception for television watchers.

Reporters and producers crowded around a roped-off podium in front of the justice building. Lumpy's head peeked above the wooden lectern in the center. Willie had to park the car outside the fence. As they walked toward the entrance, Lumpy pointed. "Here's Special Agent Tanno now."

The crowd swarmed them and microphones hung in Manny's face. Reporters fired questions, all at once. Willie shouldered his way through to make a path for Manny. He jerked away when someone grabbed his arm. "What the hell's this?"

Lumpy smiled and waved his arm across the crowd. "News conference. They're here to learn from the legendary Agent Tanno."

"I can see that. Who called them?"

Lumpy grinned. "We've been inundated with questions about the progress of the investigation. I'd field the questions, but we're out of the loop. It's your investigation, Hotshot."

"But I didn't prep for a news conference."

Lumpy's toothy grin again.

"You're about as useful as a mint-flavored suppository," Manny called to Lumpy's back as he disappeared into the justice building.

Manny turned to the crowd and held up his hand. "One at a time."

"Sonja Myers." Her voice was soft, faint, and other reporters quieted to listen to her. "Have you identified the prints on the war club that killed Jason Red Cloud?"

Manny fought to keep his train of thought. Blond hair over-filled a *Rapid City Journal* ball cap and she stepped closer to the podium. She wore her jeans a size too tight, and her shirt a size too small.

"The prints? Can you identify them?"

"Who told you there were prints on the murder weapon?"

"Sources."

"Then ask your sources. I can't comment on that just now."

"Then when can I have that information?"

Manny ignored her and called on another reporter.

"Were you assigned this case just because you're an Oglala?"

"What kind of question is that? Who are you?"

"Nathan Yellow Horse. *Lakota Country Times*."

"I was assigned this case in part because of my background at Pine Ridge."

"And if you don't find Red Cloud's killer, your being Oglala is supposed to appease us country Indians?"

"Nonsense," a voice whispered, barely audible. Sonja Myers stepped toward Yellow Horse. "Agent Tanno's here because he's solved every homicide in his career. Isn't that so?"

Manny nodded. If eye candy were real calories, Manny could get fat just watching her.

"Agent Tanno certainly has some ideas as to Red Cloud's killer, don't you?"

"Nothing's conclusive yet." He'd conducted enough news conferences to know how to stall, to parry reporters' questions, to feed them just the right amount of bullshit to get him out of the spotlight.

A KELO reporter pushed his way through the crowd, a cam-era perched on the videographer's shoulder like it was a parrot waiting to throw back whatever Manny had to say. "Is an arrest pending?" The reporter's hair remained pasted to his head, moving not a wisp in the strong wind. Too much hairspray. Or starch. "Will the resort go forward now that Jason Red Cloud is dead?"

"Either way, he leaves the rez when the case is solved." Yellow Horse stepped closer to Manny, and Willie stepped closer to Yellow Horse. "When he's done when this, he won't care one whit about the resort or us."

"Of course he will." Sonja stepped beside Manny and turned to the crowd. "Agent Tanno is doing the job he was assigned. He has roots here. Of course he cares about the project over and above the homicide investigation."

Sonja's hair whipped across her face, and brushed Manny's cheek. He drew in a breath as he caught her essence floating by.

Two other reporters interrupted Yellow Horse, who stepped in front of the KELO man. Manny held up his hand as they jostled for position. "There's nothing I can say." He turned to leave when someone gently squeezed his arm. "Can I call you later?" Manny tried reading something other than professional curiosity in Sonja's blue eyes. "When you have something new?"

"Of course. Call here. The dispatcher will be able to reach me." He didn't trust himself further, and hastily walked inside the justice building.

He stopped just inside the door and listened. Cars started and voices grew fainter. "What the hell was that?"

"We haven't had the press flock here since the Wounded Knee takeover, from what Aunt Lizzy says. We're just not used to it."

"We're just lucky to get through that unscathed."

"You don't know how lucky." Willie handed Manny a cup of coffee and led him to the break room. "If that looker out there, Sonja Myers, had her way, she would have torn into you. Literally. You might have been walking around with just your BVDs."

For a moment the appealing thought crossed Manny's mind

but he brushed it off. A beautiful woman tearing into him. Unlikely, unless it was to get an exclusive on the investigation. "You can bet she has other reasons for coming to my aid out there. Besides, I've got other things on my mind this morning, like how to approach Reuben."

Willie dropped into a chair across the table from Manny. "What are you going to say? It's been thirty years since you talked with him."

Manny shrugged. "You know my brother?"

Willie whistled. "Who around here doesn't?"

"Trouble?"

Willie shook his head and sipped his coffee. "Never. Since he was paroled from the state penitentiary, none of our officers has had official contact with him. He keeps to himself, spends most of his time lining up masonry jobs for his Heritage Kids. But Reuben carries a reputation from his AIM days that would stop a wildcat."

Manny had researched Reuben and learned that most of the Heritage Kids were high school dropouts, troubled Lakota youth from dysfunctional homes, kids who just needed a strong hand to guide them. Reuben Tanno was that strong hand. Manny heard good things about Reuben's kids: Many had cast off their wild streaks and become productive. But Reuben could not help them all, and some of his kids never changed. Some mirrored Reuben, unable to be tamed. It brought back conversations with Unc, how Reuben had been sent to an Indian boarding school but ran away so many times that they gave up bringing him back. "Reuben's a hard worker. Or rather, he sees that his kids are hard workers. He drives them until they're too tired and beat to get into trouble."

"All their construction contracts here on the reservation?"

"Most, because of Reuben's natural intimidation, as much as the quality of their work. Even if Reuben wasn't a 'Nam vet, people remember him from his AIM days and he lands most contracts here."

Manny finished his coffee and tossed the cup into the round file. Reuben had enlisted in the Marines when Manny was only four years old. He had missed his brother, but Unc kept Manny's adoration alive by reading Reuben's letters about actions in South Vietnam. Except for their parents' funeral, he had seen Reuben only once in all those years, when he was wounded landing in a hot LZ near Hue and spent a month recovering at home. Manny wanted to be just like him then.

When Reuben was discharged, he joined the American Indian Movement just in time for the takeover of Alcatraz in 1969. Manny was only eight then, yet he pleaded with Unc to let him join his brother. But Uncle Marion's disdain for Reuben had escalated with the violence and heavy-handed tactics AIM used to enforce their ideologies, and his mood turned foul whenever Reuben's name was mentioned. "He'll only end up with a bullet in his head in some ditch, or making license plates in a federal lockup somewhere."

"But if I could only see him for a little bit, just talk with him, Unc, I know he'd listen to me. What he's doing is good."

"But it's not good." Unc had hefted Manny on his enormous lap and spoke as a father speaks to his child. "Their objective is right: Indian sovereignty and Lakota rights. But their militant methods will destroy us."

Unc told him little about Reuben after that, but Manny heard things whispered around the reservation from AIM supporters: Reuben in the middle of the AIM takeover of Mount Rushmore when Manny was ten; Reuben at the Custer riot in 1973; Reuben in the lead of the Wounded Knee takeover the same year. Reuben's name had been venerated around the reservation for masterminding campaigns that brought the government to its knees. Even his being a suspect in several deaths on Pine Ridge couldn't dampen Manny's idolization. Reuben would never—could never—murder anyone. Especially another Lakota.

Until Billy Two Moons's death when Manny was fifteen. Reuben confessed that he murdered Billy Two Moons and everything changed. People looked differently at Manny, and Manny grew to loathe Reuben's AIM connections ever since. And even though he knew Reuben's confession was sound, that it was obtained legally and without coercion, a small part of him believed Reuben was innocent. Killing another Oglala to save himself, perhaps, but not murder.

"What do you know about the Two Moons killing?"

"Jeeza. That's required reading with Lieutenant Looks Twice. Billy Two Moons, who never had a pot to pee in, drove a new Chrysler 300 to deserted China Gulch right out of Hill City. That'd be . . ."

"In 1976," Manny finished. "Same year they found Anna Mae Pictou-Aquash with a bullet in her head."

Willie nodded. "Rumor was floating around back then the FBI got their hands dirty with her murder."

"But you know that's wrong?"

Willie nodded. "The lieutenant goes out of his way to educate every new officer on that period. 'So history won't repeat itself,' he says. Lot of things that AIM spouted back then were wrong. Lot of things came to light, like some AIM women helped drive Anna Mae from that safe house in Denver to where she was murdered here."

"And Billy Two Moons was just another AIM victim."

Willie nodded. "Some guy from Mitchell with a cabin back up in China Gulch found Two Moons with five .45 slugs in him, and an open can of Pabst Blue Ribbon in his lap."

"And Alex Jumping Bull, who went missing the same night, was never found." Manny dug deep into the mind of a fifteen-year-old boy whose love for his brother had just been trashed.

"No one saw or heard from Jumping Bull again," Willie confirmed. "Even though he and Two Moons were inseparable. There was speculation that Reuben killed him, too, and dumped him somewhere that same night, but Reuben never confessed to killing Jumping Bull."

"I know." Since joining the bureau and teaching interviewing and interrogation at the academy, Manny had studied Reuben's confession so many times that he knew it by heart. And every time he read it, something on the fringes of his mind told him the confession was soured. Reuben admitted to the murder with little prodding by the detectives, but he couldn't remember little details of the murder scene, such as the position of the Chrysler, or the brand of beer littering the car. Reuben told sheriff's deputies he didn't know such details because it was dark, and he was drunk. Manny wanted the confession to be bogus, because he wanted Reuben to be innocent. As a naïve youngster, he had wanted to see his brother exonerated. As a veteran lawman, he knew Reuben's confession was legitimate. Reuben was a murderer.

But now Manny was back on Pine Ridge, close enough to his brother that those feelings surfaced again. "Am I the only one that thinks it strange that Two Moons would be on that dark road alone?"

"Why so strange?" Willie opened his snuff can and took a dip. He put it in his lower lip and rubbed the excess on his pants leg. "I go for drives all the time by my lonesome. Nothing odd about that."

"Do you park in the middle of nowhere? Drinking by yourself?"

"I don't drink."

"Then park with your girlfriend?"

"I don't have a girlfriend."

"All right then. The point I'm making is a man doesn't drive miles into the country to sit and drink alone. Someone must have been with Two Moons. The Pennington County Sheriff's Office called in the State Department of Criminal Investigation. Their evidence techs pulled Two Moons's prints from a beer bottle, but they also found another set on the car-door handle. They didn't have enough points for identification because the prints were either rubbed or smudged. The only thing the fingerprint tech could say with certainty is that the second set didn't belong to Two Moons."

"Or the store owner."

"The deputies ran that angle down. They rolled a set of elimination prints from the liquor-store clerk in Custer where Two Moons bought the beer. Nada."

"How about Alex Jumping Bull? He went missing the same time as the killing. Even Lieutenant Looks Twice thinks that Jumping Bull was in the car with Two Moons that night."

Manny nodded. If Reuben had copped to killing Two Moons, admitting to killing Jumping Bull wouldn't have added any more time to his sentence. "All I know for certain is I'm no closer to nailing Reuben—if he's Jason's killer—than I was this morning. Let's drive."

>‹›‹›‹

Willie slowed as he turned onto Highway 41 toward Oglala. This road conjured frightening memories of bodies dead in the roadway, pools of blood drawing an army of ants on a humid summer afternoon. This road memorialized a black culmination of the violence that was Pine Ridge in the 1970s. Unc tried shielding Manny from the realities of living in the poorest county of the nation, and the most violent. But whenever Manny huddled with his school buddies, they swapped stories about the bodies that had been found scattered around the reservation like White kids traded rumors of their favorite sports stars. And this road leading to Oglala was connected directly to that violence; this road could take them to Cuny Table, then on to Red Shirt Table if they wished.

But they wouldn't be driving there, as Agents Williams and Coler had been on that June day in 1975. Williams and Coler had been ambushed on the anniversary of Custer's defeat at the Little Big Horn. Manny had just gotten out of school that day after a wrestling meet, in which he trounced Lumpy on the mat. Manny met some friends at Big Bat's for celebration burgers when the news came in: Two FBI agents were shot to death on the road to Oglala. "Do you know we require academy students to study the ambush of Williams and Coler to learn how not to make a traffic stop?"

"I guess I got mixed feelings about them," Willie said. "No one had a right to kill those guys, but they foolishly chased those militants into their own stronghold in an unmarked car."

Manny felt just the same back when it happened. The moccasin telegraph quickly got word around back then, and people said the agents had been harassing AIM members. When the agents tried to stop a pickup-load of Indians, they fled, and innocent, peace-loving Lakota merely defended themselves against government intrusion.

Manny swore by that version until he became an FBI agent, when the incidents would be studied, the tactics dissected. He learned that the agents had no chance that day. He read eyewitness accounts of the militants shooting them so many times they couldn't have survived, even if help had arrived on time. Manny, the rebellious teen who wanted to follow his big brother's path, believed they deserved their fate. Manny, the eager FBI agent who wanted to stand up for justice, came to look with contempt upon those who murdered Williams and Coler. Peltier was the only man convicted in the murders, and had remained in jail since. Manny despised the FREE LEONARD PELTIER bumper stickers that could still be seen on reservation cars even today.

They crested a hill overlooking a shallow valley with trailers on forty-acre lots. "Which one is Reuben's?"

Willie pointed to a beige colored single-wide sitting past three others a quarter of a mile away. On the east end of Reuben's trailer, a corral jutted out. A paint gelding stood three-legged in the intense morning heat, his tail methodically swatting flies. Across from the corral, a lean-to frame held wood stacked shoulder high, and smoke billowed up from the rear of the trailer. "What's he burning back there?"

"Who knows with these *wicasa wakan*."

Manny turned in the seat. "Reuben claims to be a holy man now?"

"Not claims. He is. Like a lot of convicts in stir, he found religion behind bars. He's been studying with Ben Horsecreek up by Cuny Table, and most folks hereabouts consider Reuben to be a sacred man now."

"A holy man," Manny breathed. "I would never have believed it." How does an AIM enforcer who murders and goes to prison suddenly become a sacred man people look to for spiritual guidance?

Dust settled around the squad car as Willie stopped in front of Reuben's house. "You sure you want me to come along?"

Manny nodded. "I may need a witness. Or at least someone who'll keep me honest until I see where this goes."

Manny climbed out of the cruiser first, and caught in his peripheral vision Willie unsnapping his holster. Manny smiled. He was comfortable around Willie, assured the young policeman could handle most things that came his way, including ex-felons more than twice his age. Maybe it was Willie's attitude, or his size, that caused Manny to feel safe, and he was thankful that Willie was with him.

As they walked toward the back of the trailer, cedar smoke hung heavy in the air, pungent yet enticing enough that Manny forgot for a moment that he came to question a murder suspect. They walked around the corner of the trailer, and Manny saw his brother for the first time since Unc's funeral sixteen years ago. Reuben sat facing a fire that crackled and snapped from cedar and pitch pine burning. He bent over as he worked on something, oblivious to the occasional ember that escaped the fire ring and landed in the dirt at his feet. *This is a holy man?* Reuben's sweatpants had fallen a bit too far south, exposing his plumber's smile. His long gray hair was tied in a ponytail that ended midback, matted with what appeared to be yesterday's lunch.

They didn't sneak around the trailer, but they weren't noisy either. Reuben called over his shoulder, "I figured you'd be paying me a visit soon."

Manny jumped.

Reuben stood to his full height and faced them. He wore a dirty T-shirt that said My Heroes Have Always Killed Cowboys. Patches of white hair covered his temples. He had gained forty pounds since Manny last saw him, but he carried almost no fat. The wise old men, the *nige tanka*, would have said that Reuben possessed *bloka*. The Big Bellies would have said he projected the power of masculinity, symbolized by the buffalo to describe a man's bravery and strength. Despite his age, his eyes remained bright and clear. And transfixed on Manny. He stepped forward. *"Hau, kola."*

Reuben's hand encircled Manny's; his grip firm, though not punishing. Manny turned Reuben's hand over, his skin soft and supple and smooth. The last time Manny shook his hand it displayed the deep, dry cuts of a mason's palm. "You give up bricklaying?"

"Naw, I still do some. But my kids do most of the work." He pointed to formed wet clay shaped into a bowl glistening on a potter's wheel. "I picked up pottery in the slammer. Keeps me sane. And my hands soft as a baby's behind."

Reuben turned to Willie. "My little brother took my hand after all these years, but he's not polite enough to introduce us. I'm Reuben Tanno."

"William With Horn." Willie hesitated before he shook Reuben's hand. Reuben smiled. "Tribal. Good. At least you're not BIA. Or worse, some . . ."

"FBI?" Manny finished.

"You said it, little *misun*," Reuben said. "But you didn't come over here to jaw about your cushy job. I hear you've been assigned to investigate Jason Red Cloud's murder."

Reuben didn't wait for an answer as he turned his back and motioned to a chair and a tree stump. Willie took the stump and Manny sat in the chair opposite Reuben. He walked barefoot, holding a small, circular knife in one hand and tanned deer hide in the other. He cut narrow strips of hide and allowed them to drop to the ground while he spoke.

"Making some repairs," he said. He pointed to a pair of well-worn moccasins warming by the fire. "You guys want some tea? Lemonade? I'd offer you something more substantial, but we all know hooch is illegal here on the rez. Besides, I quit it for good while I was in Sioux Falls. Never got the urge to start again."

Willie shook his head, and Manny ignored the offer. As he studied Reuben, he wondered if all this posturing, all this mock-friendlessness had a purpose. "We really don't have time for that," Manny said. "I just want to know—"

"You forget your manners since you escaped to the big city? First we country Indians jaw a little before we get around to talking about your investigation. It's been so long since I saw you, little brother."

"Unc's funeral." Manny cursed under his breath. Reuben had sucked him right into a conversation he'd dreaded.

"That was long ago." Reuben picked up one of his moccasins and threaded the new string through the top. "In all that time, you never wrote your big brother in prison, never indicated that you cared if I was still breathing or not."

Willie stood and started for the car, and Reuben rested his hand on Willie's arm. "Stay awhile, Officer With Horn. This bit of reservation history might interest you."

"I'll wait in the car. I've got some school notes to go over anyway."

Manny waited until Willie disappeared around the trailer before facing Reuben. "You know damn well how I felt. It's not every day a boy's brother murders another Lakota."

"But you strutted around your little friends because of my involvement with AIM. That was cool back then, wasn't it?"

"Being involved with AIM wasn't synonymous with murder."

"What the hell do you think we did back then?" Reuben put on his moccasins and stomped his feet to feel the new string. "We weren't exactly Boy Scouts."

"But you didn't murder." Manny was a teenager again, pleading with Unc that Reuben didn't commit the terrible crime he was charged with; pleading that Reuben didn't kill Billy Two Moons, or Alex Jumping Bull as people rumored.

"You may have been suspected of killing, but I just knew you never murdered anyone. Some other AIM, but not you. You stood up for Native rights and I always knew you couldn't murder anyone, especially another Oglala."

Reuben looked down at him. "Didn't we kill each other? How about the sixty-odd dead found scattered around the rez in the years after Wounded Knee? Some died of exposure, compliments of the booze. Some staggered onto the highway and got themselves waffled. Wilson's goons killed some. But AIM was at least as responsible as they ever were."

Tribal president Dick Wilson's bodyguards shadowed him wherever he went, and he needed them. AIM swore they would see Wilson buried, and Wilson swore he would do whatever it took to rid Pine Ridge of AIM thugs. "There goes Wilson's GOONS," people would comment behind their backs. "The mighty Guardians of the Oglala Nation."

Manny stood and put his hands up to shove his brother back. "But not you. I knew you enforced AIM's policies, and I lived with that all right. Right up until you killed Billy Two Moons. That changed everything, Reuben. A justifiable killing was one thing. People died because they defended themselves. But a murder—cold and confessed. You became like the rest of them. You shamed me and Unc."

"Manny," Reuben said, his voice softened now. He took a step toward him, but Manny backed away. "I remember when I came home for the folks' funeral and I held a little five-year-old boy just long enough to bury our parents, then return to 'Nam."

"What the hell's that got to do with murder?"

"You're the only family I got left. Sure, I confessed to the murder, and yes, I served my time."

"You paid the price? Is that it?"

Reuben nodded. "I paid a bigger price than you'll ever know. That gated community of the state penitentiary wasn't exactly paradise, you know. You forgot me. But I never forgot you. Or the pride I feel for what you've become. I may publicly denounce you because you joined the FBI, but I'm still proud of my *kola*."

Manny dropped onto the tree stump and grabbed his handkerchief from his back pocket. He wiped the sweat from his forehead and face. He didn't want to be Reuben's *kola*. He didn't want memories of a time when he adored Reuben. He just wanted to solve his case and get away from Pine Ridge. "I didn't come here for a social visit. Like you said, I'm here to investigate Jason Red Cloud's murder."

Reuben nodded and sat back in his lawn chair. He grabbed a pipe from his back pocket. He filled the bowl from a Prince Albert can and lit the pipe with an Ohio Blue Tip and tossed the match in the fire. *Stalling*. Manny read Reuben's smoke ritual as taking time to anticipate questions and have answers ready in his mind. "All right. Ask away."

Manny dug a small notebook from his shirt pocket, not because he needed to refer to his notes, but as a distraction while he gauged reactions to his questions. "When was the last time you spoke with Jason?"

Reuben blew another smoke ring and shrugged. "I can't recall."

"Besides the argument at Big Bat's?"

Reuben laughed. "You have been busy. My ears on the rez heard right after all."

"The argument?" Manny asked, fishing now as he often did in interviews. He thumbed through pages in his notebook as if he possessed secret information that would trip Reuben.

"OK," Reuben said. He tamped out his pipe bowl on the side of the chair and pocketed it. *Killing time. Concocting his answer.* "Jason and I argued. His resort needed retaining walls built along with pads for the showers and RVs. We haggled on the price, and he awarded my Heritage Kids the contract. A few nights before he was murdered—last Wednesday—I was in Big Bat's when Jason came in and I confronted him."

"About?"

"I heard he'd given the job to a contractor from Black Hawk, and screwed my kids out of work. He blew me off. He said he'd thought it over, that it would hurt the corporate image if he hired an ex-con. He laughed and said it was just business."

"And you were mad at him."

"Livid."

"Enough to kill him?"

"Slowly. Deliciously."

"And did you?"

Reuben laughed, but deep creases furrowed his forehead. "I

got no intention of going back to the joint. But as a matter of record, I grabbed him and threw him against the wall by the pop dispenser. Hard enough that a picture hanging on the opposite wall crashed to the floor."

"Your contacts from the old days didn't do you any good?"

"Not one bit."

As Manny sat across from him, a deep sadness for Reuben overcame him that had nothing to do with Reuben's butt sagging through missing slats in the seat of his lawn chair. It was Reuben's choice of associating with the likes of Jason Red Cloud and AIM back in his youth. Jason had been there with Reuben at all of AIM's major headline grabbers. But the year Reuben was sentenced for the Two Moons murder, the year Jason's parents died in that wreck, Jason quit AIM for the easy life of college and the family business. Even now, Reuben held a grudge against Jason.

"Why the hell didn't you get an attorney and make him honor the contract?"

Reuben retied his moccasins and flexed his foot for the feel. "A verbal contract with an ex-con, a murderer who lined up work for a bunch of delinquent kids? Who the hell would believe me?"

Reuben was right. Jason's reputation as a businessman was beyond reproach, and Reuben would have been laughed out of any courtroom.

They looked at each other, saying nothing, for there was nothing more to say between them. They had rehashed the past. They had traded guilt trips. Manny had the information he came here to get: Reuben and Jason had argued, but for different reasons than Elizabeth thought. And Reuben, by his own admission, had been angry enough to kill Jason, and was quite capable of it.

Manny stood and stretched. "One other thing: How long would it take you to drive to Wounded Knee?"

Reuben chin-pointed to the corral where his pony still panted in the heat. "I don't drive anymore, *kola*. Don't even own a car. There's a whole lot of dangerous drunken Skins on the road to worry about. I'll stick to my pony. And by the by, you're free to come around here any time. Maybe someday we'll patch things up, no?"

"Patch things up? You tell me what really happened the night Billy Two Moons was murdered. Then maybe we'll pass the pipe."

"Where'd that come from?"

"That night," Manny pressed. "What happened?"

"I told it all already. Dozens of times. Billy was going to buy beer and meet me by Hill City. When I saw him driving that fancy White-man's car, I knew he'd snitched for Dick Wilson or the FBI, and I just lost it."

"How many times did you shoot him, big brother?" Manny had committed the information to memory.

"Six times. Six rounds of .45. One would have been enough, but I was always thorough."

"Why would Henry Lone Wolf claim he saw you with Elizabeth that night?"

"Because he did see me at Lizzy's. But he was wrong on the time. I left Lizzy's early that night and drove to meet up with Billy. Don't you know I would have used Henry as a witness if I thought it could have helped me?"

Manny always believed something else happened that night, that Reuben was involved in more than just the murder of a suspected AIM informant. And even though he was still tormented by the thought of Reuben being the murderer, reopening a thirty-year-old case to satisfy his own curiosity wouldn't help him solve Jason Red Cloud's death.

Reuben started to speak, but Manny turned on his heels and left before he had to listen to his brother anymore.

CHAPTER 5

Willie closed his textbook. "You all right?"

"Do I look all right?" Manny shut the car door. He rested his head on the seat back and rubbed his forehead.

"You look like you need something. Maybe a stiff drink."

"I don't drink either."

"Well, you need something. You're shaking worse than a dog passing a peach pit."

Manny's hand trembled as he reached for the pack of cigarettes. A smoke would hit the spot: an old friend helping him through stressful times. Most men had a wife to comfort them. Some a dog. Manny had a damned Camel—or used to before he quit being a two-lighter-a-day smoker. His Camel would have been there if he hadn't been so foolish to quit right before coming back here. "It's just been so long since I talked with my brother."

They started down the gravel road away from Reuben's trailer. When they pulled onto Highway 18, Willie turned in his seat. "Did I hear Reuben call you 'kola'?"

Manny nodded. He had hoped that had gotten by Willie, but Manny figured few things got by Willie. "Reuben first called me *kola* at our folks' funeral, and I can't shake it."

"You got no choice. Margaret says a man's *kola* is a lifetime commitment. The *wicasa yatanpi*, the shirtwearers of the old days, praiseworthy and honorable men, taught that a man's *kola* was his for life. If a man's *kola* went down during battle, he had to rescue him."

Once Manny had been proud of being Reuben's *kola* when Unc explained the obligations. "A person must never betray his *kola*, never reveal secrets about him. The old ones cherished this relationship, and a *kola*'s bond is greater than *tiospaye*, than family. You have both a brother and a *kola*." Could he arrest his *kola* for Jason's murder?

"A man's lucky to have one in a lifetime."

"I don't feel very lucky."

><><><><

Ten minutes out of Pine Ridge Manny got cell service and his phone vibrated. He checked the numbers. One he didn't recognize.

"Might be someone with information," Willie said.

Manny was skeptical and called the number. "I'm so glad you got a chance to return my call." Even over the phone her voice resonated with that mellow, bedroom-soft tone. Manny felt as if he'd just called one of those porn lines.

"Ms. Myers, I—"

"Sonja."

"Sonja. How did you get my private number?"

"Lieutenant Looks Twice was kind enough to give it to me. Do you have time to talk?"

"Not right now." Manny was beat, and he didn't feel up to phone sex. "Perhaps another time."

"Then I'll call tomorrow." She hung up.

"Damned ignor-anus."

"Who? And what's an 'ignor-anus'?"

"Your lieutenant. He's stupid and an asshole. He knows better than to give out my number."

"Who's the other person that called you?"

Manny sighed. "The Pile. I better call him."

Niles answered on the first ring and gave Manny no time for small talk. "That was one shitty news conference. You didn't have squat to give the press. If you're hiding something, they'll eat us alive. Tell me you have something more for them."

"I'm making progress," Manny lied, then promised to keep Niles posted. He closed his phone and slipped it back into his pocket.

"We are?"

"Are we what?"

"Making progress."

Manny laughed. "Hell no. But that prick doesn't need to know it."

Manny punched in the Red Cloud Development number again and talked with the operator he had spoken to before. "I really do need to speak with her."

"I'll give her the message again."

"Problems?"

Manny shut his phone. "Clara Downing. If I didn't know better I'd say she was avoiding me."

They pulled into Pine Ridge and Willie drove toward Manny's apartment. "I'm feeling a little gaunt. Buy you a burger."

Willie slapped the wheel. "That's what I forgot. Aunt Lizzy gave me an invite for supper tonight. I'm sure she won't mind setting another plate."

"Thanks for the offer, but it's getting late and I'm beat. I'll just grab a quick bite before I get some road time in." Manny had slacked off long enough from his daily routine of jogging three miles. It helped him think, helped him forget about how he missed his home in Virginia right now.

Willie stopped the car by the gas pumps at Big Bat's. People stared through the windows of the convenience store. Manny read their looks, their hatred, their mistrust, their hostility. It was the 1970s all over again. Such looks would be upon him during his entire stay on the reservation.

"Pick me up at o-seven-hundred?"

"O-seven-hundred," Willie answered, and motored east toward Elizabeth's house.

A typical evening crowd dined at the only spot in town to get a hot meal. Manny ignored the stares as he walked to the counter. A young man reeking of wine nudged hard against him. Dirt and fine white powder flaked off onto Manny's shirt and he slapped it off. The kid's grin taunted Manny. He ignored him and ordered a burger combo, then decided to skip the fries. He wanted a preemptive strike against his middle-age spread. He was fighting to keep on his diet until he could return to Virginia, back to where his life was in order. Where he could concentrate on his diet. Besides, greasy fries would make him puke during his run later tonight.

He filled his cup with Diet Coke and picked an empty booth. His trousers caught on something sticky on the plastic seat, but he was too exhausted and ignored it. He took his time eating as he listened to the conversations around him. Over George Strait crooning about "Amarillo by Morning," he heard a couple in back of him plan on a beer run to White Clay.

Two booths down, four teenage boys talked about driving to North Rapid to party with friends. And a man twice his age snored in the booth in back of him. A typical night on the reservation. What the hell possessed him to accept this assignment? Why had he come home? Thomas Wolfe was right, of course, but who the hell would even want to go home again to this? Whenever Manny was jerked from his academy assignment to take the latest Native American case, he wanted to ask Niles if the bureau could please hire more Indians. But the Pile threatened to assign him recruiting duty, to go to reservations around the country to hire those same Indians Manny prayed for. And no matter how Manny insulted him, Niles was smart enough not to fire him. The only thing left for him was to quit the bureau.

In the end, he had no choice. Police work had first crept into his bloodstream as a tribal cop. He needed investigations to challenge him. Police work, particularly investigations, invigorated him, made him something more than the criminals he pursued.

"I don't know why you don't jump at the chance to go back home for a case," Niles had told him. "See old friends. Have a good time. Do the tourist thing while you're working on this Red Cloud murder."

"You ever been to Pine Ridge?"

"Never had the pleasure."

"Then come along if you think it's so nice there."

"I would, but the wife and I got that Orlando vacation package all lined up."

"We got other agents capable—"

"Well," Niles said. "We got several training positions that need to be filled in Iraq right now. Who better to teach eager Iraqis investigation techniques than Manny Tanno. Or there's still that field agent opening in Greenland . . ."

"Enough. I'll go to Pine Ridge. But under protest."

If Niles had been twenty minutes slower in finding him, Manny would have been gone to the Poconos on a sudden annual leave. When Manny heard FOX News break the story of Jason Red Cloud's death, he started packing his clothes. He knew Niles would assign him the case if he found him. "But you know the tribal police never want our help," Manny argued.

"Don't worry. We'll get some cooperation. I'll make a couple calls. Get the stud duck in charge out there on the horn." It was that stud duck who interrupted Manny's meal.

"People! Look here!" Lumpy yelled above the din of talk and music as he filled the doorway. "We got a genuine federal lawman in our midst." Lumpy reeked. Sweet, loud Aqua Velva mixed with the sickening odor of beer that reached Manny even before Lumpy staggered over. Despite being drunk, Lumpy was Pine Ridge's fashion plate. Lumpy's Wranglers had creases so sharp that a man would cut himself if he ran his hand over them. His paisley double-breasted Western shirt had concrete cowboy written all over it, and his ostrich boots jutted like two large snowshoes beneath his stumpy legs. Pomade pasted his shiny hair against his head, and a silver and turquoise watchband glittered as he waved wildly at the crowd. "Mister Agent Man is going to solve our murder for us."

Manny washed his burger down. "You're drunk. Go home and sleep it off."

"He can't," someone yelled from behind Lumpy. "His girlfriend just dissed him again."

Lumpy turned to the heckler. He lost his balance and caught himself on the back of Manny's seat. "Who the hell said that?"

No one answered. Though he was drunk, people knew Lumpy was still smarter than the average man in Big Bat's. And he wouldn't forget such taunts if he knew who threw them. Manny stood to leave.

"I'm not done with you, Hotshot."

"Yes you are," Manny called over his shoulder.

The cool air chilled his cheeks. A full moon peeked between charcoal clouds, and the fresh coming of a thunderstorm reached Manny's nose. Summer Febreze.

"Don't walk away from me!" Lumpy called from the doorway and stumbled after him across the parking lot. The crowd had followed Lumpy outside and cheered him on. Poking the bear. Getting him riled up. He spun Manny around, and swung a looping roundhouse at his head. Manny jerked his head out of the way of the punch. Lumpy staggered back, lost his balance, and fell on his butt.

The crowd roared and clapped. Lumpy glared at them and gathered himself on all fours, then stood and teetered on wobbly legs. He dropped his head and charged Manny like a bull. Manny sidestepped. Lumpy continued headlong, tripped over the curb, and fell into the street.

People clapped. One girl whistled while another urged Lumpy to get up. A man did his best bull imitation while Lumpy lay in the street, his head hung down, trying to get his legs under him. A pickup sped around the corner toward him, but the driver swerved sharply and missed him by inches. The crowd roared. People laughed while Lumpy tried to stand, but he rolled over like a turtle caught on its back and started sobbing. The show was over for the night. The crowd walked back into Big Bat's, and Manny looked down at Lumpy. "You're drunker than hell."

Lumpy craned his neck up. His slick black hair had fallen down into his eyes, and he peeked around a clump of locks as he held up an arm. "Help me up."

Manny wrapped his arms around him and lifted him. Lumpy fell against his shoulder. "Where are you living?"

He draped his arm around Manny. "The housing."

An odd couple, they staggered toward the finish line in an uncontested drunken three-legged race as Manny struggled to keep the shorter, heavier Lumpy from falling. They stumbled the four blocks to Lumpy's building and he motioned to a downstairs duplex. He jabbed at the keyhole, failed, then handed Manny the keys.

Manny helped Lumpy inside and dropped him on the couch. *Psychology Today* and *National Geographic* magazines fought for what little space remained on the table in the tiny, claustro-phobic apartment. Beside the table were stacks of *Law and Order* and *Police Times*. There was a narrow path toward the kitchen barely devoid of empty Budweiser cans, and another pathway that led to a bathroom that reeked of Lumpy's Aqua Velva.

How had Lumpy come to this? Sober, the man was the most knowledgeable lawman Manny had met on any reservation. Drunk, Lumpy was just another down-and-out Lakota chasing his next buzz into a blackout. In some perverse way, he supposed he was one of Lumpy's few friends, if rivals could ever be friends.

Manny turned to leave.

"Lizzy's not my girlfriend."

"Is that who those people back at Big Bat's were talking about dissing you? Elizabeth?"

Lumpy nodded. "But she's not my girl. I thought she was once, back in the day, but now she's just too damned good to be with me on a Saturday night."

"You see her tonight?"

Lumpy laughed and grabbed a pack of Marlboros from beside the couch. He shook one into his hand, and four more dropped onto the floor. He ignored them and grabbed his matches. When coordinating matches and cigarettes failed, Manny helped him. *Not my brand when I was smoking, which was what, a month ago. But damn they look good.* Manny felt that trembling he got whenever he had the urge for a smoke, the jitters that only nicotine could calm. He fought down the temptation to snatch one from the floor and light up, and concentrated on watching the Indian Marlboro man bring his lips to the cigarette.

"I saw her in the finance office tonight. I came back from White Clay with a case of Bud. I saw Lizzy's office light on and sat out-side. When I ran out of beer I figured my courage was up enough to talk to her. But she was too good for me. She said she was busy, but I know she wasn't doing anything official there tonight."

"What did you want to talk to her about?"

"Just talk," Lumpy answered. "A man likes to talk with a woman now and again. Especially an old flame. At least I thought she was an old flame once. Right after Desirée left me."

"So you said. Get some sleep."

"Lizzy and Jason were having an affair!" Lumpy blurted out as Manny turned again to leave.

"You see this yourself?"

"Yeah." He belched and flicked his ash into an empty beer can. It bounced off the rim of the can. Manny tamped out the ember that had landed on the carpet with a shower shoe growing mold. "A couple weeks before he was murdered, I was on my way home from work when I saw Lizzy's Impala at the finance office. It was dark and I was surprised to find the lights were still on. I was even more surprised to find her door unlocked. Remember when we had to check building doors when we were rookies?"

Manny nodded.

"When I went inside, I heard a commotion. Terrible yelling from her office. Shit hitting the wall. Lizzy and Jason were fighting something awful. There was file folders scattered all over. One file drawer had been ripped from the cabinet and turned upside down. Another was wide open. Lizzy never had a thing out of place in that office, and Jason was going through drawers, with Lizzy yanking on his arm. She tried to pull him away, but he was too big. Things would have been a lot worse if I hadn't put the run on him that night."

"What were they arguing about?"

Lumpy brought his face to his cigarette for another drag. "Don't know. But there's only one reason a man and woman fight like that: lovers' spat. After I kicked him out, I thought she'd be friendlier. But all she wanted was for me to leave, too."

Lumpy paused, and Manny knew that the pause would last until morning. Snores arose from Lumpy's head, tilted back on the pillow. Drool formed on one corner of his mouth and dripped on his shoulder.

Before Manny left, he took Lumpy's cigarette from his fingers and dropped it into a beer can. He propped Lumpy's limp legs on the couch and slipped his boots off. His head lay off to one side of a cushion, and a hollow snoring continued from his open mouth. Lumpy had popped the top buttons of his shirt, exposing his flabby, hairy chest. Manny laughed. *I've found the elusive Lakota yeti.*

Manny started out of Lumpy's apartment and noticed a portable evidence kit among the rubbish. He opened the case and glanced over the contents until he spotted what he was after.

>‹›‹›‹

Raindrops peppered Manny's neck. He looked up at the moon peeking around dark storm clouds. He never noticed storm clouds in D.C., though he was certain they lingered somewhere between the smog and the fog that occasionally rolled in from the ocean. Either he was too busy to look, or the pollution prevented such a sight. He was glad to see them again.

Kids stuffed into a multicolored International pickup drove by him and shouted obscenities. They disappeared around the corner, but soon they drove by him again, tires squealing, dark smoke billowing from a broken exhaust manifold. Three kids sat in the truck bed. Their pants were pulled down, and their bare butts waved to him in passing. Manny laughed. Not because he wanted to, but because these kids represented all the kids on all the reservations, so far behind the times. He wanted to run them down and tell them that mooning died out about a century ago, but he was too busy laughing. If it made them happy to moon an FBI agent, let them have their fun.

He finished stretching his hamstrings, checked his laces one final time, then started off for a run that would take him past the powwow grounds and around the housing toward Oglala Lakota College. Within the first mile, his lungs lost their familiar burning and he settled into his pavement-eating gait. It was the same lope that he had as a cross-country runner in high school when he tried so hard to impress Desirée Chasing Hawk. The same lope that followed him during his army days. The same lope that caused him to fall far behind his younger academy instructors, then allowed him to pass them miles farther down the road. No matter how hard he'd tried altering his running style, no matter how hard he worked to increase his speed, his lope was predestined. Unc said it was that lope that all Lakota warriors possessed, back in the days when it meant something to be able to run for hours without stopping.

He knew that the abuse he'd piled on his body wasn't supposed to be part of his heritage. Unc had died from diabetes, the bane of the Oglala. Manny was determined to live long enough to be a pain in the ass—like old Chief Horn.

The fresh scent of the impending thunderstorm helped him through the first agonizing mile, and he entered his zone, where thoughts came fast at him like arrows on steroids. The zone slowed down those arrows just enough that he could catch each one and analyze it. Nothing had changed on Pine Ridge. He knew he wasn't welcomed here by the tribal police. The Lumpys of the reservation, the progressives, saw themselves as the future of Pine Ridge; they wanted to put the run on traditionalists whenever they could. Traditionalists wanted things to remain just as they used to be, without the need for federal intervention. In many ways, they wanted what AIM and all the Reubens of the reservation had wanted: to return to the very basics of life that once made the Lakota the strongest nation on the Plains, their defiant independence their staunchest ally. In any case, no one on the reservation had any use for the Mannys.

Sweat stung Manny's eyes and he wiped it with his sweatshirt as Reuben popped into the zone. Manny recalled how conversational he had been when he interviewed him, like they had only parted the day before. Like they were two brothers who weren't separated by Reuben's twenty-five-year stint in the state pen and Manny's decision to enter law enforcement. Reuben had answers for everything. Manny knew his brother had his lines memorized. It was his challenge to look for the opening that would finally prove—or disprove—Reuben was Jason's killer.

A car came up on his six, and he hugged the side of the road. A single headlight followed him, closer than it should be, and he shot a look behind him. The car veered right for him, tires biting the gravel, accelerating. Manny took a dive for the ditch as a car door opened in passing. The door clipped him on his shoulder and sent him rolling to the ground. He caught sight of two boys as the car passed by and sped off.

Manny stood and brushed dirt off his running shorts and pulled his shirt down over his paunch. He stretched his shoulder where the car door had hit him, and a deep scratch across one delt was throbbing, but he was in one piece. He resumed his run, vigilant for the car. When he came around the corner by the pow-wow grounds again, he slowed to a fast trot, then a slow walk. He sucked in air to purge the fire in his lungs and bent over when a stitch came to his side. After a minute, the pain disappeared and he walked the remaining three blocks to his apartment.

Low growling from behind caused him to jump as he neared his door. A patchy border collie crouched as it advanced on him, its hackles standing straight on its back. Manny squatted. He had always had a way with animals. They trusted him. Liked him. *It was a Lakota thing.* The dog's hackles flattened, its teeth receded back into its mouth. Manny held out his hand while the dog approached. Close. Close enough to lick his hand.

The dog lunged. Manny jerked away, but the dog buried canines into the web of his hand. Manny instinctively reached for the gun on his belt—the gun that he hadn't carried since he began teaching at the academy. Manny looked for something to fend the dog off, but the mongrel turned and trotted down the street in search of fresher meat.

Manny cursed himself for not bringing a gun. Why had he reached for it after all this time of not wearing one? Not enough dangers lurked in the academy classroom to warrant carrying a gun. He had gotten used to not carrying, though he qualified as best he could every quarter, but the first thing he did tonight when danger faced him was reach for a gun that wasn't there. As a tribal policeman, he'd practiced the basics of police work, including marksmanship and tactics. Even though he had never actually had to fire it on duty, he was always prepared back then.

Even rookies have more street sense than he did right now, and being back here on the reservation revealed the dangers of losing his edge over the years of being—what?—civilized? Even the Living Legend needed to keep his wits about him.

He straightened and held his hand high. Two gaping holes where the dog had nailed him dripped blood down his hand and wrist to pool in the crook of his arm. He fumbled for his door key with his other hand, as he held his injured hand away to avoid bleeding on his new sweatpants.

He found the keyhole. Dropped the keys. Bent down to pick them up when the door next to his apartment opened. Desirée stuck her head out and looked to the street. She wore a sheer teddy that revealed everything, and Manny didn't want to have to fight her off tonight. After a day getting no closer to solving the homicide, getting into a lame fight with Lumpy, getting waylaid by a couple kids in a one-eyed car, and getting ambushed by a Trojan mongrel, the last thing he wanted to do was come up with some excuse not to keep Desirée out of his apartment. He scurried around the corner and squatted while he willed his breathing to stop. He was certain she heard his heart beating as she stepped into the cool night air. She looked around a final time before she shut the door.

Manny breathed again, aware that something wasn't right. He was a young tribal cop whose awareness told him someone waited around the door with a butcher knife at a domestic fight. Or some other obscure danger that awaited him.

He stood and swayed, light-headed. Did he stand up too quickly? Or was the dog returning for a rematch?

A sound behind him, coming fast. He turned as something arced downward. He shot his arms up and blocked a blow that glanced off the top of his head. Dull pain turned to a stabbing sensation in his scalp, and he fell and rolled, bringing his arms over his head for protection. Blood, sticky and wet, seeping through his fingers, flowed through a wide scalp laceration as he braced himself for the next blow.

The grim reaper, face hidden in a dark and ominous hood, straddled him. Held something thick and heavy in one hand, poised to strike again. Manny tried standing. His legs buckled. He fell back down onto the sidewalk.

Then voices in the night. Faint, nearing voices. Running toward him. In a heartbeat the grim reaper was gone, replaced by others bending to help. He blinked the blood from his eyes and wiped his head with his dog-bitten hand. Strong hands lifted him and he jerked back. Just before he passed out, he looked up at Desirée. Brown eyes rimmed with just the right amount of makeup to allow her to once again look like the beauty he'd panted after in school. Just before he passed out, he imagined this as what it would be like in Purgatory—having both the pleasant and unpleasant at once was eternal punishment, and his cursed *wanagi* would roam the Spirit Road forever.

CHAPTER 6

Willie leaned over and opened the cruiser door. "Let's see the stitches."

Manny slid into the passenger seat and eased the bandage away from the side of his head.

"Jeeza. You were lucky."

"Why the hell do you always say I'm lucky? I get three stitches in my hand from some damned dog, and more from some a-hole with a club, and you say I'm lucky."

"Could have been worse."

"Could have been better—I could have kicked the shit out of them."

"Maybe breakfast will help." Willie drove to Big Bat's without waiting for an answer.

Music blared from speakers hung above the gas pumps: Waylon, Willie, and Johnny sang about the "Highwayman." *Odd music to eat breakfast by.* Manny felt so out of his element here. He was used to entering a five- or four-star restaurant at the least, with the Three Tenors piped in to aid the digestion. Or live performers drifting between tables taking requests to help set the mood of the meal. Yet a part of him enjoyed this music and the rustic atmosphere here. He was becoming comfortable with the reservation—and that worried him.

With Willie and Manny her only customers this morning, Angelica smiled as she recognized him from the night with Lenny the loser. She handed the order slip to an old, short, fat man in a sleeveless T-shirt sweating over the griddle. They filled their coffee cups and took a seat facing the street while they waited for their food.

"What's so funny?" Willie asked.

"Does it show? In D.C., chefs prepare a work of culinary art. I forgot what this was like."

"You'll be pleased when Franklin there gets done with your order." Willie jerked his thumb to the cook, who wielded his spatula like a swordsman limbering up his rapier. "Who do you figure for that little souvenir?" He nodded to Manny's head.

"That's what I've been wondering." Angelica brought their food, and Manny waited until she left before he took his first bite of the sandwich. The sweetness of the sausage, the gooeyness of the cheese melted over the egg that ran down the side of the bun surprised him. "Reuben would be capable of this. He's slung masonry hammers long enough." Pain shot through his head, and Manny tried to ignore the intense urge to scratch at the stitches, so he occupied his good, unbandaged hand with his coffee cup. Stitches always hurt the worst for the first few hours, and he just had to keep himself busy and distracted.

"When I talked to Reuben yesterday, he was friendly enough. He even acted like a big brother for a few moments, given that we haven't talked in years."

Johnny Cash sang how he would rest his spirit if he could. Manny put his sandwich down and pressed a hand against his head, which was throbbing along to the beat of the song. He wished he could join Johnny in resting his own spirit this morning.

"Your brother's damn well unpredictable enough. He'd be at the top of my list."

"And who's right underneath him in the suspect cesspool?" Manny had grown accustomed to bouncing ideas off his fresh mind. "There's others here besides Reuben who would love to see me gone."

Willie dropped his eyes. "Like Lieutenant Looks Twice?"

"You heard about our discussion last night?"

"The jungle drums. Or at least the reservation drums. One of the guys called me last night after someone attacked you. Word is that you embarrassed the lieutenant big-time here last night."

Manny took small bites of his sandwich. At least tiny bites didn't aggravate the pain. He washed it down with coffee before giving Willie the headline version of the argument. "As far gone as he was when I left him, I doubt Lumpy could have crawled to his own bathroom, let alone stagger to my apartment."

"He sure doesn't like you. He might have been faking it."

"Might have," Manny agreed. Then dismissed the idea, since as a tribal cop he'd dealt with enough drunks to spot a scammer. Lumpy was dead drunk last night, and Manny would lay odds he was still drunk this morning. "I don't think that's his style." Lumpy would have played on his panache and set Manny up on another unannounced press conference to make him look like a boob. Or give some other reporters Manny's personal phone number to call and pester, as he had Sonja Myers.

Willie refilled their cups and sat across the table. "Who else did you talk with yesterday?"

"Just your aunt Elizabeth. But you two had supper last night."

Willie shook his head. "I was late for supper, 'cause the lieutenant dispatched me to a call right after I dropped you off.

When I finally got to Aunt Lizzy's, her note said she'd gone into the finance office for a while and to help myself to tuna casserole. So I popped a plate in the microwave and watched the Braves play the Phillies in a twilight doubleheader. I caught the last half of the game. When it was over, I crashed in the spare room. I couldn't wait up for her any longer."

"What time did she come home?"

Willie shrugged. "All I know is that she was there when I got up this morning." Then his head jerked up and he dropped his sandwich. He leaned across the table, close enough that Manny could smell the egg and bacon as he spoke. "You don't suspect her of attacking you last night? I know my aunt Lizzy, and—"

Manny held up his hand to stop him. It could have been a woman. It could have been Elizabeth. But he had known her since they were teens, when she and Reuben first became an item. More than former in-laws, she and Manny remained friends. That, and she had too much to lose, with her finance officer position, her status here on Pine Ridge. Yet with the hatred of federal law enforcement still prevalent around here, anyone could be guilty. When his attacker had bent over for another strike before being frightened off, all Manny had seen was the hood. His head pounded from the swelling that surrounded the stitches, and the fresh itchy pain snapped him back to the present and he fought to keep from scratching.

"I doubt your aunt did it. I got more old enemies still living here that'd love a piece of my ass than to suspect her."

"How about that car that tried running you over, that peckerwood that opened the car door on you? When they didn't get the job done the first time, maybe they came around for another try."

"I've thought of that, too." Manny sipped his coffee from the side of his mouth that pulled less on the stitches. "I got the impression they were only trying to scare me. They could have run me over with little effort; when I get in the zone, I run with my head up my rectum."

"Jason's killer would want you dead," Willie blurted out. "Somebody doesn't want you solving that murder."

Their investigation had stalled yesterday. Reuben's interview had yielded little new information. "We're not much closer than when we started, but someone must think we are." Whoever thought he was close enough to the truth was getting nervous. And dangerous.

They finished their meal and stayed. They were on Lakota time now, in no rush. "What did the investigating officer tell you?"

Willie grabbed a spiral notebook from his shirt pocket and flipped pages. "Martin Slow Elk said two young couples were walking toward your apartment when someone attacked you. They saw you go down and started for you, but Desirée Chasing Hawk beat them to it. She held you until the paramedics came."

"I didn't know."

"Close. To her bosom. Slow Elk said he couldn't even see you when he ran up. All he saw was Desirée Chasing Hawk bent over you and cradling your head. Took three of them to pry her loose, but he didn't mind."

"Didn't mind?"

"Didn't mind grabbing her all over and pulling her away." He winked.

"Did she see the person?"

Willie flipped pages again. "No. She came outside just in time to see you going down. She saw what the others did: somebody with a hoodie running off.

"The couples?"

"Their description won't help much. It was dark, and they only got a glimpse. Short to medium height, not fat. If there were no bulges under the sweatshirt, that rules out Reuben."

"Unless he was hunkered over," Manny suggested. "And none of the witnesses recognized the runner?"

"None." He stirred creamer into his coffee. "Hoodies can cover a lot of sins. The one thing they all agree on is that your attacker wielded that hammer like it was an extension of an arm."

"What else did Slow Elk say?"

"Only that Ben Niles called for you when the doc was patching you up."

"Now what did the Pile want?"

"He just left the message that school starts in a week. What's that mean?"

"It means I'll have a permanent desk on some reservation if I don't wrap this up in time to start the next academy class."

"Jeeza!" Willie slammed his cup on the table so hard that it bounced off and rolled onto the floor. He sprang from his seat and ran to his police car. He returned with a manila folder under his arm, and dropped back into the booth as he fumbled through the folder. Some papers fell out, and Manny recognized one as an Oglala Sioux Tribal incident report on a stolen car. It bore yesterday's date.

"Stolen car yesterday?" Manny's eyebrows arched. Stolen vehicles should be big news to a young tribal cop, and he wondered why Willie hadn't mentioned it to him.

"That was the call the lieutenant sent me on last night after I dropped you off. I had to run back out to Oglala. Crazy George He Crow wanted to report his car stolen. So I took the report is all."

"You don't sound too enthused."

"I'm not. Crazy George is one of our chronic bitchers. He's always making some harebrained report on something or other. Last night he wanted to report someone stole his beat-to-hell old Buick at ten thirty night before last."

"Did he see the thief?"

"See him?"

"The car thief. He sounds positive of the time."

Willie laughed. "Oh, that. Crazy George's junkyard horse raised hell at precisely ten thirty, he told me. That's how he knows."

"Junkyard horse?"

"Mean-ass roan mare of his. Got a hell of an attitude. Stomp a man quicker 'n Mike Tyson. No one gets around Crazy George's place without that mare letting him know. Damned thing's better than a watchdog. He's positive on the time."

Manny finished his coffee and reached for a cigarette in his empty pocket. Of course it was empty. Would he ever get over craving a smoke at the end of a meal, of reaching for a pack that wasn't there? Just a drag. One small draw from Mr. Camel. "But the thief was able to distract the horse long enough to steal the car?"

Willie shook his head and retrieved his can of Copenhagen. "The car was parked by Crazy George's toolshed. It's outside the corral, so the horse couldn't get to the thief. Odd thing is the car was still there when Crazy George woke up that morning."

"Then why does he think it was stolen? Did his horse whisper it to him?"

"Mileage," Willie winked. "Crazy George knows it was stolen because there's exactly two hundred fifty more miles on the odometer than when he drove it last."

"That's a pretty good memory."

"Crazy George is crazy," Willie said. "Not stupid."

Manny eyed the fresh sandwiches. On cue, his stomach growled in mock hunger. He felt a tug at his waistline from a belly bigger than he wanted, and passed on another sandwich. Jenny Craig wouldn't approve, and neither would his side stitches when he hit the road tonight. "What's all the rest in that folder?"

"Lab tests," Willie answered. "At least some results are back on the homicide." Willie rifled through the papers. He licked his thumb, then turned a page. Lick and turn. Lick and turn.

"You going to tell me what the tests results are, or just watch me squirm?"

Willie dropped the folder on the table and handed Manny the fingerprint report. "They developed a set of partials on the handle of the war club," Willie pronounced as if educating a jury. "Five points on one latent, seven on the other. Report says they appeared smudged and unreadable."

"Wiped?"

Willie shrugged. "Can't tell. Not enough points for an ID. But there was a second set of prints." He handed Manny another report. Twelve full points had been developed on this second set, enough to identify a suspect. "The lieutenant sent the prints into Pierre and faxed a set to Quantico."

"And the prints on the blood around the handle?"

Willie grabbed another sheet. "Unidentifiable, same as the other set."

"DNA?"

Willie laughed. "Here on the rez? Now where would we get the funds for a private lab to do DNA testing?"

"I'll take care of that. I'm certain the blood will match Jason's."

Willie stood to refill both cups again when two girls walked into the convenience store. "*Han, sic esi*," one said to Willie. She smiled as she passed him.

"*Hau, hankasi*," he answered back, and matched her smile. Willie's glance wandered down to the girl's tight Levi's.

He didn't take his eyes off the girls as he walked back with the coffee. Was Manny ever that young? Not worried about what to do about his diet, not worried about what to do about his nicotine withdrawal, not worried about what the hell to do with himself when retirement came. "Pretty friendly there." Manny snapped his fingers in front of Willie's eyes. "Girlfriend?"

"Who, Doreen? Nah, she's in one of my college classes." When Manny just looked at him, Willie blurted out, "She's a Big Eagle. Moved here from Crow Creek this last year to go to college. She's just a friend."

"Well, you talk the talk pretty good with her."

"Margaret's been teaching me that, too," Willie said, and leaned sideways around Manny to watch the girls. "Besides teaching me the healing ways, Margaret's teaching me Lakota. She says if we don't keep our language alive, it will die as surely as the *mazaska*, the corn, dies every fall."

Manny once sat across from Unc at the base of a cottonwood, a blanket between them holding their afternoon snack. They hiked the steep cliffs of Buffalo Butte to gather elderberries that afternoon. "*Tunska*, if we don't talk the talk," Unc told him as he addressed him in the traditional word for nephew, "we'll be like a man losing an arm or a leg. Our society will never recover our heritage without constant stumbling."

It was up to the youth of each generation, Unc told him, to carry on traditions that White people scoffed at, and Manny often regretted not keeping up with his Lakota language. He intended to get back into it when he was discharged from the army and working on the reservation as a tribal cop. He'd even attended a Sun Dance that first summer to get his mind right with the old ways. But when the FBI hired him, he'd figured his Lakota language skills would be useless in Virginia. He'd been wrong. As many times as he was assigned cases on reservations, being able to converse in Lakota would have been useful. At least being back on the Pine Ridge again was bringing back some of his dormant skills.

"Why don't you take Doreen somewhere for a nice meal and a movie?"

"Oh, I couldn't," Willie blushed. Manny laughed. The very large man in front of him had turned into a shrinking, intimidated little boy, and Manny empathized.

He let Willie off the hook. "You said other tests were back."

"So I can quote you by saying Jason's blood was found on the murder weapon? Along with unknown prints?" Sonja Myers stood beside their table and sipped delicately from a Coke cup. "May I?" She slid in the booth beside Manny and scooted close. Her legs touched his, but he was as close to the window as he could get.

"How did you know where to find us?" Then he answered his own question. "I'll bet that nice Lieutenant Looks Twice."

"Why, yes." She looked sideways at Manny, her flowing hair cascading down her—what?—"bosom," as Willie would say.

"We really have nothing new . . ."

"Well, this is new." She reached for the lab report. Manny snatched it and jammed it into the manila envelope. "We have nothing more. I can call you when we do."

"Look, Agent Tanno. I got a job to do same as you. If I don't give my editor something on this Red Cloud case, it's back to the mail room for me. Can you see me exiled to the mail room?"

Be a damned shame to stuff her somewhere people couldn't see her. "I'll call you when I have something I can release."

She feigned disappointment, then smiled. "That's a promise?"

"Promise."

"Don't force me to look you up."

"I won't. But I'd bet the lieutenant will have new information. We haven't checked in with him this morning yet."

"You might be right." Sonja stood and smoothed her white blouse, and her eye contact lingered a moment longer than Manny thought the occasion warranted. "We'll meet again soon."

"Of course," he stammered.

Now it was Manny's turn to watch tight Levi's walk away.

"You could ask her out. A nice meal, maybe a movie."

"I got other things on my mind right now. Like the lab results?"

"Oh, yeah." Willie flipped through the papers until he found another page and handed it to Manny.

"That stuff we thought was sweetgrass? It was. And that leaf you thought was cut-grass: It was."

The report showed that the material embedded in Jason's trouser cuffs was concrete dust.

"That'd fit your brother." Willie seemed to be reading Manny's mind.

"Or it could have been picked up on Jason's pants legs when he was inspecting the construction site. More people than Reuben work with concrete around here." What the hell was he doing, defending Reuben? Manny dismissed it as being just the open mind of a trained investigator, not a *kola* protecting his brother. "Who else works around concrete?"

"Can't say."

"Think." If he could get Willie reasoning on his own, one day he would be a top investigator. And spare Manny another trip to places like Pine Ridge. "Who else could have deposited this at the crime scene?"

"The Heritage Kids," Willie said. "There's six of them by last count. How do we narrow it down among them?"

"Not so fast." Manny reached deep into his pocket and came away with a piece of Nicorette gum to take the edge off his craving. *Unless the gum could be rolled and smoked.*

"But they work concrete all day."

"Construction is pretty common here. New foundations, footings for houses, curb and gutter work. That doesn't mean one of them killed Jason."

"I see your point. Just one more thing to add when we put all this together."

"Now you're learning."

Willie smiled and sat a little straighter in the booth. Manny knew the praise of a senior officer. His first pat on the back by Chief Horn had raised his rookie head inches one day. It was the end of a long night, when Manny had tracked a runaway boy from the Red Cloud School to the edge of the Stronghold region. The kid had been a runner, but Manny had humped these hills with Unc, and still ran when he got the chance between work and college classes. When he caught up with the runaway, the kid was as surprised as the rest of the officers were when Manny returned to town with him.

"Oh, and we got some info on the war club." Willie smiled and spread papers on the table. This time Manny allowed Willie to explain the report at his own speed.

"The war club—which, to the lieutenant's chagrin, was an original—was stolen. Along with other artifacts from the Prairie Edge store in Rapid City three weeks ago. Forty grand worth."

"When the other antiquities surface, we might know more."

"They have." Willie handed Manny a list of stolen Lakota artifacts dating back to pre-1890: a bone whistle, a medicine pouch in the shape of a turtle, a pair of beaded moccasins, a stunning pink and rose colored star quilt. "All original. And all returned."

"Returned?"

Willie paused as if speaking to an anxious crowd. "The morning of Jason's murder, someone left them on the front doorstep of the Prairie Edge. They were all stuffed into a Sioux Nation grocery bag, undamaged."

Returned undamaged. Manny rolled that around in his mind. Someone stole forty thousand dollars' worth of artifacts, then just returned them. "Have they been seized?"

"They have." Willie slid a pinch of Copenhagen under his lip, dragging his explanation out like a skilled attorney. "Rapid City

PD seized them. Detective Harold Soske told me they developed some good prints from the bone whistle, and some partials on the grocery bag. He'll call if they get a suspect."

Manny stood abruptly. He grabbed their paper plates and tossed them into the garbage. He patted his pocket for his notebook, and checked his watch for the first time since entering Big Bat's. "You going to be on Indian time all day?" he called over his shoulder. "I need to get some work out of you today."

Without waiting for an answer, Manny walked to the patrol car with his hand on his throbbing head to ease the itch in his stitches, grateful that he had the case to take his mind off the pain.

CHAPTER 7

Willie slowed to allow a cow and her calf to cross the road. "If I had a brother, I wouldn't want to have to arrest him either. Even if he is an ex-con."

Dispatcher Shannon Horn located Reuben's jobsite from construction permits he had filed on behalf of his Heritage Kids.

"I keep telling myself it really doesn't matter if Reuben is the killer or not. Just as long as I do my job. See justice done. All that ideological bullshit. It would easier if it was someone else, though. But right now he's our best suspect."

Willie pulled over and stopped the car. He reached into his briefcase and came away with a handgun in a brown shoulder holster.

"I don't need a gun."

"You need one here."

"I haven't needed one in years, except for qualifications."

"Last night should have taught you that you need a gun on the rez. You need to be armed. As many homicides as you've investigated should have taught you that an armed man will kill an unarmed man with monotonous regularity."

"I'll pass."

"Hell, you're safer walking around Watts or Harlem un-armed in the middle of the night than you are Pine Ridge."

"You're right. It is foolish of me, but I'm kind of rusty with guns."

"Don't worry." Willie slid the Glock 9 mm from the holster. After dropping the magazine and clearing the round from the chamber, he handed it to Manny. "It's like a revolver. Just point and shoot. There's no safety to worry about, and there's seven-teen rounds in that thing, plus this spare mag."

"Don't let Lumpy see you saving my butt."

"He won't know a thing. This is my own gun."

Willie drove while Manny wrestled with the adjustment straps. He hadn't worn a shoulder holster since he first started with the bureau. It had been cool back then, in a Don Johnson-*Miami Vice* kind of way. But experienced agents were right: Real cops didn't wear shoulder rigs. He fidgeted until he got it com-fortably positioned under his armpit, eased back in the seat, and thought of what he'd say to Reuben. He'd told Willie the truth: It didn't matter if Reuben was Jason's killer, Manny would ar-rest him. But it did matter. He wanted Reuben to be innocent of Jason's murder like he'd wanted Reuben to be innocent of Billy Two Moons's murder. And if he'd read Reuben right yesterday, they might have an outside chance of patching things up.

He envied Willie's relationship with his aunt Elizabeth and their extended family back at Crow Creek, envied how they looked after one another. *Tiospaye* had always been the corner-stone of Lakota society, where family ties took precedence over everything else. *Tiospaye* determined how people conducted their lives.

Manny and Reuben were the last of their *tiospaye*. Manny

admitted that he wanted some relationship with Reuben, even if only limited. He'd lie awake many nights, fighting to drive his brother from his thoughts, to forget old promises from Reuben that he would always be there if Manny needed him. If only he hadn't talked with Reuben yesterday, this would just be another assignment to complete before he returned to the academy. He damned his brother now as he damned him untold times after he went to prison.

Willie hit a rut, and the shoulder strap bound into Manny's armpit. He wrestled with it until it was loose, then settled back in the seat and listened to Willie. After his folks had drowned at Big Bend Dam near Fort Thompson on the Missouri River in South Dakota, Elizabeth had brought him to Pine Ridge to live with her and Erica. He told Manny how he had no other living relatives except for his aunt Lizzy and his cousin Erica.

In many ways Willie and Manny shared similar backgrounds. Like Manny, Willie was left orphaned. And like Manny, a loving relative took Willie in as her own. Elizabeth had welcomed Willie into her family and treated him as an equal with Erica. Again the importance of the *tiospaye* reminded Manny of the Lakota way, going back when warriors failed to return from a hunt or a war party: the surviving family members raised the orphaned children as their own.

"Aunt Lizzy said your uncle raised you since you were five."

Manny smiled. He always smiled when he thought of his uncle Marion. "My aunt Sadie died of complications from diabetes the year I was born, and Unc's only son died at Chosin in Korea. When my folks died in a car wreck, he took me in even though he couldn't afford another mouth. We were so poor, the only pet we could afford was a tumbleweed."

Willie laughed. "We didn't have much either, but we didn't want for anything."

The reservation was peppered with the Willies, people who

possessed none of the things that White people worked so hard for. Yet the Willies were happy with their lot. Deep inside, Manny wished he could reconnect with that life he once had. If only Quantico wasn't on another planet than Pine Ridge.

The droning car motor helped Manny drift in and out of sleep. The aching in his head was now just a dull thud, and he was grateful for the chance to close his eyes. The thump-thump-thump of the tires on highway expansion strips acted like the sound machine he used back home to drown out traffic noise. He dozed in and out, the exhaustion of the last three days evident in his aching muscles and sore joints. In just a few days, the reservation had beaten him to a draw on the homicide case, and had aged him.

When the car had left pavement for a washboard dirt road, Manny awoke massaging his stitches. *Damned thing's more a two-track than a road.* He tried to place where they were. Cows, whose ribs and spines threatened to burst from their skin, stood grazing on sparse scrub bushes on one side of the gravel road. In the ditch on the other side of the road, a Chevy van sat abandoned, every multicolored fender shot full of holes. A six-pack of empty beer bottles littered the grass around the van. "Modern Indian artifacts," Unc used to say. Willie swerved to miss the glass.

"Where are we?"

Willie smiled and turned the radio down. "Just turned onto Route 100 from 18. Your snoring drowned out the radio for the last half hour." He turned KILI off. "They give you something strong for the pain there at the ER?"

As if in response to Willie's question, the squad car hit a rut, and pain shot sharp and deep into Manny's stitches. A reflex reaction jerked his hand up to his head, and he hit his forehead. Now the throbbing stitches in his hand took his mind off the pain in his head.

"I kick myself in the ass now that I didn't take the painkillers they offered."

They drove the remaining eleven miles on Route 100 in silence, until Willie slowed for the dirt road leading to the construction site. Fine dust built up on the windshield. They turned and caught a crosswind, and dirt and mortar dust blew off a large concrete-block foundation. Willie stopped the cruiser in front of a dirty Dodge pickup with a magnetic sign on the side announcing that a *Lakota Country Times* reporter was on-site. "Damned Yellow Horse," he muttered.

Manny couldn't see Yellow Horse, but tops of people's heads bobbed just above the basement rim as they walked back and forth. "He's got to be down there."

"What's he doing here?"

"Making my life miserable."

Willie and Manny walked around the brick pile and peered over the edge. Five feet down, Reuben straddled a chalk line. He held a trowel in one hand while four boys, stripped to the waist and glistening in the hot morning sun, handed bricks to another boy. The fifth boy, larger and older than the rest, broke block for a corner piece. He tossed the brick to another boy, also stripped to the waist. "Lenny."

"You met him?"

"First day when I rolled into town." Lenny tossed the brick to one boy and accepted a clean one from another boy. "What's the skinny on him?"

"That's Lenny Little Boy. And that kid that's sixteen-going-on-twenty is his brother, Jack. They're a couple bad ones. They've been in more shit than ten plumbers."

Jack slung the hammer effortlessly. "Wielded the hammer like it was a part of him," the witness had told Officer Slow Elk. Each time the boy struck the brick, the sound carried to Manny's head and he winced while he fought to leave his stitches alone.

Nathan Yellow Horse, holding a reporter's notebook, stood in front of Reuben. Yellow Horse wrote while Reuben worked the concrete on the trowel while he talked. Reuben had just grabbed the corner brick from Jack Little Boy when he spotted Willie and Manny. After dropping it, Reuben put his hands on the small of his back and arched. Sweat ran down from his face and chest and soaked his jeans.

"*Kola*," he called out. Yellow Horse looked up at Manny and pocketed his notebook. Reuben grabbed a bandana from his back pocket and dried his neck. He ran the bandana over a wide scar that ran diagonally over one pectoral muscle. Reuben had picked up that wartime souvenir when an incoming RPG hit the Con Thien mess hall one morning in 1967.

Another scar, the result of a fight with some Minneapolis policemen three years later, started at his neck and ended at his upper shoulder. The eagle tattooed across his chest flew a little lower these days, its wings drooping across tired muscles. Still, Reuben was well preserved for his age, and Manny patted his own potbelly without thinking.

"*Kola*. Come down here, and help me and Nathan. Real work will do wonders for you."

"I can see Yellow Horse is working up a sweat." Manny stepped to the edge of the hole. The boys stopped working. They glared at Willie's black Oglala Sioux Tribal Police uniform, then at Manny, who they now knew was an FBI agent. One boy stood clenching his fists, his bare pecs flexing, while another spit his chew into the dirt and glared at them with taut neck muscles. Another boy slipped a knife from a belt sheath and picked his nails, holding it so that the sun glinted off the blade and reflected in Manny's eyes.

Jack Little Boy elbowed his way in front of the others and clenched the hammer while he tapped it against his thigh. He cinched up on the handle as if he had intentions to use it.

"Come down and we'll visit," Reuben repeated.

"Let's talk up here," Manny said.

"Suit yourself." Reuben dropped his trowel and started the climb up from the hole in the ground. He grabbed the block pile and hoisted himself out of the basement. He winced in pain and massaged his leg. "Don't ever grow old, little brother."

He offered Yellow Horse his hand and pulled the thin man up.

"What you doing here?"

"Follow-up," Yellow Horse answered. "Getting the native perspective on Red Cloud's murder. Anything you want to say?"

"Not particularly."

"Then you won't mind me interviewing your prime suspect?"

"Who said he was my prime suspect?"

"Two interviews with Reuben in two days is more than coincidence."

"Who said I talked with him already?"

"I have my own ears on the rez." Yellow Horse smiled.

"Which I confirmed." Reuben limped to a large pile of mortar bags sitting on a pallet. He grabbed a bag and dropped it beside a Coleman cooler. He eased himself onto the bag as he rubbed his leg. "A touch of arthritis. It's hell getting old. But I'm not too old to rehash old times for Nathan here."

Yellow Horse flicked on his pocket recorder and thrust it at Manny. "Tell me why you automatically assumed the killer is Lakota?"

"Leave."

"And why pick on your own brother? You got something to prove, Agent Tanno?"

"You're interfering with my investigation. Leave."

Yellow Horse stepped closer and held the recorder to Manny's mouth, prompting Willie to step between them. "Man told you to leave, Nathan."

"We'll see what Lieutenant Looks Twice has to say about

this." Yellow Horse turned on his heels and tripped over a concrete bag that had broken open. He fell to the ground as dust rose and engulfed him. He sputtered and beat his hands against his pants as he walked to his car.

"Give Lumpy my best," Manny called out, and turned to Reuben. He'd opened the cooler and set the water bottles aside before he tipped it over his head. Water cascaded down his face, chest, and back, and he shook his head like a wet sheepdog as he ran his hand through his gray hair to get it out of his eyes.

"Water?"

"Not for me," Manny said. Reuben's Heritage Kids peeked over the edge of the foundation.

"At least sit so I don't get a stiff neck looking up at you."

Manny grabbed a concrete block and sat across from Reuben.

"It's so nice to have another visit from you tribal boys today."

"Another visit?"

"Your esteemed Lieutenant Looks Twice waddled over here. He felt compelled to check our building permit."

"Why would he do that?" Willie asked. "Not our job to enforce building codes."

Reuben shrugged. "Guess he's still stuck in the past. Trying to be like one of Wilson's goons. Back in the 1970s, they did all sorts of things that didn't come with their job description, like whatever the tribal chairman wanted. Which often had nothing to do with police work. By the way, Officer With Horn, has my brother been teaching you anything about the lost art of homicide investigation?"

Willie stiffened. "He has."

"Why'd you tell Yellow Horse I talked with you already?"

"He already knew it."

"How?"

"You're the FBI, you figure it out. Like maybe he's been following you around."

"Or maybe he's got someone checking the radio log for him," Willie said.

Reuben grinned. "Sure. Like your old school chum Lumpy. But you didn't come here to solidify our budding relationship."

He ignored Reuben's comment and told him about the artifacts, as much to gauge his reaction as to explain his visit. When he said the antiquities had been returned to the Prairie Edge, Reuben sat expressionless.

"I am glad someone returned them." Reuben fished into his pocket for his pipe and tobacco. He tamped his bowl with a used Sun Dance skewer. Manny thought of that skewer once piercing Reuben's chest muscles and he shuddered as much out of fear as respect. "They should have been returned. The Lakota artifacts would be impure in the hands of someone who doesn't deserve them."

"But they'll be resold," Willie said. "Some are near priceless, and I don't know any Indian who can afford them. Some *wasicu* will buy them."

"Then the White dude will come by them legally," Reuben snapped. His face flushed. The old Reuben's anger rose to the surface. Then he was calm once again, talking low, talking evenly. "If a Lakota was in possession of stolen artifacts, it shames us all."

Like the shame Unc and I felt, shame enough to cry ourselves to sleep because you killed Billy Two Moons. What was it that Unc had called Reuben's disgraceful actions? Owakpamni. In the old times, men were expelled from the village forever for dishonoring themselves. Owakamni. "So you and your kids here know nothing of these items?"

Reuben hung his head for a dramatic moment. He winced as he stood and hobbled to the basement hole. "Come up here, boys. They're not going to arrest you or anything." They scrambled out of the basement and stood beside Reuben. They glared at Willie, his uniform the symbol of authority. Reuben caught their look, too, and faced them.

"Enough." His voice rose and he gestured to Willie and Manny. "How many times have I told you boys that you're in your predicament because of choices you made. What you did, not what the law did to you. And especially, not these cops."

Jack Little Boy stared a hole through Manny that matched Lenny's stare. Jack was built as if he'd tossed brick all his life, lithe yet muscular with the hardened look of someone who had walked on Reuben's side of the line all his life. He tapped the chipping hammer against his thigh, and Manny's elbow brushed against the Glock beneath his jacket. Instinct? As a tribal cop he had packed a gun, and as an FBI field agent he'd had to carry one. But he doubted he could even use one now, especially against this boy.

"Jack! Lenny!" Reuben looked straight into their eyes. Lenny flinched as if Reuben intended to hit him, but Jack took a step closer in defiance.

"That's enough. Put the damned hammer down."

"But they're not one of us. Especially that FBI man. He left—"

"I said, that's enough."

Jack looked to Reuben, then back to Manny before breaking his stare and dropping the hammer. Reuben turned to Manny. "Ask your questions."

Manny looked into each boy's eyes. As with all interrogations, in the field or the interview room, Manny first asked simple, nonaccusatory questions. He watched reactions to those questions so that he would have a base of reference when he later asked the tough ones.

"The Prairie Edge had thousands of dollars worth of Lakota artifacts stolen. Then returned." He needed answers about the theft. If he discovered who returned the artifacts, he was certain he would find Jason's killer. Before another attempt on his life was made.

He studied each boy's face as he asked about the theft of the antiquities. Brows furrowed at the implication that they were involved. Jaws clenched when they were accused of stealing. There was the twitch in one boy's face that had been absent before, and the nervous spitting of tobacco juice from another. Others stared deadpan as they answered Manny's questions. When he was finished, he concluded they concealed information well if they knew anything about the theft.

Then he sprang another question on them, one that reminded him of the pain and itching that still caused him to wince whenever he moved. "Any of you know who attacked me last night with a hammer? Maybe with a masonry hammer?"

"Are we suspects?" Jack asked.

"No."

"Then you're just fishing."

"Someone tried killing me last night—"

"So we heard," Reuben interrupted. He turned to the boys. "Finish up that last row and we'll take a lunch break."

They started down the hole again when Manny called out, "And get that headlight fixed."

"Don't worry. I'll get it fixed as soon as I get to the Pronto," Jack called over his shoulder.

Reuben waited until they disappeared into the foundation hole before he faced Manny. "What was that about the headlight?"

"Nothing." Manny wanted to tell Reuben he suspected it had been Jack driving the car that tried running him over last night, and probably Lenny who had flung the door open and knocked him into the ditch. Both boys would be good for the assault, but he wasn't certain if Reuben was involved. Perhaps he gave orders to his kids off the jobsite as well as on.

"I heard someone attacked you, but I didn't know it was that serious. Let's see."

Manny tugged at the cloth tape holding the gauze to his

head. The bandage caught matted blood, and he winced again as he pulled it away. He was certain a stitch tore loose, and again he fought the urge to run his hand over the stitches.

Reuben whistled. Manny replaced the tape, which only partially stuck to his sweaty forehead.

"I heard someone just wanted to scare you away, but that's serious. My kids laughed when they heard it, but I told them Manny Tanno couldn't be frightened off."

"Thanks for the vote of confidence. And everyone in that hole is a suspect."

"I think I'd know if any of my kids attacked you. They'd be bragging to each other about it, and then one of them would whisper it to me."

"You think?"

Reuben paused just long enough that Manny knew he didn't have as much faith in his kids as he professed. "Of course I'd know."

"Then where were you last night?" Reuben didn't fit the description of his attacker, but Manny wanted to keep his brother guessing.

Reuben smiled. "I went over to the White River south of Red Dog Table—"

"Drive?"

"I rode my horse."

"That's a good three-hour ride from your place."

"Like I said, I don't drive. And yeah, it took me three hours of hard riding."

"And why'd you ride all the way up there?"

"I was conducting a Hunka sing at the time you were being attacked. The Little Creeks and Drapeauxs were always close, and they wanted to get closer last night. The Hunka ceremony is where one person in a family ritually adopts another to bring the two clans together."

"I do remember some of the old ways."

"So you said."

"And how long was the sing?"

"All night. I rode home just in time to grab a bite and head to work. Look, none of us had anything to do with you getting whacked last night." He rubbed his leg. "Now if there's nothing else, I got to get back to this job so we can finish it on time."

"Wait for me in the car, please," Manny told Willie.

"You sure? Those kids don't like you much."

"It'll be all right. On some level, I know my brother won't let anything happen to me here."

When Willie disappeared around the mound of dirt hiding the cruiser, Manny turned and looked down at Reuben, who asked, "Something else, *kola?*"

"Something's been bothering me for a while."

"What?"

"Where were you the night Billy Two Moons was murdered?"

"I said it enough times. I was with Lizzy. We'd separated, but we weren't divorced then."

"Maybe you were there all night. Maybe someone else killed Two Moons."

"What's it matter now, anyway?"

"Because I believed you didn't do it!"

"So that's what this is all about, *kola*—that you can't accept having a murderer in the family. You're too much like Unc, aren't you?"

"Did you kill Two Moons?"

"My confession is a matter of public record."

It is. But before I tie up this Red Cloud investigation, I'll know the truth about that night with Billy Two Moons.

CHAPTER 8

Lumpy looked over his half-glasses first at Manny, then at Willie seated next to him. Sober this afternoon, Lumpy said nothing about last night. He cupped his face in his hand to hide the large purple stain covering one cheek and part of his ear. The other hand sported a spot matching the grotesque color of his face. Lumpy had opened the door of his new Mustang this morning after someone had smeared indelible thief powder over the door handle, and he was trying to make his futile attempt to hide it appear nonchalant.

Manny suppressed a smile. While still a rookie, he had responded with Chief Horn to Big Bat's one morning to investigate a break-in. The chief had used thief powder. The manager reported money missing from the till and suspected an employee. Chief Horn had smeared the oily substance on the underside of the cash register, and the new janitor got it all over his hands late that night when he went for more money. He had stained hands for more than a week, and they caught their suspect. Now

Lumpy's face and hand would be stuck with the deep purple stain, impervious to any known cleaning agent.

Lumpy slid a teletype across the desk. "Rapid City PD got a break on the stolen artifacts from the Prairie Edge," he said. His words came out mumbled from the hand cradling his mouth.

"What did you say?"

Lumpy spoke again.

Manny shook his head. "Can't understand you."

Lumpy pulled his hand away to speak and Manny fought back a laugh. Out of the corner of his eye, he saw that Willie looked away as he fought down his own snicker. "Seems like it was some kid who lives across from the air base in Ellsworth stole the stuff. The Rapid City detectives are interviewing him now."

"Why the hell didn't you tell them to hold off until I got there?"

"None of my business, Hotshot. I figured whenever you checked in here, I'd give this to you." Lumpy smiled. "And I have."

"Then we'd better get up there as soon as we can."

"I'll go change into civvies—"

"You'll be going solo." Lumpy winked at Manny and leaned back against Elvis. He hooked his thumbs in his duty belt somewhere under his belly. "Willie's needed here today. With his own people." *Retribution has already begun.*

Lumpy propped his big feet on his desk and took his glasses off, while he kept smiling at Manny. A call to Niles would grease the wheels for Lumpy to cooperate, including the availability of young Officer With Horn, but Manny wouldn't give the Pile the satisfaction.

"Now if you don't mind, Hotshot, Willie's got work to do."

They started for the door when Lumpy called after them, "Close the door on Agent Tanno and me."

Manny turned back to Lumpy after Willie closed the door. "What the hell was that all about? I need Willie today."

Lumpy dropped his boots on the floor and used Elvis to stand. "You think this shit's funny?"

Manny smirked. "It'd be funny if you did it to me."

"That a confession?"

Manny shook his head. "I never confess to anything. How about you? This confession time?"

"Confess to what?"

"Butting into my investigation." Manny walked to Lumpy's candy machine, but dropped his change back in his pocket as he remembered how hard the run was last night. "You didn't go out to Reuben's jobsite to check his permits."

"You're more observant than I remember."

"Why'd you go there?"

Lumpy's smile faded and he stepped closer to Manny. "I drove there because of your assault, Hotshot. Witnesses said a car damned near run you over right before you got clubbed. A car with a busted headlight. I knew the Little Boys would be good for it, and I made the building permit an excuse to check their car out. Only now you're pissed 'cause I'm a step ahead of you. Like I always was."

"Not hardly. Little Boy admitted he drives a car with one headlight."

"Oh it's Jack Little Boy's Pontiac all right, but I'm biding my time. I'll bring him in when he figures he's gotten away with it."

"You could have told me."

"Your assault is a tribal case. I intended telling you when I got a confession out of them. Get over it."

"You're still an asshole."

"Why? 'Cause I even work my ass to solve the assault of some fancy damned city Sioux that hasn't even been back home in years?"

"I've been busy with academy classes."

Lumpy laughed and stood in front of the candy machine,

looking at it like it was a television and he wanted to change channels. When the clink of change fell into the coin box, he pushed a button. "While you were off rubbing elbows with every *wasicu* in D.C., I was back here working my ass off for my people. Your people, too, in case you don't remember."

"Oh, I remember. I remember a ruthless patrolman who edged everyone out for sergeant, then used his position to stick it to us."

"Street sergeants have a job to do, too."

"You didn't have to be such a jerk about it. But it looks like you made it just to lieutenant and stopped."

"People had it in for me."

"Bullshit." Manny sat on the edge of the desk. He recalled this was one of Lumpy's absolute no-nos, and he glared at Manny. "It's the same all over, Lumpy. People in authority go too far left, too far right, and they start making bad decisions. You walked the progressives' road . . ."

"You think I want those AIM thugs popping up here again? Like Reuben?"

"You deserved Desirée."

Lumpy's mouth drooped and he broke his gaze. "I didn't deserve what she did to me."

Manny realized he had gone where he had no right, and he stood from the desk.

"You're always digging in the knife about my battles."

Manny straightened the papers he'd sat on. "I won't mention her again . . ."

"Just go to Rapid. And send in Willie on your way out."

Willie walked Manny to his car. When they got outside, Willie laughed. "Hell, that stain on his face couldn't be worse if some kid tagged him with a can of Rust-Oleum."

Willie laughed again, then the smile faded and deep furrows creased his forehead. He eyed the fresh gouge along the driver's-side back quarter panel of Manny's rental. "Wish I could go along with you today. You look like you could use a driver."

Willie was dying to ask about the fresh damage. Manny had rehearsed his story just in case: The gas pumps at Big Bat's moved a bit too fast and clipped the rental. The accident had been in self-defense.

"I was looking forward to sitting in on one of your interviews."

"I'd like you there, too." Manny would miss their discussions, Willie's fresh insight. Besides, Willie was right: He drove better. "But keep your ear to the tracks. You never know when some tidbit of useful info will come your way."

He waited until Willie went back inside the station before he called the Red Cloud Development office. Again. "I gave Ms. Downing the message," the receptionist said. "She said she would call you when she could."

Manny closed his cell. Maybe some soothing Six Fat Dutchmen riding with him to Rapid City would ease his anger. And his confusion.

>‹›‹›‹

Two hours later, Manny walked into the Rapid City Police Department building. He badged the receptionist, and she buzzed him through the security door into the inner office.

"Harold Soske." Soske's smooth, well-manicured hand applied just the proper amount of pressure to let Manny know there was strength in that grip, yet not strong enough to cause pain to his bandaged hand.

Manny smoothed his white shirt and bloodred tie. The bureau required agents to dress as if they were going to a business meeting, but Manny always felt stiff and out of place, like he was dressing for a wake. He fidgeted, awkward, standing in front of this young detective. Soske wore a dark blue herringbone suit that complemented his amber shirt and maroon tie, all of which exuded effortless professionalism. *Professional, hell. The kid looks like he stepped out of the pages of* GQ.

"An honor to meet you." Soske dropped his hand to the manila folder he carried. "You're here to speak with Ricky Bell."

Manny nodded. "Your evidence techs matched his prints to those found on the bone whistle from the Prairie Edge burglary. What did he tell you about that?"

Soske shrugged. "Nada. The kid clammed up tight when I asked him about the stolen artifacts. He invoked Miranda right off. We can't even ask his name without his lawyer."

"I have no intention of asking questions. I'll just be talking to him. Does he have a lawyer?"

"No. Kid don't have squat. He'll end up with some public defender."

As Soske led Manny to an interview room, he filled him in about Richard Bell from notes tucked away in the file folder. "We got more than a few contacts on Ricky. Minor contacts: shoplifting, public intox, joyriding when he was a juvie. But Pennington County nailed him on an agg assault three years ago, and he did a stint in Sioux Falls for that stunt."

"Parole?"

"Served and released. He did just enough hard time to learn the tricks, like we can't question him without an attorney."

They came to a door separating the long hallway from another set of offices, and Soske held it open.

"How did Ricky gain entry to the Prairie Edge?"

"The kid's pretty stout. He just pried the back lock off."

"Alarmed?"

"Not then, but Brinks installed a system yesterday."

"What do you make of the items just being left on the doorstep?"

Soske stopped. When he finally answered, he chose his words carefully. "I figure someone is trying to set Ricky up. Ricky's prints coated the stuff we found. He's been through Criminal College 101 in Sioux Falls, and he'd never leave prints all over it like that."

"I understand the bag was a Sioux Nation brown bag."

Soske nodded, and opened a file. He took out a stack of photographs. "This is just how the bag was found, with the items stuffed in there in no particular order." Manny studied the photo. The bone whistle was resting on the star quilt that covered up and hid the other items. And the quilt was folded strangely, in a unique way of tucking the edges into one another to keep the material together. He would ask someone about that later. Soske unlocked interview room two. Two large fluorescent bulbs overhead looked like overkill in the tiny room. The only furniture was two straight-backed metal chairs and a card table. Pens and a stack of statement forms sat on the table.

A muscular man younger than Soske sat in one of the chairs, arms folded as he eyed Manny sitting across the table. He leaned back against the wall with the front two legs off the floor. Soske leaned against the opposite wall.

"I already told you a-holes I wasn't going to talk without my mouthpiece."

"And who might that be?" Manny asked. "F. Lee Bailey? Gerry Spence? Fact is, Richard, you're looking at some snot-nosed public defender, who just squeaked by the bar exam, getting between you and a murder rap. You're going to end up playing leapfrog with some horny cellmate for a long time. You want to put your future in the hands of some flash-in-a-bedpan right out of law school?"

Bell smiled. "Murder? Who am I supposed to have murdered?"

"Jason Red Cloud."

"Jason?" Bell laughed. His voice wavered and his eyes darted between Manny and Soske. "Now why would I murder my own boss, kill my way out of the only job an ex-con can get in this town?"

Manny looked at Soske and motioned him into the hallway. "Bell worked for Red Cloud?" he asked when the door was closed.

"Bell's a janitor at the Red Cloud Development building. The victim hired him fresh out of the penitentiary two months ago."

"Any more surprises?"

Soske shook his head. "But don't be shocked when this kid comes up with an airtight alibi. Cons have been tutoring him the last three years."

Manny nodded. He didn't like surprises, and this one in particular. He led the way back into the interview room.

"Take a hike, Indian," Bell said before Manny could speak. "I'm invoking my Fifth Amendment rights, and I ain't speaking to you or anyone else."

Manny pulled his chair around the table and scooted it close to Bell. "Good. Exercise those rights and sit still while I do the talking." Without waiting for a response, Manny continued, "The tech found your prints all over the artifacts stolen from the Prairie Edge two weeks ago. One of those items, a Lakota war club, was found buried brain-deep in Jason Red Cloud's skull."

Bell dropped the chair onto the floor and leaned closer to Manny. "So I heard, but I ain't killed no one, so go screw yourself. I got nothing to say to you." His voice broke. Perspiration formed on his brow. Bell folded and unfolded his hands and studied them as he avoided looking Manny in the eye.

Manny shrugged and turned to Soske. "We're done here. Have your detention officers prep Richard here for transport."

"Transport?" Bell asked, his voice breaking once more. "Where the hell to?"

"Pine Ridge, of course. You'll be spending some time there in the lockup until I can house you in a regional federal lockup."

Bell stood abruptly and his chair fell against the wall.

He stepped toward Manny, but Soske stepped between them and shoved Bell back into his seat. "He can't do that, can he? He can't just take me out and lock me up, can he? I'll be the only White dude in that jail."

Soske picked up on the ruse. "Of course he can. His murder case takes precedence over our burglary. And the murder was on the reservation. Federal jurisdiction." Soske started for the door. "I'll have the detention officer grab the belly chains," he called over his shoulder. "I take it you'll be transporting?"

"Wait!" Bell yelled at Soske's back. "You can't let him take me to Pine Ridge. Those Indians will kill me in there."

Soske's face drooped in an exaggerated display of sadness. "Sorry, Ricky, but that's your choice. You invoked your Miranda rights, and we can't ask you a thing without your attorney."

"Hold it. What about if I tell you guys what I know?"

Beads of perspiration widened and ran across Bell's forehead. Sweat dripped into one eye, and he wiped at it with his hand as his eyes darted between Manny and Soske.

"I uninvoke," Bell pleaded. "Whatever I got to do, I'll do it. I don't want an attorney. Just let me tell you what I know."

"We're listening," Manny said.

"Let me talk with that public defender first. Then we'll deal."

Manny picked up his briefcase and headed for the door.

"Where are you going?"

"Brief the transport officers."

"Wait!"

"When I go through that door, the offer evaporates and you take your chance on the reservation."

"All right. All right." Ricky ran his fingers through his hair. "What you need to know?"

Manny reached into his briefcase and placed a recorder in the middle of the table. After noting the time, date, and place of the interview, he asked Bell to state that he had received an explanation of his Miranda rights and had voluntarily waived them. "Now we can begin."

Manny sat back in his chair and patted his pocket. Whenever he had scored a victory in the interview room, he would grab one of his little buddies from his pack and light up. He would have to find some other way to celebrate later.

"Jason Red Cloud hired me to steal the stuff." Bell must have read the doubt in their faces. "It's true. I'm a night janitor at the Red Cloud Development building. Jason got hold of me a couple weeks ago. He says, 'Ricky, I need you to do me a special favor.' He hands me a list of shit to steal from the Prairie Edge. I spend one afternoon inside the store looking around. They got no alarm. No guards. It's a cakewalk, and the next night I waltz into the place."

"And you stole these items for him out of the goodness of your heart?"

"Not hardly. Jason paid me ten percent of what the stuff was worth, two hundred bucks. Not bad for a few minutes' work one night."

"The things you copped were worth at least forty thousand dollars," Soske said.

"That bastard," Bell breathed.

"No honor among thieves," Manny added.

"Now I don't have to go with him?" Bell jerked his thumb toward Manny. "I can stay here in the Pennington County lockup, right?"

"As soon as you tell me why you brought the artifacts back."

Bell looked from Soske to Manny. "You talking trash? I never brought anything back I stole. Ever. What would I do that for?" Bell hunched over. He cupped his face in hands as he stared at the floor, silent, offering nothing else. When Soske told Bell he would remain at the Pennington County jail, he slumped in his chair with relief, like he'd been granted an eleventh-hour pardon from the governor. Outside the interview room, Soske asked if Manny thought Bell had been truthful.

"What do you think?" Manny asked.

"He was so scared he nearly fell off the chair. He knew that if he jerked you around, and you caught him in a lie, you really would take him back to Pine Ridge."

Manny nodded. "I think he was truthful, too, but I had a problem when I asked him if he had killed Jason. He hesitated when he denied it."

"But what would he gain by killing him?"

"Jason could finger him for the Prairie Edge burglary. With prior pen time, it would be enough to get five years added to the sentence."

"But that would mean Jason would have had to testify he'd hired Bell." Soske shook his head. "That would have ruined his business. What was left of it."

Manny fumbled for the key to the rental car.

"If Ricky killed Jason Red Cloud, he isn't telling us all he knows about the burglary," Soske said as they walked to the parking lot.

They shook hands again before Manny opened the door.

"It was a pleasure watching you work," Soske said. "Where are you off to now?"

"Shopping for artifacts."

Manny pulled out of the parking lot, and failed to see a city garbage truck driving in the same lane he turned into. Brakes squealed. The odor of burnt brake lining drifted inside the rental car as the truck driver laid on the horn. From the rearview mirror, Manny watched the woman driving the truck mouth obscenities as she stabbed her middle finger out the window. Manny smiled and waved, then sped to get out of her path. Once again, his *wopiye* saved him, and he patted the medicine bundle tucked deep into his jacket pocket. Perhaps there was something to the powers of the old ones after all.

CHAPTER 9

Manny draped his coat over his arm as he enjoyed walking in downtown Rapid City. Old Town's touch of the West reminded him of the area's roots. Bronze frontiersmen stood mute, guarding the corners, symbols of the hardy souls who had first settled here. Or rather, had driven the Lakota off their rightful land, away from their sacred Black Hills to the desolate reservations they occupied today.

Since coming back to Pine Ridge, Manny fought the cynicism. Hadn't the bureau been good to him, hiring a Native American? Except for the reservation assignments, the bureau treated him as an equal with White agents. He kept telling himself that all Pine Ridge meant to him was a childhood full of painful memories, yet with each passing day he wished there were something he could do to change things there. He fought the feelings, convinced that they would subside once he returned to Virginia after this assignment.

Manny smiled at each person he passed. Each one would

look him in the eye and throw out a genuine "Good morning" or "Good day" or "How's it going?" as if they were actually interested how life was treating this stranger from another place. They couldn't tell he was a temporarily displaced FBI agent from the East. All they knew was that they had spoken to an Indian man in passing. Indian–White tensions of the early 1970s had indeed eased, and he looked forward to the next person who wished him a good day so he could return the gesture.

The Black Hills air was crisp and clean, and he picked up the pace, walking without being winded thanks to his stepped-up road regime every night. He thanked Jenny Craig for his diet, and he thanked those young agents who took time from their workout at the bureau gym to help and encourage him. And oddly, he thanked Niles the Pile for sending him out here, even though he'd have to hustle to solve this homicide in time for the next class. By the time Manny walked the mile to the Prairie Edge, it was late afternoon, and the heat of the day faded into a cool puff of air that followed him into the store.

A bell tinkled above the door. He stopped just inside and listened to the mellow music that surrounded the room. He closed his eyes, and cherished the falsetto of the flute, the bass drum in the background setting the beat of the song. How many powwows had he attended where such music was sandwiched between the Shawl and the Jingle dancers? How many had he missed being away so long? Maybe that's why he liked polka, with its distinctive beats reminiscent of his native music.

He opened his eyes, and drew in a deep breath. Sage and sweetgrass burned somewhere in the room. It was another thing he missed: the fragrance of sacred, burning grasses.

A rawhide war shield hung from one wall, and Manny stepped closer to examine it. A traditional geometric pattern was beaded in the colors of the sacred winds: black, red, yellow, and white. Each row of beads was perfectly aligned, too perfect to be an original. The price of two thousand dollars was steep for a replica. But an original Sioux war shield would have cost ten times that amount.

He turned to another wall where a brain-tanned deerskin shirt hung. The pale, milk-supple hide had been beaded on every inch. Like the war shield, it detailed intricacies that original artifacts never possessed. Beaded rattles and drums and knife sheaths hung beneath the shirt, awaiting buyers wealthy enough to afford them. "If something moved, an Oglala woman would bead it" was a saying he had heard often growing up.

In an adjacent room were gifts that tourists, not purists, would buy. Knives and mass-produced beaded purses and pouches sat in glass display cases. Their quality was shoddy compared to the art made by native hands, which the price difference reflected. People unfamiliar with the culture would parade these things in front of their friends to show they had something genuinely Sioux and say they supported Indians by buying them, perhaps taking off the "made in Hong Kong" stickers before showing their friends.

In the back room, bins of beads waited for artisans to purchase them. Trade beads, they were called in the days when the White man traded the pieces of glass made in Europe for valuable fur to sell in the cities. Two old women stood hunched over the bins. One squinted through reading glasses missing one bow, while the other fingered a small leather coin purse as she dug for enough to cover the price of their beads.

Manny returned to the main room and spoke with a young woman behind the counter wearing an elk-hide vest adorned with imperfect rows of beads. It was ancient, beaded perhaps a hundred years ago by a Lakota woman on a winter night. When the clerk spoke, a distinct Brulé accent greeted him, thicker and more inclined to draw out the nasal vowels than the Oglala dialect.

"I'm looking for the manager."

"Ms. Horkley is upstairs." As she spoke, she cut strips from a piece of suede with a razor blade. She saw him watching her. "For moccasins," she said. "We can buy commercially made moccasin strings, but these are authentic. Besides, they last longer."

He thanked her and walked upstairs. The books for sale were arranged with Western settler history separated from Indian history separated from books about the Dakotas. The room had the air of a well-organized, albeit small, research library. A plump lady who could have passed for Manny's grandmother squatted beside CDs marked "Language."

"Ms. Horkley?" Manny opened his ID and badge wallet.

She gasped as she pushed her gray hair behind her ears. "Don't tell me I have to go to the police station and identify that Mr. Bell again?"

Manny shook his head. "I'm just here to ask you some questions about the break-in."

"The thefts could have been a disaster for us." She set the CDs on a table, and used the side of the bookcase for support to stand. She turned to a desk and took three Oreos from a pack, and offered Manny a cookie. He hadn't eaten this afternoon, and he accepted two cookies. "We deal in replications by a select group of artists, mostly local and mostly Lakota, though sometimes we acquire some Cheyenne and Crow pieces. All those are replaceable. But not the artifacts that were stolen. They were all original Oglala and Sicangu."

"Detective Soske said you remembered seeing Ricky Bell in here before."

"He showed me a whole page of pictures, and I spotted Mr. Bell right off. He browsed the store the day before the break-in. I understand he worked for the Red Cloud Development Corporation, which is a coincidence."

"How so?"

Ms. Horkley once again turned to the Oreo pack to give her strength to continue. "Jason Red Cloud was the best customer we had for authentic Lakota antiquities. I was delighted that he was able to purchase them, being Oglala himself."

"Did he buy things often?"

"Heavens, yes." She smiled. "Mr. Red Cloud bought something every month."

"Every month?"

"Yes. Except last month there was an unfortunate problem."

Manny waited until she'd swallowed her cookie before continuing. "Mr. Red Cloud came in to buy a star quilt. At least he intended buying it. Very old. Rumored to have been made for High Back Bone."

"Who?"

"Hump."

Manny flushed with embarrassment. He should know old Lakota leaders as well as this White woman did. "Jason paid with a corporate check, as he always did. Even for the best of customers like Mr. Red Cloud, we do a bank verification for any amount over a thousand dollars, you understand."

"Fully. But there was a problem?"

"Yes." Ms. Horkley sat on the edge of the desk. She brushed cookie crumbs off her dress into her hand. "When I checked with the bank, there were insufficient funds to cover the purchase. Mr. Red Cloud became very angry. He said he'd be back when he got it straightened out with his banker and stormed out. But he never came back to pick up the quilt."

"Did his checks ever bounce before?"

"Never. The bank always honored them. This was the first time the bank declined it. I thought they'd made an error. But when I called the bank president personally, he said there was no mistake. He said there just wasn't enough money in the Red Cloud Development account to cover the purchase."

"Tell me," Manny said, recalling the photo of the quilt when it was returned, "did you usually fold in the edges of quilts like that?"

"Heavens, no." She took a small step back as if Manny had called her a profane name. "We always store our quilts like those." She pointed over the balcony to four quilts in the art section of the store; each hung on individual wooden presentation rods. "That's the proper way to store antique quilts."

He thanked Ms. Horkley and had started toward the door when she stopped him. "What do you think will happen to Mr. Bell?"

"He'll be prosecuted under state statute. With his prior arrest record, he'll go back to the penitentiary."

"That's such a shame," she said, eating the last of the Oreos. "They don't feed them very well in jail, do they?"

>‹›‹›‹

"I thought I'd never find you." Passing cars nearly drowned out Sonja Myer's voice. She locked an arm in Manny's.

"Don't tell me. That nice Lieutenant Looks Twice?"

"He's been so helpful. Now all I have to get is your help with my story and I'll be all set."

Sonja moved closer and her fragrance once again overwhelmed him. Her face was inches from his. "I'm not jerking you around, I just don't really have anything new," Manny lied.

"Then we'll just go someplace where we can talk. Where I can enjoy intelligent conversation for a change."

Manny could not think of a single reason not to go somewhere with this beautiful woman. Except, like any other beautiful woman coming on to an over-the-hill man, she had other motives. He'd go with her, as much out of amusement as curiosity about what she knew.

She led him past small shops, past other bronze statues he

was only vaguely aware of, and sat at an outside table in front
of a small bistro.

"Would you like to hear the specials again?" The enthusiastic
young waiter had postgrad written all over his handsome face.

"Please. I didn't catch all that."

The waiter started reciting the specials again, then he stopped
midsentence and put his pencil back behind his ear. "I thought I
recognized you. Can I get an autograph?"

Manny was once again speechless. "Sure." He reached for
the waiter's pen and pad, but the man jerked his hand back and
turned to Sonja. "I've been a fan of yours ever since you came
here from Denver."

Sonja signed the waiter's pad, and Manny looked after the
kid as he disappeared into the bistro.

"A closed mouth gathers no feet."

"What?"

Manny forced a smile. "I thought he was talking to me."

Sonja laughed and rested her hand on his arm. "I get that a
lot around here."

"Did you work in the media in Denver?"

"Part-time television. Or I should say my other job was part
time: Denver Broncos cheerleader."

Manny nodded as if he knew what she was talking about.
He couldn't recall the last time he saw a football game, but if
the cheerleaders looked like Sonja, he thought he'd become a
fan.

The waiter brought their order and lingered, looking at Sonja
a little longer than Manny felt was appropriate. After the waiter
left, she scooted her chair close to his. Her leg touched his lightly,
and Manny tried reading anything else into it besides the story
she was after.

"I'm really struggling to have new information by dead-
line." She dabbed mustard from the corners of her mouth with

a checkered napkin. "Anything, however slight, that might fool my editor into thinking I've been doing my job."

Manny put his sandwich down and sipped his latte. He decided he hated lattes. *Give me the last dregs of the coffeepot anytime.* "I can tell you public information, that Jason was strapped financially and his project funding had been matched by the Oglala Sioux Tribe. Thirty million dollars that the tribe stood to lose if the resort failed."

"And was it failing?"

"No comment."

"Did he reinvest the money the tribe fronted him?"

"No comment."

"You're not giving me much to go on." She leaned closer to him and her breasts brushed against his forearm. "Is that man you just interviewed at the police department a suspect?" She flipped through a reporter's notebook. "Is Ricky Bell?"

"Who told you that?"

She batted her eyes. "There are always desk sergeants willing to listen to the requests of their citizens."

"Sergeants or lieutenants?"

She ignored him and smiled. "I assume the 'no comment' is your way of telling me I'm right, that Red Cloud's resort was failing, and that this Ricky Bell was connected somehow. Like maybe your suspect in Red Cloud's murder."

Manny composed himself. He sat up and slid his chair away from her so he could look at her across the table. "Ms. Myers . . ."

"Sonja."

"Ms. Myers. I really wish I had more information for you. The fact is, the investigation is moving along as expected but there's nothing more I can say. When I do have more, I'll call you."

She batted her eyes at him. "No need. I'll be calling on you again soon."

CHAPTER 10

Manny stood when Erica glided into the restaurant. Heads turned and people stared as she picked her way gracefully through the tables. Her black hair hung midback, straight and shiny, in a ponytail held by a beaded dream catcher. Manny looked up to her as she strode toward him like a model on a runway. Erica's height had helped the Pine Ridge Lady Thorpes to the state championship her senior year, and like her mother, her height enhanced her exotic look. And as with Elizabeth, more makeup would have distracted from her natural beauty, from the light skin and lower cheekbones she inherited from Reuben.

"Uncle Manny." She bent and hugged him tight. She pulled back and stared, and frowned as she looked first at the bandage on his head, then at his gauze-wrapped hand. "Mom said you'd been attacked, but she didn't say it was this bad. You look worse in person than you did on the news last night."

"Has everyone seen that botched news conference?" He forced a smile over the pounding in his stitches. "Anyway, it's not as bad as it looks. But let me look at you." He held her at arm's length and admired her. A year had passed since he'd met Erica and Jon in D.C. for the Indian Rights conference, and five years before that since he had given her away in a small wedding near the Capitol. She'd changed so little in that time.

"You look even fitter since the last time, Uncle Manny. Still running?"

He nodded and blushed, his cheeks warm. He knew when he was being politely lied to. Even though he had embarked on his diet and exercise regime, he had gained ten pounds since last year, and what little hair he had left had grown grayer around his temples. Still, in her presence he felt young again. "And you," he said. "You never change."

She smoothed her maroon linen sheath dress before sitting. "No Jon tonight?"

"He got tied up in deposition, but he sends his best."

"Ah, the bane of an attorney." Manny feigned regret.

Erica began to speak, then dropped her eyes.

"Trouble?"

Erica nodded. "It's the resort project. It could ruin Jon."

"How?"

She glanced around their table and lowered her voice. "His law firm here in Rapid City—and in particular Jon—handled the project. He vouched for Jason, even when he couldn't back up Jason's big ideas with the feasibility study the tribe required. Jon figured everything Jason touched turned to gold, and trusted him implicitly."

"But the Red Cloud Corporation backed the project. Out West here, that's better than posting a bond." He hadn't believed it when Elizabeth told him Jason was going under, and he found it difficult to believe it coming from Erica.

"That's another thing that Jon covered for him," she whispered. "The Oglala Sioux Tribe waived a thirty-million-dollar bond on Jason's reputation, and on Jon's and my assurance that the project would progress on schedule. But with Jason dead, it's not going to happen."

"Why not?"

"There's no one to run it."

"Couldn't someone else in the corporation run the project? Surely the board will see that it would still make a bundle for the corporation and the tribe. From what I've heard of Jason's ambitions, the project would have been a slam dunk."

The waitress brought their tea and Manny asked for a little more time to order. He dropped the sugar packs and used the Sweet'N Low as he waited for Erica's explanation. "There is no board. The corporation was a corporation in name only. He took over after his parents died, and he made all the decisions."

"I understand there's Jason's executive assistant, Clara Downing. Have you thought about working with her? Proceeding with the project?"

Erica flushed. Her lips quivered as she leaned closer to him. "Clara Downing is inept. She'd be even more of a disaster than Jason."

"Have you worked with her before?"

She shook her head. "I haven't, but Mom has. She can't stand Clara."

"Why?"

Erica stopped and studied her sweating water glass, running her finger over the sides. "Well, I guess Mom just doesn't trust her. There's nothing she can put her finger on. It's just women's intuition, Mom says."

"But you personally have never seen Clara Downing's work?"

Erica lowered her eyes. "No. But I trust Mom's judgment."

"OK. But apart from Clara Downing, Jason had all those projects. That Skylight Hotel in Breckenridge. The Deer Lodge Ski Resort outside Billings. Surely he must have—"

"He threw them up by the seat of his pants. Believe me, I learned there was nothing sound in anything Jason did in business. And I know business." Erica had landed a full ride to Harvard right out of high school, one of the few Oglala Sioux to attend an Ivy League school, and she'd made the most out of it. She had excelled in her business administration major, and Jason hired her to help the Red Cloud Resort project get off the ground. Erica put her heart and soul into the project to make it a success, but now it wasn't going to happen.

The waitress hovered over their table. Erica ordered a Cajun chicken salad, shaming Manny into dropping his yearning for a fatty prime rib and ordering a salad, too. When the waitress left, Manny leaned closer. "The bottom line then: How solvent was Jason?"

Erica shook her head. Her hair shimmered in the light of the votive candle on the table. "Clara Downing might tell you more. Jason wasn't solvent at all. He squandered what money he had left these past few years, and made some bad investments. Then there was the failed high-rise in Aurora that nearly wiped him out, until he could come up with something else to build. But the worst thing is he put the tribe's money in trust, just like I suggested to the tribal council, except Jason controlled the trust. It will look like I was in on it with him."

"What trust money?" Manny whispered.

"Nearly all the money the tribe had in its coffers. We—that is, I—convinced the council that the Red Cloud Corporation would match the tribe's money dollar for dollar. The more they invested, the larger and more successful the project would be."

"The crucial question is when did you realize that Jason planned to take the tribe's money and run?" The timing involved could be the difference between a poor choice of business partners and a prison sentence for fraud. "When did you find out he intended ripping off the tribe?"

Erica wiped tea from her lip and paused before answering. Manny thought the pause a little more than necessary, as if she needed time to concoct a story, but maybe he allowed his agent's suspicion to get in the way of an uncle's good judgment. His niece was an honest person, but with Jason dead, she would shoulder the brunt of any fraud allegations.

"It was about two weeks ago. I thought Jason had hired me because I had such a good consulting track record. I was actually patting myself on the back until I figured out that he didn't hire me because of my Harvard degree. He hired me because I was from Pine Ridge, like that would make a difference to the tribe."

Erica's voice quivered and tears formed at the corners of her eyes. He wanted to hug her as he did when she was a child, wanted to tell her everything would work out. But she was right about the reasons Jason hired her: Her Harvard degree would impress tribal council members, and they would trust one of their own even more. The Oglala had a history of being stomped on and taken advantage of by outsiders, and they would have been wary of anyone other than another Oglala endorsing the project. People knew Erica had overcome tremendous setbacks to get ahead, and knew she'd grown up under the burden of her father doing time in the state pen for the Two Moons murder. She would later become a star basketballer and excel academically, only to be rejected from every top college despite her athletic and scholastic accomplishments. When she unexpectedly landed a scholarship to Harvard, people on the reservation cheered her on. People would remember all these things about his niece and trust her judgment. But right now, that judgment had tarnished her reputation, and it might ruin her career.

The waitress brought their salads, and Manny cut a slice off the hot mini-loaf of garlic bread resting on a wooden board. He passed it to Erica, then cut another slice as he steeled himself for his next round of questions.

"I need to know something. There was rumor around that you and Jason were having an affair."

"An affair with Jason! He's as old as—"

"Your own father. That's not uncommon today."

"No. I wasn't having an affair with him. The man made my skin crawl. How could anyone even think that we were involved?"

"You and Jason spent a lot of time together on the project after he came to stay on Pine Ridge."

"Once he moved into the tribe's house, I spent nearly every day with him. Except for a couple days he was gone, and that business trip to Minneapolis for a weekend, we spent every day together. A project of this size takes a lot of work, and we couldn't afford to be slackers, even for a day. But an affair? No way."

Manny selected the raspberry vinaigrette from the three small cruets the waitress had brought. He read the label and put a little on his finger before replacing the cap. He grabbed the ranch dressing: too many calories and too much fat. He returned that bottle and went back to the raspberry, trickling some over his salad. Perhaps Erica was being truthful and knew nothing about Jason's scheme to bilk the tribe of their money. Still, there was the argument Henry Lone Wolf overheard.

"Someone overheard you and Jason arguing a week before he was murdered."

Erica took the dressing from Manny, and matched his look while she dribbled dressing on her own greens. "I found out Jason intended stealing the tribe's money. He said he was going to invest it in a winter resort project in Jackson Hole, said that would keep his head above water long enough for him to make good on the Pine Ridge resort."

"Witnesses say you threatened to tell Jon it was over. That sounds like you were going to come clean on an affair."

Now Erica laughed, either out of nervousness or relief, Manny couldn't tell. "I threatened to tell Jon that Jason intended to embezzle the tribe's money. I told Jason I would work up the case myself and take it to the U.S. Attorney for prosecution. When he heard that, he exploded—that damned temper of his. He grabbed me. Violently. I never saw him that mad before. He was always so . . ."

"Charming? That's how most people who didn't know him well described their meeting with Jason. Except he was about as charming as a carbuncle."

"Exactly!" she said. She put her fork down midbite and leaned closer. "He was charming. So much that it surprised me when he grabbed me. It frightened the wits out of me. He looked capable of killing anyone who got in his way, and I was in his way. So when he finally let me go, I told him I would give him the chance to do the right thing. I told him to go through with the project, that he didn't have to steal the tribe's money. He promised me he would, and we planned on the ground breaking the day he was killed."

Manny was sorry he had to ask her those painful but necessary questions. "Jason's 'charm' sold the tribe on the project. The last one you should blame is yourself. You were so committed, you knew the project just had to succeed."

Erica looked up from her salad and straightened in her seat. "I suppose you're right, but it doesn't make it any less painful. That's my home, my people he was about to sell out. And I was part of it."

"It was his home, too, long ago," Manny reminded her. "Did you tell anyone else about the embezzlement?"

"Just Mom. I tell her everything. And she's the tribe's finance officer; she needed to know what was coming down. She needed to stay on top of things in case any tribal members needed updates. Besides, she heard Jason and I had a huge argument and asked about it."

Manny nodded. He was content to spend the next hour in the company of his niece, charming in her own right. They discussed the state of the Pine Ridge and Rosebud reservations in the wake of the recent tribal court shake-ups. They talked about the positive things developing there since she'd returned to the area. They talked about the local economy, how the tribe was attracting new businesses, and how Russell Means might change that if he were elected tribal president. They talked about all these things, but one thing Erica never once asked about was Reuben and how he was doing. Perhaps she had finally forgotten her father.

Why was Manny fighting the urge to ask Erica how she was able to put her past, her pain, her father behind her and get on with her life, even coming back to the reservation? Maybe her answer would help him bury his past, but she had enough troubles of her own right now. So, he ate and enjoyed the company of his niece for the rest of the evening.

CHAPTER 11

"I know the crazy coot'll be there," Willie insisted. He turned onto the road leading to Crazy George He Crow's secluded five-acre lot. "You think this ties in with Jason?"

"Remember what I said," Manny cautioned. He fingered his empty pocket for the pack of Camels. "Whatever we find will be just one more brick in building our case, nothing more. Certainly no smoking gun. It would be a hell of a coincidence, though, and I don't believe in coincidences."

Manny recalled the lightbulb coming on last night when he returned to Pine Ridge from Rapid City. He'd marked down the mileage in his government-issue log book, as policy dictated. Give or take, the trip odometer of the rental showed two hundred and fifty miles. Just about the same mileage Crazy George said someone put on his car before they returned it. What if someone made a round trip to Rapid City with George's car?

"And what if it had been stolen? I'll guess I'll look like the ass."

Manny smiled. "You and every tribal cop that doesn't take Crazy George seriously, but don't worry. Every agency has a chronic bitcher that all the cops ignore. Just be grateful if this pans out."

"I should have spent more time on Crazy George's complaint. Bet you didn't screw up this bad when you worked here."

Manny laughed. "You have Crazy George. We had Helen Afraid of Horses. And afraid of everything else in this world. She complained once that her neighbor's cows ate so loud it kept her awake, and once that a passing train caused her to grow plantar warts on her feet."

"We don't have trains here."

"That's what we told her. Then one evening she called, convinced that the Soviets were conducting weather modification right above her house as she spoke, that they'd conjured up a tornado that was headed straight for her. Our whole shift cracked up laughing when that call came in to dispatch. That is, until we started getting calls from the National Weather Service that a twister had touched down west of Kyle. When Lumpy and I raced to Helen's house, we found her shack scattered over the prairie for a hundred yards in either direction. But no Helen."

"Where did they find her?"

"Never did. Sometimes I look up expecting the crazy old bat to drop out of some wall cloud. Perhaps she just clicked her heels and returned to Kansas with Toto."

Willie laughed as they neared Crazy George's trailer, which sat at the edge of a treeless prairie, a single-wide made in the 1960s, early 1970s at the latest. One side had been repaired with free-for-the-taking railroad ties, blocking out any windows that might have been there. There was no propane tank, but firewood stood stacked by the door, and duct tape covered two broken windows. *The poor bastard must knock icicles off his ass every winter trying to heat that shack.*

Crazy George hunkered down drawing in the dirt with a long stick. When he saw the police car, he grabbed the corral fence and stood.

Manny took in a quick, short breath. George wore a plaid dress that stopped just above his knees, and he teetered on high heels several sizes too small. His hairy legs exposed below the dress made him look like he was wearing a pair of woolly chaps. He used the stick for balance as he picked his way toward the road in his elevated shoes.

"He fancies himself a *berdache*." When Manny's look failed to register comprehension, Willie explained. "A cross-dresser. The old ones used that term to refer to men who were dressed like women and took on female roles. George thinks he's the last of the *berdache* cult."

"I'd rather be remembered as the last of something else besides a cross-dresser, especially if I was as ugly looking as he is in that getup."

George bypassed Willie and stopped in front of Manny, pausing to smooth his dress before he spoke. "Who're you? You're too damned old to be a tribal cop." Crazy George held a stump of cigar between fingers stained dark yellow.

"I'm Senior Special Agent Tanno. FBI."

George tilted his head back and cackled while he looked sideways with the whites of his eyes showing. Manny understood why people called him "Crazy George."

"Since when does the FBI give a damn about an old man's car?" He stepped close enough to Manny that the stench of his sweat permeated the air between them. "Don't you guys usually investigate bombings? Threats to the president. Fake money. Crap like that?"

"Your car may have been involved in a murder."

"A murder! Hot damn!" Crazy George slapped his leg, and a wide smile spread across his cratered face. "I told young With

Horn here that my car was stole, but he figured it weren't. He figured that old Crazy George just reported one more crazy thing. Didn't you?"

Willie looked away.

"I wasn't here the other day, Mr. He Crow, when—"

"Crazy George. Everyone calls me Crazy George 'cause I see a lot. And report a lot to these yokels." He jerked his finger at Willie. "Not that it does any good."

"Let me see your car."

Crazy George's skirt fluttered as he sashayed around to the far side of his shed. As they neared the corral, a roan mare nickered. She hung her head over the top of the corral and pushed against the rickety boards that bowed with her weight. She plowed the ground with one hoof, and her teeth snapped as she stretched to reach Manny.

The mare's eyes followed his as she looked sideways at him, much like Crazy George did a moment ago, and Manny knew she would stomp him if she could. Unc had taught him some things about horses, and his inveterate Lakota knowledge filled in the rest. He had not been close to a horse in years, yet he knew this one would kill him if she had the chance.

He often got close to the mounted police horses in D.C., felt the need to stroke the animals' withers, to somehow communicate with them. But then he'd always had a way with animals. He rubbed the stitches in his hand. *All right, except for the dog that bit me the other night and this loony horse, I have a way with critters.*

"Don't mind Clementine." George stepped to the corral and cradled the horse's head in his arms. "As long as you're on this side of the fence, you're safe."

George led them past the corral to a barn with one side caved in from age. The collapsed roof listed dangerously far to one side, threatening to fall over. On the far side of the barn, George pointed to his old Buick. "I don't drive this here car much, but I do keep it running good. When I do got to use it, I know it won't leave me stranded along the side of the road in the middle of a blizzard."

Except for one faded brown fender, and one door still in primer, the Buick's sky blue color showed shiny beneath a layer of fine dust. Manny walked around the car. Tiny rubber flecks still stuck out of the sidewalls. "New rubber."

"Guess I missed that the other day," Willie said from somewhere behind them.

"No harm." Manny was certain Willie wouldn't make the same error again.

"What's that you say?" Crazy George blurted out. "No harm! The thief—the killer—has two days' head start on you. How are you ever going to find him?"

Manny ignored him and walked around the car again before opening the driver's-side door. Keys dangled from the ignition switch. "You always leave your keys in the ignition?"

"Of course. No one would ever steal a beater like this."

"Until a few nights ago." Manny bent and peered inside. The seat was too far forward for Crazy George, who towered over Manny and had a protruding belly several inches bigger than his. If George drove it, he would need the seat back farther than it was. "You drive with the seat that close?"

"Hell, no. That's what I tried telling young With Horn the other day, but he looked at me like a cow looking at a new gate."

Out of the corner of his eye, Manny caught Willie writing in his pocket notebook, taking for gospel everything George said now.

"So the driver was a lot shorter than Crazy George," Willie announced.

"Not necessarily," Manny said. He stood up, and his knees crackled and popped. "It might have been someone shrewd enough to know that seat position is something we'd look for. Could have been a taller person who just moved the seat up when they brought it back."

Willie nodded and wrote in his notebook before he looked in the car. He grabbed a small SureFire from his duty belt and shined the light onto the floorboard. "What do you make of that?"

Manny followed the beam of light to a piece of leather under the brake pedal. He bent and grabbed it. "A piece of leather thong," he said as he held it to the light. "Could be from anything. A moccasin thong. A choker. Maybe a jacket pull. Could be used for most anything."

Manny shined Willie's flashlight on the floorboard. He lifted the mat and picked up a small, dried stem and held it to the light. "What's this?"

Willie studied the foliage. "*Peji wacanga*. Sweetgrass. Same as we found at the murder scene. This significant?"

"You tell me." Manny used the car door to help him stand. He knew he'd have to lose a few more pounds. "You've been studying with Margaret Catches: What do you use sweetgrass for?" Like an attorney asking a witness questions that he already knew, Manny wanted Willie to think on his own. He had asked Willie that question at the murder scene, and now he wanted to know if Willie had been thinking about it since then.

Willie faced Manny with that deer-in-the-headlights look, until finally his own bulb came on. "Ceremonies. Sings. Just like Reuben said he was doing the night Jason was murdered."

"But Reuben isn't the only holy man on the reservation. Or holy woman. Sweetgrass can be picked up most places a person walks in these parts. Someone could have walked through sweetgrass before climbing back in the car."

"But Reuben lives only a half mile from here."

"Whoa." Manny held up his hands. "We don't even know

that this car was involved with Jason's murder. George has other neighbors that live close besides Reuben. Call for a wrecker. Your evidence tech needs to process it."

"Just wait a minute." Crazy George stepped between them. "You're telling me my car's been stole. But I got it back. Only now you tell me the police are going to steal it again."

"We'll release it as soon as we can," Manny said. "Until then, maybe you can ride that mare of yours around." *If you can find a sidesaddle*, he thought as he admired George's dress flapping in the breeze. Then he told himself he'd better be good to George: with his own age and paunch going against him, this might be the closest Manny got to a skirt anytime soon.

CHAPTER 12

Manny ran through the slosh and the mud and jumped into Willie's truck. He brushed the rain from his shirt and trousers before he took the cup of coffee and breakfast burrito from Willie.

"This hits the spot."

"The rain or the coffee?"

"Both. It's long overdue. The rain, that is." Manny sipped the coffee. "You going to a cowboy funeral or cowboy wedding?"

Willie's powder blue, double-breasted Western shirt fit tight against his chest. Faux pearl buttons secured the shirt, except for the top one, which Willie left unbuttoned to make the shirt lay open at a sharp angle near his neck. His Wranglers were creased at least as sharp as Lumpy's jeans the other night, and they hung bunched at the bottom against a pair of Justin ropers that looked a size too small for such a large man. A tan 5X beaver Stetson poised at a self-assured slant completed his dress, and he only needed a matched pair of pearl-handled Colts to look the spitting image of a Lakota Tom Mix.

Great. I'm working with Hopalong Lumpy and Willie Mix.
"You don't have to go," Manny said as they turned onto Route
18. "Lumpy'd have a cow if he found out you came along."

"This is my day off. Besides, one more minute lying to the
lieutenant about where you are and I'll break down and tell
him."

Willie had called this morning to warn Manny that Lumpy
was on his trail. Niles had talked to Lumpy and demanded he
find Manny. Lumpy wanted to find him so he could tell Niles,
and so he could jump him about the thief powder, which office
rumor had it that Lumpy had proof Manny was the perp.

"Maybe you should call him."

"Piss on Ben Niles. Maybe he should catch the next flight
here and see what the hell I've been putting up with, see if he has
any better luck than we're having. The one thing I'm certain of is
if Lumpy finds out you spent the day with me in Rapid City, he'll
assign you to animal control for the duration of your career."

"I'll take my chances," Willie said, but he scooted lower in
the seat until they left the town limits. "I'm sure I won't be in as
much trouble as you are."

"How's that?"

"Here. Front page." Willie handed Manny the latest *Lakota
Country Times*. The front photo showed Manny and Sonja Myers cozying outside the bistro in Rapid City.

"What the hell did Yellow Horse do, follow me?"

"Must have, but it gets better. Read it."

Nathan Yellow Horse quoted Sonja Myer's recent follow-up
article in the *Rapid City Journal*. Manny had told her information he refused to share with other journalists. Native journalists. Yellow Horse said Manny had given Sonja the name of the
murder suspect, and told her that Jason might have squandered
the tribe's money.

"You read the *Journal* today?"

Willie nodded. "Sonja Myers said you told her Ricky Bell was your prime suspect, and she quoted you saying Jason's resort project was going belly-up."

Manny sipped his coffee as he followed the story to the next page, with Yellow Horse accusing Manny of giving inside information to a sexy White woman that he wouldn't share with a Lakota reporter. "That's bullshit. She turned my 'no comments' into affirmatives. She's got it all wrong. And so does Yellow Horse."

"It's your boss you'll have to convince, not me."

"Great. All I need is that prick on my ass." Manny's cell phone rang. He checked the number. "This asshole got Psychic Friends on retainer? How the hell would he know we were talking about him?"

"You going to answer it?"

Manny put his cell phone back in his belt holder. "Naw. Like you said, there's not very good reception here on the rez."

><><><

Manny dropped Willie off at the *Rapid City Journal* office. "Humor me," Manny said.

"But that was twenty-some years ago."

"The Red Clouds died twenty-eight years ago in that car wreck, to be exact. See what you can find. I'll call you on my cell when I'm done."

"But my truck."

"What about your truck?"

"You have a pretty crappy track record in the driving department."

"It's not that bad."

Willie grimaced. "If I believe half of what the lieutenant says, you're such a bad driver that you'd have to go a long ways to upgrade to being called shitty behind the wheel. No offense, but he said when he worked with you, you wrecked more squad cars driving normal speed than all the rest put together running code."

"I've improved since then."

"Not by the looks of your rental. I just don't want my truck dinged up."

Manny hoped his laugh would convince Willie his pickup would be safe. "Relax. If anything happens to your truck, you have the full backing of the FBI. Fair enough?"

Willie nodded. He stroked the hood affectionately, and dramatically. Manny shook his head at Willie's lack of faith, then pulled out into traffic and nearly hit a passing car.

>◇◇◇<

Manny drove past the Jack First Gun Shop and Coke Plant to the Red Cloud Development Corporation building. The front of the three-story structure would have looked more at home in Old Deadwood than in Rapid City. The first-floor false front depicted bawdy scenes: soiled doves waved kerchiefs out windows to attract passing cowboys while they leaned ample breasts over a railing. The second floor's gunfighter mural pit Wild Bill against a hapless victim in a street showdown. Bill had just touched off a round and watched through black-powder smoke as the fallen fighter bled in the street. On the top floor, Lakota and Cheyenne warriors armed with only bows and lances fought Crow and Pawnee braves shooting Henry repeaters.

Manny stepped inside the building Jason had designed six years ago. *Parade* magazine had done a spread on it, and they had shown off his talents well. The lobby was decorated in Old Western motif with a scarred hardwood bar that ran the width of the room. A mirror reflected the backside of the receptionist behind the bar, and Manny felt his face flush. She smoothed her ruffled lace dress, which showed off her shapely figure inside a skintight bodice. Her hair was up in a bun, and her makeup was so heavy you couldn't tell if she blushed, like saloon girls of old. She leaned forward and revealed more cleavage than a woman had a right to show a stranger.

"Is there anything I can help you with?" She batted her eyes, reminding him of Sonja Myers yesterday.

"Jason Red Cloud's office, please."

Her smile faded and she pointed to the elevator. "Third floor."

The *Parade* article said Jason had rescued the manual elevator from the old Biltmore in New York. The elevator operator played with his white handlebar mustache as he waited for a fare to take upstairs. The building's legend posted beside the elevator showed the Red Cloud Corporation consumed the entire third floor. Manny bypassed the elevator and headed for the stairs to work off the breakfast sandwich. By the time he reached the third floor, a bead of sweat had formed on his forehead and he dabbed at it with his handkerchief. He sucked air, winded, but not as winded as he was last month taking stairs in D.C.

At last Manny's heart rate slowed, and he stepped into the Red Cloud office. The receptionist faced the elevator so she could greet anyone coming off that floor. She was a Lakota half his age, and sat jotting on a memo pad as she cradled a phone on her neck.

Manny waited, thankful for the time to look around the office. Large photos framed in rustic, graying barn wood hung every few feet, some aerial shots and others close-ups. He put on his reading glasses and looked at the captions. He recognized the Salt Lake City Celestial, the tallest hotel on the Great Salt Lake when it was built. The before-and-after photos showed Jason had transformed a barren hillside into a flourishing resort.

Manny admired more pictures showing how efficiently— almost magically—the Red Cloud Corporation had developed land that other developers had passed up as useless. The most recent date of any picture was six years ago.

"Can I help you?" The receptionist smiled easily at him.

Manny unfolded his badge wallet. She looked first to the ID, then to Manny and handed it back. "I'd like to talk with Clara Downing."

"Ms. Downing is awfully busy," the receptionist stammered, then stopped and took a deep breath before continuing, "I can set up an appointment for you."

"Is she in?"

She shot a glance at a door marked with Jason Red Cloud's brass nameplate. "She's so busy today, with the death of Mr. Red Cloud and getting the firm in order for auditors."

Manny leaned over the counter. "I've been calling here every day to talk with her. Now do I need to issue a summons for her to appear at the Rapid City FBI field office?"

She dropped her eyes and stood. "This way, please." She escorted Manny through an enormous door that appeared far older than any he ever saw in a modern building. One gouge on the door looked like a giant chain had drug itself across the wood, leaving a deep, insulting wound. Another scar may have come from a huge fork once imbedded in the wood. Worms had gotten to the pith and eaten holes in random fashion on the front of the door.

Manny stepped onto hardwood floors, glossy and reflecting the sunlight from a row of windows. The floors matched the door, with nail holes and gouges in deep planks of varying shades of brown and gray. The wood had been used hard for a hundred years before being salvaged for this office.

One wall was paneled with decrepit, cracked, graying barn wood. A barbed-wire display hung on the wall, completing its Western motif. The wall opposite the windows hosted the heads of animals: deer and antelope, black and grizzly bears, a mountain lion bigger than any Manny had seen on the reservation.

But it was the last display that fascinated Manny the most.

A wall-to-wall glass case containing original Lakota artifacts stood in front of a painted mural depicting Plains Sioux Indian life. A forty-tipi *tiospaye* camped along a meandering creek. Off to the right, Indians on horseback hunted buffalo, their bows cocked at the ready. Farther yet another group crouched low, bows across their backs and arrows clenched in their hands, and stalked enemy Crow warriors.

Manny gasped. Next to the hunting scene hung an original Ghost Shirt, the brain-tanned deerskin adorned with painted geometric patterns across the breast and sleeves. He was no expert in Lakota artifacts, but he thought the notation "1890" was correct. Images came to him: unarmed women, along with the elderly and children, fleeing cavalry troopers at the massacre of Wounded Knee. He closed his eyes and said a silent prayer for the innocents who journeyed the Spirit Road before their time.

Beside the Ghost Shirt hung a quiver, which was beaded to match the shirt, the same design that the warriors had on their backs as they stalked the enemy. Four flint-tipped arrows jutted from the quiver.

Manny squinted. An original Colt Army .45 caliber revolver, the patina faded on the case-hardened frame, dangled from an elk-horn peg beside the Ghost Shirt. The checkering on the chipped plastic grips was worn smooth from years of hard use, and the revolver's front sight tilted to one side where it had once struck something hard. Dried powder marks caked the front of the cylinder, but it showed no rust and looked as if it could have been picked up right there and fired.

In the bottom of the display, a small leather pouch sat on a driftwood shelf beside a red catlinite clay pipe, from a Pipestone, Minnestota, quarry. Teeth marks made perhaps a hundred years ago were deeply cast into the pipe's stem. A beaded turtle medicine pouch like the one Manny carried around his neck was hanging from a rust-browned Springfield .45-70 rifle. Manny imagined a Seventh Cavalry trooper firing it at the Greasy Grass.

"Jason liked old things," a voice called out. A woman in her midthirties faced him, tall as he was even as she leaned against the doorway with her arms crossed. A wry smile that accentuated her high cheekbones played at the corners of her mouth, and a single hoop earring peeked out from behind sandy hair. Her hand thrust out from her gray pinstriped business suit. "Clara Downing. I've been expecting you."

"Now how would you be expecting me when you haven't returned any of my calls?"

"What calls, Agent Tanno?"

"If I was one to jump to conclusions, I'd think you had something to hide."

"What calls?" she repeated.

Manny took his cell phone from his pocket and checked his outgoing calls. "I tried to reach you here four times in the last couple days. You promised to call me back, but you didn't."

Clara glanced at the closed door and her jaw tightened. "Emily sometimes takes it upon herself to protect me."

"Do you need protecting?"

"Maybe," she grinned. "You volunteering?"

"If it means getting straight answers from Jason Red Cloud's executive assistant, then I'm volunteering."

Clara smiled. "Then straight answers it will be, and I'll deal with Emily later. Now can we start fresh?" Clara continued to smile, and her bright eyes disarmed Manny.

"Fair enough. Manny Tanno. You started to tell me about Jason's collection here."

"Clara Downing." She stepped to the display case and tapped the glass with her ring finger. She was single. "Jason was an ardent collector of all things ancient belonging to the Lakota."

Then she paused. "I'm sorry. I seem to have forgotten you are Lakota also."

"No need to apologize. Please continue."

"Jason collected these antiquities at great expense. The Ghost Shirt was such a powerful symbol of the Lakota plight; it took him years to get an old man on the Rosebud to finally sell it. And he claimed the medicine bundle was Chief Red Cloud's own. Jason said he had thoroughly researched it, said the pouch wasn't buried with the chief there at the Holy Rosary cemetery, and he just had to have it. He claimed that it was part of his heritage. But Jason never was related to Chief Red Cloud, like he boasted."

She paused. He wanted to respond, but her beauty distracted him and he fought to come up with something that would sound brilliant. But he couldn't.

"They tell me you have an uncanny ability to look at cases objectively," she said. "To shuffle through the heap of information and come away with just the right pieces that fit the puzzle."

"Who are 'they'?"

Clara laughed. "*Newsweek* for one. CNN for another. They say you're the only one who can catch Jason's killer."

Manny's face warmed. "I landed the assignment, so I'm stuck on the reservation until I solve the murder."

"Is that so bad?"

Manny shrugged. "I didn't leave anything on Pine Ridge that I needed to come back to."

He was speaking frankly to this woman he had just met, and he checked himself. "I take it this was Jason's office?"

"It was." She motioned for Manny to sit in a black and white cowhide chair that rested on a tattered rag rug. Manny placed his arms on stag-horn armrests while she sat on the edge of Jason's desk. "What do you want to know, Manny?"

He hadn't told her to call him by his first name.

"You're in charge of the Red Cloud Corporation now?"

Clara smiled. "As much as I have been the last five years. Jason called me his executive assistant, but I had to be more than that. I had to do a lot of his day-to-day paper shuffling. Office acrobatics. You know, parry a bill collector here, fend off a paper server there. Protect the 'Donald Trump of the West.' "

"So it's true, he had made poor investments. Enough that he was on the brink of losing the business?"

"He almost filed Chapter 11 last year, but we pulled through." She turned to her phone and ordered coffee. "Jason was a gifted architect, but as a businessman he was a dismal failure."

"This is the first time I heard that. I'd always heard he was some kind of icon for Oglala prosperity."

"He had his successes, but I took the blame for any failures of the business."

"Even if the failure was his fault?"

She nodded. "If people blamed him for botched projects, they might not have faith in future Red Cloud ventures. In the business world that Jason inhabited, I was the assistant that screwed things up now and again."

"So that's why she thought you were inept."

"How's that?"

"Nothing," he said, thinking back to his conversations with Elizabeth and Erica. "How long had you known Jason?"

"Since before I came to work for him."

The receptionist carried a silver serving tray into the office and set it on the desk. Clara handed Manny a cup and cradled hers in her hands.

"My folks ranched on the Rosebud, on the same place my grandparents did. The Red Clouds' ranch butted against ours, right across the reservation line in Pine Ridge. They hadn't been active in their ranching operation for some years; the development business took all their time. When Jason's folks were killed in that car wreck, my parents helped him settle his affairs. He had been out of college and working for the corporation only a year when they died, so he was pretty unsure what to do. My folks helped him through that."

"Growing up on the Rosebud must have been interesting for you."

Clara nodded. "When I graduated from Rosebud High, I was the only White girl walking down the aisle to get her diploma. But I never felt out of place. I was always at home there. After graduation, Jason called me and asked if I wanted a job. I think he felt obligated to my folks and knew they didn't have the money for my college. I was grateful that Jason hired me."

Manny sipped the coffee. "I got the feeling Jason was lucky to have someone loyal working for him."

Clara chuckled. "Jason was like a big kid. He would lose his show-and-tell books when he met with clients. He would forget appointments. He would go away weekends to the casinos and never say when he'd return. Before long, the business suffered. He was constantly distracted. He had a series of failures, projects that could discredit him, all kept hush. This Pine Ridge resort was his chance for a comeback."

"But how did he keep his business problems a secret?" Manny's cup warmed his hand, and he felt the warmth from Clara as well. "If he had that many failures, someone would know."

She stood and refilled their cups from a carafe. "Like I said before, I'd always take the heat for his screwups. Besides, there was always that 'legendary' Jason Red Cloud charm. People just believed whatever he said. Like the Jackson Hole project."

"Tell me about that."

"There was no Jackson Hole project. Jason designed the Wyoming resort to compete directly with Teton Village. Skiing. Shopping. Five-star restaurants. But it was just one more pipe dream to sell people on the corporation." She pointed to an artist's rendition of a resort built on the side of a mountain in the Grand Tetons of Wyoming, eight miles from Jackson Hole. "He landed some high rollers, big investors. Until he lost his shirt on the stock market and gambling. Then the investors—some were less than honorable themselves—threatened him. They pressured him to come up with either the resort or their money—with interest. That's where the Red Cloud Resort on Pine Ridge came in. It was Jason's escape from a nasty situation, from the threats he got every week."

"Who threatened him?"

Clara shrugged. "All he'd say is that people had bad intentions toward him and he needed to come up with the thirty million the tribe was going to lay out for the resort. He claimed he'd have enough leftover after paying off the investors to get the Jackson Hole project under way. But I always knew there was no Jackson Hole project."

"How could he rope investors into something that didn't exist, on just his architect's rendering?"

"That, plus the strength of the Red Cloud name. This company has never had to forfeit a bond in any project it promoted. But there's more to your investigation?"

"There is. A lot more. Though I'm not certain where it's leading." Manny told her about the artifacts that Ricky Bell stole on Jason's behest.

"That doesn't surprise me. I can see him hiring Bell to steal those items for him, just to get his mojo back. Put himself on top once again."

"And Lakota antiquities would help him get back on his feet?"

Clara nodded. "My folks said that when Jason first started working here out of college, the Red Clouds allowed him leeway to develop clients on his own, get his feet wet, get a feel for what it took to become successful. Early on he made some bad decisions, and the company lost a bundle. But after his parents' death, he got the hang of the business. He always said Chief Red Cloud's spirit was helping him succeed. He had a string of successes that boosted the firm's reputation and helped expand the corporation. The Red Clouds had built up a thriving development business, reclaiming land thought unusable by any other developer: desert land deemed too harsh to live in or forest acreage that no one else wanted to fight the permitting process to acquire. When they died, Jason was the sole heir. There is no corporation."

Manny stood and stretched. "How'd he handle his success?"

"People who worked here before me said Jason was almost giddy after his parents died. People here chalked it up to the stress of losing both parents at once. Jason's success and the power of the company made him intoxicated on his own ego. But each time a project came up short of his expectation, he'd be devastated and despondent for weeks. I know he placed a lot of store in old artifacts, in things that he could call upon for luck. I can see Jason praying to his collection just to get himself back on track. Keep himself from wandering."

Manny's own mind wandered off track as he took in the beauty of the office, and especially the beauty in front of him. He took in her primrose perfume that suggested springtime, took in her flawless makeup, took in the way she carried herself as she spoke. He found himself uncharacteristically daydreaming. And got caught—

"What's that?"

"Is there anything else you wish to know?" she repeated.

"What about Jason's associates? Anyone want him dead besides his gambling cronies?"

Clara shook her head. "I've wracked my brain over that. I can't think of anyone, but I might find something when I start going over his things. I have an audit of the books scheduled in a few days."

Manny thanked her and had started for the door when she called after him: "Will you be in town long? Perhaps we could catch dinner tonight."

Manny turned and faced her. His face warmed with a blush that he prayed wouldn't be obvious. He had never been asked on a date before. The thought of dinner with Clara had earlier crossed his thoughts, before being beaten back as improbable. "I would love to, Ms. Downing."

"Clara, please."

He smiled. "I would like to, Clara, but I have a young tribal policeman I have to pick up and take back to Pine Ridge. Rain check?"

She smiled back, a warm smile that brought out even more blushing. "A rain check it is. Now don't let me down. I won't eat a bite until I eat it with you."

Manny turned on his heels and quickly excused himself. A lovely woman asking him to dinner? Where Sonja and Desirée had their own agendas for coming on to him, he could only think of one that Clara would have: She knew more than she was telling him about Jason and the business, and wanted to find out how much Manny knew. Still, Clara was one woman whose company he was certain he'd enjoy. This time he bounded down the stairs two at a time, feeling young, thinking about cashing in that rain check soon.

>‹›‹›‹

Manny pulled up to the curb outside the *Rapid City Journal* office. Willie got up from the wino bench and walked around to the driver's side. Manny slid over and Willie started climbing behind the wheel when he froze. He frowned as he ran his hand over the dented fender.

Manny looked at him and anticipated the question. "A light pole came at me a little faster than I could avoid it. Let's just say it was self-defense." *Again.*

"Must have come after you pretty quick. The tire's rubbing against the fender."

Manny nodded. "Get it fixed and give me the bill. Price is no object. Your tax dollars at work." He forced a laugh, but Willie didn't. "What did you find out?" Manny asked to get Willie's mind off the damage.

He slid the seat back before he reached into his rear pocket for his notebook and flipped pages. "There was a ton of info about the Red Cloud Corporation," he began, "but not much about Jason. I researched the date of his parents' accident that Verlyn Horn investigated. The *Journal* quoted him as claiming the brake lines had been cut, not ruptured as they'd initially reported. The Red Clouds came down that long hill just south of Interior and lost their brakes and plunged off a steep ravine. They lay there four days until a rancher found them."

"What? I didn't catch that."

"I know you didn't," Willie agreed. "It's like you're in a dream or something."

If Manny were in a dream, Clara Downing was there with him.

"I said, Verlyn Horn was certain they lost their brakes on that steep hill out of Interior."

"I know the hill he was talking about."

"Me, too," Willie said. "The one before you come to Badlands Grocery. I could see them losing control if they had a head of steam and no brakes."

"What else did you learn about the accident?"

"Not much." Willie pinched Copenhagen between his thumb and forefinger, then offered the can to Manny. He shook his head, and Willie put the can back in his shirt pocket. Manny looked lovingly at the tobacco. *It could be rolled tight in a piece of paper, and if it were dried just a little bit, it might light.* "Because the accident happened on the rez, there wasn't much coverage. The only reason it got written up at all is because the victims were Red Clouds."

"Any mention of AIM's involvement?"

He handed Manny a photocopied front page of the *Rapid City Journal*. Yellow marks dotted the copy where Willie had highlighted parts he felt were important. "There was mention of the Red Clouds opposing AIM, despite their son's former involvement with the organization. Why do you ask?"

Manny shrugged. "Call it a hunch. A man should always listen to his hunches in this business. That car wreck had AIM written all over it, just like Jason's murder."

"AIM involved in Jason's death? They haven't been active for decades."

"But they're not all dead. There's some holdouts still lurking on Pine Ridge."

"Sure, they have the occasional AIM member run for councilman from time to time; Russell Means made an unsuccessful run for tribal chairman a few years ago, even made it to the primary again this year. But they're just a bunch of hangers-around now. Just old men playing dominoes and wishing they had the power again like they did in the 1970s."

Manny grabbed a piece of gum from his shirt pocket and peeled back the foil. It was gooey from body heat. He popped it into his mouth and licked his sticky fingers. "Jason's resort was to be at Wounded Knee. On sacred ground, at least that's the way it's been played in the media. Wounded Knee is sacred to AIM."

"Most people I know on the rez think the massacre site is sacred, too. AIM doesn't have a monopoly on that."

"That's true, but AIM's been more vocal about it. Some members are opposed to any outsiders even coming onto Pine Ridge at all. They've pushed to ban Whites from even watching a Sun Dance."

"Then how did the permits for the resort get through the tribal council?" Willie asked. "AIM doesn't have the muscle it once did, and I doubt the threat of protests hold fear like it once did. But I'd have thought there would be an uproar over allowing the project to be built on sacred ground."

"Economics." Manny reached for the radio, found powwow music faint and breaking up on KILI, and turned it low. "People are no different here than they are elsewhere. Jason promised prosperity for the tribe. He claimed the resort was just the start. People got hungry, got greedy, and the measure passed the council."

"That brings us back to AIM involvement."

"So we better talk with whatever militants are left."

"I only know one," Willie said. "Reuben. He'd be the first one I'd visit with."

Manny agreed. "But I better talk with him alone this time. Find anything else?"

Willie flipped another page in his notebook. "Sonja Myers. That's one shark that's out for herself."

Manny recalled the softness of her voice, the way she sat close to him at the bistro. He wouldn't describe Sonja as a shark. Opportunistic and conniving, but not a shark.

"The networks have their eyes on her," Willie continued. "She has the looks and the education. The ability to make people tell her things, all sorts of things. All she has to do is break one story and she's rocketed right out of Smallville to the big time."

"That what *Journal* people told you?"

Willie smiled. "I found a lot of people who'd talk with me about her. Except for her making the majors, everyone would like to see her move on—soon. People warned me to watch her, so I'm warning you. She took things out of context before and she'll do so again."

"Thanks for the advice." Manny settled back in the seat while his mind switched from Sonja to Clara.

They drove out of Rapid City past the green fields that melded into prairie grasses as tall as antelope. Both sat quiet, and Manny was thankful for that. He had other things on his mind: Clara Downing. She had been something more than charming. She had allowed him to forget his problems with Nathan Yellow Horse and Sonja Myers and Niles the Pile and the stitches in his head and hand.

He fought down the urge to rip the bandage off and rub his wound raw. Instead, he concentrated on remembering his time in the Red Cloud offices. Clara had treated him as an equal. Even though Manny had been hired as a minority in the bureau, he had a reputation as a top investigator and academy instructor. But he never quite lost the feeling that people treated him as Indian first and senior special agent second. The bureau always went out of its way to be racially tolerant with other minority agents. Indians were treated differently, although Manny could not exactly quantify it.

But here where Indians were populous, old racial biases rose to the surface once again. Relations had improved since he'd lived here, but his Lakota heritage was never far beneath the surface when he talked with people. But Clara had respected him. He wanted to cash in the rain check for dinner sooner than later.

Then Reuben pushed thoughts of Clara aside. Though Manny never concluded a case in his mind until he had uncovered sufficient facts, he had to admit that Reuben rose to the top of the dung heap as the prime suspect in Jason's murder. Tomorrow he might have his answers from his brother, for what happened to Jason as well as what happened to the Red Clouds nearly thirty years ago. Tomorrow he would reinterview Reuben.

CHAPTER 13

The entire trip back to the reservation, the tire thump-thump-thumped against the crumpled fender. It didn't help any that Willie's tires had less tread than his boots had. By the time they crossed the Pine Ridge line, chunks had begun to break off. One flew into the air and was caught by the rearview mirror before falling away. Willie strained to control the truck as it darted into road ruts. He slowed down to a crawl as they approached Manny's apartment.

"I'll park it here. Call a wrecker tomorrow to cart it away to the body shop. Maybe get a new paint job, a new set of tires, since price is no object."

Manny could say nothing in his defense. He unlocked the rental car and slipped behind the wheel. Willie stood by the open passenger door.

"Get in, I'm not that bad of a driver. You'll be all right. I'll regale you with tall tales of my exploits."

"All right." Willie folded himself into the car. "But drive careful, and tell me about your exploits later, when you're not behind the wheel. I'd rather you tell me something about Aunt Lizzy's AIM days. She doesn't talk much about that."

Manny drove slowly, carefully to Elizabeth's house, so as not to cause Willie to jump out of the moving car in fear of his life. "What do you want to know?"

"She said that she, Reuben, and Jason were all close once, back in the day."

Manny jerked his hand away from his bandage. "The three of them were inseparable back then. Except when Elizabeth was pregnant with Erica, they attended every AIM function together."

"Aunt Lizzy always laughs and tells me she met Reuben in prison." Willie grabbed his can of Copenhagen. The pungent odor caught Manny by surprise, and he yearned for a cigarette.

"She did. When AIM took over Alcatraz prison in 1969, Reuben was one of AIM's special enforcers, someone who kept the peace internally during the occupation. Elizabeth was one of the occupiers. That's when they started their relationship—behind the bars of Alcatraz."

"She talks about Reuben now and again," Willie said. "Talks fondly, even after all these years. She must have loved him a lot."

"I'm certain she did." Manny drove past the Batesland Store toward Elizabeth's house. "But when he killed Billy Two Moons, she had to do what was best for Erica. She's always done what she had to do for Erica, and I can't fault her for having ambition."

Willie nodded. "She worked her tail off for that finance position, and it fits her. Everyone on the rez knows she's honest and thorough, and people look up to her for that. I'm as proud of her as she is of herself."

They turned onto Elizabeth's gravel driveway and Willie grabbed his overnight bag from the backseat.

"Will she be gone long?"

Willie shrugged. "Hard telling. When Aunt Lizzy goes shopping, she may be gone for hours. Especially when she's with Rachael Thompson, who's a shopping legend around here."

Manny had never been married, never been close enough to a woman to know her shopping habits, but he had married colleagues who stood around watercoolers talking about their wives' shopping marathons. If Elizabeth would be gone that long, Manny understood why she would want her nephew to house-sit until she returned. Elizabeth's business associate had been killed recently, and her FBI agent ex-brother-in-law had been attacked. Willie's presence would ease her fear.

"I'll pick you up in the morning, and we'll go over those recent lab results. I want to be prepared when I interview Reuben."

Willie unbuttoned his shirt as he walked toward the house. Manny waited until he retrieved the house key from the flower bed before he drove away, and the washboard gravel road leading to the highway jarred his thoughts. How would he interview Reuben tomorrow? He'd finalize his attack when he ran tonight, when thoughts came more clearly. From a thousand interrogations, he'd pull pieces of what had worked and what had failed in his interviews.

As he drove past the shelter belt along the road, his mind wandered. He found it hard to think of Reuben and the investigation. He let Clara Downing fill his thoughts, remembering how she had leaned against Jason's office door, one lithe leg crossed over the other, hair falling freely onto her shoulders. She had the most wry smile he had ever seen, projecting that "Want a good time, sailor?" look. Yet she was no tawdry madam but a sophisticated woman, and that made her flirting with him especially intriguing. He longed to return to Rapid City and cash in that rain check.

But he had little time for his own wants. The investigation had stalled, and he was not much closer than when he began. On the bright side, Clara Downing was part of this. She had vital knowledge he needed, and for that, he would have to visit with her again. Soon. Perhaps tomorrow after he talked with Reuben. Perhaps.

Headlights suddenly filled his rearview mirror. In a heartbeat, something slammed into the rear of his car. His forehead hit the steering wheel. His head whipped around. Behind him. Coming fast. A truck. Manny floored the accelerator and stiffened his arms on the wheel. The truck hit him again. His arms buckled. A back tire caught a crumpled fender and he skidded sideways in the road.

Manny gripped the wheel, but the Taurus skidded across both lanes, ran over a delineator post that punctured the radiator, and stalled. Steam rose from the dying motor while the truck's lights illuminated him. Motionless, Manny strained to see the driver as the truck lurched forward and T-boned him on the passenger-side door. The car rolled. And rolled, and rolled. Manny scooted down in the seat, bracing himself. The car teetered once before it stopped with the passenger side up.

Manny lay against the driver's door and forced one eye open. The other was stuck shut. Sticky warm blood oozed between his fingers as he gingerly touched his head. Glass, gritting on his skin, mixed with blood as it trickled down his forehead, the stitches in his head pulling apart and breaking open. He closed the open eye against the blood and glass and spat out a broken tooth. His labored breathing came in short gasps, and he sprayed blood over the windshield from a split lip.

He tugged at the seat belt. *Stuck*. Pulled harder. Pain shot through his chest. He stopped when he heard a door slam. *Close*. Close enough that footsteps approaching in the dry grass echoed in his ears. Purposeful footsteps, footsteps that approached to ensure the truck had done its job. He bit his lip to stay conscious. To analyze. Was there one set of footsteps, or two? Were they hard steps, or soft?

He tried reaching the Glock. Three steps. *Closer.* Reached again. Steps stopped outside his shattered window. He lay on his arm, trapped, unable to get to the weapon. He willed his labored breathing to stop. He told the rising and falling of his chest to be still. He lay quiet, listening, praying to God he could pull it off. His hand fell automatically onto his medicine bundle.

Someone shined a flashlight into Manny's car. Through his closed eyelids, Manny saw all this as if he was sitting in a theater watching some dark, foreboding movie. Light played across his lids. He wanted to open them, wanted to get a look at his attacker, but he didn't. The driver squatted inches from him, close enough that Manny felt warm puffs of breath on his neck through the window. He struggled to remain conscious. His cop side took over, and he listened for anything that would later identify the driver. If he lived through this.

For the first time since childhood, he clutched his medicine bundle and prayed to *Wakan Tanka,* the Great Mysterious of the universe, giver of all things. He prayed his attacker wouldn't realize he was still alive. *Wakan Tanka, unsimalaye*, he prayed. *Wakan Tanka, pity me.* He had no time to reflect from what part of his distant memory the old words came, and he slowed his breathing more.

His sight returned, yet his eyes remained closed. Even as a boy during the *hanbleceyapi*, when he had sat for four days and nights crying for a vision, he had not had one. Hoofbeats neared, while the sweet scent of lilac reached him. Was this how a man faded into the other life to journey south along the Spirit Road, the *Wanagi Tacanku?* Amid collective memories and forgotten teachings? Maybe he was that close to death that his vision would come to him now. He wanted to cry out to the meadowlark he heard in his head, for he knew the meadowlark spoke Lakota, but no sound came from his lips.

The hoofbeats grew louder. Riders neared. Bugles blared.

The wailing of mothers louder than the horses. What were the surviving sisters and wives shouting to him? Where were they pointing? What did they want of a man lying near death, fighting for his life in a wrecked car along a dark reservation road? Before losing consciousness, Manny thought that these ancients had finally arrived to carry him home along the Spirit Road.

>◇◇◇◇<

Manny heard muffled talk somewhere to his left. He opened one eye, the other blocked by a gauze bandage. Desirée stood over him, her face inches from his, her lips painted like they had bad intentions.

"I thought we'd lost you," Desirée said.

He tried sitting, but fell back down onto the pillow. He drew in a quick breath. A stabbing pain in his chest caused his breath to come up short. Elastic constricted, and he knew he had broken or bruised ribs. He closed his eyes. Shallow breaths now, coming quicker as he tried to match his breathing with the throbbing in his head.

Antiseptic stung his nostrils, like someone running ammonia under his nose. He was certain that the hospital staff had used about a gallon on him before patching him up. The room shone clean, unlike the would-be-rental-car-grave he last remembered. "I'm at the hospital?"

She smiled a wide set of perfect pearlies. He looked at her as if for the first time since they were in school, since that time she left him for Lumpy. Slight crow's feet tugged at the corners of her eyes, just enough to reveal she'd aged as he had, except she looked like she was ten years younger. She bent over, showing more chest than he needed to see right then. "I came as soon as I heard you were admitted."

"Let me guess: Lumpy told you I was here."

"What are ex-husbands for?"

"*Hoka hey.*" Willie filled the doorway. He held a foam cup of steaming coffee. His grin was exaggerated, but his face was ashen and bags had formed under his eyes. "How you feel?"

"I feel like you look."

"Been up all night since I heard you'd been in an accident."

"That was no accident," Manny said.

Willie turned a chair around beside the bed and sat backward on it. He rested his beefy arms on the chair back as he sipped his coffee.

"Where . . . ?" Manny craned his neck to look at Desirée with his one good eye. "I'm afraid Officer With Horn has some confidential information to share with me."

Desirée frowned, then a smile lit her face. "Well, the least I can do is take care of you when you get released. Just rap on the wall and I'll come over." Just before she walked out of the room, she glanced back over her shoulder and blew him a kiss. Willie waited until the sound of her footsteps had died.

"Guess you have a new love interest."

"Just an old flame wanting to rekindle, not for any good purpose I can figure out. What you got on the accident?"

"You're one tough bastard, I got to say that for you." Willie flipped through a stack of Polaroids and showed one to Manny. The Taurus had been shortened several feet as a result of the rear-ending: it was at least half as tall because of the rollover, and there wasn't an intact window left. "Most men would have been dead. Maybe it's because you had this." Willie held back a corner of the bedsheet to expose Manny's beaded turtle. His medicine bundle, still hanging from the leather thong around his neck, watched over him. "Officers said you clutched your *wopiye* like you planned to walk the Spirit Road with it. Maybe you're not dead because of it."

"I ain't dead?" Manny wanted to tell Willie about his experience waiting for the truck driver to finish him off. But such a highly personal vision would have to wait before he shared it with anyone. "What do you know about the wreck?"

"We know we damned near got another agent sent out on this Red Cloud investigation," Lumpy called from the doorway. He waddled across the room and stood beside Willie, who, sitting down, was about even with Lumpy's shoulders. "I passed Desirée in the hall. She said you were doing just fine. I told her I'm sure she had brightened your day."

"Thanks a hell of a lot." Manny tried sitting and got a couple inches higher up on the pillow this time. "Will someone tell me what the hell happened?" He propped himself on one elbow. Pain, intense and biting, radiated from his chest to his navel, and he eyed Lumpy through his one unbandaged but bloodshot eye.

Lumpy smiled. "Well, Hotshot, seems like someone stole an F-350 and ran you off the road."

"You found the truck then?"

"A dozen yards from where you rolled, but no one was around. Whoever did the deed left you for dead. Probably caught a ride from someone else, probably also involved. Means more than one suspect, I'm thinking."

Manny peeked around the bandage at Willie. "Anything in that truck that could ID the driver?"

Willie began speaking, but Lumpy interrupted. "The truck was stolen from Reuben's jobsite. It belongs to a contractor installing the electrical. The owner leaves the truck there when he knocks off work and grabs a ride from another electrician back to Hot Springs. The guy didn't even know it was stolen until the Fall River County SO talked with him. We're bringing in Reuben with all his little urchins for interviews as we speak."

"Any prints?"

Lumpy nodded. "We lifted a ton of clear prints, like the killer wanted to get caught. We already faxed them to Pierre for identification, and Hot Springs took a set of elimination prints from the truck owner for us."

"Anything else?" A rib rubbed a lung and pain shot down through Manny's entire body. He dropped back down onto the pillow and sucked in shallow breaths.

"Shoe prints," Willie said. Lumpy glared at him.

Manny smiled. The kid was growing cojones after all.

"Big shoes," Willie went on. "Someone stood next to your window, probably checking if you were dead."

Manny vaguely remembered the bright light that had filtered through his bleeding eyelids. "How big were the shoes?"

"Like we found at Jason's murder, but not the same tread. This one is distinct. I'll dig up the shoe book later and see if I can get a match." He reached for his can of chew, then quickly put it back into his pocket when a nurse poked her head into the room.

"Everything all right?" she asked.

"Just fine," Manny answered, and waited until she left before pressing Willie.

"So, size ten or thereabouts?"

"Lots of people got big feet," Lumpy blurted out.

Manny glanced down at Lumpy's feet.

"Thank God, or we'd all be suspects," Elizabeth added from the doorway. She walked to the bed and glared at Lumpy. He excused himself and left without wishing Manny a speedy recovery.

"Is that hot coffee I smell?" she asked Willie. "Maybe you could get your old aunt a cup."

"Sure enough, Aunt Lizzy." Willie turned the chair around for her and disappeared through the doorway. When Willie left, Elizabeth sat on the chair beside Manny's bed. "I'm sure you've told it a dozen times, but what happened?"

Manny turned his head so he could look at Elizabeth. He knew people could often remember things from their childhood, but couldn't recall what happened a few moments before an accident or traumatic incident. It surprised him that he remembered the details of last night with such clarity.

"So you saw the driver?"

Manny shook his head. "I never opened my eyes. I played possum as best I could. It must have worked, because I'm still kicking, though not as high or as easy as yesterday."

"Then you got no idea who?"

"None."

Willie lumbered into the room with coffee for Elizabeth and Manny. "Just don't tell the nurses here or they'll scalp me for sure."

Manny forced a wink. Sympathetic movement of his injured eye shot pain back across his forehead. "I won't breathe a word. Hell—I won't hardly breathe."

Elizabeth bent and kissed him lightly on the cheek. Her lips brushed his bruised skin. It was soothing, the fragrance of her perfume. The fragrance of—what, another forgotten memory?— whatever perfume she used was pleasant compared to the sanitary smell of the hospital room.

They sipped their coffee, and Willie showed Elizabeth the photos. She shook her head. "It's amazing you're not dead, by the looks of this car."

Willie smiled. "Like I told him, he's tough."

Elizabeth finished her cup and tossed it in the trash as she stood. "Have to get back to the grind. I'll come see you when you get out." She bent and kissed his cheek once again before she left.

Clara Downing briefly shared the doorway with Elizabeth. "Hello, Clara."

"Well, hello, Elizabeth." Manny swore the temperature in the room dropped several degrees. "You don't have to leave."

"The tribe doesn't pay me for socializing."

She brushed past Clara, who watched her go, before she turned to Manny.

Clara held a large bouquet of roses in front of her like it was a magic wand that would mystically heal him. The flowers, and especially Clara, perked him up enough that he felt on the road to Wellville already. She searched for a vase, and found one in a cupboard beneath the sink. She filled it with water and set the flowers on the tray table next to Manny's bed. She looked at Willie.

"This is Officer William With Horn," Manny introduced him. "And he was just going to say good-bye to his aunt Elizabeth."

Willie looked like a big kid caught dipping into the cookie jar when he finally caught Manny's meaning. "Yeah, better catch up with Aunt Lizzy."

"Did you just happen to pop in?" Clara scooted the chair closer to the bed after Willie left. Her perfume was different from Elizabeth's, not as sweet, more subtle. It took him back to their first meeting at the Red Cloud offices. "Just happen to be in the neighborhood?"

Clara laughed. "No. I came home to the Rosebud for a day visit and called the OST police dispatch for you. I had some things I wanted to run by you concerning Jason, when they told me you almost died in an accident."

Manny's laugh shot pain through his chest. "It's not quite that bad, and it wasn't an accident. Someone deliberately ran me off the road, but I was lucky. I just got some superficial cuts, and my eye will be swollen shut for a few days by the feel of it, and floating ribs on my one side took a beating. Other than that, I'll be up and around soon."

Clara smiled. His face flushed. "You said you had information for me?"

She nodded. "The corporation—that is, I—ordered a full audit on Jason's books. Dunn, Dunn, and Winthrop out of Billings worked on it, and they found some odd irregularities."

"Such as?" He struggled to sit up, and Clara propped a pillow behind his back. Her hand rested on his shoulder for only a second. He felt stirrings that confirmed he was very much alive after all, stirrings he could get used to. "What irregularities?"

"Jason sent Harvard Business School gobs of money every year, from 1989 to 1995."

The answer came to him easily. "Erica."

"Your niece?"

Manny nodded. "She attended Harvard those years." He sat up straighter, and reached for his coffee on the sliding tray beside his bed. Without thinking, he confided in Clara. He told her about Erica's full-ride Harvard scholarship, with a healthy stipend each month. "Erica was the first Oglala to be awarded such a scholarship. And even though she was an outstanding high school athlete and her GPA was through the roof, folks were left scratching their heads as to how she landed it."

"So it wasn't a scholarship, after all," Clara said. "Jason footed the bill for her education. Why would he do such a thing?"

"Perhaps she's really Jason's daughter." The answer rolled quickly off Manny's lips before he could suck it back. But it was possible that Jason could have been her father. He told Clara about his dinner date with Erica, when she'd pointed out that Jason was old enough to be her father. "During the whole time she never once mentioned Reuben, never once asked about him. I thought that maybe she'd decided to forget her father, to disallow him in her life."

"And maybe," Clara reasoned, "it was because she finally found out that Jason, and not your brother, is her natural father. Maybe she doesn't want any contact with Reuben because of that."

"You're turning into a first-rate FBI agent."

"Not me." Clara frowned. "All this is a little scary as it is. But you said yourself she looks like Reuben."

"I said she has Reuben's cheekbones, his skin tone. But Jason had those same features."

Clara nodded and poured ice water into a cup from a plastic pitcher on the bedside tray. She sipped from a straw as she continued. "There is one other thing, though. Remember I mentioned Jason made a trip to Minneapolis a couple weeks before he was killed? Well, I found the boarding stubs from a charter airline in Rapid. Jason flew out of Rapid City Regional to Minneapolis. And the auditors found he was sending money to a Clifford Coyote monthly, by way of a post office box in Pine Ridge."

"Who is Clifford Coyote?"

"Not a clue," Clara answered. "But just as strange is Jason flying to Minneapolis. He never flew anywhere. He had a phobia of flying, and if he had gone to Minneapolis on business, he would have driven."

He understood Jason's fear. Manny had developed an acute fear of flying in the army while in Germany, where he had to fly often. The bureau required him to fly, but he always opted for driving when he could, even though his driving was more dangerous. Years of working to overcome his flying phobia had helped him enough that he could control it, but had Jason been able to do the same thing? Suddenly, he swung his legs over the bed.

"What are you doing?"

"Investigating." Manny hobbled over to the closet to check for his clothes. "And the one person who might have some answers just walked out the door."

><><><><

Clara drove while Manny held his bandaged ribs. They pulled into Big Bat's just as Elizabeth disappeared inside. He opened the car door, but Clara put her hand on his arm. "My guess is she'll take her lunch to her office. Better to confront her there, I think."

"See, agent material in the making."

They waited until Elizabeth emerged. Manny got out of the car and started after her. He couldn't walk fast enough to catch her and called out her name. She stopped. When she saw him, panic brushed her face a split second before a frown furrowed her forehead.

"Manny, what are you doing out of the hospital? The nurses told me you were going to be there at least a couple days."

"We've got to talk. It's important." His words came out in great gasps as he clutched his ribs.

"We can talk in my office." She led the way across the street. He flashed five fingers twice to Clara behind his back. Ten minutes. He followed Elizabeth into the finance office. He had to stop and catch his breath, and found breathing less painful if he bent over. Elizabeth was at his side. She put her arm around his shoulders and helped him into her office. She eased him into a chair beside her desk. He started speaking, stopped and held up his hand, and finally spoke when he caught his breath.

"What did you forget to ask me at the hospital?"

Manny knew there was no easy way to ask the question. "Is Jason Erica's father?"

"What the hell kind of question is that?"

"One that I need to know."

"What prompted all this?"

When Manny taught interviewing and interrogation, he always explained the many ways people avoided answering questions. One way was stalling until they could think of an answer that sounded convincing. Elizabeth was stalling now, and Manny pressed home his question before she could regroup.

"Jason funded Erica's college the entire six years she was in Harvard. He somehow made it appear as if she'd received a scholarship. He wouldn't have paid her way unless he had a good reason—like he was her father."

"How dare you ask me that."

"I dare because it's my job. The question is simple, even if the reasons may not be."

Elizabeth put her sandwich on her desk and sat in the chair opposite Manny. She rested her arms on the desk and leaned close. "Reuben is Erica's father."

"Elizabeth, I already have an agent running down the info from the college end," he lied.

Elizabeth dropped her eyes. Those interviewing classes again: Manny had won.

"We were all in AIM, we lived AIM together," she began. "A year before Reuben killed Billy Two Moons, Jason graduated from college and moved to Rapid City to work in the family business. When Reuben went to prison, Jason came around here a lot. He and Reuben were best friends before the Two Moons incident, and Jason was like Erica's godfather. He took her to concerts in Rapid when he could, took her on day trips other times. He took her to the powwow on Standing Rock once. Jason always treated Erica as if she was his own daughter."

"That still doesn't answer why he would pay for her college and grad school."

Elizabeth sat back in her chair. "Erica landed a scholarship to Harvard out of high school. Thank God and affirmative action, they scooped her up. But the tuition was only a small part of what she had to pay for. There were books, lab fees, dorm fees, and just day-to-day expenses that she had no money for. So Jason came up with the idea to supplement the scholarship.

"But we didn't want anyone thinking just like you do now. We didn't want anyone whispering that Jason was really Erica's father, so we concocted a ruse. Jason sent money to Harvard every month, and they told Erica it was part of her scholarship."

Elizabeth made sense, at least on the surface, but digging below the surface was something Manny did well. "I had to ask."

Elizabeth nodded. "Your job, right?"

"Sure, my job." He used the edge of the desk to stand. He limped toward the door and paused. "Do you remember Alex Jumping Bull?"

Blood drained from her face. "I remember him vaguely. He moved away from here years ago."

"Moved, or disappeared?"

She shrugged. "Why?"

Manny shrugged. "His name came up, is all. Thanks, Elizabeth. And I am truly sorry for the questions."

"I believe you are," she said. This time she didn't move to help him.

Manny used the wall for support. He had to cock his head to look through his good eye. People he passed in the hallway witnessed a Halloween caricature of the mummy come trick-or-treating a few months early, but that was all right. With the information he had gathered the last few hours, here and at the hospital, he might not have to be around the reservation much longer for people to stare at.

CHAPTER 14

Clara stopped the car beside the curb outside Manny's apartment.

"Pull up a little farther."

"Why?"

"There," Manny pointed. "I don't want her to see me." Desirée stood framed by the window. She hadn't seen them yet, and Manny hoped she would continue looking the other way until he drove off.

"An admirer?"

"More like an old nightmare."

Clara pulled the car a hundred feet ahead and stopped. She turned in the seat and faced him. "I'm not so sure about this."

"It'll be fine. I still got one good eye I can drive with." He winked it, bringing sympathetic pain to the bandaged one. "I can still drive good enough," he insisted.

"But my car. My baby. Willie said you're not the best of drivers with both eyes working, and cracked ribs that double you over in pain every time you hit a bump won't help any."

"Is that all you're worried about? Your car?"

"I'm worried about you, too." Clara looked at Manny and leaned over the seat. Her lips brushed his cheek.

Manny felt the blood rush to his face and blurted, "What can I hit just driving the few miles to Reuben's?"

She sighed and ran her hand over the Cadillac's leather seats. "I guess it isn't that far. Besides, you need someone here to sign for your new rental car when Hertz delivers it."

Clara had put the key in the lock before Desirée realized someone was next door, and Manny drove away before she saw him.

He turned onto the highway and digested the happenings of the last few days. He needed to do some road work, to run, to get into that zone where he sorted things out. But with his injuries, all he would be able to manage was a pained shuffle, and he'd have to think without the runner's high. He had uncovered some facts about Jason's murder, which caused someone to run him off the road and bury a hammer in his head. Then someone, presumably the same person who failed with the hammer, struck him with the stolen truck and left him for dead. And even though there would be many people on the reservation who wanted him out of the way, all roads led to Reuben.

As Manny continued west on Route 18, he thought of the truck that rammed him. If he hadn't stayed motionless, his attacker would have killed him, but the thing that kept invading his thoughts was the vision he'd had as he lay hurt and bleeding inside the car. He had never experienced a vision, despite Unc's insistence that he participate in the *hanbleceyapi*. He "cried for a vision" like other Lakota boys did at puberty when they exiled themselves to pray to *Wakan Tanka* for a dream that would guide them through life. Manny had trudged through deep snow to get to the low butte in back of Unc's house, where he'd prayed and fasted and wrapped the buffalo robe tightly around him to keep out the cold. He clutched the pipe he had made and prayed for that vision, while frigid air stung his exposed legs and ice clung to his breech clout. After the sacred four days, he was deemed worthy to enter the sweat lodge. His vision had eluded him as a boy, only to come visit him when he was a middle-aged man in a wrecked rental car.

He'd drifted in and out of consciousness, unsure what the apparition wanted. Among the wails of mothers and sisters and wives, the *wanagi* had approached, its features obscured. But the pain in its twisted face cried to Manny that it needed his help. He hadn't been able to keep awake. He had passed out in the crumpled car, certain he would never awake from his dream, certain he could never help the *wanagi*.

When he awoke in the hospital, he didn't understand the meaning of his vision and he desperately needed a holy man's guidance. But he was about to question the only *wicasa wakan* he knew about a murder. He couldn't allow his personal quest for the meaning of his vision to interfere with his duty.

The FBI had hired him, trained him, and made him one of the nation's premier investigators. He had given back far more than he had received, however, and had forsaken his heritage for his position. Duty wasn't one of the four Lakota virtues. Even before he thought of excuses not to maintain his loyalty to the bureau, he had his answer: Uncle Marion. Duty, Unc told him, was as important as the traditional virtues. Duty is what kept a man walking when he should be crawling, crawling when he should be lying on his deathbed. Generosity, fortitude, bravery, and wisdom were the four Lakota virtues. Duty was Manny's virtue.

Then Manny's thoughts turned to Niles the Pile. Niles had always resented Manny's abilities as an investigator. Assigning Manny to every Indian reservation case that came along was the Pile's way of making things rough enough that Manny would quit, but Manny wouldn't quit, and Niles had never had cause to fire him. Until now. If Niles gathered enough evidence that the investigation was stalling because the assigned agent was spending too much time romancing women, Manny would be down the road kicking rocks. And the Pile, and Lumpy, would have won.

Manny had no doubt Niles had been fed information from Lumpy and the media, outlining the time Manny had spent with Sonja Myers and now Desirée Chasing Hawk. He imagined Niles had some distorted visualization of Manny cavorting with more women than Caligula had. But the Pile didn't know that Manny hadn't been with a woman in so long that he forgot what to do if he had been.

He turned off the blacktop onto the gravel leading to Reuben's, and the Cadillac floated over the washboard road. Manny was grateful that the car softened the bumps, and he was able to breathe without the pain stabbing his ribs every time he hit a rut. The car filtered the dust and noise and allowed him to focus on how to question Reuben. The last two times he had tried to talk to Reuben, he had been evasive, even cagey. He knew he was the target of Manny's investigation and told Manny nothing new.

><><><

He drove by Crazy George He Crow's. Crazy George was not there, and neither was his Buick. The OST evidence tech hadn't finished processing it yet. Crazy George remained convinced that the tribe had stolen his car, and Manny made a mental note to speed things up.

He continued past a ramshackle shanty that was missing all the windows on the west side. With winter approaching, Manny hoped that whoever lived there was able to board up the holes against the wind and snow, but he knew that wouldn't happen. When the snow flew in the fall, the people living there would huddle against a garbage can in the middle of the floor, burning whatever they had gathered during the summer, and pray to *Wakan Tanka* to see them through until spring. He had been there with Unc many winters, making do with what firewood they could muster before winter set in. For a brief moment, Manny's heart sank, knowing he was powerless to help those people.

Past the shanty, four children played with sticks in the dirt. They checked out the passing Cadillac, then returned to their games. They could have been Manny's children, if he had remained on the reservation. Was it empathy he felt for people here? Certainly any good interrogator could empathize with people to get a confession. He wept when they wept, acted frustrated when they became frustrated. But he wasn't about to wring any confessions from these people. They didn't want his sympathy. They didn't even want his empathy. Pine Ridge was smack in the middle of the poorest county in the nation, yet all its people wanted was respect.

His thoughts turned back to Desirée. He rubbed his medicine bundle and silently thanked Lumpy for taking her from him. Those kids could have been his, playing in the dirt while the old man made a run to White Clay with the little lady. Desirée had become conniving and manipulative. He admitted that even Lumpy deserved better.

He turned down Reuben's driveway and coasted the rest of the way in, feeling the reassurance of Willie's Glock beneath his light corduroy jacket. He stepped out of the car and eased the door shut, then walked toward the house. Reuben's pony hung its head in a feed bucket but glanced sideways at Manny before returning to the grain. Manny shielded his eyes from the afternoon sun as he looked through the windows, but Reuben wasn't inside, and he walked around to the back of the trailer where they'd spoken that first time. When he cleared the corner of the trailer, Reuben called out from somewhere in back.

"No need to sneak around, *kola*. I'm down here."

Manny looked for a surveillance camera, certain Reuben must have one hidden somewhere. He walked toward the sound of Reuben's voice, but didn't see him.

"Down here."

"Down where?"

"By the creek."

Manny walked to the edge of a bank leading down to a shallow stream where Reuben tended a fire ten feet down. He squatted as he fed the fire in front of a heavy bark-and-mud covered dome: an *ini kagapi*. Past the sweat lodge a trickle of water meandered in a twenty-foot-wide stream that flowed into White Clay Creek.

"Come down here, brother." Reuben gestured over his back with a metal poker, then turned and added more cedar branches to the fire. Manny double-checked the position of the pistol before he picked his way down the bank. Reuben wore long shorts that stopped just below his knees. Sweat beaded on his naked chest and trickled down his legs to wet his moccasins, the worn-out deerskin contrasting with the one new string. Reuben set the poker by the fire and turned to Manny, and his smile faded as he eyed Manny's head.

"I heard you got banged up again, but I didn't know it was that bad."

"How did you hear about it?"

"Drums."

Willie had said the same thing about the information highway here on the reservation. "You got no enemies here. Come sit for a bit while I finish preparations."

"For what?"

Reuben laughed. "It has been a long time since you been home. We're going to sweat."

"I don't have time for that. We need to talk."

"About things that happened here on the rez before you came? And things that's happened since?"

Manny nodded.

"Then we'll have a lot to talk about, but we'll talk about it after we cleanse ourselves. I insist. If you want your answers."

Reuben grabbed a deer hide water bladder and limped to the entrance. He faced east for the sacredness, the source of power and life, and bent low to signify his humility as he disappeared into the lodge, then reemerged. With a small pitchfork he scooped rocks the size of softballs from the bottom of the fire pit and started for the entrance. He stopped and reached into his pocket and tossed Manny a half pouch of Bull Durham. Loose tobacco spilled onto the dirt.

"For an offering when we're finished," Reuben said, and once more disappeared inside.

"Shit," Manny murmured under his breath. He caressed the white cotton tobacco pouch. What pure pleasure it would be to roll a smoke, to feel the cigarette firm in his fingers, to watch the smoke rings drift skyward.

Then he was back to his bigger problem: Participating in a sweat was not on his agenda right now. He hurt and his head pounded, and even the minimal exertion of walking from the car to the back of Reuben's house taxed his muscles. His healing hand from the dog bite made it difficult to hold the tobacco pouch, and he was unsure if he could withstand the heat of the sweat lodge. But if this was the only way to talk with Reuben, he guessed he had no choice.

He picked his way along a worn path to the *inipi*. He stripped, and hid the Glock under his jacket on the ground before he draped his trousers over a lawn chair and reluctantly took off his BVDs. Naked, he walked barefoot over sharp rocks to the lodge entrance and bent low to enter.

Instantly Manny felt twelve years old again, when he had

crawled into the sweat lodge following his fasting and crying on the hill in back of Unc's house. "Enter Mother Earth's womb with reverence," he heard the sacred man instructing him. "So you can receive what *Wakan Tanka* wishes for you."

Manny had entered and found himself with four other boys sitting in a semicircle around the *wicasa wakan*. The holy man had given each boy a buffalo tail to whip himself while he flicked water on the hot rocks with a straw broom.

"The hot stones will be the coming of life," the sacred man said. "Feel the creative forces of the universe being activated with the steam." He flicked more water on the rocks. Soon, all the boys except Manny moaned, wrapped up in the visions that had descended upon them as they sweated in the lodge. Manny envied them, never knowing why his vision had eluded him. Even now it disturbed him.

Manny parted the canvas door. Reuben sat cross-legged on the far side of the lodge and he directed sage smoke over his body with an eagle feather. Manny shook at the thought of his crazy brother attacking him in the confines of the lodge. But Reuben was his best suspect, and this might be Manny's only opportunity to question him.

Manny stooped low and duckwalked into the lodge.

"*Yuhpayo!*" Reuben said: Close it.

Manny threw the heavy canvas door flap closed. The lodge was plunged into darkness, the only light the glow of the rocks, the heat already intense in the enclosed space. Manny patted the ground around him as he tried to recall where he was in relation to Reuben. The bed of sage pricked his bare butt and legs, and he gingerly put all his weight on his bottom.

Manny's eyes adjusted to the darkness. He squinted to make out Reuben, momentarily lost in the fog as he sprinkled water on the hot rocks with a buffalo horn. Steam erupted. Heat rose. Manny gasped in shallow, painful breaths.

"Where do I sit?"

"Where?" Reuben's face rose above the steam as he nodded his approval. "At least you have some respect for the old ways, even if you forgot the knowledge. Sit there. Facing east."

"East to give one wisdom."

"So you do remember some things that Unc taught you."

"I remember a lot of things he taught me. Taught both of us. But you forgot the important things he stood for. You tossed what integrity you had away and became—"

"A murderer, little brother? You don't have to remind me of that. But I won't argue with you here, not within the lodge. Maybe you should just sit back and pray, contemplate why we're here."

Reuben ladled more water onto the rocks. Fog engulfed him. His head poked through the steam and looked detached from his body. Manny rubbed his eyes, feeling the injured one open from the steam. He swayed and fell forward. He caught himself and sat up. His chest heaved. His breaths came at great expense.

"You don't look so good, *kola*. I heard you got a nasty concussion last night. Maybe you shouldn't be in here right now."

Manny's head pounded. He wiped sweat from his eye. "I got questions that need answers, and don't have a lot of time to find them out."

"Ask away." Reuben took a small pouch beside his feet and tossed the medicine plant into the air. "*Peji wacanga.*"

"Sweetgrass."

Reuben nodded his approval and trickled more water from the horn onto the rocks nestled in the pit in the center of the lodge. Steam rose. Reuben disappeared in the steam. Manny rubbed his eye, and light-headedness returned. When Reuben reappeared, a single eagle feather jutted from his hair and his head appeared to float above the steam cloud.

"You really don't look so good. Maybe you should step outside where it's cool. You never know with a concussion."

"The sweetgrass." Manny ignored him. "There was sweetgrass found besides Jason's body where he was killed, and more found in Crazy George's car. Maybe it came from that pouch."

Reuben grinned a jack-o'-lantern smile against the glow of the hot rocks. "Haven't you heard? I am now a *wicasa wakan*. I use sweetgrass in ceremonies. But I tell you, there are other people here on the rez that use it. Like your young With Horn. I understand he's been studying with Margaret Catches. I'm certain she uses it, too."

Reuben didn't wait for a response, but added more water. He set the horn at his feet, and began a soft chant, rocking gently as he closed his eyes. Reuben would soon be entranced, and Manny needed answers quickly. "The night someone attacked me with a hammer: Was it one of your Heritage Kids?"

Reuben's expression showed no emotion. His fists clenched. And unclenched. His jaw tightened. And relaxed. In chewing-gum fashion. Could Manny reach the gun outside in time before Reuben was upon him? As quickly as Reuben's rage had surfaced, it was gone, replaced by an equanimity that surprised Manny. "Some of my kids are less saintly than I'd like them to be, but I asked each one about the attack, and they all denied it."

"And you believe them?"

"I got to, until I have a good reason not to. I hurt too many people in my life by not believing them."

"Did you drive the truck that hit me?" Manny's head throbbed, and he wished he could detach it from his body as Reuben seemed to do. Manny wiped sweat from his forehead and his eye, and caught himself from falling forward and leaned back. His shallow breaths came with great labor as sharp pain radiated from his ribs down to his toes. "The truck that rammed me was stolen from your jobsite. Either you or one of your kids stole it and ran me off the road. What say you, *kola*."

"I told you, I don't drive anymore. Besides, Ben Horsecreek and I went to the Rosebud for a wake last night. He drove. That'll be easy enough for you to check out."

Manny nodded. It would be an easy fact to check.

Manny drifted. His mind wandered away from the investigation. He held the side of his head, watching Reuben add water to the rocks. The hissing steam consumed him. What had the sacred man said during his *hanbleceyapi*, that the stones within the lodge represented the coming of life, and the steam was the creative forces of the universe being activated. Reuben mouthed something that Manny couldn't understand; his voice sounded as if he mumbled through a hollow culvert. Manny fought to stay conscious, but his eyes drooped shut.

When he opened his eyes, Reuben was gone. Manny no longer sat cross-legged in the sweat lodge, but lay on the prairie grass, tall buffalo and gama grass that cushioned his head. Voices woke him from his deep sleep. Gone was the aching in his head. Gone was the bandage covering his eye. Gone was the throbbing of his ribs that had reminded him of the incident that nearly cost him his life.

Voices roused him. Those same voices he had heard as he lay fighting for his life in the rental car. Women crying. Children crying. Frightened voices, rising over the distant noise of gunfire. He was powerless to move, unable to help.

A tall white marker jutted out of the ground over the mass grave for the 1890 Wounded Knee Massacre victims. Horse soldiers of the Seventh Cavalry rode to the hill overlooking Chief Big Foot's village, down along the banks of Chankpe Opi Wakpala, Wounded Knee Creek. Manny shouted a warning, but no words came out, and he watched in revulsion as the soldiers opened fire on the villagers.

Manny blinked and was once again fifteen years old, leading other teen sympathizers past the FBI roadblock at Red Arrow outside the Wounded Knee standoff. They inched their way toward the Catholic church, which American Indian Movement members occupied.

"Get down!" he ordered the others when an armored personnel carrier loaded with U.S. Marshals approached. They drove past without stopping.

"Clear," Manny whispered, and ran bent over, then crawled the last few yards in the gully leading to the church.

Manny told the others to wait in the gully behind the church while he made certain that the AIM people inside knew they were there to help, and he crawled toward the building. Sagebrush tore his jeans, and his hands bled raw from the rocky ground. He had paused and was listening at the back door when a gun cocked close to his ear, and someone thrust a rifle barrel into his face. Strong, lean, muscular hands grabbed him by one chubby arm, hoisted him, and dragged him inside the church. Twenty or more women sat in different places. Some cared for children. Others sat on the bare wooden floor, stirring tripe on fires made from pews they had chopped up. The odor made Manny retch, but he was too frightened to puke. Men held guns and peered intently out windows. The overpowering stench of urine and feces gagged him, and again he fought down the urge to vomit.

"What you doing here, *kola*?" Reuben shouted from across the room. Manny stood as Reuben picked his way through women and children. "Unc will skin you alive if he finds out you're hanging with me. What're you doing here?"

"We're here to help."

"Who's 'we?'"

"Friends. Hiding in the gully out back."

Reuben sat on a pew in front of Manny, and rested his hand

lightly on the boy's back. "I appreciate your heart, *misun*, but this here's a journey you gotta sit out. I don't know where this is going, but it's not going to get any easier. We've already been here nearly two months with no end in sight. Go. Take your friends out of here."

Buddy Lamont, one of Reuben's AIM friends, who would eventually die from a gunshot at the occupation, led Manny from the church that night. As he skirted FBI and Marshal roadblocks, a voice called out to him. The same voice he heard the night he was rammed. The voice that moaned for help.

He was back at the church, but this time there was no church, just the hill overlooking the village where the Seventh Cavalry waited. Hotchkiss guns pointed toward tipis, and troopers stood poised with Springfields as other soldiers searched lodges for weapons.

Manny shouted a warning, but no sound came out. He waved his arms wildly, but no one noticed. A young Lakota pulled a .36 Navy Colt from under his Ghost Shirt and began firing into the air. Hotchkiss guns opened up, cutting down half the village in the first rapid-fire barrage. Women, children, old men fled, and soldiers shot them in the backs as they ran. Survivors dropped into a ravine in back of the village. The soldiers re-aimed their Hotchkiss guns and fired another volley.

Manny turned away. His stomach heaved while he forced a look back at the massacre. A young mother caught his eye as she ran clutching a baby in her arms. Looked over her shoulder. Fell. Picked herself up. Bloodied. Then the guns ripped her deerskin skirt apart. More blood. Screams, and she fell again. Her baby flew through the air and landed on corpses already melting the snow with their cooling bodies. The baby cried, and a single shot stopped it.

Manny was beside the burial party days later. He cried as civilians, hired by the soldiers at two dollars a body, pried corpses from the frozen ground, then used the same shovels to lever them into the mass grave.

Manny cried, and another voice cried with him. The figure that had guided him to Wounded Knee approached and Manny couldn't see his face, couldn't see through the cloud that covered his mind. The specter held out his hand and Manny reached for it. The apparition withdrew it and walked away, wailing with each burdened step.

Still, Manny couldn't look away from the genocide as burial crews performed their grisly task.

"Wait!" Manny shouted. He ran after the apparition. "I'm here to help."

It kept just beyond his grasp.

"Wait!"

It remained just a step ahead. "Wait!" Manny cried again. And again. And again.

"Kola!" Reuben shook him. *"Kola!"*

The scene, and the apparition, faded. Manny looked up at Reuben, shirtless over him, sweat dripping from every pore of his body, a concerned look across his glistening face. "Come out of it."

Reuben had thrown back the covering of the door, and cool air dimpled his body with goose bumps. Reuben trickled water over Manny's face and shoulders, then carried him outside. Reuben propped him against a cedar log, and handed him a folded towel. Groggy, Manny had to concentrate to unfold the edges that were tucked into each other.

"You're all right now," Reuben said. He held a pot of water and Manny dipped the towel into it and wiped his face.

"It was horrible," Manny breathed, toweling his nude body. "Is this what a vision is supposed to be? A nightmare?"

Reuben dried himself and slipped on a T-shirt that proclaimed HOMELAND SECURITY. It depicted the faded images of four Apaches posing together as they eyed the camera with a dour look. "Part of the journey you just took involves having someone help interpret your dream. You need a *wicasa wakan*."

Manny laughed. Reuben didn't. "My brother, the holy man I came here to question about a murder? What kind of fool do you take me for?"

"One that needs help with his vision before it drives him mad. Besides, you got any other sacred man to talk to?"

Reuben crouched beside him, genuine concern etched across his face. Was this a true holy man kneeling beside him? Manny thirsted for answers, and he slipped on his trousers. "Let's take a walk."

"Now?"

"I think better when I'm moving." Manny used the cedar log for support and stood, stretching his legs, getting the circulation going. Reuben draped a towel over his shoulder and started walking beside him. Although Manny was still light-headed from the sweat, and the pain caused him to wince with every step, he thought he might just be able to outrun Reuben even now. Reuben limped to keep up, rubbing his leg.

"Bursitis," he said when he caught Manny eyeing him.

"I thought it was arthritis?"

"It's one of those -itis brothers." And they both laughed together for the first time in so many years.

>◇◇◇<

When the heat overcame Manny and the stress of his vision wore on him and weakened him, Reuben had called Willie to give Manny a ride. Willie left his patrol car at Reuben's house, and proudly sat behind the wheel of Clara's dusty Cadillac. "So what was it like?" Willie asked when Manny dropped onto the seat beside him.

He wanted to tell Willie that his brother, sacred man and

chief suspect in Jason Red Cloud's murder, had guided him through the meanings of his vision and helped him understand things afterward. He wanted to tell Willie that the specter in his vision was a wandering soul, destined to roam eternity, destined never to find the Spirit Road without Manny's help. Manny was this *wanagi*'s savior and the instrument by which this lost *wanagi* would find the road home. Most important, Manny had no idea who the spirit had been in life. But he couldn't tell Willie, or anyone, about this most personal of experiences, so he changed the subject.

"I found out some things. I don't think Reuben stole that truck and ran me off the road. His story that he and Ben Horsecreek attended a wake can be easily verified. He said he doesn't think any of his Heritage Kids are involved, though his reaction told me he was less than certain of that. But Reuben did say something, when both of us were lost in our visions. Something he denied later. But I distinctly heard it."

"What was that?"

"Reuben screamed out something about Jason Red Cloud's folks having their car tampered with. I swear he accused Billy Two Moons of killing them."

CHAPTER 15

Willie turned onto Route 18 leading into Pine Ridge Village. "You want me to talk with Verlyn Horn about the Red Clouds' accident?"

"Do you know him?"

"I talked with him at the Rosebud powwow last year. A grouchy, unpleasant bear. Cantankerous as hell, but I'll pay him a visit if you want me to."

Manny forced a grin. "I used to get along with him pretty good. I should've stopped to see him before now anyway."

When they arrived at Manny's apartment, Clara came out and walked around her car. "Was that Willie?" She pointed at the cruiser whisking Willie back to Reuben's to pick up his own squad car.

Manny nodded as his eyes darted to the apartment houses.

"Relax, Desirée left an hour ago. Guess she got tired of waiting."

"Thank God for that."

Clara nodded to her car. "It's still in one piece. Not a scratch on it. Other than the dust, it looks fine. Guess I got Willie to thank for that."

"I told you I'm not as bad a driver as I'm made out to be."

"Then why was he driving?"

Manny explained that he had become overheated in the sweat lodge and was too weak to drive. "I feel good enough now to go talk with Chief Horn."

"Am I ever going to get to spend time with you?"

Heat rose from his neck to his face as if he'd just stepped out from the *inipi*. "When I wrap up this investigation . . ." He let it trail off.

She smiled. "I'll hold you to that."

"I'll call you tomorrow."

"That reminds me. An Agent Niles called for you. He said time's running out. What's that mean?"

Manny sighed. "It means my time's running out. I'll call you."

><><><

Manny let the cool water take away the heat of the sweat lodge, and he had to force himself to get out of the shower. After putting on clean khakis and a polo shirt, he drove to the Cohen Home. Shannon Horn had told Manny that her grandfather resented living at the retirement home the past few years. She warned him that his rosy disposition had soured, but Manny couldn't recall Chief Horn ever having a rosy disposition.

Manny doubled over when he stepped out of the car and caught his breath. The pain in his ribs subsided, and he straightened and entered the home. A petite woman in her early twenties sat reading *People* magazine at the service desk. He leaned over the counter. "Is Verlyn Horn here?"

She put her magazine aside. "Why do you wish to see him?" She stared at Manny's bandage. "Did he do that to you?"

"No. I haven't seen the chief in years. He's an old friend of mine."

"Your name?"

What difference does it make?" Manny snapped. "Why the third degree? I just want to talk with him." He realized he was the one usually giving someone the third degree. "I'm sorry. I know you're just doing your job and protecting the people living here."

She laughed. "It's you I'm protecting. There's a reason his granddaughter is his only visitor."

Manny reached into his pocket, withdrew his ID case, and flipped open his badge wallet. She frowned as she read it, and her demeanor changed from suspicious to outright hostile. "So you're the agent they sent on the Red Cloud murder. What's the FBI want with Chief Horn?"

She must have had friends or relatives who were pro-AIM, anti-Wilson back in the day. She was too young to have experienced that conflict, but it probably influenced the way she viewed federal law enforcement.

"Look, I used to be a tribal cop here. Chief Horn was my boss back then, and I just want to visit him."

Her facial muscles relaxed, and she walked around the counter. Was everyone on the reservation these days taller than him? Everyone except Lumpy, anyway. "I guess that wouldn't hurt, but don't get him wound up—that's all I need is another night of reassuring the other residents that the chief's not really going crazy."

Manny followed her down a long hallway. Apartment doors on each side stood open to allow air to pass through. The apartments appeared spartan, yet neat and tidy, and he caught her watching him.

"There are two people to a room. At two hundred dollars a month, conditions can't be too luxurious."

"Two to a room makes it pretty cramped."

"Except for Chief Horn's room. He's the only occupant."

"No roommate?"

She shook her head. "No one that can tolerate him for any length of time." She stopped at the end of the hallway and rapped lightly on the door. When she got no answer, she knocked louder.

"Who the hell is it?" Chief Horn's voice bellowed, the same timbre and tone that used to chew Manny's butt almost daily.

"You have a visitor," she spoke to the door.

"Don't want one."

"This man's FBI."

The door flew open and hit the wall behind it. The doorknob fit neatly in a hole in the plaster, an old wound on the wall from the knob slamming into it. Manny looked up at Chief Horn, with a beer poised in his right hand as if intending to hurl it. Although his posture stooped, he still towered above Manny. "Manny Tanno."

"Chief Horn." The old man's hand wrapped around Manny's, and he felt like a rookie again.

Horn scowled at the receptionist. "Can't you see we want some privacy."

"See what I mean?" She turned on her heels and walked swiftly toward her desk at the end of the hallway.

"What the hell's that mean?"

"Nothing, Chief. Can we talk?"

Chief Horn stepped aside. Beer cans from an overflowing garbage pail littered the floor, and a fresh case of Falstaff waited on a stove beside an overflowing pot of macaroni and cheese that had burnt sometime yesterday. The only chair in the room sat in front of a small television set growing coat hangers for rabbit ears. Horn motioned to the back sliding-glass doors. "Why don't we sit out under the cottonwood." He grabbed a partial six-pack and led the way outside.

He motioned for Manny to sit in a lawn chair, while he plopped into an Adirondack chair missing one arm. There were four beers left on the plastic stringer, and he placed them on a picnic table beside him. He popped the top on a beer and downed half the can in one gulp.

"What manners. Have a cold one."

Manny shook his head. "Never got the taste for it."

"Suit yourself, kid, but why the visit? I thought you were an instructor at that FBI academy there in Quantico."

He wanted to tell Horn he wouldn't be in Quantico for long unless he found Jason Red Cloud's killer soon. "Sometimes I get field assignments."

"I know." Horn's grin showed a full set of perfect pearly whites, despite his age. "Whenever I hear your name bandied around, I remind people I trained you."

"And you did well." Chief Horn wanted his new officers to be aggressive and to enforce tribal statutes. But he also pushed them to demonstrate honesty and integrity. It was those virtues Manny learned as a tribal cop that he was struggling with now, and he couldn't get his *kola* out of his head as the murderer.

"I hear you have a case right here on Pine Ridge." Horn chugged his beer, placed the can between his large hands, and crushed it. He hollered and grinned at Manny. "The old fart's still got some lead in his pencil, huh?"

"That you do, Chief."

He peeled another can off the plastic. "You didn't come here to jaw about old times."

Manny brought Horn up-to-date on the Red Cloud investigation. Chief Horn possessed a fine analytical mind, and Manny hoped he could tap into that logic. "I think Jason Red Cloud's death ties in with his parents' car wreck."

Horn slammed his fist on the picnic table. It bounced and

came back to rest on all four legs. "That was no accident. I said so that day we found the car."

"Why did you think it was deliberate?"

Horn opened the beer and took a long pull. He slammed it on the table and wiped his mouth with the back of his hand. "Those brake lines were cut. Not sloppy, so you'd know it, but professional-like. I had a repair shop in Gordon check it out, and they thought they had been cut, too."

"You're certain it was no accident?"

Horn leaned closer. "I investigated enough accidents through the years where the brakes had failed. Like LaVonne Drapeaux's wreck that time, with the brake lines cut, not ruptured. Someone sliced those lines on that Red Cloud car."

"Is the car still around?"

"That red Impala? Naw." He picked up his beer and sipped it more slowly. He had come to the part of his story he was sure of, and didn't want to rush it. "The crusher came through here a few years after that and bought up junkers for scrap, the Red Clouds' Chevy among them. But they'd always kept their cars in top shape. Traded every other year. There's no way those brakes could have failed."

"Who would have wanted them dead, and who would know how to rig a murder to look like an accident?"

Horn shook his head. "I've asked myself those same questions a hundred times, and it's always bothered me. Jason was the only one who profited from their deaths, but he never had a harsh word with his folks. AIM had more bitter enemies than the Red Clouds, so that was an angle I thought held the most promise." Horn finished his beer and tossed it into a sack beside his chair. He reached for another. "As for who could have done it, any knowledgeable mechanic could have. It wouldn't have been hard to pick a time to cut the lines, either. The Red Clouds drove to Scenic every Saturday night to play bingo at the

Episcopal church. Anyone familiar with their routine could have picked that time."

"What about my brother? Reuben was one of AIM's enforcers."

Horn stood and stretched. "I interviewed Jane Afraid of All two nights after the wreck. Reuben was on my short list of suspects, and Jane had the apartment below Lizzy's. I thought if anyone knew if Reuben was there or not, it would have been Jane."

"And she saw him there?"

Horn nodded. "Jane saw Reuben going into Lizzy's apartment about sundown that night. She knew Reuben was there until morning because the bedsprings upstairs kept her awake half the night. Reuben couldn't have killed the Red Clouds."

Horn opened the beer. Manny declined once more. "Trying to cut the waistline some."

Horn tilted his head back and laughed. "Kid, you get to be my age, you start worrying about that. For now, live a little and don't sweat the small shit."

"That's what I'm trying to do, Chief, not sweat the small shit. It's this big shit—this Red Cloud murder—that has me puzzled. A lot of things don't add up. Like Billy Two Moons's murder."

"How does that fit in?"

Manny shrugged. "Maybe it doesn't. But tell me what you recall about him."

Horn set his beer on the table and leaned back. "Billy was a sneaky little bastard. He did a bit of everything, never for any length of time, just 'til he got his paycheck so he could make a run down to White Clay with the other alkies." He rested his hands on his protruding belly. "You know, I condemned people like that back then. Now look at me."

Manny let that pass. "What kind of work did Two Moons do?"

"Day jobs. Sometimes he'd help Harlan out at his shop fixing tires or doing tune-ups. Him and that other worthless piece of shit, Alex Jumping Bull. I threw the pair of them in my hoose-gow for one reason or another about twice a month. When Billy was in jail, at least I got free tune-ups and repairs for the squad cars."

"So Two Moons had some mechanical ability?"

"Considerable, though he was rarely sober enough to take advantage of it."

"Was he ever connected with the FBI or the BIA?"

"Never, though we tried to turn him more than once, to get him to snitch for us. He wouldn't bite, said he had another source of lucky bucks that would be coming due soon, and he didn't need government money. Besides, he made it known that he'd join AIM if they'd have him."

"But they didn't?"

Horn shook his head.

"Then the rumor that he was an FBI informer was false?"

"Totally. But most folks thought he was a snitch anyway, like they thought Anna Mae Pictou-Aquash was a snitch."

"But she wasn't."

Horn shook his head. "All that mattered is the wrong people thought she was. That's another case that's bothered me through the years. If I could ever have identified those women that hustled her from that Denver safe house, I would have been a step closer to nailing her killer." He eased back into his chair, and the wood slats creaked beneath his weight. "But getting back to Two Moons, the weasel didn't hang with anyone except Alex Jumping Bull."

"Whatever happened to him?" Manny asked.

Chief Horn shrugged. "He disappeared the same time Two Moons was killed. I always thought Reuben was good for that, too, but he just wouldn't come off it. Jumping Bull's body was never found, and the Pennington County deputies searched that area around China Gulch for days, but came up short. I always figured some deer hunter would come upon his body at the bottom of a deep ravine someday. For all I know, he could still be alive still getting drunk somewhere."

Chief Horn's eyelids drooped, and Manny switched subjects to the old times, amazed at how sharp the old man's memory was. They talked about their old department, and the growing pains it experienced following the AIM–BIA feuds of the 1970s. They talked about Lumpy, and Horn regretted not firing him before he retired as tribal police chief. The chief said Lumpy was a political animal even back then, and would get ahead by whatever means he could.

Chief Horn's head nodded, then settled onto his chest. He woke long enough to say good-bye, and Manny left him sipping beer under the cottonwood as he stood quietly to leave. He wished he had Horn's investigative talent. The chief had fingered Two Moons for the brake-line job, and with the Red Clouds' anti-AIM stance, killing them might have curried favor with AIM members and they might have accepted him. And if that was the case, did Jason find out about Two Moons cutting the brake lines that killed his parents? If Jason learned that and then killed Two Moons, then Manny could lobby for a pardon for Reuben. Thoughts filled his head fast, and what he needed most right now was to feel well enough to put some miles in his running shoes—he needed to get into his zone to sort things out.

As he drove away from the Cohen Home he passed Nathan Yellow Horse's truck. Manny watched in the rearview mirror as Yellow Horse got out of his car and started into the Cohen Home. He knew Yellow Horse would interrupt Chief Horn from his nap. And perhaps the chief would take care of Manny's reporter problem for him.

CHAPTER 16

Manny pulled into the public safety parking lot beside Lumpy just as he grabbed on to his doorjamb and, with a grunt, pulled himself out of the car. He gently closed the door of his new Mustang GT, white and sporting-blue racing stripes running the length from the hood to the trunk, and sauntered to Manny's car.

"What you here for, Hotshot?" The dark purple stain from two days ago was lighter. Lumpy put his hand over his cheek to hide it. "If you're here for Willie, I can't spare him today either."

"I'm checking on any more lab results that might have come in."

"None yesterday." Lumpy grinned as he eyed Manny's rental, then glanced back at his own car. "What kind of ride you got there in Virginia?"

"Nothing like that fancy machine you got, just an eight-year-old Accord. How long you had that?"

Lumpy smiled wide. "I got it last month. Still got the dealer tags on it. Why, you looking to upgrade?"

"Not me," Manny said. "Guess we don't get paid what you tribal cops do. I was just looking at those new tires. Kind of odd."

Lumpy laughed nervously as if he had missed an important point in their debate. "What's your point?"

Manny hung his head out the window, and looked down at the tires. "They're new, just like those impressions of new tires we found at Jason's murder."

"What the hell's that supposed to mean?" Lumpy stepped between Manny and his car, as if shielding the Mustang from suspicion. "You implying something?"

Manny held up his hands. "Of course not. Just not many cars here with new rubber. That's why it's so important that old Crazy George's car be processed, just in case those tire marks at the crime scene match his old Buick."

"I'll get Pat Pourier on it this morning." Lumpy turned and tripped over his own feet, caught himself, and disappeared into the station. Manny had too easily convinced Lumpy that processing Crazy George's car was a priority, but he had scant moments to savor his small victory when his cell phone rang. "Niles here. Good morning." The Pile didn't intend it to be a good morning for Manny. "How's the investigation going?"

"Slowing."

"I'm not surprised. What the hell you doing out there in the Wild West? Reports I get, you've been chasing skirts rather than chasing leads."

"Don't tell me: Lieutenant Looks Twice."

"And a reporter for the local rag, a Nathan Yellow Horse. Seems like his paper is up in arms that you're lovin' this babe Sonja Myers, who landed an exclusive. How's that going to look for the bureau?"

"Take a breath, Niles." *And rub yourself with some Preparation H.* "I'm not sleeping with her."

"Bullshit! Yellow Horse says Lieutenant Looks Twice and you are feuding over her. He swears you've been dissing his paper because this Myers woman has been sleeping with the lieutenant, and you gave her a story to woo her back."

"First I've heard about it. Look, the fact is that I've run up against a stone wall here. Actually, a stone wall would have felt much better." Manny filled Niles in on what little information he had uncovered, and how his injuries from his two assaults had delayed things. "That sound like I'm having fun? How about you come out here. Give me a hand."

Niles laughed. "You know I don't do fieldwork."

"Then how about sending a couple agents from the Rapid City office down here?"

"Can't do," Niles said. "Like I told you before, we don't have any other agents with a background in Pine Ridge."

"But Harlan LaPointe's Lakota from Rosebud. I talked with him a couple days ago in Rapid. He doesn't have anything on his plate right now."

"But he's not full blood," Niles said. "He's one-eighth Sicangu Lakota. That'll just remind people there that he's seven-eighths White, and he'll get nowhere on Pine Ridge. But I'm not telling you anything you didn't already know." Then, after a long pause, he added, "I called you just as a friendly reminder that the academy begins in a week. And I need you to leave that woman alone."

There was no convincing Niles that he wasn't womanizing, so Manny promised to be at the academy when the next session began. When Manny hung up, he wasn't so sure he would. And Niles never even asked him how he was doing after being attacked. He had little time to be pissed at the Pile when his phone rang again.

"The auditor finished and I need to go through Jason's things," Clara said. "Would you like to meet me here and we can go over his report?"

Did Manny detect something more than business in her voice? "Sure." At least he hoped he did. "I'm doing no good here today. I'll meet you there in two hours."

><><><

Manny bounded up the stairs at the Red Cloud Development Building. At the first landing, he doubled over from the pain in his ribs. When he caught his wind, he continued up as he held his side.

"Ms. Downing is expecting you. Please go in." Manny detected some hostility in Emily's tone, probably because Clara had chewed her out for not relaying his messages all week. She put her headset on and resumed typing without looking up.

Manny reached for his comb as he walked to Clara's office, formerly Jason's, then realized he didn't have enough hair to comb and left it in his pants pocket. He paused at the door long enough to pop a piece of gum in his mouth before he swung the huge old door open.

Clara sat in Jason's chair pouring over papers scattered across the desktop. She smiled and dropped her glasses. They dangled from a silver chain around her neck, and rested in brimming cleavage. Manny averted his eyes and concentrated on the green business suit and black pumps that illustrated her professionalism.

"I'm glad you could make it."

"How could I refuse?" They fidgeted as they eyed each other. "You said you had something to show me."

"Of course." She shuffled through papers on a corner of the desk. "I found where Jason has been mailing checks to a Clifford Coyote at a Pine Ridge post office box."

"How much?"

"Two thousand dollars. Every month since 1976."

Manny couldn't recall Clifford Coyote ever coming up during the investigation or in his memory, and few people on the reservation actually had post office boxes. Most received their mail General Delivery. "Who's Clifford Coyote, and why the monthly checks?"

Clara shrugged. "Don't know. Jason didn't confide in me where he spent his money. With him, it could have been anything." Manny made a mental note to call Willie and have him check on that post office box, and to see if the post office had a residential address for Coyote.

"You said there was more."

"There is." She put her glasses on and walked around to the back of the desk. She shuffled through papers and snatched one from the pile. She handed it to him and leaned closer, and her perfume distracted him. The receipt marked BUSINESS VOYAGES showed that two weekends before Jason died he had booked a round-trip flight to Minneapolis on the charter service based in Rapid City.

"But you said he often traveled on business."

"He did." She walked around to sit on the edge of the desk next to Manny. "But he never flew. This trip must have been so important he sucked it up—or it wasn't Jason who flew that day. I also found this." She handed Manny a note ripped from a spiral notebook. It was written in clear, neat letters, threatening to expose Jason if he didn't resume payments. The note was signed "Alex."

"Tell me you know something about this Alex."

"I wish I could, but I don't know any more about him than I do any of Jason's associates."

Chief Horn was adamant that Alex Jumping Bull and Billy Two Moons were inseparable. Was Alex Jumping Bull still alive all these years, as the chief suspected? If he was, what did Alex have on Jason? And why send Clifford Coyote a check every month?

"Do you think this Alex may have known Jason intended embezzling the tribe's money?"

Clara shook her head. "I don't know. Jason had a lot of contacts, knew everyone, and he could have told this Alex. Maybe Alex was in with Jason on the scheme."

"That's a thought. Do you have a paper sack I could have?"

Clara nodded and stepped out of the room. She returned with a brown paper Albertson's grocery bag. Manny placed both the envelope and letter from Alex inside, and sealed it with tape from a dispenser on the desk. "I'll overnight this to Quantico to get the letter and envelope fumed for prints."

"They can do that on paper?"

Manny smiled. "Ve have our vays," he said. It came out as a silly impression of Colonel Klink of Stalag 13. "There's a lot of prints on the envelope by now, but maybe I'll luck out. Because you handled the letter, you'll have to go down to the police department here and have a set of elimination prints taken."

Clara nodded and her face lit up as she looked at the clock over her desk. "Speaking of lucking out, it's quitting time and I'm famished. We have a great Olive Garden by the mall. Be my treat."

Before Manny could stammer his way out of the offer, she had threaded her arm through his and started for the door. As they left, even Emily wore an approving smile.

CHAPTER 17

Manny drove across the reservation boundary along Highway 41, past Red Shirt Table and later Cuny Table, though he didn't notice the scenery as his mind relived the night's dinner conversation with Clara. They stayed until the restaurant closed, drawing out their time together, until Clara drove him back to his car parked at her office. As he climbed out of her car, she pulled him back in and kissed him full on the lips. A good-night kiss, nothing more. But her lips had lingered there longer than they should have. Manny didn't object and kissed her back.

He pulled away, breathless, and her perfume conjured up images of things forbidden at this point in their relationship. And it conjured up something else: how different it was from the scent he had smelled that night his car was rammed, and later as he lay in his hospital bed. He fought to think where he had smelled it before, but another kiss erased all thoughts of anything except Clara.

"Let's do this again soon," she said. "When we have more time."

Manny thought he had agreed, though he didn't remember that part very well. He only recalled Clara inviting him for a romantic rematch.

He came to the stop sign at Oglala, and a dark-colored Dodge pulled beside him. He was vaguely aware that the Dodge's passenger window rolled down. The darkness obscured the driver, but not the passenger who pointed a long-barreled pistol at Manny. The image took a moment to cut through his brain, foggy with thoughts of Clara. Quick movements eluded him as he reached for his gun in the shoulder holster. Was it stuck, or was he just drawing slower than he should?

His firearms instructors at Quantico had talked about the phenomenon that slows a man's perceptions in a crisis and causes everything to move in slow motion, as it was doing now. The shooter cocked the hammer on a single-action revolver, like in Old West movies. Except it wasn't the Old West, it was the New West, starring Manny Tanno, who didn't want his ass ventilated by any gun, let alone a movie hogleg.

He jerked the Glock free and hurled himself across the seat just as the man fired. Muzzle flash bright. Night vision destroyed. Tiny explosions of yellow light popped across his one good eye. Another shot. Glass shards cut his cheek, and one piece tore his ear as the side window shattered.

He looked over the jagged window as the shooter cocked his gun again, and the slow motion faded. Manny was pissed.

He fired through the open window at the driver. He fired again. And again. The Dodge spun gravel. Manny shot twice. Double tapped. Double tapped. A round struck a taillight, and Manny floored the accelerator.

The Dodge swerved across the road and hit a reflector post, the back end breaking away and the driver almost losing control. The car straightened and sped toward Pine Ridge Village, swerving across both lanes. Manny shot. The back window shattered and the car careened off another post, but the driver re-gained control. Manny gained on the car.

Manny jammed the Glock under his leg and fumbled for his cell phone. He hit speed dial. Tribal Police dispatcher Shannon Horn's voice calmed him as he screamed that he was in a pursuit. She urged him to breathe slowly, speak slowly, and he sucked in a deep breath, the pain sharp in his ribs. He blurted out he was in pursuit of two men who had shot at him, driving recklessly, wildly, possibly from a bullet that struck the driver.

Before Shannon could confirm his position, the Dodge braked hard and Manny slammed into its trunk. His cell phone flew beneath the seat as his head hit the steering wheel, pain shooting deep into his injured face. Fresh sticky blood ran down his forehead and into his eyes. He brushed it away with his sleeve as he squinted to see the road in front of him.

The Dodge accelerated, dragging the front bumper of Manny's car with it. He hung the pistol out the window and pulled the trigger, but the slide was locked back: empty. He clawed at the inside of his jacket pocket for the spare magazine.

Manny pressed the magazine release and the empty clip dropped on the floorboard. He squeezed the gun tight between his legs and slapped the magazine into the butt of the weapon. With one hand, he hit the slide release while he wrestled the steering wheel, struggling to control his car. Pieces of his tire flew into the air and a chunk landed on the windshield, obscuring his vision for a moment before flying off.

The Dodge dropped over a hill and Manny came fast on brake lights. Someone rolled into the ditch just before the Dodge accelerated and pulled away from Manny.

On the first hill east of Oglala, three marked patrol cars blocked the road. One blocked the Route 18 and Route 33 intersection, while the other two cars set up a choke point to funnel the Dodge over hollow spike strips laid across the road. It drove over the strips and they flew violently in the air seconds before the two blocking patrol cars squealed tires and pursued. Manny slowed, driving around the spikes still laid across one lane, the thumpa-thump of a flat tire loud in his ears. He cleared the first curve a half mile farther, where the police had apprehended the driver, whose car had three of its four tires flattened.

Manny was careful to stay off the brakes as the steering wheel jerked in his hands to the side of the flat tire, and he stopped just before the police roadblock. He controlled the urge to run up to the shooter and screw the barrel of the Glock in his ear. He stepped out of his car and his legs shook. He leaned against the Taurus for support as he brushed shards of glass from his clothing. Cuts from tiny pieces of glass had peppered his face, and his cheek oozed blood from a dozen slices. A flap of skin hung from his ear like a grotesque earring, and the head wound from the steering wheel caused blood to stream into his eyes. *Shit. More stitches.*

He walked closer to the traffic stop. Over his PA system an officer commanded the shooter to toss his keys out the open window and thrust both hands out and step from the Dodge. Manny strained to see the man's face but it was covered by a hooded sweatshirt. As he walked to the sound of the officer's voice, the driver stumbled and fell. A shotgun slide chambered a round somewhere to Manny's left. Another officer scurried for safety behind his car door. The driver recovered and stood, holding one arm high and the other limp and bloody at his side. At least one of Manny's rounds had connected.

The driver obeyed the command to turn and verify he had no guns in his waistband. As his face turned to the bright police headlights, all Manny could tell at this distance was that he was Indian. He was handcuffed and strapped on a gurney attended by two paramedics from the ambulance service. A large officer dressed in the black Oglala Sioux Tribal uniform disappeared in back of the ambulance with the shooter. Willie.

A tribal officer approached Manny from the traffic stop. He shook his head and introduced himself as Robert Hollow Thunder. "Talk hereabouts is you got some bad luck, but the way I see it, you got some incredible good luck following you. Hit?"

Manny brushed glass shards from his collar and wiped fresh blood on his trousers. He checked himself and was grateful he hadn't pissed himself—he'd witnessed officers do that before under stress. That's all he needed, for Nathan Yellow Horse to print that Manny had messed his Dockers.

"I'm all right. Some glass cuts and my stitches busted out, but nothing that'll kill me. Can't say the same for my car." The shiny Hertz sticker was still intact on the fender, and for the first time, Manny noticed that the first bullet fired at him had taken out both the driver-side and the passenger-side windows. Two more bullets had struck his door but not penetrated. Manny would have the door taken apart later: He was certain the window and door lock mechanism had stopped the rounds and saved his life.

"Who's the shooter?" Manny asked.

Lumpy Looks Twice interrupted Hollow Thunder. He had parked his cruiser within feet of where they stood and walked over to them. Lumpy stood with his thumbs hooked into his gun belt as he spoke to Hollow Thunder, as if Manny weren't there.

"Get a wrecker on the way for this heap of shit." He jerked his thumb at Manny's car. "I want it impounded."

He turned to Manny as if he saw him for the first time. "We'll need to process your car, and your gun."

Manny grabbed Willie's Glock from the holster, and cleared the weapon before he handed it to Lumpy.

"Thought you didn't carry a gun."

"I reformed."

"Where'd you get this one? FBI doesn't issue Nines."

"The Gun Fairy put it under my pillow. Now get off my ass and do what you have to, Lumpy. I'm in no mood for your crap."

"You're just pissed 'cause us dumb-ass Skins out here in the sticks know something about law enforcement, like we know when to process a crime scene. Hertz will get that car back when we're done with it."

"Then you know there's also a secondary crime scene about eight miles back, where I was first shot at, that has to be processed, too."

"Step ahead of you. Already got a unit heading that direction to process. You'll never admit that we might just be the equal of you FBI here on the rez."

"Where's the shooter?"

"There. In custody."

"That's the driver. The car slowed and the shooter rolled out about a mile back. You might send some officers back there to look for him."

Lumpy grabbed his portable radio and barked orders for two more units to begin searching a mile east along the road. He turned to Manny. "Done. And I'll need a statement from you."

"I'll give you a statement if you'll drive me to the hospital to get checked out."

Lumpy agreed, and Manny reached through the shattered window, pieces of glass still in the frame catching his jacket and tearing the sleeve. He grabbed his briefcase before he climbed into Lumpy's cruiser. "Who's the driver?" Manny asked, as they followed the ambulance to the hospital.

"Kid by the name of Lenny Little Boy."

Manny knew that name well from his childhood, and from studying the violence on Pine Ridge in the 1970s. Frederick Little Boy from Gordon, Nebraska, had been an AIM instigator involved in the protest over Raymond Yellow Thunder's death in Gordon in 1972. Little Boy led a meeting at Billy Mills Hall in Pine Ridge, and the following day AIM descended on Gordon.

"Is he Fred Little Boy's kid?"

"He is. Or was. Fred was gunned down some years back south of Porcupine on a BIA traffic stop. Made the kid all the more hateful of law, especially federal cops. Seems like no one hereabouts likes you feds."

"That was a little before my time here."

"You wouldn't have done anything different if you were BIA back then." Lumpy spit out the window as if to punctuate his disdain. "While you had your fancy Washington, D.C., job, I was back here on the rez, doing what I could to help kids like Lenny."

"Doesn't seem like it's done much good."

"For every fifty kids that are flushed down the cesspool here, we manage to save one. But not Lenny. He just never had a real chance."

"I know I recognize that name from somewhere else."

Lumpy turned his head and smiled wide. "Lenny Little Boy is one of your brother Reuben's Heritage Kids." A snicker started at the corners of Lumpy's mouth, turning into raucous laughter. Manny would later remember that Lumpy laughed all the way to the hospital.

>◇◇◇<

Manny paced the ER waiting room while Lumpy interviewed Lenny. When they had first arrived at the emergency room, Lumpy blocked Manny from entering the examination room. "This is a tribal case, Hotshot. You can talk to him when I'm finished with him, after they patch up the leaks you put in him."

Manny had his own problems with fluid leakage. After nurses cleaned him up with carburetor cleaner or something as stinging, the ER doctor shuffled into the room with a gleam in his eye. He held the suture kit in front of him like he wanted Manny to know what was coming.

After the stitches, Manny poured a cup of lukewarm mop water from last week's complimentary coffeepot into a foam cup.

He usually drank it black, but this time he grabbed up packets of Sweet'N Low, then dropped them back. He felt too crappy to worry about his diet, and added two packs of raw sugar to his coffee. At least he'd feel good until the lidocaine in his head and pieced-together ear wore off.

He paced the waiting room, worried that Lumpy might foul up the interview and he wouldn't be able to get any information from Little Boy. Manny wanted to bust into the room, throw a full nelson on Lumpy as he did in their wrestling days, and toss him out. But Lumpy was right: The assault was a tribal case, and he had to sit this one out until he was allowed in.

Lumpy scowled when he walked into the waiting room, and Manny knew he'd had no luck with Little Boy.

"They put the kid in ICU. You were right about one thing: You hit him. Twice. A round that penetrated the trunk of the car grazed his thigh, and another hit his shoulder and fractured his scapula. If that had been me he was shooting at, I'd have drilled him right off, and there wouldn't be a need for a trial."

Manny ignored Lumpy's insult because he needed answers. "Why'd he want me dead?"

Lumpy shrugged. "Haven't the slightest. He invoked right off. Like most of your brother's delinquents, he has been through the system enough to know he doesn't have to talk."

"Then you have no objection if I try?"

Lumpy laughed. "Have at it. Lenny hates us tribal cops, but he hates you FBI even more."

When Lumpy turned on his heels to leave, Manny saw there was a silver lining to Lumpy's arrogance. The large but fading dark purple stain still covered the back of his neck, and it would still be visible for a few more days.

Manny tossed the rest of his coffee in the garbage can and walked into Lenny Little Boy's room. Willie stood guard over him, his lips pursed, his fists clenching and unclenching as he glared down at Little Boy. But when Willie spoke, his voice was controlled and deliberate.

"Lenny here won't say a thing," Willie said. "Not because he can't, but because he invoked his right to counsel."

"That so?"

A bandage covered a wound on Lenny's cheek, and he peeked around the gauze dressing. He tried sitting up and his sheet dropped off, revealing jailhouse tattoos, nebulous and indistinct, inked on the smooth skin of a lacquered casket across his chest and shoulders. All Manny had to do to read Lenny's record was study the tats.

Willie anticipated Manny's question. "The kid here resisted arrest," he said, motioning to Lenny's face. "Then resisted once or twice more when we got here, right after he invoked his Miranda rights."

Manny nodded and turned to him. "That so, Lenny? You invoke Miranda?"

"That's a fact, Mr. Agent Man. I got an attorney out of Hot Springs who'll chew you up if you violate my rights. And With Horn here for beating me."

"Fair enough," Manny answered.

He turned a chair around by the bed and rested his briefcase across his knees. He looked up at Willie and motioned for another chair. "Guard duty, huh?" he asked, ignoring Lenny.

Willie smiled. "I don't mind. Lenny might resist a time or two more before the night's up. Besides, you know what rolls downhill. I just happen to be the lowest Indian on the totem."

"I thought we Sioux didn't have totem poles?"

"Well, when we get around to having them, my face will be on the bottom."

A nurse walked into the room and scowled at them. She said nothing as she walked to Lenny's bed and checked his IV and dimmed a monitor before leaving. Manny waited until she left the room before speaking to Willie.

"I need a snitch. Now maybe Lenny here would like to be my eyes and ears while I'm here on the reservation."

Willie picked up on the ruse. "Well, the kid here tried to kill you for certain. But you think someone else has been hunting you besides Lenny and he might know who it is?"

Manny nodded. "Lenny could find out if he had a mind to."

"Go screw yourself. I ain't no snitch."

"Why, because you don't like the law?"

"Mostly."

"And maybe because you know what happens to snitches here on the reservation?"

Lenny forced a laugh. He grabbed his shoulder and winced. "You got that shit right. A snitch on the rez will last about as long as a case of Budweiser on a Saturday night."

"At least you know what's up here," Manny said, and turned to Willie. "I'll get you cleared to leave as soon as I talk to Lieutenant Looks Twice."

"You think he'll have someone relieve me so soon?" Willie looked at Manny with doubt in his eyes. He motioned to Lenny. "Someone's got to watch this turd."

"There'll be no need for you to stick around here after I talk to the lieutenant. As far as I'm concerned, Lenny here's a free man." Manny watched Lenny out of the corner of his good eye and waited until he had Lenny's attention. "I'm not prosecuting. I'll talk with your lieutenant about dropping the assault charges. Lenny of course will have running that roadblock hanging over his head, but with just that charge, he can walk out of the hospital a free man."

"Why?"

"If I don't press charges on him, what's that tell everyone

hereabouts, especially the other Heritage Kids? It tells them he cut a deal good enough that he's not being charged with assaulting a federal officer. Most folks would figure that would take some serious snitching."

"Bullshit!" Lenny shouted. He propped himself up on his pillow. He leaned forward and caught himself falling from the bed. "That's bullshit. No one will believe I told you anything."

"Lenny, Lenny," Manny said. "You know the only one reason you wouldn't be charged with attempted murder is because you cut a deal. Sang like a warbler. Folks will know that, and word will get around that you belong to me."

"But that's like sticking a shiv in me. I'd be killed for certain."

"Eventually," Manny answered. "After your friends have some fun with you." He stood and started for the door. He glanced back over his shoulder at Willie. "I'll get you out of here in a few minutes."

"Wait! At least give me a chance. What do you want to know?"

Manny faced him. "I can't ask you anything until that high-class lawyer from Hot Springs says you can."

"All right. I'll waive my rights, I'll talk. But maybe you could put in a word to the judge, tell him I cooperated."

"I don't know. You being a juvenile and all . . ."

"I'll be charged as an adult, right? You'll have to keep me locked up. Right?"

Manny nodded. "I'm sure with your record—and you being so close to eighteen—you could be tried in adult court."

Lenny nodded. "What do you want to know?"

"Let me get this straight. You'll tell me what I want to know—knowing full well that I'll charge you for the assault?"

"It beats the alternative of you guys finding me some morning lying in a ditch with a knife stuck in me."

Manny smiled and winked at Willie, then scooted a chair

close to the bed. He rested his briefcase back on his knees and took out his mini-recorder. After noting the time, date, place, and waiver of rights, he began his interview.

>◇◇◇<

Two hours later, Manny put his recorder and notes in his brief-case and stood, the interview concluded. He started to say something, then doubled over as the pain in his ribs throbbed with the exertion. Willie started for him, but Manny shook his head.

"I'll wait for you in the lobby," he said, and left the hospi-tal room. He knew only minutes remained on Willie's scheduled four-hour guard watch, and he started for the coffeepot. It was the same coffee as before. Something akin to river sludge floated on the surface—or had someone soaked his feet in it? He passed on the coffee as Willie headed toward him.

"I got my relief. Need a lift?"

"That was the idea." He followed Willie to the cruiser. Man-ny's muscles ached and he strained against the fresh pain in his head since the lidocaine had worn off, causing him to feel older than he should have as he fought to keep up with Willie. When they had started out of the parking lot, Willie turned to him.

"You really wouldn't have charged him?"

"Of course I would have." He found himself putting on his seat belt, something he seldom did, but he had been violently ed-ucated on the merits of buckling up since arriving on Pine Ridge. "Someone who tried as hard as Lenny did to kill me shouldn't be running around free. And even pled down, with federal sentenc-ing guidelines, that kid won't be out of the slammer before he's joined AARP."

On the way home, they talked about the reasons Lenny at-tacked Manny. Lenny knew Manny was on Pine Ridge inves-tigating the Red Cloud murder and he feared, as did many of

the Heritage Kids, that he would figure out that Reuben killed
Jason.

"Because Reuben didn't like Jason," Lenny had confessed.
"Reuben said Jason was an AIM turncoat, that Jason should
have stayed in the movement rather than sell out for the family
dollar. Reuben must have found him parked at Wounded Knee
that night. He must have killed Jason. I know I would have."

Manny believed Lenny would have killed Jason had he been
the one to find him that night. The Heritage Kids were a tight
group, with their hero worship of Reuben, and Lenny Little
Boy would have done whatever it took to protect Reuben, even
murder. Manny had pressed Lenny for other reasons he thought
Reuben had killed Jason. He finally blurted out that the morning
following the Red Cloud murder, Reuben showed up at the jobsite looking like hell, said he hadn't slept all night. When Lenny
heard of the murder, he knew it had been Reuben.

When Lenny told his big brother about his suspicions of Reuben, he and Jack concocted the ambush. They'd wait for Manny
to return from Rapid City. Lenny would drive while Jack did the
shooting.

"All they had for proof that Reuben killed Jason was that he
looked like he hadn't slept," Willie said. "That's a pretty flimsy
reason to try to kill you."

"Unless Lenny or Jack is Jason's killer."

"And they think we're close to finding out." Willie swerved to
avoid a cat in the road. "What better reason to want you dead.
They had access to that stolen truck, and both matched the description of your jogger that night."

"It's too pat." Manny adjusted the bandages on his hand.
Now they itched in time with the stitches in his scalp. "I think
Lenny actually believes Reuben killed Jason."

"Then why would he talk to us?"

"Honor."

"Of course. *Wayuonihan*. Lenny grew up in a traditional home, traditional values. Even though he's always been in trouble, in his mind it's dishonorable to snitch on your friends. Or your mentor. He'll slit your throat in good conscience, but not talk with the law. Unless he saw a chance to cut his losses, like maybe you'll go out of your way to plead with the judge for leniency."

"I'll talk to whatever judge is assigned," Manny said. "Like I promised. Tell him that Lenny spilled his guts." He massaged his hand. "Any luck on finding Jack?"

"None. We got the K9 out along 18. The dog alerted on Jack's bloody T-shirt in the ditch. That's the closest we came to finding him tonight."

They pulled into the housing area, and Willie stopped outside Manny's apartment. "Looks worse for your brother all the time."

"That it does." Manny's cheek itched fiercely from the glass cuts under the bandages and he resisted the urge to scratch. "But I know my brother well enough that if he thought I had him nailed for the Red Cloud murder, he'd kill me himself. Or maybe he put them up to it."

Willie faced Manny. "Reuben's a *wicasa wakan* now. That changes a man. Sacred men might feel they have to kill, but they wouldn't go around putting others up to doing the killing for them."

"Then you figure that Lenny told the truth about Reuben knowing nothing of this ambush tonight?"

Willie nodded. "I figure Lenny and Jack pulled this stunt all by their lonesome."

"And his denials about attacking me a couple nights ago outside my apartment? And the truck incident?"

"All true," Willie said. "At least with as little experience as I got, I figure Lenny and Jack did this without Reuben's knowledge, but I wouldn't rule out Jack on the others attacks. Either way, there's at least one other person roaming around the rez that wants you dead."

"Oh, thanks for that piece of good news." Manny opened the door and eased out.

"One other thing," Willie said. "Why do you think Jack loaded that six-gun with just five rounds?"

Manny bent down and peered into the car. "He's seen too many Westerns. Folks think Rugers are like the old Colts, that it's unsafe to load them with six, so they load five shells with the hammer on an empty chamber." Five, an odd number. *Five*. The same number of rounds found inside Billy Two Moons nearly thirty years ago. But the murder weapon was never found after Reuben tossed it. So how could Reuben have missed Two Moons with that sixth round within touching distance? Just one more question to ask his brother next time.

"Where do we go from here?" Willie asked before Manny shut the door.

"You might go to the post office tomorrow and check on Clifford Coyote. No one knows him, but he gets his mail there at least once a month. As for me, all I want to do is hit the rack and sleep for a long time. Even for us adventurous G-men"—he smiled—"it's not every day we're shot at."

"Well, you watch your backside. Jack's still out there and he'll be madder'n hell now that his brother's locked up."

Willie drove away, and Manny's arm felt for the Glock that wasn't there since Lumpy seized it. He'd gotten used to its bulk since at least one other person hereabouts wanted him dead. He checked the dark apartment before he entered, and hoped that whoever was after him would allow him one decent night's sleep.

Manny peeked around the corner of the building. Desirée's

apartment was dark, and it was late enough that he could tiptoe into his apartment without alerting her he was there.

He slipped the key in the lock. The door stuck and he nudged it with his shoulder, then stepped inside and eased it shut before he turned on the light. "That you darlin'?"

Desirée lay on the couch. A blanket over her that had fallen away revealed a bare waist. She stood and the blanket dropped to the floor, revealing all of Desirée in a lace camisole.

"What're you doing in here? How'd you get in?"

"Leon let me in. He said you might need someone to watch over you tonight to make sure your injuries didn't get any worse."

"You got to leave."

"It'll be like old times. We got a lot of catching up to do. And I'm not spoken for at the moment."

Manny backed out of the apartment and shut the door. The cool air hit him and he realized this nightmare was in real time, and he called Willie before he got too far away. "Got a spare couch in your apartment?"

"Desirée?"

"In the flesh."

"I'll be right there and get you. The last thing you need right now is to work out with her and get a heart attack."

CHAPTER 18

Manny rolled over on the couch and used his good arm to sit up. His ribs had stiffened sleeping on the hard hide-a-bed, with its metal slat jutting into his side all night. He stood to stretch his legs as he read Willie's note saying he would be back soon with breakfast burritos and coffee for them. Manny pulled the curtain back and squinted into the sun. A new Hertz rental had been dropped off sometime this morning.

Manny slipped his trousers on and hobbled outside to the car. Something attached to the steering wheel flapped when he opened the car door: a pleading note. *We're running out of cars!!!!! Be more careful!!!!!* He crumpled the note and went back inside Willie's apartment.

He hit the shower and had to put on the same clothes he'd worn last night, praying Desirée would be gone when he went back to his own apartment for fresh clothes. He walked back to the living room just as Willie came in. His jeans were as wrinkled as Chief Horn's face, and his T-shirt bore some dried food on the front. Willie had bags under his eyes, and he hadn't shaved today. He tossed the sack from Big Bat's on the table and dropped into a chair. His head drooped between his knees.

"You all right?"

"I don't know. I stopped at the post office after I picked up breakfast. I found out who rented that box under Clifford Coyote's name." Willie handed Manny a copy of a receipt dated January 2. "Elizabeth Comes Flying pays the box rent every year." He bent over in the chair and cradled his head in his hands. "She's been renting the box for Clifford Coyote for the past thirty-one years."

"Who's Elizabeth Comes Flying?" Manny sucked in a quick breath when he recognized his sister-in-law's maiden name. "Maybe she was doing him a favor."

"You really believe that?"

"I see your point. But who's Coyote?"

"There is no Clifford Coyote on the tribal books or in our system."

"Then Coyote's a bogus name?"

Willie nodded. "Georgette White Bird said Aunt Lizzy pays for the box every January. Aunt Lizzy got Georgette her first job at the post office, and Georgette doesn't ask any questions. She said Coyote gets one letter a month, and figures he drops by at night 'cause she's never seen him."

"Did you talk with Elizabeth about the post office box?"

"No. She left a note saying she and Rachael Thompson went shopping in Rapid again, but I got hold of Rachael, and she hasn't talked with Aunt Lizzy in a couple days. What do you make of her renting that post office box every month since 1976?"

"The reservation was embroiled with intrigue back then. Lots of things happened that year. Reuben was sent away for the Two Moons murder. Leonard Peltier killed Agents Coler and

Williams near Oglala. Anna Mae Pictou-Aqash was found shot in the back of the head and dumped off a cliff. Bodies littered the reservation when AIM and Wilson's men feuded in the years following the Wounded Knee takeover."

"But why do you think she rented that box under an assumed name?" Willie pleaded, as if Manny could pluck answers for anything right out of the clouds.

Manny shrugged. "The only reason someone receives monthly checks for that long is a house payment. Or blackmail."

"You mean Aunt Lizzy was blackmailing Jason and cashing his checks all these years?"

Manny sat and rubbed his head while he thought. "Clara told me Jason squandered his money. She discovered in the audit that he has been sending Clifford Coyote two thousand dollars every month. Hard to imagine Elizabeth blackmailing anyone, but she was active in AIM, and WARN. As an officer in Women of All Red Nations, she'd had access to inside information. Maybe she knew something that could damage Jason, or maybe she cashed that information in once he became sole owner of the Red Cloud Corporation."

"Jeeza. There's gotta be a logical explanation."

Manny knew Elizabeth was as important to Willie as Uncle Marion had been to him.

"There's got to be a good reason she rented a box under that name," Willie persisted. "We just have to find her and let her explain it. I'm going back to her house and wait for her. She's bound to return, then I can straighten this out. I just can't see Aunt Lizzy doing anything illegal."

Willie's face twisted in anguish. When the man Manny idolized toppled from his pedestal, he knew the sorrow Willie now experienced. Once, Manny believed Reuben could never have murdered anyone. He stood by that faith until Reuben confessed to killing Billy Two Moons. Now, Willie's world was turned upside down, and Manny knew that if Elizabeth were mixed up in anything illegal, her relationship with Willie would never be right again.

><><><

Willie called Manny's cell. "She's not back yet. She might've gotten wind we wanted to talk with her and wanted to avoid an embarrassing explanation."

"Do you work today?"

"Yes, swing shift. I'd better get cleaned up."

"I'll check her house later. If she shows, I'll give you a call."

Manny hung up the phone and headed for Martin. If anyone knew where Elizabeth was, Rachael Thompson would.

><><><

Asking Rachael to betray her friend shouldn't bother him, but it did. When he had arrived at Rachael's house, Manny played the concerned brother-in-law, asking about Elizabeth's well-being, worried since he hadn't talked with her today. Rachael hadn't seen her either, and they hadn't gone shopping today. Or three days ago, like Elizabeth claimed.

"Maybe she's running," Rachael said. "She's been training for this year's Black Hills Classic."

Manny recalled the running shorts hanging on the line that first day he visited her. She kept herself in top shape, and had looked as if she could run two marathons back-to-back. He left Rachael's house with her promise to call him if she heard from Elizabeth, and he started for her house.

It had been three hours since Willie left Elizabeth's house for work. Manny cleared the shelter belt and saw her Impala parked by the back door. Manny parked beside it and painfully stepped out. He used the handrail to step up on the deck. His ribs rubbed against the binding and sent sharp spasms of pain throughout his body, and his legs ached as much from driving the last hour as from the accident. He stretched against the house. Elizabeth's clothes were drying on the line: two pairs of running shorts and sports bras hung beside a set of paisley sheets.

He knocked on the door with his good hand, and rapped again before he poked his head inside. "Elizabeth, it's Manny." He stepped inside and strained his eyes to see in the dark. "Elizabeth?"

In the living room that smell drifted past his nose. *Lilac*. He smelled lilac the night his car was rammed, and lilac when his attacker checked if he was dead, lilac when Elizabeth visited him in the hospital, lilac when she helped him stand in her office. The smell grew stronger. Someone watched him. A corner lamp clicked on.

Elizabeth wore running clothes drenched in sweat, and held a gun leveled at Manny's midsection. Light bounced off dark eyes that held no emotion.

"Elizabeth. It's me."

"I know who it is."

"Then put that gun away."

"Can't do that." She took a step closer and raised a small revolver to his chest as she cocked the hammer. Manny's firearms training classes raced through his mind. He knew that the chances of surviving a single handgun shot was ninety percent. Unless the small .38 caliber held the hot +Ps, which would do more damage when they struck. If he rushed her and she shot him, he might survive, but he knew he wouldn't be able to cross the room before she got off a second shot, or a third. His ribs made it nearly impossible to breathe at times, and seeing out of only one eye made depth perception nonexistent. No, the odds were slim indeed that he could cross the room and disarm her before she pumped several slugs into him.

"What do you want, Elizabeth?"

"It's too late to have what I want." He listened to her voice as a trained interviewer would. She sounded hollow, one-dimensional, with no warmth in her voice. The Elizabeth he knew was gone. The woman he now faced was used to imposing her will on other people—and getting her way.

"I wanted you to leave the rez that first night. You got too close and I tried to scare you off. I waited for you outside your apartment, knowing that if I used a hammer then somebody else would be blamed, somebody like one of Reuben's little shithead Heritage Kids he's always defending. You deflected my blow just like I thought you might, rolled with the punch, but that was OK because I really didn't want to hurt you seriously. I just wanted you gone."

Manny's legs buckled, and he leaned against a chair. "But why?"

"Erica. You hung around and found out about Erica and Jason."

"Erica and Jason what?" Elizabeth's arm muscles tightened, and again he calculated his chances of rushing her. "Erica said there was nothing between them. They argued about Jason embezzling the tribe's money. Not about an affair."

"People will think the worst here on Pine Ridge. People always think the worst. They'll think you covered her involvement because she's your niece, and that would make us both look bad."

Manny still leaned against the chair and stretched his calf muscles, slowly. Too slowly. Stalling. Could he make it across the room?

"People will say she was in knee-deep with Jason on his scheme to bilk the tribe out of the money. Her reputation will be ruined, her marriage will be ruined, her life will be ruined, and they'll look at me like I put her up to it, and I'll be ruined, too."

Manny forced himself to stand upright, but his motions came

agonizingly slow. Was this the fight-or-flight syndrome his instructors spoke about? It was the flight option that appealed most to him as his eyes darted to the door. Could he make it before Elizabeth reacted?

"Think about what you're doing." Manny tried not to sound as if he was pleading. But he was. "Even if you kill me and get away with it, it'll stay with you the rest of your life."

"Like that would bother me," Elizabeth laughed. "Like I haven't had to kill before. After all, I was in AIM when I was young, remember. What's another body to bury somewhere?"

He watched her eyes. The telltale dilating of the pupils meant a shot was imminent, and he willed his muscles to relax, telling himself that tense muscles reacted slower. What were the odds of throwing himself away from the muzzle blast when it came? Elizabeth's knuckles whitened. Gun arm outstretched. Muzzle hole swallowing Manny's attention.

Someone shoved Manny hard from the side and he fell against a coffee table. Pain shot through his body as his ribs scraped his lungs, and he lay on the floor gasping for breath. Willie stood between him and Elizabeth. In the dim light, Willie's black OST uniform blended with the background, but his face seemed illuminated by an outside light.

"You can't do this, Aunt Lizzy."

Willie glanced down at Manny. "The techs identified Aunt Lizzy's prints from the stolen truck," he said to explain his presence.

"Nonsense! My prints aren't on file anywhere."

"You're wrong. Remember when you and the others were arrested in that Mount Rushmore occupation in 1971, the one time you were arrested and printed at booking."

Willie glanced down at Manny. "I hoped to make it back here before things got this bad."

"Step out of the way."

"You can't do this Aunt Lizzy."

"I have to. He'll ruin Erica with his investigation."

"He's only doing his job."

"Right. The FBI has always 'only done its job' here on the rez." Elizabeth shuffled to the side to aim at Manny. Willie stepped to shield him.

"Give me the gun."

"Erica's the only good thing that came out of my marriage to Reuben, and you want me to throw that away? And give up my finance officer position to boot? Never. Now move away."

Willie stepped toward Elizabeth. "And what am I? We're of the same *tiospaye*, you and I. What kind of person would I be if I allowed you to shame yourself by killing Manny? I won't let you do it. You'll have to shoot me first."

Willie took another step toward her, and the muzzle of the .38 drooped. Another step, and she dropped the gun. Willie draped an enormous arm around Elizabeth's shoulder and gently led her to his cruiser for the ride to jail.

>‹›‹›‹

"I owe you my life." Manny and Willie had just spent the last four hours in the interview room listening to Elizabeth rambling. Exhausted, they shared a pot of coffee in the OST break room. The night shift was out on patrol or taking calls, so they sat alone. "She would have shot me, you know."

Willie nodded. "I couldn't let her do that. Even though she raised me, I couldn't let her shoot you. I was only doing my job."

"That's right. He was just doing his job." Lumpy waddled through the doorway and grabbed a chair. He turned it around backward, and draped his portly arms over the back. "It looks like we solved the case of the truck stolen from Reuben's jobsite."

Lumpy looked happier over solving the stolen truck case than clearing both cases of assault, the hammer and the truck.

"I missed the signs," Willie said. "How could I have missed the signs?"

"Easy," Lumpy said. "Folks got used to seeing Elizabeth around. Sometimes running, sometimes doing things job-related. No one connected her." Manny detected a bit of humanity in Lumpy's voice as he tried to let Willie off the hook. "She was like the UPS delivery man no one sees because he's always there, or the wino that's always passed out along the curb. No one notices them after a while."

"He's right." Manny refilled their coffee, and poured Lumpy a cup as well. "We're just now getting reports that people saw her running to Reuben's jobsite. They saw her, but they didn't connect her with the stolen truck."

"The night she attacked Manny with the hammer, she ran into town," Lumpy added. "She always ran along the road, day or night, and people were used to seeing her."

Willie held his head. His eyes burned red from crying during the interview. Elizabeth was more his mother than his aunt, and she'd just confessed to attacking Manny with the hammer and trying to kill him by running him off the road in the stolen truck. His life would never be right again.

"But why the charade about shopping with Rachael Thompson?"

"Too easy to verify or refute," Manny suggested. "Elizabeth knew that no one would question Rachael Thompson. And no one did until I drove to Martin today and talked with her. As for the truck, Elizabeth knew—through you—that one or more of the Heritage Kids was suspected in the ambush at my apartment. What better way to misdirect than to make us think one of Reuben's kids stole the truck right off their own jobsite."

Willie's eyes dropped, but Manny was quick to prop him up. "It's not your fault. She fooled me, too. There's just no good news today."

"Don't be so sure," Lumpy said. He rose slowly and refilled his cup, then put the pot back on the burner without refilling theirs. "We matched the tires on Crazy George's car to those found at Jason's murder." He smirked as if vindicated for Manny's earlier implication about his own car tires.

"Any match with the latents?"

Lumpy frowned. "We lifted enough partials to know the driver didn't care if we found them or not. Just not enough points to ID anyone."

"Smudged?"

"Who knows, the evidence tech just couldn't pull enough points."

"Then do something for me," Manny asked. "Tomorrow, have your tech pull Jack and Lenny Little Boy's prints. Ricky Bell's, too. See if anything comes close to matching the prints found in Crazy George's car."

Lumpy nodded. "That I can do."

Manny stood and stretched, his exhaustion reaching a new level. "As for me, I've had about as much fun as I can stand for one night. Take me home, please."

On the way to Manny's apartment, Willie remained quiet, and Manny knew the guilt was gnawing at him. "You couldn't have stopped her. Elizabeth chose to do what she did."

"But I should have seen it coming." Willie stared out the window. "I told her everything we did these last few days. I might as well have given her my incident reports, passed my field notes to her. I trusted her. And she stabbed me in the back."

"She felt she had to protect Erica."

"Does Erica need protecting?"

"No," Manny answered instantly. "Elizabeth had it in her mind that Erica knew all along about the embezzlement of the tribe's funds, but when I talked with Erica about it, she hesitated. I plan to have one of the Rapid City agents reinterview her, but I'm certain Elizabeth had it all wrong about her own daughter."

"Do you think Aunt Lizzy knew there was no Clifford Coyote?" he said, barely audible.

Manny nodded. "She knows. When I confronted her about it, she hesitated. She admitted that the big fight with Jason in her office a week before he was killed was over Jason's demanding Coyote's physical address. She caught him rooting through her files trying to find it. He might have gotten it if she hadn't threatened him with the same gun she held on me. She knows. Jason sent Coyote checks to his Pine Ridge PO box all those years. Elizabeth picked up the checks and deposited them into her Edgemont Bank account, then drew cash. She knows who and where Clifford Coyote is, if he even exists. But we'll never break her down."

"What'll happen to her now?"

Willie had all but lost his family, and Manny wished he had words of comfort to give, but he had none. "She'll be psychiatrically evaluated. Her mental condition will preclude her from standing trial for the attempted murder charge and the assault charges, but she'll need help. The best you can do for her is to be there for her, despite her betrayal."

Tears formed at the corners of Willie's eyes, and Manny hurried to get out of the car. The last thing Willie needed right about now was for Manny to see him crying again.

>()()()<

Manny squinted in the dark and jabbed the key into the apartment lock. The door swung in, unlocked. Manny froze and strained to hear anything inside. Anger replaced fear as he realized Desirée may have used her key to get in again. She could be inside, waiting for him in some provocative pose.

Scraping noises came from the bedroom. Or was it crying?

He reached for the gun and cursed under his breath for letting it be seized after the chase. Manny crouched and pain tore through his chest as his breathing became increasingly labored. His hand felt for the light switch. Stopped. Whimpering came from the bedroom, pained whimpering, followed by muffled sounds.

Manny groped in the dark and his hand found the upright ashtray made from an old aluminum piston, and he silently thanked Lumpy for furnishing the apartment in Old-West-slum. He hefted it close to the base, felt the power he could wield. He duckwalked toward the bedroom, and his foot kicked the coffee table. A woman cried from behind the closed door. Manny stood and his hand found the light switch just as someone rushed him. Light reflected off a knife thrust at his throat. Manny jerked back and swung the ashtray as light flooded the room. The piston glanced off Jack Little Boy's shoulder, and he staggered before he disappeared outside.

Manny hobbled to the door and peeked around the corner. Jack was gone, but crying rose from the bedroom again. He eased himself along the wall and buttonhooked the door. Desirée Chasing Hawk lay on the bed, her hands tied with sash cord, and duct tape held a pair of Manny's socks in her mouth. He ran to her and peeled the tape from her mouth and untied the cord that bound her hands.

She threw her arms around him, and he gently pulled her away to examine her injuries. One of her eyes had closed shut from swelling, and her lower lip protruded where blood pooled from a blow. "He said he'd kill me if I made any noise."

Manny eased Desirée back on the bed. He called 911 before he grabbed a cool, wet washcloth and began dabbing at her lip and eye. "He was going to kill you."

"Tell me later, after the EMTs transport you to the hospital."

"No!" She snatched the cloth away. "He's crazy and I need to tell you this. He wants you bad." She brushed hair out of her eyes and wiped her bloody nose with the back of her hand. "I used the key Leon gave me to come in tonight. I looked real good. Had my hair fixed. Makeup just right. Though you wouldn't know it now."

Manny smiled. "You look just fine."

She winced in pain as she forced a smile. "As soon as I flipped on the light, he grabbed me. He was waiting here for you with that damned big knife. And for sport I guess he passed the time working me over. Way I figure it, he'd have killed us both and been off the rez before our bodies were found."

Manny nodded as sirens approached. "We'll get him. What you gotta do now is get better."

"But he'll come after me again." Desirée sobbed and buried her face in Manny's shoulder. "I'm afraid."

"I'll get Lumpy to post a guard at the hospital. We'll find him."

An EMT burst through the door toting his jump bag. He glanced at Manny in passing as he pushed him aside, and he knelt beside Desirée and started assessing her injuries as another EMT maneuvered a gurney through the door.

Manny used the edge of the coffee table to stand, and he watched as Desirée squirmed when the EMT prodded her for injuries. Yesterday she was a manipulating, conniving woman who wanted to wrap Manny around her little finger and get whatever she wanted from him. Now she lay as a victim in need of his empathy. And his concern.

CHAPTER 19

Manny dreamed of days on Pine Ridge when he was a boy, and days of the Lakota before he was born, when all a warrior had to worry about was where to store all his surplus buffalo meat for the winter, or when he would next count coup on a Crow or Pawnee.

Then the figure that had haunted his vision reappeared and beckoned with his bony hand. Manny knew that following the dream figure could be dangerous, even fatal. The spirit of the man who taunted him yet lived, and this *wanagi* would do what he could to entice Manny into the dark part of the afterworld where he didn't want to go.

Danger followed the spirit, but the warrior lured him to crawl from his dream bed and go with him. Manny took two steps when his cell phone rang. He startled awake, sweat dripping from his nose and his face, and he fumbled for the phone on the nightstand.

"Bob Andrews here. Minneapolis Office." It took a moment for Manny to clear his head and connect Andrews to the homi-

cide investigation. After the "Alex" letter Clara had given him
had been processed for prints, Manny sent out an Attempt To
Locate for matching prints to FBI field offices in the five-state
region. "We've got a positive match on your latents. They came
back to an Alex Jumping Bull."

Chief Horn thought that Alex Jumping Bull might still be
alive, that he might have fled the reservation when Reuben killed
Billy Two Moons. This might be the same Alex Jumping Bull,
alive and not murdered that night with Two Moons. Manny just
didn't believe in coincidences.

"What kind of contacts you have with Jumping Bull?"

"Nothing since 1984," Andrews answered. "It's just dumb
luck that a set of majors was sent in back then by the Hennepin
County SO. Jumping Bull was arrested on a public intox charge
where he told the booking officer he was Clifford Coyote. The
detention officers got hinked by the way he acted, evasive when
they asked him standard intake questions. They thought there
was more to Mr. Coyote than what he was telling them so they
rolled additional prints."

"So Clifford Coyote is an alias for Alex Jumping Bull?"
Manny asked as he realized his question had already been answered. "Can you put the grab on him?"

Andrews chuckled. "I can, but it would be a mighty cold grab.
He was found shot to death in a south Minneapolis apartment."

"When?"

"Two weeks ago. Coyote, or Jumping Bull, lived in a flea pad
among other dregs. One of the upstairs tenants heard shots, but
the meth-head was tweaking at the time and waited until he'd
wound down to call the Minneapolis PD. He told them Jumping
Bull had been shot five times."

"Certain about the number of shots?"

"Quite. The witness is a Gulf War veteran. Meth-head or not, he knows his weapons. He said he thought it was so odd that the killer shot five times."

"Odd in what way?" Manny asked, somehow feeling he knew that answer, too. He always thought it was odd that Billy Two Moons had been shot five times, not six as Reuben claimed, just as he thought it was odd that Little Boy had loaded his revolver with only five rounds the night he attacked Manny. *What the hell, did everybody count their rounds with their toes?*

"He thought it was strange that the guy didn't shoot six times. Six-shooters are a lot more common than the five-shot revolvers. And if he was shooting an auto, there'd have been a lot more rounds fired."

"Maybe the shooter used something like a Chief's Special .38," Manny said, thinking back to Elizabeth's snubbie. "Maybe a Charter Arms. Something that's designed to hold five rounds."

"No. The ME dug .45 caliber slugs out of Jumping Bull."

"What kind of .45?"

"What's that?"

"The round, what kind of .45 slug? Was it a ball round? Lead? What was the exact diameter of the bullet?"

Andrews said he didn't know, but promised to fax Manny a ballistics report at the OST Office when he had the answers.

Manny remained on the line for one more surprise from Andrews: Alex Jumping Bull was murdered the same weekend that Jason Red Cloud flew to Minneapolis.

>‹›‹›‹

Manny held the car door open for Clara. She slid into the seat and fastened her seat belt even before shutting the door, and read his questioning glance. "Because if you don't wreck your cars, someone else does it for you."

"Can't argue there." Manny buckled his own seat belt before starting for Rapid City Regional Airport. Between his crappy driving and people trying to kill him, a little insurance in the form of a thin web strap couldn't hurt. "Tell me about Jason's flying phobia."

"He abhorred flying," she began as they left the Red Cloud building. "He'd start shaking just talking about it." By the time they had cut through Rapid Valley on their way to the airport, she'd convinced Manny that Jason had not flown to Minneapolis the weekend Alex Jumping Bull was murdered.

"You're certain he didn't catch a bout of brave just one time?"

She shook her head and winked. "Jason wouldn't mind me opening his mail just this once." She took an envelope from her handbag. It was a receipt from the Crook County, Wyoming, Clerk of Court for a ninety-eight-dollar speeding ticket on I-90 just out of Devils Tower. "Jason got the ticket the Saturday that he should have been in Minneapolis."

"In law enforcement," Manny grinned, "we call that a clue."

Clara grinned back, a wry smile that melted Manny's thoughts, and he turned his attention to his driving.

They pulled into the airport and followed the signs to Business Voyages Charter Flights. An elderly couple waited in a small lounge, while a young receptionist greeted them from behind a service counter. "And you wish to go where today?"

Manny was tempted to tell her back to Quantico before he lost his instructor's slot, but he kept it to himself and showed her his ID and badge. "He would have flown out that Friday evening on one of your charters."

"I remember him," the receptionist said. She sat in front of a computer terminal. "Mr. Red Cloud flew out of here that Friday at 2:24 in the afternoon."

"Alone?"

"Oh, yes. He insisted he wanted no company on the trip. After all, he did charter the flight."

"Are you certain it was Jason Red Cloud?"

She stepped back, her poker face faded, and anger replaced her congeniality. "Of course I'm sure. When he called, he paid by credit card."

"Company?"

"Personal card. When he arrived here, I insisted on the verification number, which he gave me."

"Could you please describe Mr. Red Cloud," Clara said.

The receptionist warmed to Clara, and turned her back on Manny as she spoke. She described a man shorter than Jason, stocky, but in shape. "I heard so much about Mr. Red Cloud, I thought he'd be a much older man."

"Is this him?" Clara handed her a publicity photo of Jason. The picture was of a younger, thinner Jason Red Cloud, wearing a fringed buckskin jacket and beaded headband that held his long braids together.

The receptionist shook her head. "No. That's not him."

Manny threw Clara an "I-told-you-so" glance. "Could the man flying as Jason Red Cloud have gotten a gun on the plane?"

The girl scowled. "He did. Mr. Red Cloud had some Indian artifacts he was taking to Minneapolis for a museum loan. Among the items was an old cavalry Colt he claimed was used at Wounded Knee in 1890, but it didn't work."

"How do you know it didn't work?"

"He told me. He said it was too old to shoot, so I let him have it on the flight with the other items."

"Anything else you can think of about the man who posed as Jason Red Cloud?" Manny asked.

The girl looked to the ceiling for a moment. "Not much. Unless you think it would be important that he looked like a weight lifter. And had a pronounced limp to one side."

"Good God!" Manny led Clara out of Business Voyages. He dialed Harold Soske as he shuffled to his car.

>‹›‹›‹›‹

Manny didn't object when Clara took the elevator to the Red Cloud Development floor. She led Manny through the outer office and into Jason's office. "You're certain of this?"

"Pretty sure. Ricky Bell fit the receptionist's description, and Soske confirmed that Bell has a pronounced limp from a prison fight."

By the time Clara found the key and unlocked the sliding door on the display case, Manny had put on latex gloves. He reached into the case and took the Colt Army revolver from the wooden peg holding it to the wall. He stepped away from the case and held the gun to his nose, then held it for Clara to sniff.

She drew back. "I don't much know guns, but this thing's been fired recently, long after Chief Red Cloud owned it. But how's that possible? It's been hanging here since I've worked for Jason."

"That Gulf War vet living above Alex Jumping Bull in Minneapolis heard five shots that night. Five shots, which he thought was odd, and I did, too."

"But this is a six-shooter," Clara said. "If someone would have used the gun, they would have shot six times, not five."

Manny shook his head. "These Colts, even the ones manufactured today, have no hammer block to prevent an accidental discharge. People who know guns load these with only five, leaving the cylinder under the hammer empty in case it's dropped or caught on something. Ballistics will find only five chambers recently fouled on this gun. I'm certain."

Manny folded the top of a paper sack around the gun. "I'll

call you." He kissed Clara on the cheek and left before she spotted his embarrassment.

>‹›‹›‹

Manny met Detective Soske at the Pennington County Detention Center. "Ricky Bell's in interview room one." He led the way down the long corridor and unlocked the door. "I'll be outside if you need anything."

Bell sat with the legs of his chair tilted back. He met Manny's gaze, then dropped his chair down, his muscular arms remaining crossed, and he mustered defiance as he spoke. "I told you everything I know."

"About the burglary, not the murder."

Bell sat upright. "What murder, Jason's? You can't pin that on me."

Manny didn't answer, but placed his briefcase on the table and opened it.

"What kind of crap is this?" Bell's voice raised an octave.

Manny placed his recorder on the table, and dropped a manila envelope beside it. He noted the time, date, location, and that he'd read Bell his Miranda rights. When he was finished, he made a little tent with his fingers and sat looking over his hands at Bell.

"I didn't kill Jason."

"Why should I believe you? You had every reason not to trust him. After all, he arranged for you to fly to Minneapolis and kill Clifford Coyote. 'Alex Jumping Bull' to you. If Jason would have talked, you'd be looking at life in Stillwater."

Bell slumped in his chair looking like a balloon that had just been pricked with a needle when Manny mentioned Alex Jumping Bull. He looked down at the floor as he spoke. "What bullshit is this?"

"You got this huge problem, Richard. You tell me what I want to know, and I let Minnesota have your young ass on a state murder charge. You might cop a plea to second degree if you're lucky, out in ten. You jerk me around and make me work for this, and I'll see you're charged federally for Jumping Bull's murder. And federal sentencing guidelines what they are, you won't see the light of day until you're too decrepit for Social Security."

Bell fidgeted in his chair. "I don't know what you're talking about."

Manny opened the manila envelope and slid photos across the table to Bell. "You'll recognize that old Colt: It killed Jumping Bull, and it has your prints all over it."

"Of course it does, I'm the janitor. I clean Jason's office every night."

Manny ignored him, and grabbed a photocopy of the flight agreement with Business Voyages. "You took a charter out of Rapid under Jason's name. The receptionist identified you from your booking photo," he lied. "She remembers checking that gun with the other artifacts. And one of our Minneapolis agents found a witness watching you coming out of Jumping Bull's apartment right after you shot him," he lied again. "What you got to say, Richard?"

Bell remained silent. Manny rapped loudly on the door, and Soske opened the door. "Take him back to the cell block. I'm going federal with him."

"Wait." Bell's shoulders drooped and he slumped in his chair. "I got nowhere to go, but I sure don't want to end up in a federal slammer for the rest of my life. What kind of deal you giving me?"

"I don't deal," Manny said. "That's the prosecutor's job, but I got a lot to say about which jurisdiction hears a case. I can recommend to the U.S. Attorney that we decline the Jumping Bull murder and remand it to state court, at which time Minnesota tries you. But I guarantee, Stillwater is whole lot softer time than Leavenworth."

Bell sighed and picked up the photo of the Colt pistol. He nodded slightly, resigned, and answered Manny's questions.

>‹›‹›‹

Manny emerged from the interview room and forced a smile. Clara paced the police department lobby as she clutched an empty foam cup. A dry, dark stain that matched her scowl trickled down one side of the cup.

"Three hours." She tossed her cup in a round file. "You really know how to show a girl a good time. I can only read so many *Sports Illustrated* and *American Rifleman*." She nodded to the magazine rack beside the chairs in the waiting room.

"Bell started singing. His voice just mesmerized me, I guess."

She laughed. A curl fell across her forehead and she brushed it out of the way. "That's the biggest bunch of cock-and-bull I've ever heard." She grabbed Manny's arm. "But I know you have a job to do." She led him out of the lobby to his car, where she suggested they find a quiet place to eat.

>‹›‹›‹

"What did he say?" She slid into the seat beside him. Manny noted that her faith in his driving hadn't improved as she fastened her seat belt. "Did he admit killing Jumping Bull?"

"Finally. Jason bought Bell a ticket to Minneapolis under his name. He knew Business Voyages was just scraping by and the charter could only get down-and-outers to work there, desperate people that needed a job, people who wouldn't know Jason Red Cloud from Chief Red Cloud if they both came through their boarding line. He didn't figure on that receptionist having such a good memory about one passenger flying as Jason Red Cloud."

Manny pulled into the Millstone Restaurant. Clara locked her arm in his, and he felt at peace with her beside him. The hour was late, the patrons few, and they had a secluded corner table to themselves. The waitress handed them menus, explained the day's specials, and left.

"Jason called him into his office late one night. He paid Bell the money he owed him for stealing the artifacts from the Prairie Edge, and they started drinking."

"So that's what that was. One morning a couple weeks ago, Emily found a whiskey bottle in the trash. Jason said he thought the janitor had been drinking when he was supposed to be working. I was going to call Bell in and confront him, fire him if he admitted it, but Jason told me to forget it."

"That makes sense. Bell said they drank heavily that night. He'd seen Jason drunk before, but nothing like that. Jason rambled on about the resort, and how he had to fool the tribe just a bit longer. He ranted on about Elizabeth and Reuben, and smashed a whiskey bottle against the wall. He yelled that Elizabeth and Reuben still loved one another. He was furious."

"So all this time, Elizabeth and Reuben have been having a relationship?"

Manny shrugged. He waited until the waitress brought their salads and left. "That's what I'll have to ask Elizabeth about, if she'll talk to me again. If that's true, then everything I told Willie has been going to Elizabeth, and from there straight to Reuben."

"Don't blame Willie. I get good vibes from him. He's a good officer. He trusted Elizabeth implicitly, being family and all."

Manny swallowed both his pride and a sip of the iced tea. "I know it wasn't his fault."

Clara peeled a plastic wrapper from a cracker. "When did Jason hire Bell to kill Jumping Bull?"

"That night. They'd drunk their first bottle and were well

into their second bottle of Johnny Walker when Jason threw out the offer of big money. More money than Bell had ever seen. Five thousand dollars. 'Who do I have to kill for that kind of green?' he asked—joking, according to Bell. 'Alex Jumping Bull,' Jason shot back, and they struck the deal then and there."

Clara held up her hand and waited until she had swallowed before speaking. "With Jason's finances as bad as they were, he didn't have that kind of cash. I know. Where did he get it?"

"He didn't. Jason agreed to pay Bell when he returned from Minneapolis, after Jason was certain that Jumping Bull was dead, but Jason never paid up. He claimed that he couldn't get confirmation that Jumping Bull was dead."

"And Jason's gun?"

Manny stared into Clara's eyes. He took in the essence of her perfume while he admired her beauty from across the table. Had he been stalling this last week? Was he certain he wanted to leave Pine Ridge as soon as this investigation was over?

"The gun?" she repeated.

"When he told Jason he didn't own a gun, Jason unlocked the display case and grabbed the Colt. Bell said the thing looked like a museum piece too old to shoot. But Jason assured him it could, said he'd used it before, so he knew it would work. Jason explained how to get it through check-in at Business Voyages, and told him to pack some cheap imitation artifacts with the gun."

"But what did he do when Jason didn't pay him?"

"He thought Jason was stalling and confronted him."

"Overlooking Wounded Knee perhaps?"

Manny shrugged. "Bell had every reason to kill Jason. He owed Bell for a murder that could put the kid away if he pushed too hard for the money. Bell stole the artifacts, and he could have been the one that returned them to the Prairie Edge after he killed Jason. Remember, Bell's prints were all over the war club. With his temper, he could have killed Jason with no more than a thought."

"But if he used that old Colt to kill Jumping Bull, why would he go to the trouble, and danger, of killing Jason with that war club? He could have shot Jason with the same gun as he used on Jumping Bull."

"That's just what I thought, and I asked him about it. He said he knew nothing about Jason's murder. He claims he was in Sturgis at the time scoring an eight-ball of crystal meth from some chick. When I suggested that he met Jason that night, and the war club made it a murder of opportunity, he stuck by his story. And he stuck by his claim that he put the Colt back in the display case after he came back from Minneapolis and hasn't touched it since."

"But he could have gotten it back out again."

"If he planned on meeting Jason with the specific intent of killing him."

"Then he must be telling the truth," Clara said. "If he admitted to killing Alex Jumping Bull, admitting to killing Jason wouldn't make much difference."

"But it would. He can work a deal with Minnesota prosecutors for Jumping Bull's homicide, hold out for second-degree murder, manslaughter if he's lucky, catch an eight- to ten-year sentence, out in four. If he cops to Jason's murder, he faces federal murder charges on a reservation and lethal injection is likely."

"Then we're right back where we began."

Manny thought that sounded good: He and Clara on this case together, at least in her mind.

"No, we're way ahead. We know Jumping Bull had something on Jason big enough that Jason hired Bell to kill him."

"Sure." Clara laughed, nearly choking on her coffee. "Now all we have to do is ask Alex Jumping Bull."

Manny grinned. "Too late for him, but I can talk with a man who might know of these things, a genuine sacred man who can hot-wire me to the spirits."

"Your brother?"

"Who else," Manny answered, and started on his prime rib.

>‹›‹›‹

They talked long after their meal was finished, oblivious to anyone else who might have remained in the restaurant. Manny lost himself in Clara's soothing voice that took away the stress of completing the investigation, the stress of planning on seeing Reuben once again, the stress of worrying about losing his academy instructor's slot.

"Elizabeth doesn't much like you."

"That's an understatement." Clara sipped her afterdinner wine. "She loathes me."

"You and she have words or something?"

"'Or something' is close. I accompanied Jason down to Pine Ridge the first few times he drove there to set up his contacts for the project. Between us, we knew most people and convinced a lot of folks to at least hear Jason out."

"And that angered Elizabeth?"

Clara scooted her chair closer. Her perfume intermingled with the aroma of the wine. Manny was getting giddy and he hadn't even drunk anything. "She was the finance officer. Powerful position on the reservation. She felt people would think less of her when they realized a couple outsiders like Jason and me had success with getting land lined up for the project. Jason picked up on that, too, and he stopped having me come with him. He needed to get in tight with Elizabeth."

Manny became aware that two waitresses and the maître d' stood beside their table, checking their watches repeatedly. "It looks like we have to leave."

"Do we?" Clara asked. "It's not often I get the chance to have an intelligent conversation with a charming man."

Manny's face warmed and he nodded in the direction of the waitresses. "I think it's past their closing time."

Clara glanced over her shoulder and sighed. "I suppose they're right. It is late."

"And I have a long drive back to Pine Ridge."

Now it was Clara's turn to check her watch. "Drive this time of night? There's all sorts of things you could hit at night out there. The road isn't safe for you in daylight. You have to stay over."

Manny shrugged. "You're right. In the daylight on good roads it's iffy whether I could get back without wrecking my car. I'll grab a room here in Rapid for the night."

"You will not. You can stay with me."

Manny's eyebrows arched of their own volition.

"I mean, I have a guest room," she sputtered. "You're welcome to it for the night."

"I have per diem." Manny was unsure what else to say, though he was finding it difficult to argue with her.

"We can save the good taxpayers of the United States money if you accept my offer."

He struggled hard for a logical reason not to go with her. It was late at night in the middle of tourist season, and it would be hard to find a room at a decent motel. If he stayed anywhere, he would like the Alex Johnson, but that was always packed this time of year. He had an overnight bag in the backseat that experience taught him to always carry in case he got stranded, which happened often in his line of work. And it was true that he would save the government money for a motel room. "I guess it would make more sense to accept your offer."

They left the Millstone, and Manny's mind drifted between a vague fantasy of what would happen once they arrived at her home and the directions she was giving him. Clara lived on Sky-line Drive in a ranch-style three-bedroom with a view overlooking Rapid City. He parked in the driveway long enough for her to grab her keys from her purse and go inside. The whir of the garage door opening echoed off the hills.

"Pull it in here."

Manny looked at the garage doubtfully, then reasoned that even he could park in an empty three-car garage, and eased in until Clara held up her hand. He grabbed his overnight bag and followed her into the house.

She adjusted kitchen and living room lights with a remote as she nodded to the couch. "Make yourself at home." Cupboard doors banged from the kitchen, and he peeked around the corner. She put water in a measuring cup and heated it in the microwave. "One Sweet'N Low?" she called from the kitchen.

"You remembered."

"How could I forget."

She came out with two cups of tea and sat on the couch beside him. "Do you think you'll have Jason's homicide solved soon?"

Manny read concern in her eyes. Or disappointment. He wasn't sure. What he was sure of was that he wasn't certain he wanted go back to Quantico after all.

"I'm close," he said abruptly.

"Then you have new leads?"

"No."

"Then how do you know?"

Manny knew from a hundred other investigations that he had all the information he needed to find the killer, he just had to put it all together. "Just a feeling."

"Then you'll leave and go back to Virginia in time for the next academy class?"

Manny nodded. "Have you ever been there?"

Clara shook her head. "I'm just a Western hick."

"Then maybe you could go back with me. I have extra rooms, too. There's so much to see. So much you could experience . . ."

"I'd be like a female Crocodile Dundee." She forced a smile. "If I'd ever get to the city, I'm afraid I'd wither and fall to pieces. I'm not sure if I could take all that commotion. Besides"—she frowned—"I'd worry about you even more, with crime the way it is back there. I don't have any right to be, but I'm uncomfortable with you having the job of solving these types of crimes. The danger . . ."

"I've been attacked more in this one trip on Pine Ridge than I ever was in the D.C. area."

"I'll keep that in mind."

After they finished their tea, Clara stood and took his hand. She led him down a short hallway. "Your room," she said. A double bed was fitted with sheets depicting a prairie scene. A mission oak dresser matched the headboard. Manny estimated the set to be at least a hundred years old.

Above the dresser an oval mirror hovered, secured between two uprights that allowed it to tilt. As Manny hoisted his overnight bag on the dresser, he noticed his reflection. Heavy bags had formed under his eyes, and he appeared to have aged ten years in the ten days since returning to Pine Ridge. "I need to splash some water in my face or something," he said.

"In back of you. Your bath."

He saw it in the mirror and turned to face her. "Thank you for the room. And for the evening. I needed to wind down a little."

She laughed. "I should be thanking you. It's been a long time since I thought of a man other than in a business sense."

Manny felt his face flush again, but Clara didn't give him time to recover. She took his face in her hands, and drew him close. Her lips brushed his, then she kissed him. He kissed her back, reveling in the softness of her skin, in her perfume that seemed to draw them together. Then they both eased back a step.

"Whew," Clara looked wide-eyed like a schoolgirl just caught with the town Romeo in back of the barn. "I could get carried away."

"Me, too."

She smiled. "Yes, some day. Now we both have to get some shut-eye."

"Good night." Manny watched the sway of her hips as she walked away from him. He turned to his overnight bag and grabbed his toothpaste. As he started for his bathroom, he thought that, in the morning, he would shave especially close. Just for Clara.

><><><><

Manny fell asleep the moment his head hit the pillow. His mind wandered and drifted, his body detached from his mind. He was reliving the vision from his sweat with Reuben, when a distant familiar voice called faintly to him. Manny tried to open his eyes when the hollow voice talked to him, and he probed the recesses of his mind for the origin.

The mist faded, and a figure appeared blanketed by fog. The *wanagi*. The ghost of someone recently dead beckoned him. In the recesses of his memory, Unc told him that should he ever encounter a *wanagi*, he had to run. Run—not walk—away, because the ghost, the soul of the dead, wants company and will do whatever it takes to trick the living into joining him. Manny couldn't fight the pull, couldn't fight his mind following the *wanagi* south toward the Spirit Road.

A face appeared for a brief moment in this indeterminate time, a face he would never forget. A face etched in his memory. In a crime scene photo. Jason Red Cloud's face was contorted. Gruesome. A war club dripping blood and brain matter protruded from his skull. Manny followed him, now running to catch up, but Jason's *wanagi* remained just out of reach. Manny called, stretching out his hands, almost touching the vision. Crying. Crying. Crying for that vision that eluded him as a boy. Breaths came in great heaves in his chest. Manny's heart raced at the *wanagi*'s presence, yet he cried out a final time. "Wait!"

Manny felt himself being pulled back to the here and now. The *wanagi* grew fainter in the distance, and Manny gasped as someone shook him roughly by the shoulders. "Manny!" Clara shouted. "Manny, wake up."

He reached a final time for the *wanagi* as it melted into the mist. His eyes fluttered open. Clara sat on the bed, bent over him, shaking him. "Manny!"

He coughed hard, fighting to normalize his breathing, and the intense pain from his cracked ribs helped to bring him back. His bounding heart threatened to burst from his chest, and for once he was grateful that he had quit smoking. "I'm awake." He gulped and tried to sit up, but fell back down on the bed.

Clara put her hand behind his back and helped him sit, then propped a pillow behind his neck. "You had some kind of nightmare, but it's all right now."

"Yes. Some kind of nightmare." He wanted to leave it there, but he began telling Clara about his vision, about the many times he had seen the apparition, when he had not known the spirit or what it wanted from him. He told her he now knew it was Jason's *wanagi* that kept appearing in his dreams.

"He'll leave me alone once I solve his murder. I know that now." Manny had to solve this homicide, for a reason more important than any Niles could dangle in front of him. Jason's *wanagi*, and his wandering soul, made it personal.

Clara walked to the bathroom and soon she returned with a cool washcloth. She ran it over Manny's sweating face and neck. "Did he give you anything that might help your case?"

Manny thought of that for the first time. Unc taught him the old Lakota ways, about teachings in a time that most Oglala forgot or chose to forget. "Jason died unexpectedly, and no one performed the *Wanagi Yuhapi* for him, the Ghost Keeping ceremony. The fact that he still lingers here tells me someone wept for him, someone prayed for him."

"But who would do that? Jason had no family, no friends."

"Even the bandit has his confessor," he quoted an old Welsh saying. "Someone must have felt some pity for him."

Clara nodded as she put the washcloth on the nightstand, then shut off the light. She lay on the bed beside Manny and held him. What was absent now was the stirring in the loins, as the Big Bellies had a way of saying, and Manny felt content to be cradled in Clara's arms, and to drift off to a dreamless sleep.

CHAPTER 20

Willie closed the break-room door. He grabbed a chair and sat backward, his arms threatening to rip his uniform shirt. "You're asking a lot. I feel like I'm betraying my entire family."

"I know how you feel, but we need that information and Elizabeth won't talk to me. You heard her the last time we spoke in that interview." Anger in Elizabeth's voice had cut him short with resentments going back farther than Manny realized, and he knew she wouldn't talk with him again.

Willie reached over to the coffeepot and emptied the dregs into a ROSEBUD POWWOW cup. It flowed so slowly that it appeared curdled, but Willie drank it without mention as he stared at the floor. "Why would she tell me? If she's kept quiet all these years about Jason paying Alex Jumping Bull, aka Clifford Coyote, she'll clam up on me, too. She knows honor is important, even more than loyalty to one's *tiospaye*. She knows it would be my duty to report what she said. She knows I would."

Manny paced the room. "Nothing she tells you will affect her outcome. She knows that as well. After her psych eval, she'll be ruled incompetent to stand trial. This is her chance to get everything off her chest. If the question is posed in the right way."

Willie drank the rest of his coffee and wiped a hand across his lips. "All right. I'll do what I can."

"I know you will," Manny smiled. "Did you get a chance to check in with Desirée?"

"She'll be all right. The lieutenant put a guard on her after they admitted her to the hospital. He talked with her for quite a while today. Guess she's still scared to death of Jack Little Boy."

"Any word of him?"

Willie shook his head and his hand dropped to his gun as if he expected Jack to come into the room at any moment. "We've been hunting him, but there's still enough AIM sympathizers living here that'll hide him out if they figure he's got a hard-on for an FBI agent."

"Guess you guys are doing all you can. Now tell me what you found out about the murders here in the 1970s."

"Not much. Sixty-odd murders here on the rez in the three years following the AIM occupation of Wounded Knee. AIM blamed Wilson's goons, and Wilson's men pointed the finger at AIM. Most victims were killed by gunshot, but just one with a .45. Ballistics showed the slug measured .451 inches. A .45 auto round, not one from an old Army Colt. You still think Jason might have used that gun to kill someone here before?"

"I don't know what to think. From what Clara said, Jason might have been a real horse's ass, but he wasn't violent. Still, we'd better check out old files: Somewhere around here I bet there's a cold case or two involving that old hogleg as the murder weapon."

"Already checked," Willie said. "There's no unsolved homicides here on Pine Ridge involving a .45. Maybe Soske will dig up something from Pennington County. Or the sheriff in Hot Springs."

"Maybe," Manny answered. Willie had asked Soske if he could research their homicides for the past thirty years, from when Jason was active in AIM, for anyone killed with a .45 Colt. Ditto for the Fall River County Sheriff's Office. Manny hoped someone in the two counties bordering Pine Ridge might have an old homicide involving a .45.

Manny and Willie sat silent. They had no more to say. Manny had asked Willie to betray his aunt, and he had agreed. Manny hoped by the time he returned from talking with Reuben, Willie would have the answers he needed. He started for the door, and Willie called out after him.

"Be careful when you see him."

"Careful of my own brother? Now why would a sacred man hurt me?"

Manny had started to leave when Lumpy called to him. "Come in here, Hotshot."

Manny turned around and walked into Lumpy's office. Nathan Yellow Horse sat across from Lumpy and smiled at him as if they shared a secret. They did. "Nathan's been in contact with Ben Niles. He ordered you to give Nathan an exclusive."

"Just to offset that skirt from the *Rapid City Journal*," Nathan said. "The one you've been feeding information to—in exchange for what, I can only assume."

Manny started for Nathan, but the reporter jumped back in his chair just as Lumpy stepped between them. "Don't blame Nathan, here. You're the one that's been chasing her."

Manny sighed deeply and pulled up a chair across from Nathan. "I only have time for a few questions. Alone."

Lumpy laughed. "No problem, use my office. I'll read about it in the paper, anyway."

Manny waited until Lumpy shut the door before turning to Nathan. "Ask away."

>‹›‹›‹

Manny chuckled to himself. For the first time, he wished the local newspaper would come out early so he could see what Nathan Yellow Horse wrote. He had asked pointed questions, leading questions, questions that would compromise the investigation if they were answered. But Niles had ordered him to talk to Yellow Horse, and he had. Manny told Yellow Horse that Elizabeth had attacked him with a hammer that night, and that she had driven the stolen truck three nights ago.

Manny told Yellow Horse the investigation had a leak as big as the White River. Yellow Horse pressed. Manny stonewalled. Yellow Horse pressed again with the threat to call Niles one more time. Manny relented—Lumpy had been in the company of Sonja Myers more often than he—and left the implication there. Yellow Horse needed to know specifically if there was a connection between Lumpy, Sonja Myers, and the leak. "No comment."

>‹›‹›‹

Manny shut the car off and coasted down Reuben's driveway. He stopped in front of Reuben's trailer and cracked the car door, listening. A scraping noise came from somewhere behind the house, and he eased the door shut. He brushed his arm against Willie's Glock, and he thanked Lumpy for returning the gun. He knelt and peeked around the back of the trailer. Reuben stood bare-chested hunched over a smoking fire. He held an eagle feather in his hand and passed it through the smoke, directing it over his body as he chanted softly in a language Manny only vaguely remembered from his childhood.

Reuben opened the tiny medicine pouch hanging by a thong around his neck and pinched a small amount of sweetgrass and sage, tossing it into the air away from his body. Then he made a quarter-turn, and repeated the process in all four sacred directions. Manny watched in fascination as his brother performed a ceremony that had not changed with the Lakota since oral tradition was their vehicle of history.

As he turned, Reuben's moccasins made faint depressions in the dirt that lasted seconds before disappearing in the wind, while Reuben prayed to Wakan Tanka. Unc insisted on Manny's pursuit of the traditional Lakota ways, but Manny had fought against it and let them go.

Reuben prayed and ended the ceremony facing Manny's direction, but didn't acknowledge his presence until he had bowed once more to the four directions and passed the eagle feather through the smoke one last time. Reuben placed the feather and medicine pouch inside a small cedar chest beside the fire, then turned to Manny.

"It's good to see you. If I knew you were coming, I'd have waited so we could worship together."

"I worship my own way."

"Of course," Reuben grinned. "Unc's Catholicism. But there's still room for Native ways in your world. Many of our people share dual beliefs."

Reuben was right. Many Lakota shared their belief in traditional ways alongside Christianity, finding no difference between Wakan Tanka and God, but now was not the time for a theological discussion. "This isn't a social call."

"It never is." Reuben bent to a cooler and grabbed a Snickers bar. He tossed it and a Diet Coke to Manny without asking. Manny caught both as Reuben grabbed a Diet Coke for himself before dropping into his lawn chair. Manny looked at the Snickers: Reuben knew his weaknesses. How the hell did he know how long it had been since Manny ate? And how long since he ate a candy bar? Manny peeled the wrapper off the Snickers, and guilt visited him for only a moment. The Diet Coke would even out the calories in the candy bar.

Manny's lips smacked Snickers. Reuben slurped Diet Coke. Two brothers on Lakota time sharing moments that did not pass, in a hurry to be nowhere while the aromatic cedar smoke of Reuben's fire passed over them.

"Where's Jack Little Boy?" Manny blurted out.

Reuben sipped his soda slowly, all the while matching Manny's stare. "I heard about that stunt he pulled in your apartment . . ."

"Rez drums again?"

"If I knew where he was I'd put the grab on him myself. Can't have someone running around trying to kill my only brother."

"Then at least tell me who Jason would have killed when he was younger." He wished he could drag it back, but he couldn't.

"You teach that in your interrogation classes? I thought you were supposed to lead up to touchy questions, gain my confidence first before you pop the big question."

"I also teach that tough questions make men stall when they don't want to answer. Like you're stalling now. It's a simple enough question. You knew Jason back in his AIM days. Who would he have killed back then?"

Reuben finished his soda and crushed the can in one hand before tossing it into a trash sack with others. Reuben spoke deliberately, calculating each word he said now. "Jason couldn't have killed anyone. He was never an enforcer, never involved in the tough things we had to do. He was a milquetoast. Why do you ask?"

"Because he told Ricky Bell he killed someone before," Manny interpolated.

"Who's Ricky Bell?"

"The guy who stole the artifacts from the Prairie Edge, the one Jason hired to kill a man in Minneapolis."

"What man?"

"Clifford Coyote."

"Never heard of him."

"You may have known him as Alex Jumping Bull when he lived here on Pine Ridge."

A noticeable twitch attacked the corners of Reuben's eyes. Manny always pointed out to his students that slight tics were involuntary and indicated non-truth.

"You do remember him?"

Reuben reached for another Diet Coke. Stalling again. "Last I knew, Alex Jumping Bull disappeared about the time I killed Billy Two Moons. FBI goons came to visit me at the lockup in Rapid City to question me about that. I didn't know anything about Jumping Bull back then, and I don't now. But it sounds as if your Ricky Bell does. If Jason paid him to kill Jumping Bull, that lets me off the hook as your main suspect. I'd say Bell had a lifetime of reasons for wanting Jason dead."

"Not entirely." Manny paused while he felt the last of the caramel from the Snickers bar slide down his throat. A sliver of goo stuck on his lip and he licked it away. "Bell may be crowding you out from the top of my suspect list. But just a bit."

"And why not put him higher?"

Reuben was fishing, trying to find out what Manny knew. That was all right. He'd tell Reuben things that might help him lose sleep at night, things that would cause him to make a mistake if he killed Jason. "If Bell murdered him, he would have driven here. Maybe not with his own car—he doesn't own one—but in a stolen car if he had to."

"What makes you think he didn't?"

"Crazy George's Buick," Manny answered. "It had two hundred fifty miles on it, just enough to get to Rapid City and back. You're within walking distance of Crazy George."

"I don't drive anymore, remember? Scares the hell out of me."

"That doesn't mean you can't."

"Did you ever think it was pure coincidence that Crazy George's car was stolen the night of the murder? As I recall, you and a couple other kids swiped a car and went joyriding when you were about twelve or thirteen."

Manny thought he'd forgotten that incident when he and Freddie Leaping Star and the oldest Collins boy had taken a car double-parked in front of Billy Mills Hall. They drove it around the reservation until they ran out of gas. They had been caught, but not prosecuted. The owner, who was passing through on his way to Chadron, didn't want to return to Pine Ridge for court. They would have returned the car eventually, if the gas had held up. Maybe Reuben was right, maybe joyriders had taken Crazy George's car and returned it before it ran out of fuel.

"I don't believe it was kids joyriding that old beater of Crazy George's," Manny said. "And I don't believe in coincidences. Especially where murder's involved."

There was nervousness in Reuben's laugh. He stood and dropped the soda can into the sack. He grabbed another from the cooler along with a cold towel that had been trifolded with the ends tucked neatly into each other and handed it to Manny. He opened it and wiped the sweat from his neck and face, then draped it over his neck.

"Indian air-conditioning," Reuben said, and they both laughed. Reuben remembered some things Unc said, after all. They laughed together, and sat awkwardly looking at one another until Reuben asked, "Are you still running?"

"Every day, when I can."

"I bet you a can of pop this old man can run circles around you with arthritis and all."

"With my ribs being bruised, that'd just about make us even. Let me slip my shoes and shorts on and I'll meet you in front."

Manny grabbed his gym bag from the trunk and slipped his running shorts and shoes on. He was just donning a T-shirt when Reuben came from around the trailer. He started at an easy lope, one that seemed to favor his arthritis-aged leg.

"I hear tell Lizzy's going to the state mental hospital in Yankton for evaluation. She ever say why she wanted you dead?" Reuben's words came in gasps now, matching Manny's grunts every time his foot hit the pavement.

"Erica," Manny huffed, again wishing he could pull it back. His brother was better at playing this game than he was, but then Reuben had always been able to lower Manny's guard. He picked up the pace so he could get into his zone to think more logically. "Elizabeth told me she thought Erica and Jason were having an affair. She thought Erica would be implicated in Jason's embezzlement scheme."

"Lizzy's dead wrong," Reuben wheezed, struggling to keep up with Manny. "Erica could never do such a thing, she's a good kid. Makes me proud."

A piece of buffalo grass blew across the road and caught in Manny's teeth, and he spit it out. "You knew Jason was footing the bill for Erica to attend Harvard those six years."

"Lizzy finally told me a couple years back."

Reuben was once again the composed ex-convict, hard to read, unemotional and in control. Manny needed to shake him up, destroy that confidence. "I'm convinced Jason killed someone before. And I think you know who it was."

"Bullshit."

Manny picked up the pace, fighting his own battle to exchange air with his aching lungs. He started leaving Reuben behind and he had to slow. "No bullshit, big brother. When I mentioned Alex Jumping Bull a moment ago, you damned near choked. You know who Jason killed, just like you knew Jumping Bull."

Reuben ran his hand through his hair to get it out of his eyes, and gestured with his arm to the vast prairie beyond his barren forty acres. "Much of this land remains in tribal hands because of things we endured in AIM years ago." He paused to gulp dusty air. "We led a resurgence in Indian sovereignty and Lakota pride. If Alex Jumping Bull got himself killed, it's got nothing to do with AIM. Or me. If he pissed off AIM now, all he'd get is pissed off Indians. Even I will admit that AIM doesn't have the power it once had, but that's got nothing to do with me. I haven't been involved since they sent me to the prison."

"Just what do you remember about Jumping Bull?"

Reuben slowed, then stopped. He bent over, hands on his knees, breathing, coughing. *Stalling.* "I remember he was a weasel like Billy. What do you want from me? I did my time for killing Billy. All I want to do is live the rest of my life here as it was intended. I made mistakes, now I am trying my damndest to rectify them."

"And to maintain this life, would you kill again? Would you have killed Jason to keep it?" Manny started off at a pace that allowed Reuben to keep up.

"I didn't kill Jason. If this Ricky Bell killed Jumping Bull, he could have killed Jason with little effort, given the kid's rap sheet you mentioned. As much as I like your visits, *kola,* maybe we'll run back to my trailer and you can leave me while I am still in control of myself."

Reuben was still capable of killing if he saw the need. "Come on, big brother. Kick yourself in the ass, unless you want to concede."

Reuben found a burst of speed that overtook Manny for ten

yards until Manny picked it up and passed him. He kept just ahead of Reuben on their way back to Reuben's trailer. He beat Reuben by a hundred yards and squatted down, waiting for him to catch up. Reuben's hand rubbed one leg as he limped over and sat on the ground beside Manny. He hung his head between his legs and coughed.

"You know who Jason killed in his AIM days, and somehow this is mixed up with his murder," Manny said when he caught his breath.

"That might be," Reuben said, calm once again. "But that's no concern of mine. And especially no concern to a *wicasa wakan*."

>‹›‹›‹

Manny's cell phone beeped a message to call Soske. "We had several unsolved homicides around here in the 1970s," he said. "But only one killed with a .45. That was Billy Two Moons."

".45 auto or Long Colt?"

Papers shuffled on the phone. "The autopsy report doesn't say, except that the coroner recovered two intact slugs from the body. The other three hit bone and were too deformed to help."

"Does it mention the type of bullet, the style, or the weight?"

Papers shuffled again. "Solid lead slugs. Semi-wadcutter design. Each weighed 255 grains."

Manny knew officers from the Hostage Rescue Team who shot Colt .45 auto pistols, but they shot hollow points with a sharper nose for feeding reliability, not the semi-wadcutter, blunted-style lead bullets recovered from Two Moons.

"Tell me the evidence from the Two Moons case is still available."

"I'm certain it is," Soske said. "The sheriff's office here never gets rid of anything involving a capital offense."

"Can you overnight those two intact slugs to Quantico?"

"Sure. Just a matter of clearing things with the SO."

Manny told Soske the address of the FBI ballistics lab at Quantico. He figured that both slugs and the old revolver he seized from Jason's display case would arrive there at about the same time.

><><><><

On the way to the OST police building, Manny detoured and pulled to the curb at the Cohen Home. The same young woman at the front desk glanced up at Manny and waved him on. He started for Chief Horn's room, even now feeling like a young tribal officer reporting for duty. Manny rapped on the door and Horn jerked it open. He held a beer in one hand and what was left of a sandwich in the other. A smile spread across his face and he stepped aside.

Manny thought he'd fallen into the twilight zone as he stepped into the apartment. Gone was the mound of empty beers overflowing the garbage can containing last week's leftovers. The kitchen table was visible this time, though a stack of papers hid one corner. Horn motioned to an overstuffed chair. Manny was unsure whether it was there on his previous visit.

"It wasn't my idea." Horn seemed to be reading Manny's mind. "My granddaughter Shannon thought I should clean up my act if I have the FBI visiting. I told her it was just Manny Tanno, but she insisted on cleaning it anyway."

"I like it."

Horn's smile broadened as he basked in the compliment. "I don't get many visitors. Shannon said I might get more if I keep my place clean. That, and maybe be more sociable. What do you think she meant by that?"

"I haven't a clue," Manny lied.

Horn finished his beer and set his sandwich on a paper plate on the table. "But this isn't a social call."

Manny shook his head. "I'm still struggling with the Red Cloud murder. You said something the other day that struck a chord, Chief. You said Billy Two Moons and Alex Jumping Bull hung together a lot."

"Inseparable. If one got tossed into the hoosegow, the other did; just for solidarity, I always thought. Or maybe they were lovers." He tossed his head back and laughed.

"Where was Jumping Bull the night Two Moons was killed up by Hill City?"

Horn shrugged. "No one knew."

"But if you had to guess, where do you figure he was that night?"

"With Two Moons," Horn answered immediately. "Alex would have been with him that night like every other night."

"Even if Two Moons planned on meeting Reuben and partying, as he claimed?"

"Even then." Horn took another bite from his sandwich. "When Jumping Bull came up missing right after the murder, we all thought Reuben was good for that one, too. We told the Pennington County deputies investigating the homicide that Jumping Bull would have been at the scene, but they came up with a dead end on that. I always figured that they had their confession to one murder, enough to put Reuben away, and they were satisfied at that. Jumping Bull's body was never found. Oh, they put out the obligatory BOLO missing-persons bullshit, but I don't figure they worked too hard to 'be on the lookout' for a missing Indian."

Manny stood and stretched, eye to eye with his old chief sitting down. Manny explained that Jumping Bull, under the alias of Clifford Coyote, had been murdered in a Minneapolis apartment two weeks ago, at an address where he had been living and receiving checks from Elizabeth for nearly thirty years.

Horn chuckled. "So the peckerwood's been in Minneapolis all this time."

"Why do you figure he ran away?"

"Best reason in the world I can think of: fear. The little bastard was afraid of being found and killed like his pal Two Moons."

"My feelings exactly. I just had to have someone else that's sane say the same thing."

CHAPTER 21

Manny pulled into the parking lot just as Willie emerged from the OST police building. "I was coming to hunt you up, but we can jaw inside."

Manny followed him through the locked door and into the empty break room. Willie shut the door and shuffled to the coffeepot. Empty. He scrunched his nose at the burnt coffee in the bottom of the pot before putting it back on the burner. He turned a chair around and sat facing Manny. "I talked with Aunt Lizzy, but I don't feel very good about it." He looked down. The guilt Willie held inside made the room feel as heavy as a low-flying summer storm cloud.

"Did she tell you about Clifford Coyote?"

"She did. I just can't figure why I didn't see some of this."

"What?"

"There never was a Clifford Coyote."

"We knew that, but we didn't know why the ruse."

"After the Two Moons murder, Jumping Bull took the name

Coyote out of fear of being killed next. Jumping Bull was Aunt Lizzy's cousin from Crow Creek. When she moved out here after she married Reuben, she got Jumping Bull his first place to stay here in Pine Ridge, and tried to recruit him into AIM right after that Custer takeover fiasco."

"But he never made the grade."

"How'd you know?"

Manny forced a smile. "There are some things I recall about those days. For one thing, a man had to be a warrior, or be considered a warrior by some convoluted standards in order to be accepted by the others and allowed to join. From what Chief Horn said, Jumping Bull was anything but. He was just a drunk and a petty thief."

"Anyway, Jumping Bull fled after Reuben killed Billy Two Moons."

"Then he was blackmailing Jason?"

Willie nodded. "Jumping Bull knew that Jason paid Billy Two Moons to kill his parents."

"How did he know?"

"Two Moons and he were partying on the money Jason shelled out to rig that car wreck with the Red Clouds. When Reuben found the car that night in China Gulch, Jumping Bull hid in the backseat, because he knew Reuben would have him killed, too. But before he fled to Minneapolis, Jumping Bull also told Aunt Lizzy what he knew. At first, he was content to just be alive and gone from the rez. Then he got greedy and started blackmailing Jason. Aunt Lizzy felt like Reuben did, that Jason sold out for the almighty dollar rather than stay in the movement with the other AIM brothers. She was happy to help Jumping Bull bleed some of that Red Cloud money from Jason."

"You believe that?"

Willie nodded. "It's what she told me."

"Chief Horn said that Two Moons did mechanic work for

the police when he was in jail, and on his own when he was out. He could have made the wreck appear as if the brake lines had ruptured, to make it look like an accident."

Willie nodded again. "Jason's lackluster performance with the family business disappointed his parents. The year after Jason graduated college and started working for them, he lost the company's clients tons of money. The Red Clouds didn't want their business pissed away, and tasked their corporate attorney to deed their assets to the tribe when they died."

"That new car Two Moons drove the night he was murdered," Manny said. "That's how someone without a pot to pee in managed a new Chrysler."

Willie walked to the vending machine. "You're right on there," he called over his shoulder. "The new car was Two Moons's payment for rigging the wreck." When the machine spit out a MoonPie, Willie returned to his seat.

"And Elizabeth despised Jason enough that she kept Jumping Bull's whereabouts secret all those years?"

Willie nodded. "When she was in AIM and WARN, the thing she hated the most was the status quo. Jason's hiring Two Moons to kill his parents for control of the family business got to working on her. She knew she could turn in Jason at any time, but she thought it would hurt him more to be bled dry all those years."

"But things went south for Jason. Clara showed me a letter. Jumping Bull was fixing to pull the plug on his long-distance relationship with the 'Donald Trump of the West.'"

Willie nodded. "Aunt Lizzy confirmed what Clara told you, that Jason ran the business into the ground. He had a string of mediocre properties mixed with some that fell flat. He spent money like there was no tomorrow—or no yesterday to catch up with him. He bought Lakota antiquities he couldn't afford, and something had to give. So Jason thought that he could cut off his blackmail money to Jumping Bull, that after all those years no one would believe him if he implicated Jason in masterminding the car wreck that killed his parents."

"But that letter called Jason's bluff."

Willie nibbled on the outside edges of his MoonPie. "Jumping Bull sent Jason that letter threatening to expose him. He became obsessed about finding his address, and charmed information out of the new girl at the post office. He learned that Aunt Lizzy received Jumping Bull's monthly checks in Pine Ridge under Clifford Coyote's name, and figured Aunt Lizzy was Jumping Bull's go-between. He snuck into her office one night a few weeks ago and tried finding Jumping Bull's address."

"The argument that Lumpy walked in on." Manny stood and reached for his pack of cigarettes, but his pocket was empty. A Camel used to help him sort things out, like an obnoxious yet trusted friend at his side. "Lumpy said file drawers were strewn all over. Jason and Lizzy arguing fiercely. Did Jason find the address that night?"

"Now she thinks he did, and she's carrying a powerful amount of guilt because she didn't warn Jumping Bull that Jason might know his address in Minneapolis."

Willie looked at his empty MoonPie wrapper, turned it over, read the nutrition facts. The young officer had matured with his interview of Elizabeth, but Manny had one last question that needed answering. "Did you ask her about Jason's murder? If she could kill me, she could kill him, too."

Willie dropped his eyes and stared at the floor. "She told me she didn't know anything about Jason's death, even though she hated him enough that she could have killed him. She knew all about his embezzlement of the tribe's money and how he would implicate Erica if he was caught. Sure, she could have killed him, with considerable pleasure. But I don't think she did." Willie looked away. Manny knew Willie didn't believe his aunt was in the clear on Jason's death.

Manny put his fingers together, building a tent with them, as he often did when things came together in an investigation. He thought of his suspect list—when Lumpy blocked the doorway. He was backlit by the bright hall light, and he still had a fading purple stain on his right cheek from the thief powder. Manny swallowed down a smile.

"You think this is funny?" Lumpy said. "It'll be on my skin for a month."

"A week," Manny said. "A week is more like it."

"How do you know that?"

"It's what I remember when we used it back in the day, remember?"

Lumpy ignored him and tossed a manila envelope on the table between Manny and Willie. "FedEx overnight. Must be important."

It was from the FBI lab in Quantico. Manny left it unopened on the table. "Thanks."

Lumpy stood waiting for Manny to open the envelope. When he didn't, Lumpy started to leave, then turned back. "Before I forget, Hotshot, your boss called."

"And?"

"He didn't say much, but he seemed to get pretty upset when I told him you were in Rapid City visiting your girlfriend."

Manny could argue that Clara was not his girlfriend, but Lumpy probably didn't know about Clara and was referring to Sonja. "What did Niles want?"

"Not sure," Lumpy answered. "All he said is: 'Two days. Things start in two days, you tell Manny Tanno that.' And what the hell did you tell Nathan Yellow Horse when he interviewed you?"

"Why?"

"He left in a damned hurry. Didn't say a word, just brushed past me."

"Oh, I just hinted at some places where he might begin his story."

Manny waited until the sound of Lumpy's footsteps died down then propped his feet up on another chair and waited for Willie to continue. Elizabeth had told Willie more, and he was anxious to get it off his chest.

"Aunt Lizzy still has a thing for Reuben," he said. "She got used to them being a couple, got comfortable being the woman of a local celebrity, even if he was a violent AIM celebrity. I think she protected him as much as she protected Erica."

Willie reached into his briefcase and took out a bundle of letters held tight by a single deer-hide thong. Willie started untying the bundle when he dropped the letters. They scattered on the floor. "Pick one, any one, they're all alike."

Manny grabbed one postmarked SOUTH DAKOTA STATE PEN- ITENTIARY, SIOUX FALLS, MARCH OF 1989.

"They're all dated that way, up until Reuben was paroled from the penitentiary." Willie pulled up a chair and sat beside Manny. "I'll spare you reading them. Aunt Lizzy and Reuben never actually broke up, even after the murder. They were corre- sponding all those years he was in the lockup. And they've been intimate. They were divorced on paper only."

"How'd you find these?"

"Aunt Lizzy asked me to pack her some clothes for her stay at the state hospital. I found these in Reuben's old Marine foot- locker in her bedroom closet."

Manny picked up several letters, all sent during Reuben's in- carceration in the South Dakota State Penitentiary.

"She hid her love for him all these years because folks wouldn't have trusted a finance officer who was involved with a convicted killer, especially one with Reuben's reputation. And she added one thing when I asked her about Jason's funding Erica's college: She said Jason felt bad about Reuben going to the pen. She said that Jason loved Erica like she was his own daughter, and that Reuben knew from the beginning that Jason intended paying her way through college."

"But Reuben just found out about it within the past few years."

Willie shook his head. "She was quite adamant that Reuben knew it from the start, even if he told you different."

"That's just one more thing I will talk to Reuben about," Manny said. "Now let's see what Quantico has to say."

He used his penknife to open the manila envelope overnighted from the FBI lab. As he watched Willie waiting expectantly to see the contents, Manny felt like one of those Academy Award presenters about to read the winner's name. He pulled the lab slip out. "The ID section was unable to come up with a match between the latents lifted from Crazy George's car and those of Jack Little Boy. Little Boy's got six points on each finger, at the most."

"How could that be?" Willie asked. He scooted his chair close and took the report. "Everyone has at least twelve points."

"Not if you're a mason. Little Boy's been bricklaying for the last eight years, according to his rap sheet. Eight years of constantly rubbing his hands against brick and mortar will erode fingerprints."

"Then he could be Jason's killer. There was only partial prints found on the war club along with Ricky Bell's. We thought at first they were smudged prints, but they could have been Little Boy's."

Manny nodded. "And we can't use even the partials if Little Boy is our man."

He picked up the other sheet. The crime lab had failed to locate Reuben's fingerprints. The sheet suggested they contact the South Dakota State Penitentiary.

"Jeeza! How could Reuben's prints not be on file? He's a felon."

"Sealed, would be my guess. The Special Task Force on Organized Crime investigated AIM heavily in the 1970s. The Tenth Federal Appeals Court ruled they'd been unjustly targeted by the government, and most of their records were sealed. But that didn't apply to state courts. I'll call the state pen later and have them fax over Reuben's print card."

He returned that paper to the envelope and grabbed the last one. And whistled. "The .45 slugs Soske had sent to the lab from the Two Moons homicide matched that old cavalry Colt I seized from Jason's office."

Willie read the lab report over Manny's shoulder. "Let me get this straight: Billy Two Moons was killed with the same gun Ricky Bell used to kill Alex Jumping Bull?"

"Looks like it."

"But Reuben told investigators he tossed the gun after he killed Two Moons. How did Jason get Reuben's gun?"

"Good question. Apparently, Reuben lied about tossing his gun, too."

They sat, each lost in his own thoughts, until Willie broke the silence. "You know you'll have to talk with Reuben again."

Manny nodded. "Tomorrow afternoon," he said. "Clara's coming down in the morning, and we're driving to Chadron for breakfast. I'll talk to Reuben when I get back. But for now, all I want to do is get some shut-eye."

"She forgave you after that article came out?"

"Finally," Manny answered. "It took some work to convince Clara that Sonja Myers set me up for that photo op at the Rapid City bistro. I never had a woman get jealous over me."

"How'd you explain all the messages from Sonja on your cell phone?"

Manny shrugged. "I told the truth. I said Sonja called but I never talked with her."

"But you did, just yesterday."

Manny smiled. "I had to tell Sonja about my exclusive interview with Nathan Yellow Horse, and that your lieutenant had more information on the case than I could give out."

>◇◇◇<

After Manny finished stretching his hamstrings, he cracked the door and peered out into the night. The single streetlight near his apartment burned yellow, and he was careful to throw the new deadbolt on his apartment door. His beginning pace was slower than usual, but he was able to work through the pain in his ribs. When he hit stride at just over a mile, the sweat drenched his sweatshirt. He had hit his zone, and he needed to think.

Tomorrow Elizabeth would be driven to the state hospital in Yankton where she would undergo evaluation to determine her fitness to stand trial. Would Reuben interfere? Would his love for Elizabeth overrun his love for his brother and result in his killing the one person who could testify against Elizabeth and send her away? Manny doubted that, but seeing Reuben's anger flare yesterday, he knew the man was still capable of bad intentions.

A dog barked from a house up ahead and Manny strained to see in the blackness. What would Reuben's motives have been for killing Jason? If he were dealing with the Reuben of the American Indian Movement days, he'd think hatred of the status quo was enough reason. But this was the Reuben who had served his time in prison, had somehow found the Lakota way, and now advised people in spiritual matters. Had Reuben been that jealous of Jason to think that Elizabeth was having an affair with him? Again, this was a different Reuben, yet still like the old Reuben in many ways.

Manny rounded the block on his last stretch to his apartment. Sweat flowed from every pore, and he had forgotten the pain in his side from the bruised ribs. He fumbled inside his sweatshirt pocket for the key while he slowed to a walk to catch his breath.

And stopped and listened.

The streetlight in front of his apartment was out, and he stepped on broken glass. He crouched low, crunching glass where someone had broken the light. Willing his breathing to slow, his heart to quit racing, he hunkered down at the base of the streetlight, straining, listening.

Footsteps grated on gravel between his apartment building and the next one. Manny took in deep, calming breaths as someone neared, and the glint of a blade reflected light from the apartment window above Desirée's.

The figure wore a hoodie, but there was no mistaking Jack Little Boy by the way he filled out the sweatshirt, by the way he held his knife out in front of him. Like a predator, Jack picked his way cautiously in Manny's direction, but Manny noiselessly circled the base of the streetlight. Jack's head swiveled, trying to locate him, but Manny hadn't been raised a victim. Jack searched aimlessly in the dark, unsure exactly where Manny was.

The knife scraped against the metal base of the light and Manny drew his legs beneath him. How long had it been since he wrestled another man? High school? He was grateful for that, and for the custody control classes the bureau required agents to attend annually.

Jack looked away and Manny saw his opening. He pushed off from the base of the light and sprang from his crouch. His first blow slapped the knife away and it clattered somewhere on the sidewalk a heartbeat before Manny found Jack's neck with his forearm. His other hand slipped around to lock in a sleeper hold, one that would put the much bigger man out for the count. If he'd cooperate. Jack turned to Manny and dug his elbow deep into his injured ribs. The blow threatened to do what the stolen truck could not, and Manny lost his grip as he rolled away in pain. Jack reached down, clawing at Manny's throat. Manny brought his knee up and connected with Jack's nose. Blood spurted over Manny's face and got into his eyes. Jack screamed, and Manny hit him on the side of the head before Jack disappeared into the darkness.

Manny fumbled for his apartment key and half crawled to the door. For all the bad vibes he had gotten from Desirée since he'd been back here, he wished she were looking out her apartment window now, wishing she would dial 911.

CHAPTER 22

Heavy, hard, desperate banging nearly burst Manny's door. He swung his legs over the bed and paused long enough to grab the Glock from the shoulder holster before he cracked the door against the chain. Willie stood on the other side, one beefy hand raised to hammer the door once more when Manny opened it. Manny shut the door long enough to disengage the chain, then let Willie in.

"Aunt Lizzy's gone," he blurted. His breaths came in gasps.

"Of course she's gone. They took her this morning to Yankton for her psych eval."

"They were supposed to." Willie sat on a kitchen chair and put his head between his legs and breathed deeply, gathering his thoughts. "Robert Hollow Thunder landed the assignment to drive Aunt Lizzy to Yankton. Before they reached the transport van, she snatched his gun and ran off."

"What do you mean, she ran off?" Manny rubbed his eyes,

then his groin, then his eyes again in an effort to wake up. "How the hell could she grab his gun while she was restrained?"

Willie held his head. "The damned fool Hollow Thunder's head whistles in a crosswind, I swear. He said he knew Aunt Lizzy all his life, and just didn't feel right putting belly chains on her. So as he walked her to the van, she snatched his gun and ran. And you know what a runner she is. What are we going to do?"

"How long ago did she escape?"

Willie checked his watch. "Three hours ago. Robert wanted to get back to the rez tonight, so he started early this morning before sunup on the transport. She's got a hell of a head start."

Willie sat in a chair beside Manny while he pulled his trousers on. "Where are the other officers looking?"

"They're out beating the bushes, but we're spread pretty thin. The lieutenant had damned near the whole force up last night searching for Jack Little Boy." Willie grabbed his Copenhagen can. He put it back in his pocket without taking a pinch. "Everyone except Lieutenant Looks Twice."

"Why isn't he?"

A smile spread across Willie's face for a brief instant. "He finally found his car."

"His squad car?"

Willie shook his head, and composed himself enough to take that pinch of Copenhagen. "Someone called a wrecker out of Gordon to tow his new Mustang away yesterday. The lieutenant put out a stolen on it and located it this morning. The tow service called when he was in the middle of an interview with Sonja Myers, and she drove him down there to pick it up."

"Trouble with his new car?"

"The tow service in Gordon said Captain Black Bear called and wanted it towed from our parking lot. So the wrecker snatched it and hauled it across the Nebraska line."

"But you don't have a Captain Black Bear," Manny said as he put on his shoes.

"That's what the lieutenant is so mad about. He vows to get to the bottom of it." The smile had left Willie's face, but not Manny's as he imagined Lumpy thinking his car was stolen. "You better watch your ass when he finds you."

Manny quickly changed the subject. "What else do we have on Elizabeth?"

Willie frowned. "She could be anywhere. Robert said he last saw her hoofing it cross-country by the powwow grounds. If she's caught and still armed, one of our guys might cap her."

"I'm afraid you're right. Get on the road and keep an ear as to where the other units are looking. We don't want to go over ground that's already been checked. I might have better luck in my unmarked. Call my cell when you figure out where everyone else is checking. And what about Jack?"

"Nada, though we took a break-in report from the Red Cloud Housing last night. The owner reported ten bucks cash stolen and an old Marlin .30-30 wall hanger his grandfather owned. Guy said it isn't even safe to shoot."

"Jack?"

"He'd be good for it. You be careful out there looking for Aunt Lizzy. I'd hate for Jack to get in a lucky shot at you."

Willie ran out and Manny finished dressing. He slipped the Glock into the shoulder holster that, by now, felt natural. He left his apartment and started for his car just as Clara drove around the corner and pulled to the curb behind him.

"What's the rush?" She stepped out dressed in plaid pleated pants with a matching top. He thought how suited she was for a lunch date, not for driving dusty back roads looking for an escaped prisoner.

"Can't jaw now. Elizabeth's escaped. I'm going to look for her."

"I'm coming along."

Clara slid in the passenger side before Manny could object. "This might get dangerous. Besides looking for Elizabeth, Jack Little Boy's out there somewhere armed and hunting me. Remember what you said about being frightened with certain aspects of my job? This is one of those aspects."

Clara buckled up. "Then we'd better get going if we're to find her. Because you still have just one good eye right now, I might be useful. Where do you plan to look?"

For the first time, Manny realized he had no plan. He was just going to cruise the bumpy, rutted, dusty reservation roads looking for Elizabeth.

"Where are we going?" Clara asked again.

Manny thought of all the miles of reservation Elizabeth could be hiding in. Someone who knew the area could lose anyone, and Elizabeth knew the area well, having hid out on more than a few occasions from Wilson's men back in her youth.

"I have no idea where she'd go. Willie's the only family she's got here on Pine Ridge, and she knows he'd bring her in himself if he found her."

"I know where she'd go," Clara said as she turned in the seat. "Remember those letters you told me Willie found, the ones where Elizabeth and Reuben corresponded all those years he was in prison? She'll go to Reuben's."

"For what?"

"Protection. A woman, even one as self-reliant as Elizabeth, needs to feel her man will protect her. And Reuben's still her man—at least in her mind. By what you've told me, she's a strong-willed woman who would protect him as well."

"She's had enough time running to get to Reuben's place by now. You may be right. We got no other place to check right now."

They started for Oglala and Reuben's house, both trying to

figure out Elizabeth's motive for escaping. "She must know her psych eval will show she's too mentally disturbed to stand trial," Manny offered. "Even though I think she's not as crazy as she let on in the interview."

"What if she actually is disturbed? Remember when she was caught after she tried to kill you? You said she felt no remorse, like you were talking to a person with no soul."

During Manny's interview with Elizabeth, he detected no remorse, no emotion, just an intense instinct to protect anything that she loved. At the time, Manny thought she wanted to protect Erica. Now he was convinced she would protect Reuben, too, if necessary.

They turned off Highway 18 onto 41, driving past Oglala, past the forty one-acre tracts with their weathered shacks to the north. As they drove past Crazy George's house, they saw Crazy George hunkered in the dirt drawing with a stick like the first time he and Willie stopped there.

At Reuben's driveway, Manny shut the car off and coasted the rest of the way in. He told Clara to wait and eased the door shut. When he reached Reuben's front door, Clara nudged him.

"I thought I told you—"

"Shush, or he'll hear you."

Manny left the argument for later, and walked to the front of the trailer. He bent low and peeked inside. Empty. He cracked the screen door and spotted a note Reuben left taped inside it: *Gone to Ben Horsecreek's.* After a quick look around the back of the trailer, he led Clara back to the car.

"How would he get to Cuny Table?" Clara asked. "He doesn't even drive."

"He must have ridden to Ben's . . ." Reuben's paint was gone from the corral.

"What is it?"

"Crazy George's old Buick I seized for evidence. I asked

Lumpy to return it to George after the evidence tech was finished with it."

"What's that got to do with finding Elizabeth?"

"The car wasn't there just now when we drove past George's."

They drove back to Crazy George's driveway and stopped beside his trailer. George still bent to the ground drawing in the dust. He wore an ankle-length paisley dress with low-cut neckline that showed strands of white chest hair peeking out of the front. He stood as Manny approached.

"You're here to rub it in, I suppose."

"Rub what in?"

"The car." George spit tobacco juice on the ground and narrowly missed his own foot. "You guys returned it yesterday. Then you guys came and stole it back. Now you're here to rub it in."

"What makes you think we stole it again? How long's it been gone?"

"Well, you took it for no good reason the first time. Hell, you could have left it and did your evidence processing right here. But no, you had to steal it from me again."

"How long?"

"Clementine started raising hell about two hours ago. Hell, you guys use my car more than I do."

"Why didn't you report it?"

George laughed. "You guys want me to report everything now? Besides, who am I going to report it to, the same cops that stole it?"

Manny grabbed his cell and dialed Willie. "No cell service here," George chuckled. "Unless you get up on that hill." He chin-pointed to the top of road before it dropped off to the north.

Manny climbed back into his car and drove to the high spot in the road. He got a signal and told Willie he suspected that Elizabeth took Crazy George's car and might be driving to Ben Horsecreek's house.

"How do you figure she knew Crazy George kept his keys in the ignition?"

Willie answered his own question. "Maybe she ran to Reuben's this morning and found him gone. Maybe she knew the keys would be in the ignition because she used the car before."

"Maybe," Manny answered, not wanting to complicate things for Willie right now. Manny hung up and started driving toward Cuny Table.

"Maybe Willie's right," Clara said. "Maybe she used the car before, like the night Jason was murdered."

"That's a possibility. Or it may be as simple as Willie mentioning to her that George always leaves the keys in the ignition. Remember, Willie told her everything up until the time she tried to kill me."

Manny didn't want to suspect Elizabeth as the one who had planted the war club in Jason's skull. There were other plausible suspects. He thought of Ricky Bell, who had more to lose than anyone else. By killing Jason, he would rid himself of the only witness who could testify that he had flown to Minneapolis and killed Alex Jumping Bull. He thought of Jack Little Boy, who worshipped Reuben and would do anything to protect him, even kill for him, as he'd proven by trying to kill Manny on several occasions.

Then there was Reuben, stone-cold in his own right with a history of violence as far back as Manny could recall, who had more than enough reason to kill Jason. He had double-crossed Reuben's Heritage Kids on the concrete contracts for the Red Cloud Resort. Manny was now certain that he and Elizabeth had been involved all these years, and still were. So Reuben would have known that Jason intended to embezzle the tribe's money, and, like Elizabeth, he would want his daughter protected from the scandal.

They drove the next hour in silence. Although he needed to

think right now, Manny welcomed Clara's company. He knew that, when he felt like talking, she would be the sounding board he needed.

They drove over the White River, now dried up, as was Mule Creek a little farther on. Pronghorn antelope—white-bellied goats, the old ones had called them—grazed along the riverbanks. Their watchful heads followed the dusty rental car with two fenders banged up from hitting something Manny had already forgotten about. The last few years had been dry for this region, and from somewhere in the recesses of Uncle Marion's teaching, Manny knew the antelope would have a hard winter because of this drought. His own winter would be hard, away from the academy at Quantico, if he didn't find the killer soon.

"Did Jason talk about his folks much?" Manny asked at last.

Clara shook her head. "He never talked about them at all. I thought at the time that it was just his way of handling grief. But looking back, I don't remember him ever visiting their grave site. Why?"

"Even before Elizabeth told Willie, I'd suspected that Jason had hired Billy Two Moons to kill his parents so he could take over the business, just like Alex Jumping Bull told Elizabeth he knew about it, too. I figured Jason paid Two Moons quite well, judging from the new Chrysler he was seen driving around the reservation in the weeks before he was killed."

"But Jumping Bull got greedy," Clara said. "He wanted more, so he blackmailed Jason."

"He looked at all the years Jumping Bull put the bite on him, bleeding him. Jason was already bleeding great gouts from bad investments and gambling, and he figured he'd save that blackmail money if Alex were dead."

They drove another twenty minutes before reaching the intersection of Route 41 and BIA Route 2. Willie had given Manny directions to get to Ben Horsecreek's ranch, and Manny grabbed the hasty map he'd drawn and studied it. He held the paper to the light, trying to focus his one good eye on it. Clara took the map from him.

"Go east along Route 2," she pointed. "There's a dirt trail that takes off to the north after about two miles. You noted here that we should be able to see Horsecreek's mailbox and long driveway from there."

They came to the mailbox and followed the dirt trail that served as Horsecreek's driveway. Manny slowed, every bump causing his ribs to rub against his side, making breathing painful.

"Want me to drive?"

Manny swiveled his head to meet Clara's concerned look. "Now what could I hit out here?" he said and jerked his head back in time to miss a black white-faced steer on the driveway.

"The offer stands." Clara cinched her seat belt tighter.

They continued driving until they reached a rise that dropped sharply away, and coasted the last hundred yards toward Ben's house. Crazy George's Buick was parked alongside Reuben's paint pony that had been hobbled to allow it to graze. It was so tired from the hard ride here that it hung its head in shame.

Behind the car and horse stood a simple log cabin, smaller than Manny's garage at his Virginia home. He grabbed his cell phone to call Willie. No service, and he swore under his breath as he turned in the seat. "I want you to take the car and drive back the way we came. Drive until you have cell service where you can call Willie."

"What are you going to do?"

"Walk down there. It's not more than an eighth of a mile. By the time I get there, you'll have made contact with Willie."

"Bullshit." Manny was taken aback by her choice of words. He had not heard her swear since he'd known her. "Bullshit. It'll probably take miles to get where this damned thing can catch a tower. You're not getting rid of me like that. I'm going down there with you."

"I can't allow that. Elizabeth may still be armed, and Reuben is still as unpredictable as an old range bull."

"You have no choice. I might be scared to death and I might not be much good, but I'm all you got."

Manny gave up. "Well, at least do what I tell you when I tell you."

"Fair enough." Clara took off her seat belt as if readying herself to leap out of the car.

Manny inched his way down the hill, every step jarring his cracked ribs and causing him to take quick, short breaths. He expected the front door to open, expected a rifle barrel to poke at them from the door or open window, but there was no movement and they stopped beside Crazy George's car. The hood was warm. Manny unsnapped the retaining snap on his holster before creeping to the cabin door and easing it open. He tried the latch, but it was locked. From the inside? He couldn't tell, and he motioned to Clara to stay where she was while he crept around back.

He paused and listened at the corner of the house, then took careful, silent steps toward the back. As he cleared the back wall, Elizabeth sat with her back to him on a tree stump across from Reuben. She bent over him as she wrapped gauze high around his thigh. Reuben saw Manny, and called his name. Elizabeth wheeled around. She held Robert Hollow Thunder's automatic, her eyes wild with fright. And something else that Manny was quick to recognize. Clara was right: Elizabeth really was mentally disturbed.

"Come on in and sit a spell." Reuben used the back of the lawn chair to stand, and rubbed the bandage on his leg. "We've been expecting you."

Elizabeth pointed the gun at Manny's chest, her knuckles white, the same rage in her eyes as the night she was going to kill him in her house. Manny was certain now as he was then that she would fire at any moment.

"Come over here where I can watch you." Her voice had deepened. Her words slurred together. Guttural words, hateful words, coming from the mouth of the sister-in-law he didn't know anymore. "Tell your lady friend to come here, too."

Manny led Clara slowly around the corner of the house, her eyes wide and fixed on the gun pointed at her. She started to shake. Manny took her hand and squeezed, as they moved cautiously, deliberately to where Elizabeth motioned with the gun barrel.

"You'll start by shucking that gun under your coat," Reuben said.

"How'd you know?"

Reuben laughed. "I'm an ex-con. I've seen that elephant, more than once. Besides, I spotted it in that pile of your clothes that day we had the sweat."

With his left hand, Manny took it from the holster.

"Just toss it away."

Manny flung it on the ground.

"Good. Now we can all sit down and figure out what we're going to do next." Reuben nodded to tree stumps to sit on.

"You going to make your friend Ben Horsecreek an accessory to whatever you got planned?"

"He's gone for a few days," Reuben answered. "Drove to Standing Rock for a Sun Dance. He wanted me to check on his steers while he was away."

"Then what do you intend to do?"

Reuben held his hands up, palms facing Manny. "That depends on what you're going to do, *kola*."

"You know what I got to do. Elizabeth stole an officer's weapon as she was to be transported to Yankton for her psych eval. I've got to bring her in."

"I'm not going to Yankton." Elizabeth's gun hand trembled and her knuckles whitened as she took up slack on the trigger. "I'm staying right here with Reuben."

"Elizabeth, you're sick. You won't be held responsible for that night you attacked me with the hammer, and the night you stole the truck and ran me off the road. You need help. Let me take you back where someone can talk with you. You don't want to kill me."

"She won't kill you," Reuben assured Manny. "Not my Lizzy."

"Oh, yes she will. Just look at her."

Reuben stood beside Elizabeth and whispered to her as he watched Manny and Clara out of the corner of his eye. "Lizzy's much better now than she used to be. Much better than when she killed LaVonne."

"You knew about that?"

Reuben nodded and stroked the side of her head. "She came to Sioux Falls to visit me right after LaVonne's car wreck. Lizzy got fed up with the promotion system. She felt LaVonne was inept, that she'd made bad decisions that cost the tribe money. Lizzy worked her butt off getting her business degree, and she knew she could do a better job for the tribe."

"She set up the so-called accident, and you think that's all right?"

"I didn't say I condoned it." Reuben ran his fingers through Elizabeth's hair. "But she's my woman. I couldn't toss her to the wolves. She was beside herself after that. Guilt ate at her, and she talked of suicide. It wasn't easy, but between Erica and me, we managed to get her into therapy."

"Erica knows about LaVonne?"

"No." Reuben took his pipe out and filled the bowl from a small canvas tobacco pouch. He tamped the tobacco with his Sun Dance skewer. "All Erica knows is that her mother needed help.

Erica lined up a therapist in Rapid City, a first-rate shrink. No one's the wiser. Everyone on the rez just accepts the fact that Lizzy goes shopping with Rachael Thompson in Rapid once a week."

"Does Rachael know about LaVonne? About the therapy?"

"She's just my friend," Elizabeth snapped. "You leave her out of this. She knows nothing, other than she and I drive to Rapid. All she knows is that I see a therapist while she shops. She thinks it's about Reuben."

"So there you have it," Reuben said. "Lizzy just made a mistake, trying to get rid of you before you figured out Jason's murder."

"I already have," Manny said. "I know just who's responsible for burying that club in his head."

"And you'll be prosecuting the killer," Elizabeth said. "You'll be sending the killer away for a long time or the death penalty?"

"I will. It's not just reservation justice, it's the law of the land, and I've got to do it."

"I can't allow that." Elizabeth stepped away from Reuben. He took a step toward her, and she side-stepped away. "Leave us alone," she told Reuben. "Manny and his woman and I have business that I don't want you to see."

"Like what, Lizzy?" Reuben said. "Do you intend to kill them over some asshole like Jason? Do you intend to kill two more people?"

He stepped toward her.

"I'll kill you, too, if you get in the way."

Manny calculated the distance, calculated if he could reach Elizabeth before she could get off a round, or two, calculated if he could disengage his hand from Clara's viselike, trembling grip.

"You won't kill me," Reuben said. He stepped closer, his hand held out to accept the gun. "You killed LaVonne in a moment of rage, that's all. You can't kill again."

Elizabeth laughed. "Even you are too damned naïve. There was no moment of rage involved. My cousin sneaked back to the rez to rig her car."

"Alex came back here?"

"He was the only one I knew who could rig it so it would look like an accident. He got the idea from Billy Two Moons when he rigged the Red Clouds' wreck."

"So he couldn't tell anyone he helped you kill LaVonne," Manny said, "because you'd tell where he was hiding up in Minneapolis."

"Pretty good for a crazy lady, huh?"

"But you always said LaVonne was a spur-of-the-moment thing." Reuben stepped closer to Elizabeth. "You couldn't have planned LaVonne's death."

"Like I didn't tie Anna Mae up in that safe house in Denver before she was driven here and killed?"

"You were mixed up in that, too?"

Elizabeth's laugh came from deep inside and her knuckles whitened on the trigger. "She was an informant, and I had no problem tying her up and gagging her. I even helped load her into that Pinto for her ride back to the rez."

"You helped them murder Anna Mae? But she was no informant."

"I know that now. But that, as they say, is water under the bridge over Wounded Knee Creek."

"Give me the gun." Reuben stepped closer. His eyes pleaded, his hands pleaded for her to give him the gun.

In one motion she wildly swung the gun around and fired.

The bullet hit Reuben in the upper shoulder. He staggered and slumped, then regained his footing. Blood saturated his Sioux Nation T-shirt. He pulled his shirt down. The bullet had struck high in his shoulder, and his left arm lay limp at his side.

"So now you intend to kill me, baby? After a lifetime together, it comes to this? You're killing me along with my brother and his woman?"

Elizabeth looked at the gun as if aware for the first time that she held it. She lowered the muzzle and staggered toward Reuben and began crying, hysterical shoulder-shaking sobs, violent crying that wouldn't soon stop.

Reuben eased the gun from her hand, and tucked it into his waistband. He wrapped his good arm around her as he stroked her head and kissed her forehead. He looked at Clara for help.

"It'll be all right, baby," he said. "Go with this nice lady while Manny and I talk."

Clara looked at Manny. "She'll be all right now." Clara put her arm around Elizabeth.

"There's some stools to the front of the house," Reuben said. "Please take her and sit there. And be gentle with her. She'll give you no more grief."

Clara led Elizabeth around to the front of the cabin.

"Lizzy's out of it now. She won't be any more trouble."

"Good." Manny looked around for Willie's Glock. He stepped toward it but Reuben stepped in front of him and leveled Hollow Thunder's gun at Manny's chest. "I think it'd be better if you don't grab that piece right now. Just sit back down there, *kola*, and we'll jaw awhile."

"About?"

"Lizzy," Reuben said. "For a while there, I'd swear you thought she murdered Jason."

"I do."

"Rez drums have Jack Little Boy right up there for Jason's death. I hear he tried to kill you again last night. That kid always was nuts. I did what I could, but Jack looked up to me, would do anything to protect me. I figured him for Jason's murder after Jason shit on me and the rest of the Heritage Kids."

"Jack's on the run. Armed himself last night."

"There you have it."

"But he didn't kill Jason. Elizabeth did."

Reuben sat slowly back on his stump and rubbed his leg. His limp arm hung by his side as his T-shirt continued to soak up blood. "How the hell could she kill him?"

"The same way she killed LaVonne for that finance officer position. Jason represented a major threat for her. He intended to embezzle the tribe's money and go on the run, leave Erica to take the rap for it. I always thought that Jason had figured it out about Elizabeth setting up that car accident that killed LaVonne. That's why Elizabeth couldn't go to the police with the embezzlement information."

"But she'll be evaluated at the state hospital," Reuben said. "You said they'll find her incompetent when she attacked you both times."

"Those times," Manny answered. "And probably for LaVonne's death as well." As he looked at the gun, he wondered if his brother really was a sacred man now. Manny weighed his odds of solving Jason's homicide while saving his, and Clara's, life. "She won't be held accountable for those times. But for Jason's murder—that's another story altogether. I'm certain I can find enough people she works with every day to testify that she was in a proper state of mind two weeks ago. I'm sure I can find enough people who will say she was quite sane at the time of Jason's murder."

"Then what?"

"Then the federal government will prosecute her to the fullest extent of their resources."

"Hard time, like I did?"

"Harder time. Federal time."

Reuben shook his head as he aimed the gun at Manny's chest. Then the *wicasa wakan* emerged, and the sacred man lowered the gun and handed it to Manny, butt first. "I can't let you do this. Lizzy didn't kill Jason. I did it."

"I know." Manny tucked the gun in his waistband. "Now we can jaw a little, while I look at that shoulder." Manny cut Reuben's shirt with his pocketknife and tore the fabric away from where the bullet had entered. "Hurt?"

"Naw," Reuben flinched. "It feels just wonderful. I think the bullet broke the collarbone."

The bullet had entered just below the clavicle and angled up. There was no exit wound, but heavy bleeding had saturated his shirt. Manny looked around for the roll of gauze Elizabeth had dropped earlier.

"When did you first suspect me?"

"When you stole Crazy George's Buick."

"Anyone could have stolen it."

"But you live close, and we found cut-grass and sweetgrass in the car."

"A lot of folks hereabouts use sweetgrass in their ceremonies."

Manny started wrapping Reuben's shoulder to stop the blood. "But cut-grass grows close to water. There's a drought going on, in case you didn't notice. Not much water in these parts, but you happen to have a little running creek in back of your place, and I don't believe in coincidences. Then Lenny Little Boy told me that the morning after the murder you dragged onto the jobsite looking like hell—said you hadn't slept all night."

"You can't convict me on coincidences."

"No, I can't." Manny patted his pocket for his beloved smokes. "But I finally recognized the faint footprints we saw at the murder scene, footprints that looked like someone checked all around for witnesses. But you weren't checking for witnesses. You were praying to the four directions just like the last time I stopped by. Your foot patterns were just like those at the murder scene, prints made by moccasins. Ones needing new leather ties, like you were making that first time Willie and I came to your house. Like maybe one got caught in Crazy George's brake pedal and it broke off."

Reuben sighed. He held his head in his hand before looking up at Manny. "Jason wasn't one of us." Reuben's voice was calm now, grateful to get things off his chest. "But he was Lakota. He deserved whatever I could do for him. After I killed him, I performed a Sending Away ceremony. He's wandering the Spirit Road now."

"I know." Manny thought of Jason's *wanagi* visiting him in his vision. "Was it just the fact that he intended sacking the tribe's funds that led you to kill him?"

Reuben forced a smile. "After so many years, the tribe finally had a project that could get them on their feet. Folks have always criticized me and my AIM involvement, but all we wanted was the best for the people. The Red Cloud Resort would have restored Oglala pride, padded their coffers, which they dearly need. Jason's scheme would have left the tribe broke. Not to mention Erica holding the legal bag."

"Put pressure on this."

Reuben pressed the gauze into his shoulder.

"Elizabeth knew about the murder, didn't she?"

Reuben nodded and looked past Manny as if he could see Elizabeth on the other side of the cabin. "We've always told each other everything. We met the evening after I killed Jason, and I told her what I'd done. She understood why I killed him. I should have realized she would have gone to hell and back to protect me, as well as Erica, if anyone figured it out."

Manny had his murderer. But there was no satisfaction in his victory, no sense that his investigation had brought justice to Jason Red Cloud. All that remained was a hollowness that perhaps one last piece of information could fill. "I always figured there was more to you and Jason these many years. I thought you'd finally killed him because he was a rotten bastard all his life, ever since he hired Billy Two Moons to kill his folks. Then killed Two Moons himself."

Reuben looked at his pipe thoughtfully, and tamped the embers against the ground. "You know about that?"

"You said you shot Two Moons six times. But that gun had only five spent cases. Jason didn't know guns like you did. He would have heard the stories of old-timers accidentally shooting themselves because they loaded six in the old Colts. But you confessed to the murder. Was it because of Erica?"

Reuben nodded. "I was fingered for a dozen homicides in and around the rez back then. I was top suspect in that Oglala bombing that knocked out the justice building and took out the power station, and it was rumored I had a hand in Anna Mae's murder. And others. Your FBI was closing in on me, and they were going to have my ass, guilty or not—which I was not in any of those."

He continued: "Jason came to me the morning after he killed Billy Two Moons. He told me Two Moons had murdered his parents by cutting their brake lines. He said he found Two Moons outside Hill City and had killed him in a fit of rage, and he felt his parents' accident would eventually be ruled a homicide. As sole heir, he was certain they would look to him first for a motive for the murder. He knew I was suspected in some killings myself, and it was just a matter of time before I was railroaded. Jason agreed to give Erica the best education possible, one I could never afford, in exchange for taking the rap for him. Lizzy didn't like it, and she has despised Jason ever since. We agreed the best thing for Erica was me going away, so I confessed, and copped a plea to second-degree."

"When did you find out Jason paid Two Moons to rig the accident, and didn't kill him in a fit of rage as he stated?"

"In prison. Alex Jumping Bull ran right after Jason killed Two Moons, and kept low for the first year. He finally contacted Lizzy and told her about the deal between Jason and Two Moons. By then, I'd made my plea and started my sentence. It was too late for me."

Manny looked at his brother, convinced he had changed in prison. He now believed he was looking at a genuine sacred man, but Manny was still perplexed how a holy man could murder someone. "You didn't intend to kill Jason that night?"

"No." Reuben pressed harder on the gauze to stop the bleeding. "I told Jason if he didn't meet me there to talk I would go to the law, tell them about the embezzlement and about my false confession. Jason wasn't a brave man, but he didn't want to end up being someone's wife or girlfriend in the slammer. So we met at Wounded Knee. I wanted him to return the tribe's money, but he'd squandered it already. I told him nobody squanders thirty million bucks in such a short time, but he just laughed at me, said he did and there was absolutely nothing I could do to him. He said no one would believe an ex-con about the money or about Billy Two Moons's murder."

"And when he turned to leave, you killed him?"

"He made it to his truck. When he came out, he had a gun. Not a very big gun, but enough that he could have done me some damage. He said Alex Jumping Bull had threatened to expose him, and he had taken care of him, and I was the last witness to be silenced. He should have opened fire instead of opening his mouth, 'cause that gave me a chance to rush him. I slapped the gun away just as he got a round off."

Reuben kicked the dirt with his toe. "It fell to the ground. He lunged for it and I grabbed the first thing that was handy— the war club that was sitting on the seat of his truck. But he got off one shot that caught me in the leg." Reuben pulled up his shorts. A fresh gash had become infected around the makeshift stitches. "Ben Horsecreek helped me pry the slug out and dress the wound."

"But the only identifiable prints on the club belonged to Ricky Bell."

"Occupational bonus," Reuben smiled, rubbing his calloused hands.

Manny nodded. "After wracking my brain, I finally found out why you wouldn't be worried about your prints being matched up. I called the state penitentiary in Sioux Falls when I couldn't locate a set of your prints to match with the war club. The latents lifted from Crazy George's car were unidentifiable. The ID techs said there wasn't enough identification points on either hand to type."

Reuben rubbed his hands together. "I got hooked on pottery in stir. I always hoped that would help these hands heal some, but I guess a lifetime of working with brick and mortar keeps things like fingerprints rubbed away permanently. You know they even had me working stone in lockup."

Manny nodded. "So the warden told me, until they ran out of projects and transferred you to the laundry room. That was another thing that took a while to sink in. He confirmed they have a distinct way of folding sheets and towels, a specific way that tucks the ends into the middle, just like that towel you handed me after the sweat. I didn't recall much about that particular day, but I did remember that odd way you had folded your towel. The same way the star quilt was folded when it was returned to the Prairie Edge the morning after Jason's murder."

"I wasn't counting on Jason having stolen artifacts. I had to return them. If I learned one thing studying with Ben, it's that sacred things remain sacred, so I took them back and left them on the sidewalk in front of the Prairie Edge. That may have helped you catch me."

Manny smiled. "I would have figured things out eventually,"

he said. "It may have taken me longer, being boneheaded like I am, but I would have muddled through it." He paused, the faint sound of sirens growing louder, and then walked back around the house. Three marked OST police cars came fast down Ben's driveway. Willie's turtle car was in the lead.

"Guess you have to take me in now," Reuben said.

Manny stepped close and looked at Reuben closer than he had ever done before, seeing the man he once looked up to, now a holy man, a man who had killed in self-defense. And to save his daughter, his wife, and the tribe's money. A man who had killed for honor.

Honor. Honor had forced Willie to keep Elizabeth from killing again. Honor set aside his feelings for his aunt and reinterviewed her. Honor forced Willie to do things that would keep Elizabeth locked away for life. Honor would get Willie through this. Honor would justify his betrayal of Elizabeth.

But what honor did Manny have after turning his back on his people, turning from the old ways, turning from being a Lakota to being just another city Sioux working for the *wasicu*? What honor would there be in becoming what he had always considered the enemy? Reuben was his *kola*, and Manny had sworn loyalty to his brother when he was still a child, had sworn to never betray Reuben. In that, there was honor left. And there was honor in seeing justice done.

"You'd get manslaughter, about twenty years for killing Jason. Not if you'd come clean right off, but now after you've covered things up. You've already spent twenty years in prison for a crime you didn't commit. Maybe we can both forget what you just told me."

"But you're an FBI. How can you forget it?"

"It won't be easy. But it will be justice. I can't say it was right to kill Jason, but it was self-defense. Nevertheless, a jury would hang you in a heartbeat with your record—and justice wouldn't be done."

The sirens grew louder. Police cars slid up to the cabin. "Besides, what's a *kola* for, if not to protect?" Manny picked up his Glock from the ground and holstered it just as Willie ran around the corner of the house, his own gun drawn. "Wasn't sure you'd still be kicking. We picked up Jack Little Boy about a mile from here."

"He didn't put up a fight?"

Willie smiled. "He tried shooting it out with that old Marlin that didn't work. And he managed to fall down a couple times before Hollow Thunder led him to the pokey."

"And your aunt Elizabeth?"

Willie dropped his eyes. "She's being cuffed now. How about him?" He pointed to Reuben. "Do we take him in?"

Manny shook his head and gestured to Reuben. "He helped talk her down. This is one sacred man who is clear of everything."

CHAPTER 23

Workmen off-loaded metal chairs, snapping them open and arranging them in a semicircular pattern in front of the makeshift stage. The front two rows were to be reserved for dignitaries and the press covering the ground breaking of the Red Cloud Resort. Manny stood between Willie and Clara in the rear. They'd arrived early and stood waiting for the chairs, and the festivities, to begin in an hour.

"I still think you should have stood up there with Erica," Manny said. "It's as much your show as hers."

Clara smiled and chin-pointed to the stage. "This is her baby. Let her have her day. I'll have enough time for the spotlight once the resort is underway."

Erica wore a gray herringbone suit and stood beside the lectern, tapping the microphone. Feedback sent waves of high-pitched squealing from the speakers arranged around the field marked for the resort, and she adjusted the volume control. On the other side of the lectern was a raised relief mock-up of the resort. She fidgeted with it, scooting it closer to the podium, nervously eying the lieutenant governor shaking hands with tribal council members on the stage with him.

Willie nudged Manny and pointed to the parking lot filling up slowly with attendees. Reuben got out of Crazy George's Buick and walked toward them. He wore a sharply pressed white shirt closed with bolo tie, and his long ponytail was tied neatly with a new deer-hide thong that draped down his back. He cradled his injured arm in a sling as he stopped in front of Manny and held out his hand. Manny shook it, and Reuben offered his hand to Willie. Willie hesitated a moment before he accepted it.

"Thought you couldn't drive?"

Reuben smiled at Willie. "Didn't say I couldn't. Just don't like to. But this is special. Not every day your only kid invites you to rub shoulders with the neat and elite." Erica had insisted that her father have one of the reserved front seats. "Lumpy will have a cow when he sees me. Better grab a chair."

Reuben sauntered up to the front row of chairs and stood a moment to catch Lumpy's glare before he winked at Lumpy and sat. Lumpy stood apart from the others in his pressed and starched black Oglala Sioux Tribal uniform. "Security," he had bragged to Manny before the ceremony. "They wanted tribal police for security. Not you feds." Manny had smiled at that. If the organizers were actually concerned with the dignitaries' safety, they would have selected someone other than Lumpy Looks Twice to thwart danger. And if they realized how ruthless he could be, they wouldn't want him near them. In the end, Lumpy would gain the attention he wanted, attention that would be remembered when the tribal council appointed a new police chief.

Desirée Chasing Hawk's laugh turned Manny's attention to the back parking area. She leaned into the lieutenant governor's aide and threaded her arm through his as they walked from his limo. Her bruises and cuts from Jack Little Boy had either completely healed or she had covered them so expertly that she was back to her luscious self. At least on the outside. Manny wondered how long it would take before she went through the young aide on her way to some other man she could use and discard.

"You never said how Alex Jumping Bull fit into things," Clara said.

"He was witness to Jason killing Billy Two Moons," Willie said, then turned to Manny. "Sorry. Didn't mean to steal your thunder."

Manny smiled. "Not to worry. The more thunder you steal, the less pressure I'll have. But Willie's right. Jumping Bull told Elizabeth that Billy Two Moons brought him along as a witness the night he met Jason by Hill City. Jumping Bull was hiding on the back floorboard of that new Chrysler and saw the entire murder. He fled that night out of abject fear. Then greed got the better of him. He saw a chance to put the bite on Jason for some of that Red Cloud estate money."

"He bit into Jason for a long time," Clara said. "But Jason would have done himself in eventually, anyway. As I said before, he was a lousy businessman."

"That he would have," Manny answered.

Erica stepped up to the lectern and gently tapped the mike. "I'll be right back." Clara walked up to the lectern and began speaking with her.

"Is it me, or is Clara a little cold today?"

"I'm afraid it's me," Manny answered. "Just when I thought she and I were an item, she said she wants to back off. Said she was just so frightened the last couple weeks that she's not sure she wants to be involved with a lawman."

"So you two are up in the air?"

"I'm not so sure there's ever going to be 'us two.'"

"By the way, my contact at the *Rapid City Journal* called me," Willie said. "Ecstatic. Seems like that piece Nathan Yellow Horse put in the *Lakota Country Times* about Sonja Myers printing confidential information had some interesting effects."

"There was no leak," Manny said. "That was just to get them tied up scooping one another."

Willie nodded. "She was exonerated. But it still cast enough aspersions on her journalistic integrity that the networks won't touch her now. She swears she'll hurt you professionally for giving Yellow Horse that bogus story."

"At least she wasn't fired like Yellow Horse," Clara said. She'd returned from the stage to stand beside Manny.

"By the way," Willie said, "did you manage to call your supervisor Niles?"

Manny nodded. "Niles the Pile finally made a decision. One of the few decisions he's actually made since I've known him. Back in the field. He took me off the academy assignment after I told him the case had hit an impenetrable wall. When I reported that the case may never be solved, he told me he'd already filled the instructor's slot."

"So officially, Jason's murder is still an active case?"

"It's still an active case," Manny lied, and hoped Willie hadn't picked up too much from him to detect it.

"So where are you off to now?" Clara asked. "What's your assignment?"

"'A fate worse than Greenland,' is how the Pile put it."

"You're back on Pine Ridge?" Willie asked excitedly.

Manny nodded. "At least some of the time. The Pile transferred me to the Rapid City Resident Agency."

"Back taking all the reservation cases," Clara said. "That's terrible." She took his hand and squeezed it gently while they waited for the ground breaking to begin.

"Sure," Manny said, smiling and squeezing her hand in return. He had never slept better than in these last weeks following his reassignment. The *wanagi* had not visited him once during the night. He'd started rebuilding his relationship with Reuben, who was helping him sort through his Lakota issues. He'd met a woman he could grow to love if she'd have him, and a friend he had grown to trust. He'd somehow manage to survive the transfer the Pile had given him. "This is just terrible, isn't it?"